Susan Meier is the author of over fifty books for Mills & Boon. *The Tycoon's Secret Daughter* was a Romance Writers of America RITA® Award finalist, and *Nanny for the Millionaire's Twins* won the Book Buyers' Best award and was a finalist in the National Readers' Choice awards. She is married and has three children. One of eleven children herself, she loves to write about the complexity of families and totally believes in the power of love.

Melissa Senate has written many novels for Mills & Boon and other publishers, including her debut, *See Jane Date*, which was made into a TV movie. She also wrote seven books for Mills & Boon's True Love line under the pen name Meg Maxwell. Her novels have been published in over twenty-five countries. Melissa lives on the coast of Maine with her teenage son; their rescue shepherd mix, Flash; and a lap cat named Cleo. For more information, please visit her website, melissasenate.com

Discover more at millsandboon.co.uk

FALLING FOR THE PREGNANT HEIRESS

SUSAN MEIER

RUST CREEK FALLS CINDERELLA

MELISSA SENATE

MILLS & BOON

First Published in Great Britain 2019
by Mills & Boon, an imprint of HarperCollinsPublishers,
1 London Bridge Street, London, SE1 9GF

Falling For The Pregnant Heiress © 2019 Linda Susan Meier
Rust Creek Falls Cinderella © 2019 Harlequin Books S.A.

Special thanks and acknowledgement are given to Melissa Senate
for her contribution to the *Montana Mavericks:
Six Brides for Six Brothers* continuity.

ISBN: 978-0-263-27255-0

0819

MIX
Paper from
responsible sources
FSC™ C007454

This book is produced from independently certified FSC™
paper to ensure responsible forest management.

For more information visit: www.harpercollins.co.uk/green

Printed and bound in Spain
by CPI, Barcelona

FALLING FOR THE PREGNANT HEIRESS

SUSAN MEIER

To my bowling buddies
on the Tuesday afternoon league.

We may not always bowl well, but we laugh a lot!

CHAPTER ONE

ANYONE WHO LOOKED at Sabrina McCallan usually did a double take. With her blond hair, blue eyes and nicely kept curves, she was physically perfect. Add impeccable manners, poise, charm, grace and intelligence, and Trent "Ziggy" Sigmund thought the woman was class in Chanel.

Until today.

As a bridesmaid in her brother Seth's August wedding, standing by a church pew, waiting for her turn in the after-ceremony pictures, she seemed frazzled. Nervous. Plus, a strand of yellow hair had sprung from her up-do and she hadn't tucked it back in.

Which was why Trent couldn't stop staring at her.

Sabrina's partner in Seth and Harper's wedding, Trent was supposed to be aware of where Sabrina was when their names were called for the pictures, and her fidgeting confused him. He wasn't staring because he was attracted to her. She wasn't his type. She was perfect, flawless, and he liked things a little messy. Not a disaster. But wild hair on a pillow, sleepy eyes, torn jeans and scruffy tennis shoes were more his speed.

Still, something was up with Sabrina and he had responsibilities as her partner in the wedding, more as her brother's best friend. He and Seth had lived together in a run-down apartment, both earning their living as waiters, as they finished school. They'd shared spare change and food, knew the bus and subway schedules like the backs of their hands and played wingman when one or the other spotted a girl they liked. Though Seth had dropped out of his family for a time, the second McCallan son still knew "people" and that had helped Trent get his first job, which had resulted in his learning the right things at the right time to develop his genius, strike out on his own and become rich.

In some ways they were like brothers. In other ways they were closer than brothers. Trent would be a fool if he didn't realize he owed Seth. And Trent wasn't a fool.

Which was why Seth's little sister's fidgeting was like a red alert alarm. The groom, Seth, was too busy to notice. Even Jake, Seth and Sabrina's older brother, was busy with his toddler and pregnant wife. Only Trent had time to see the McCallan daughter was off her game today.

When his name and Sabrina's were called for their picture, Trent sauntered across the church aisle to stunning Sabrina. Her pale purple dress highlighted her blue eyes. Her yellow hair would have been perfection, except for that one wayward strand, which to Trent's way of thinking, actually made her more beautiful.

He offered his arm. The way he and Sabrina had grown up might have been worlds apart, but twelve years of knowing a McCallan had taught him how a gentleman behaved.

"Ready for pics?"

Sabrina smiled politely as she slid her hand into the crook of his elbow. "Yes."

He nearly told her she looked elegant and feminine in the simple lilac dress Harper had chosen for her bridesmaids, but he figured she'd probably heard that thirty or forty times already today.

They walked to the space the photographer pointed out, stood by Seth and Harper and smiled as the middle-aged man snapped a picture. He took at least a hundred more shots with Seth and Harper and the members of their bridal party, Harper's parents, Seth's mom Maureen, Seth's brother Jake and his wife, Avery, and then a few final shots of everyone—a big mob of men in tuxes, women in gowns and little girls in dresses with so much tulle and ruffles, Trent wondered how they could stay upright.

Seth's mom and Harper's parents said their goodbyes. Harper's parents were taking Harper's daughter, Crystal, home for a nap before the reception. Seth's mom was going home for a nap herself. Jake and Avery's nanny hustled Abby to their Upper East Side condo for some quiet time. The rest of the wedding party took limos to Seth and Harper's penthouse for a few pre-reception drinks.

Thanking everyone for joining him in the celebration of the happiest day of his life, Seth popped the cork on the first bottle of champagne, then servants scurried over to open more champagne, fill glasses and distribute them for a toast.

Leaning against the bar, Trent kept his attention on Sabrina. She took a glass of champagne, happily raised it when best man Jake made a toast, then pretended to sip.

Trent's eyes narrowed. She had absolutely *pretended* to sip. Three toasts later, she still had a full glass of champagne.

The bride and groom mingled through the small crowd. Waiters brought out trays of hors d'oeuvres. Seth told stories of his misspent youth, and with Harper by his side, he spoke fondly of her deceased husband, Clark, the third roommate in the trio of Clark, Seth and Ziggy, who now preferred to be called Trent. Trent joined him in one final story. Then the conversation drifted to more current topics, and before Trent knew it, it was time to go to the Waldorf Astoria for the reception.

He had to hunt for Sabrina. When he found her, she looked to have gotten lost in the shuffle. A woman who ran a nonprofit that helped startups turn into corporations did not get lost in any shuffles.

He added her obvious confusion to her not drinking and came up with a conclusion so startling it almost made him whistle—the way his stepfather always had when he realized something outlandish, something farfetched, something so out of the realm of reality that only a physical gesture or a reverently whispered "Wow" would do.

Sabrina held up as well as she could through the small party at Seth and Harper's. When Ziggy found her—again—to ride with her to the reception, she wanted to throttle him. She needed some alone time to figure things out and her brother's best friend, her groomsman partner, always seemed to be two feet away.

She'd think he'd suddenly gotten a thing for her, but she knew better. If the wild-haired waifs he dated were anything to go by, she wasn't his type. But he wasn't her type, either. He was good-looking enough. His black hair curled into sexy ringlets on his collar. His heavy-lidded dark eyes never missed a thing. But he was scruffy. He liked things like dimly lit jazz bars and kicking back with a beer by the lake. Any lake. She was pretty sure he owned houses on three of them.

Then there was his name. She'd never get used to calling him Trent. First, because her brother had called him Ziggy for at least a decade. Second, because to her the name Ziggy fit the laid-back billionaire much more than Trent.

And nobody really wanted to be dating a guy named Ziggy, let alone a high-profile professional woman. She ran a respectable nonprofit. Her public persona determined whether she got contributions and grants to assist the hundreds of people who came to her with ideas every year.

Trent helped her into one of the black limos that had pulled up to the curb in front of Seth and Harper's building.

She smiled politely. "Thank you."

"You're welcome."

The driver closed the door behind them, walked to the front of the long car and took his seat behind the steering wheel.

Trent pushed the button that raised the glass between passengers and the driver. "Are you okay?"

"What? Yes! I'm fine."

"Nothing you want to tell me?"

She gave him the side eye. "Of course not."

"I'm just saying you look like a woman who might need a shoulder to cry on or maybe somebody to offer advice."

She fought the urge to close her eyes and kept her poise strictly intact. He couldn't know that she was pregnant. *She'd* only found out that morning. One stupid week of loneliness had her flying off to Paris to Pierre—with whom she'd made the mutual decision to break up the month before—and spending a reckless weekend that resulted in a child.

She'd sensed a bit of regret on Pierre's part when she'd left to return to New York, but not enough for him to call her. Which was for the best. As a woman who didn't believe in love, she'd accepted Pierre's romantic advances four years ago because she knew there was no danger that anything would come of their affair. A gorgeous, passionate artist, Pierre was a lot of fun and they spoke the language of art. They both lived and breathed art. But Pierre was the product of a marriage more dysfunctional than Sabrina's parents' marriage had been, and he'd decided to make up for his parents' neglect by giving himself everything he wanted. He'd also taken a solemn vow never to marry or have kids. Which was okay because they weren't long-term anything. They had a safe, long-distance relationship, with no possibility of things getting messy with talk of love.

And now that she was pregnant?

Well…

They'd broken up. He didn't want to be a father. She'd never wanted him in her life permanently. Nothing had changed.

At least she didn't think so. But that was the problem. There hadn't yet been time to think this through. She hadn't had two quiet minutes since she'd seen the stick turn blue, and her nerves were beginning to fray. Part of her wanted to enjoy her brother's big day and celebrate. The other part wanted to go home and cry. Except—

She didn't know if she wanted to cry out of fear or happiness. She'd always wanted to be a mom. She'd envisioned herself having as close of a relationship with her child as she'd had with her mom, guiding her little boy or girl into a wonderful, fulfilling life, choosing good schools, taking her baby to the park, maybe even getting a dog—

She'd just always thought it would be sometime in the future.

"I'm fine."

"Okay. Keep your secrets."

An arrow plunged into her heart, scaring her to death at the way he'd made *secret* plural. *Secrets*. Being pregnant wasn't her only secret. She also painted. Temperamental, brilliant Pierre was one of a handful of people who knew Sabrina McCallan was the reclusive artist Sally McMillan. She'd taken a pseudonym because as Sabrina McCallan she was New York high society. Her one and only showing had been mobbed by people buying her paintings to win favor with her now-deceased tycoon father.

She'd been on the verge of quitting painting altogether when her mother had suggested a pseudonym. And it worked. She didn't go to her showings, didn't schmooze or pander to the public. Her art stood on its own.

Still, Ziggy couldn't know that. Seth, Jake, Avery and Harper all knew the stakes. Seth would not have spilled her secret. None of them would.

Ziggy was bluffing.

"Maybe I should ask you if *you* need some counseling." He laughed.

She lifted one eyebrow. "Afraid your business won't stand up to the scrutiny of a professional?"

"Honey, my business wouldn't stand up to anybody's scrutiny. I have a couple simple formulas. I read five newspapers a day and a few dozen blogs. Once I get all the information I need in my head, I grab a fishing pole and go to the lake, or I slip off to Spain and let it all sink in. After a few days I might make a move, or I might not."

"That's really not a business."

"Didn't I just say that?"

The train of limos arrived at the Waldorf. Doormen scurried out to release the passengers and escort the bridal party into the hotel. When Sabrina and Ziggy arrived at the four-story, two-tiered ballroom, the place was lit with dim purple lights that made the space shimmer romantically. Long, rectangular tables outlined the room, while round, more intimate tables filled the area beside the open dance floor.

Sabrina murmured, "This is lovely."

Ziggy looked around. "Your family does know how to throw a party."

His casual way of looking at things hit her all the wrong ways. "We aren't throwing a party. We're celebrating a marriage."

"Potayto, potahto."

"It's not the same thing! A party can be four guys and a beer bong. We're celebrating my brother and his wife finding love."

He faced her with a goofy smile, his dark eyes gleaming with mischief. "You're a romantic."

She almost laughed. Her? A romantic? She was exactly the opposite. She was a woman who believed romance and the mythical concept of "love" only caused problems—especially for women. She would never let herself be so vulnerable as to fall in love.

"I'm not a romantic. You know as well as anyone that our family had a rough time." A dad who couldn't be faithful and a mom with three kids who lived in fear of his temper. "I never thought either of my brothers would get married."

Ziggy nodded. "Yeah. I guess you're right."

She straightened to her full five feet six inches—five-nine with heels—and still she only came up to about his nose. Odd that she'd notice that with so much on her mind. "You're damned right, I'm right. Now, if you'll excuse me, don't follow me to the ladies' room."

He laughed.

She strode away, feeling more like herself than she had all day. There was nothing like righting a wrong to get her blood flowing. Having her spunk back helped her to weed through some of the confusion in her brain.

Number one, she wanted the baby. Because of her parents' abysmal marriage, she'd vowed never to marry, but she wanted to be a mother. This pregnancy might have sped up her timetable, but she was ready—

No. She was *eager* to become a mom.

Number two, she had to tell Pierre. She expected him to be appalled and tell her that he wanted nothing to do with their child. But she'd chosen him as a lover, someone with no intention of falling in love, not a father for her children, so that was okay. She had no qualm about raising this baby alone. In fact, she'd prefer it.

Number three and four, telling her mom and telling her brothers couldn't happen until she told Pierre.

She had to go to Paris.

She walked into the elegant lounge section of the ladies' room and leaned across a vanity to get a peek at her makeup. Now that she wasn't falling apart internally, her face had gone back to normal. She could have nitpicked every tiny imperfection. She could have second-guessed her choice of lipstick color. Except she looked like the lady her mother had raised her to be. She might not be perfect, but she was firmly in her role.

She drew a long breath and left the restroom, heading back to the ballroom. She spotted Ziggy and walked in the opposite direction. Jake was about to introduce Seth and Harper and the bridal party. She ambled up to Harper, who looked elegant in her simple satin dress. Her short, dark hair gave her the look of a pixie. Her blue eyes sparkled with love—for Sabrina's brother. Sabrina could never appreciate anyone more than she did Avery and Harper for helping her brothers to heal. Theirs were the rare unicorn of relationships that did revolve around love, exactly what her brothers needed.

But Sabrina didn't need to heal as her brothers had. A

daughter, not a son, she hadn't endured the kind of cruel mistreatment from their dad that her brothers had. Her chauvinistic father didn't see her as a businesswoman, so he had no reason to "train" her. But she had seen how he treated her mom, how her mom had cried over his infidelities and worried for her sons. At fourteen, Sabrina had promised herself no man would ever treat her the way her dad had treated her mom. And she'd kept that promise.

"Anything I can do for the bride?"

Harper hugged her. "No. We're fine. I'd just like to get to dinner already. I'm starved."

"You should have had some hors d'oeuvres at your penthouse. They were wonderful."

"I was saving my appetite for the Beef Wellington."

As Jake began announcing the wedding party, Ziggy walked up to her and escorted her to her seat. Jake then introduced himself and his wife, Avery, who joined him by the podium. He introduced Seth and Harper and the room broke into joyous applause.

Tears filled her eyes. She really couldn't express how grateful she was to her two sisters-in-law for saving her brothers, healing them, helping them to believe in love and lead normal, happy lives.

Harper finally got her Beef Wellington and the dinner progressed with Ziggy making small talk with her one minute and turning to his left to talk to her mother the next. She supposed he was an okay guy—

All right. He was sort of a great guy, considerate of her and kind to her mother. She shouldn't have snapped at him.

She never snapped at anyone.

But there was something about Ziggy today. Something about the sexy way he looked in a tux—or maybe the way he'd asked if she needed someone to talk to—

She didn't know. Her hormones were a mess and so were her reactions. But now that she'd worked everything out in her head, she could get back to normal.

The band announced Seth and Harper's first dance, and her brother escorted his bride to the dance floor. When the music ended, the band announced Jake and Avery, who joined Seth and Harper, then Trent and Sabrina, who walked out onto the dance floor with them.

The band began a slow, romantic song for the bridal party dance, and Sabrina drew a quiet breath. Trent slid his arm around her waist. She put her hand on his shoulder—his very solid shoulder.

That was a surprise. Pierre was a tall, thin man, and touching someone more solid sent a jolt through her. She hadn't expected Ziggy to be buff.

"Do you work out?"

He waggled his eyebrows. "Liking my muscles?"

She rolled her eyes. "Can you be serious for one second?"

"I tried to be serious in the limo. You shut me down."

"You weren't being serious. You were prying into my life."

"See, there you go again. Making distinctions that don't need to exist."

The music shifted into something faster for mere seconds, but Trent took advantage of those seconds to spin them around. Silly though it was, the movement lightened her mood. She laughed.

"See? That's what I wanted to hear. A laugh. A spontaneous one at that."

She shook her head. "You're weird."

"No. We're opposites."

She inclined her head in agreement.

"Which means if you told me whatever was troubling

you, I'd come up with an out-of-the-box solution that might help you."

This time she didn't try to deny that she was in the throes of figuring out a problem. "You can't help me."

Her honesty surprised Trent. Not only did it mean she trusted him, but also, he'd never been able to do a real, solid favor for Seth. The McCallans wanted for nothing. If he could do something kind for the sister of the guy who'd given him the boost he'd needed to become the success he was, he was at her beck and call. "You're so sure."

She looked away. "Yeah." She caught his gaze. "Can you keep a secret?"

Without hesitation Trent said, "Absolutely."

"There's not really anything you can do about the fact that I'm pregnant."

Trent didn't react. He'd already guessed that. "I have three getaway houses in the US and a condo in Spain. I have a yacht that's really nice for privacy when you need it. If nothing else, let me give you a place to think this through."

She caught his gaze. "I don't need to think it through. I need to go to France to tell the baby's dad. I can't use one of the McCallan jets because my family will know where I've gone. And I don't want them to know." She bit her lower lip. "At least not yet. I have to tell the baby's father before I tell my family."

He perked up. "I have three jets."

Her blue eyes filled with hope. "You'd lend me one?"

"Sure."

The hope in her eyes turned to skepticism as the song ended. "And you wouldn't tell Seth?"

He made a cross on his chest. "I'll keep all of this a

secret until you have a chance to tell everyone yourself. When do you need the jet?"

"Tonight."

"So soon?"

"I just want to get this over with. You know, get myself moving forward again."

He tucked his hands in his trouser pockets. "Okay. I'd give you the keys, but if jets have keys I'm pretty sure my pilot has them."

She laughed and impulsively hugged him. "Thanks."

The strangest feelings rattled through Trent. She was softer than he'd thought she'd be. Of course, he rarely dated women with curves, so that explained the surprise that hit him. But he felt a warmth, too. Probably the result of doing a good deed. It couldn't be attraction. She wasn't his type.

He wasn't exactly sure why he needed to remind himself of that.

But he did.

Twice.

CHAPTER TWO

THEY WAITED UNTIL Seth and Harper left their reception at ten o'clock that night. Trent told Sabrina he would arrange for a flight crew while Sabrina said goodbye to her mom and Jake and Avery. Lighter now that she had a plan, she strode over to say her goodbyes, then Trent escorted her through the hot August night to the limo and they rode to the Park Avenue building housing her condo.

He exited the limo with her, but she shook her head. "No need to come with me. I won't be but a minute."

"A minute to pack?" He laughed. "I've seen how you dress. Everything coordinates. You're probably going to have a suitcase just for your shoes."

Offended because it sounded as if he thought her trite or spoiled, she strode to her building. "I'm not that picky." She wasn't picky. She simply had a standard to uphold. If her mother had drilled that into her head once, she'd drilled it a thousand times.

You are a lady. Act like a lady. Dress like a lady. Speak like a lady.

With a quick push of her hand on the door, they entered the climate-controlled comfort of the lobby. Trent pulled a draft of frosty air into his lungs. She couldn't tell if he was happy for the cool air or uncomfortable about having to explain himself.

"I didn't say you were picky. I'm just saying you always look nice."

She worked to stifle a smile. It shouldn't please her that he thought she looked nice or that he cared that he'd insulted her.

But it had.

Puzzled, she led him to the elevator. She took out a key card to start it. "That's okay."

"Are we going to a penthouse?"

"No. Just an exclusive floor. Two condos. Half a floor each. I don't need a whole floor."

"Nice." He winced. "I still sometimes marvel at luxury."

She didn't ask him what he meant. She knew his beginnings. Her brother had told her Trent had blue-collar roots and had worked his way through university alongside Seth. Then he'd quit the job Seth had found for him to invest on his own. She admired him. It had taken guts to leave his convenient job and trust his genius. She should probably tell him that—

A funny feeling invaded her chest and brought her up short. She shook her head to clear it of the desire to figure out why she wanted to talk about that. Right now, she should be focused on throwing some clothes into a travel bag, driving to the airport, flying to France and facing Pierre—

Because she was pregnant. *Pregnant.* About to be a mom.

She pictured herself holding a tiny baby the way Avery had held Abby right after she was born. The sweet little thing would snuggle against her and, like Avery, she would marvel that she had created a life.

Warmth filled her, along with a sudden desire to cry. Happy tears. Now that she'd adjusted to it, being pregnant was like a dream come true. Her life was busy but established. She could take time off, create a nursery in her big condo, set playdates, take her baby for long walks in Central Park.

The elevator reached her floor. She stepped into the lobby with two doors. One to her condo. One to the condo of a nice, recently retired couple who traveled a lot. She had breakfast with them once a month when they were home, and if they ran into each other at the elevator, they chatted happily. They'd raised four kids and adored their three grandkids.

They'd be the perfect neighbors for a single mom.

She punched a code into her alarm to disable it, then pressed her key card to the lock and opened the door onto her pristine home.

Wide-plank hardwood floors ran through the open floorplan that included a white kitchen, formal dining space and living room with a long sofa in the center of three conversation areas.

She faced Ziggy with a smile. She'd already decided which room would be the nursery and that she could dismantle the third bedroom and turn it into a playroom.

"Okay. Now that you've nudged me, you can go. Thank you for the use of your jet. Honestly, I'll be happy to compensate you for the flight crew and the fuel when I return."

His head tilted. "Oh, you think I'm just going to hand over my jet?"

"You're not?"

He laughed. "No. I'm coming with you. You're my best friend's little sister and you're pregnant. I'm not letting you fly across an ocean alone. What if you get sick? Or just faint? For at least the first trimester, I don't think it's wise to travel across an ocean alone."

She was surprised he even knew the word *trimester*, let alone that that could be a scary time for a woman, but she let that go in favor of her real concern. "I don't need help."

"Never said you did. My coming is more of a just-in-case thing. Just in case you get sick. Just in case you faint."

She wanted to argue, but she wanted to get to Paris more. It was night. She and Trent were both tired. They'd undoubtedly fall asleep for the entire seven-hour flight. When they woke in the morning, he'd be in a tux and she'd be in jeans and a shirt, suitably dressed to find Pierre.

Before Trent could buy proper clothes for a morning in the city, she'd be at Pierre's apartment, telling him about the baby. He'd undoubtedly say he didn't want to be a dad and she'd say that was fine. She'd just thought he had a right to know he was about to be a father. Then she'd go back to the airport to fly home.

There was no point in arguing with Ziggy because she could make the timing work for her.

"Fine. Come to France with me, but all you'll be doing is sleeping on the jet. We won't even talk."

"I know the drill. I always fly at night."

"Great." Without another word, she walked to her bedroom to throw enough into an overnight bag to get her through a flight and a day in Paris.

When she returned to her main room a few minutes later, Ziggy stood by the wall of windows, staring at the twinkling Manhattan skyline. He'd removed his jacket and rolled his shirt sleeves to the elbows, revealing strong forearms peppered with black hair. He'd also taken off his bow tie and opened the top few buttons of his shirt.

Now he was just a guy in black trousers and a white shirt. He *could* go with her to Pierre's condo.

It didn't matter. Even if he begged, she wouldn't take him to Pierre's. Surely, he could keep himself busy for a few hours in the most glamorous city in the world.

He took her overnight bag. "Ready?"

She slid the strap of her purse over her arm. "Ready."

She'd chosen jeans and a peach-colored T-shirt with brown wedge-heel sandals for the flight and had combed out her long hair. Because of the curls of the up-do, it flowed in gentle waves to her shoulders.

Ziggy's gaze traveled from her hair down her T-shirt and along the line of her jeans to her sandals. When his eyes met hers, a little jolt of electricity zapped her.

Now she knew what was going on. She *was* attracted to him. Sort of. The man *was* good-looking. But electricity? Sparks? She didn't believe in those. Never had.

Forcing herself to ignore the firestorm rolling across her nerve endings, she smiled her most professional smile at Ziggy and headed for the door. "Let's go."

"Sure."

They drove to a private airstrip and boarded the jet. The front of the cabin had four cream-colored leather seats. Behind those were two rear-facing blue leather recliners angled toward an enormous TV. It wasn't the kind of luxury she was accustomed to. Her family's biggest plane had two bedrooms, a kitchen and a formal dining room. But Ziggy's little jet was obviously expensive with plush carpeting, lush leathers. And it was convenient. With no unnecessary bells and whistles, it was almost cozy.

"All the seats recline." He pointed to a cabinet tucked behind the television. "Blankets are in there."

She tossed her bag into one of the empty chairs and got herself a blanket. "Great. I'm exhausted."

"Me, too."

But when she sat on one of the pale seats, he walked back to the blue ones in front of the TV. Glad he hadn't sat beside her—she didn't care to feel the crazy jolt of electricity she got when he was too close—she reclined the seat, snuggled into her blanket and almost instantly fell asleep.

She slept deeply and eventually dreamed she had twins who sometimes morphed into triplets, and every time she took them to the park, Ziggy followed her, walking a big, furry dog on a leash that sometimes got caught in the wheels of her babies' stroller.

The chaos of it jolted her heart. She woke with a start to discover they had landed in Paris, and decided her dream was an extension of Ziggy's following her around all day at the wedding. With a long drink of air to wake herself completely, she rose from her padded seat, grabbed her overnight bag and turned to go to the private area of the small aircraft.

Rushing to the door in the back, which she assumed was a bathroom, she didn't look right or left, not wanting to accidentally make eye contact with Ziggy. Or worse, wake him. The sooner she got out of here, the better her chances of leaving alone. All she needed to do was change her shirt, refresh her makeup and maybe take a minute to think about what she'd say to Pierre—

She opened the bathroom door and gasped.

Standing in the middle of the compact room, wrestling a shirt over his head was Ziggy—*Trent.*

A broad chest with well-defined muscles that led down to six-pack abs?

That was Trent. Adult. Sexy. And oh, so male. She'd

never be able to think of him as her brother's college friend Ziggy again.

She spun away, her heart doing something that felt like a samba in her chest. "Sorry."

"No, wait. I'm done." He slid out of the room into the main cabin and tossed a duffel bag onto one of the empty seats. "Didn't want to be wearing a wrinkled tux around Paris."

"How'd you get an overnight bag?"

"There's always a go bag in my office. Had one of my assistants bring it to the plane while you were packing."

She worked not to glance down at his chest, now covered by a gray T-shirt. But the vision of his pecs and abs was firmly planted in her brain. "I didn't think you would be going to Pierre's apartment with me."

"I told you. You're my best friend's sister. I'm not going to let you go to some guy's house alone and tell him you're pregnant. God knows how he'll react."

"He's not going to hit me."

"You're damned right, he's not. I'm not going to let him."

The electricity she'd felt the night before came back with a vengeance as his dark eyes held hers. It took all the strength she could muster to keep her breath from stuttering when she said, "No. Really. You can't come with me. This is private."

"Oh."

The disappointed expression on his face knocked the electricity off her nerve endings but it tugged at her heart. This was a man who took his responsibilities seriously.

"Look. It's okay. He's going to say he doesn't want to be a dad. And I'm going to say *fine*, then fly back to New York and raise my child alone."

He gaped at her. "You don't want your baby to know his dad?"

"I do want my child to know *her* dad. But Pierre's not going to want to be a big part of her life. I won't be cruel. Pierre can visit anytime he's in New York. But I doubt that he will."

His forehead puckered. "He's not going to want his child?"

"Pierre's a narcissist. His parents had a marriage as bad as my mom and dad's and he vowed to make up for that by giving himself everything he'd wanted but didn't get as a child. I have to be practical. And honest. He told me he didn't want to have children and my being pregnant probably won't change that."

Trent shook his head. "You can't know that. You saw what happened to Jake. He about went crazy when Avery didn't want anything to do with him after she learned she was pregnant. Now he's so smitten with Abby it's almost funny. Then there's Seth. A confirmed bachelor until Harper walked into his life with Crystal."

"There was hope for Jake and Seth."

"No, there wasn't. Your dad had soured them both on relationships and made both wonder if they could be good dads…yet they pulled through."

"Neither one of them is a flighty artist like Pierre."

"But you loved him?"

"We had a relationship, based mostly on our common love of art. We also had the same kind of childhood. Pierre's not the kind of guy a smart woman falls in love with."

His eyes widened. "Wow."

"I'm just saying that Pierre and I had a lot in common and we had a great couple of years together. But we never wanted anything serious."

"Okay. I get that. But don't write him off."

She sighed. "Trent, I'm a planner. I teach other people how to look down the board and see the future. I've already played this all out in my head."

"I'll bet not all of it. You're going to want to get married someday. And when you do your baby's going to have a stepfather. *I* had a stepfather. He was a wonderful dad to my half brother and sister, the kids he had with my mom, but he never seemed to warm up to me. I was the boy my mom had with another guy. The one who came into the marriage. I wasn't blood."

Gobsmacked by the admission of something so personal and saddened for the lost little boy she pictured him to be, she said, "That's terrible."

He pulled in a breath. "Not really. The truth is he tried. I tried. We just never seemed to bond."

She stared at him. She'd always had the impression he'd come from one of those perfect, close-knit blue-collar families. "But now you get along?"

"Depends on what you mean by get along. When I left home, my mom, stepdad and half sister and brother became a tight little unit. I'd see it every time I came home for a holiday and feel more left out. When I became wealthy, I bought them a house and insulted my stepdad, who refused it and accused me of thinking I was better than they were now that I was rich." He shrugged. "So I kind of stay away."

She absolutely did not know what to say. Particularly since he'd just confirmed her decision to never marry. Even if her parents' marriage hadn't warned here off, she'd heard enough horror stories from her friends at private school, whose parents had gone through divorces. From middle school through high school she'd heard tales of wicked stepmothers and grouchy stepfathers. Having a child just guaranteed she'd never marry. She would not put her son or daughter through that.

He caught her gaze. "What I'm telling you is, if I had a choice between being raised by my real father or my stepfather, I know which one I'd choose."

Sabrina stared at him. He wasn't upset, more like resigned, but to Sabrina that made his situation all the sadder.

When she didn't respond, Trent turned her toward the small dressing room again. "Go. Change. Fluff out your hair. Do whatever it is women do to get ready. I'll be right here waiting for you."

She almost pivoted to face him again. He'd shifted gears from his own troubles to hers so easily it was as if his didn't matter.

With her problems being the ones in the forefront, she supposed they didn't. At least not now. At some point she'd circle back, ask him if he really was as okay as he sounded. But right now, she had to get dressed to tell Pierre he was about to be a dad.

She walked into the bathroom, splashed her face and slipped into her clean clothes. Though she knew what she intended to say, there were three or four ways she could approach Pierre. Strong and confident. Soft and loving. Matter-of-fact. And even strictly professional, like a lawyer stating the facts.

All the options had merit. Even after a few minutes to think them through before she left the bathroom, none of them stood out.

Trent's staff had a limo waiting. The driver opened the back door for them, and she told him the address of Pierre's apartment. As they drove along the streets, she only got glimpses of the Eiffel Tower. But it didn't matter that she couldn't see the usual sights. She loved the everyday hustle and bustle of Paris. Brick and stone streets. Tourists studying maps or ogling buildings. And the scents. Croissants. Madeleines. Éclair. Wonderful crusty bread. And that rich, dark coffee she loved so much.

But she couldn't have coffee. She wouldn't drink coffee for nine months.

When they reached Pierre's apartment building in a residential section of the city, Trent followed her out of the limo.

She stopped him with a hand to his chest. His very solid chest. She almost groaned at the whoosh of attraction that rolled through her. Instead, she shook off the woozy, fuzzy feeling and said, "This part is private."

"I'll tell you what. You let me walk you up to the door and see what kind of mood he's in. If he seems okay, I'll let you talk alone."

She wanted to argue. She wanted sexy, handsome, electricity-inspiring, nice guy Trent to disappear so she could tell Pierre he was about to be a dad.

Except, what if Trent was right? What if Pierre reacted badly? It wouldn't hurt to have tall, buff Trent in the loose gray T-shirt and nice-fitting jeans at her side.

"All right. You stay for a minute or two. Then the rest of the discussion is private."

He grinned. Her heart tumbled. How had she not noticed before how gorgeous he was with his unruly hair and seductive smile?

"Absolutely."

They entered the building and climbed the two flights of stairs to Pierre's apartment. It wasn't the best building in the world. But Pierre didn't make as much money as she did from her art. And that wasn't a lot. She lived on her salary from the nonprofit and an extremely generous trust fund.

Still, her leg muscles became rubbery when she remembered how angry he'd been when her art had outsold his at their last showing. Her steps faltered.

"You okay, there, Skippy?"

She pasted on a bright smile as she turned to face Trent, who was on the step below her. "Yes. Fine."

"If you want to turn and run, just let me know. I'm up for that, too."

Surprisingly, she laughed. For such a smart guy, with such a sad past and a serious way of making money, he had a great sense of humor.

They finally reached Pierre's floor and walked to the third door on the right. Forcing her fingers to stop shaking, she pressed the doorbell.

No answer.

After a few seconds she pressed again.

Trent sent her a confident smile and thumbs-up.

She hit the bell a third time. Pierre's door didn't open, but the one next to it did.

Pierre's short, dark-haired neighbor, Danielle, whom Sabrina had met a few times, came out of her apartment, smoking a cigarette. "He's not here."

Speaking French, Sabrina said, "Oh. Where is he?"

Danielle brought her cigarette to her lips, inhaled and blew a long stream of smoke. "He's at his house in Spain."

"Spain?" Confusion rippled through her. "He has a house in Spain?"

"He goes there at the end of every August. Pretty much spends the winter there."

Trent put his hands on her shoulders, reminding her of his presence to reassure her. "You wouldn't happen to have the address?"

Because he'd spoken English, Sabrina repeated the question in French. Danielle held up one finger. The universal symbol for "wait one minute."

She returned with the address written on a scrap of paper.

Trent said, "Thanks," took the paper, then turned Sabrina toward the steps again.

They walked down the thin stairway, her optimistic hope of telling Pierre and getting it over with, vanishing. Still, it wasn't like she had to wait forever. She just had to get to Spain.

When they reached the street, she took the slip of paper with the address from Trent's hand. "I can get a commercial flight. I don't want to bother you."

"It's no bother. Besides, I have a condo in Barcelona. We'll fly there, buy a change of clothes, eat a nice dinner and head to Pierre's tomorrow morning."

A weird kind of relief poured through Sabrina. Calm, cool and collected Trent had a plan.

Still, she didn't want to get accustomed to depending on anyone. Not ever. Her mom had been so dependent on her dad that she'd lost the biggest part of her life. Now that Sabrina was in Europe, away from her family's curiosity, she would have the privacy to do what she needed to do. She could go on without Trent.

"Thanks, but I'm fine."

"No, you're not. You're mad. The guy has a house in Spain that you clearly didn't know about. You dated him, probably told him everything about yourself but he had a house in Spain and apparently spent lots of time there, yet he never thought to mention that. How much did you guys date anyway?"

She drew in a breath. She *was* mad. "We didn't *date* date. We spent weekends together, took trips, did exhibits together." She paused long enough to think through how to phrase her explanation. "Our homes were on two different continents. Our relationship was long distance. So there were stretches of time in the winter when we didn't see each other."

"Okay. I get it. That's how long-distance relationships are. You see each other when you can."

Once again, his answer relieved her. Most of her anger with Pierre melted away. But that didn't mean she needed Trent to fly her to Spain. "Thanks. When I tell Seth and Jake about being pregnant, I'll also tell them how much you helped me these past two days."

Trent's brows drew together as he frowned. "You do realize that what you're saying is that when Seth hears I brought you to France, I'll have to explain to my best friend why I dumped his little sister in Europe."

"It's not like that."

"That's exactly how a man would hear it. Especially when your brothers find out you didn't see Pierre in Paris. You saw him in Spain."

When she said nothing, he sighed. "Look, I'm offering a plane and some companionship. You could catch a cab to the airport and then wait two days before a seat opens up on a commercial flight. My jet's just a few miles away." He caught her hand. "And once we get to Barcelona I have friends, a condo, a club I like to go to. I might just ditch you."

She laughed. Again. He seemed to always say the right thing to make her feel better. He did have a plane. Here. Waiting. He also had somewhere for them to crash overnight. If he'd owned his condo in Barcelona for any length of time, he probably did have friends he'd want to go clubbing with.

And she'd have a few hours alone tonight for a bubble bath. She could chill and get her perspective back.

Because it *had* hit her all the wrong ways that Pierre had a home in Spain and in their *years* together he'd never mentioned it.

She needed some time to unwind and Trent was offering it.

How could that possibly go wrong?

"All right. Let's go."

CHAPTER THREE

TRENT CALLED HIS PILOT. Having an international cell phone, as Trent obviously did, she was tempted to call her mom but decided against it. When he finished his chat with his pilot, they climbed into the limo and headed to the airport. They landed on a private airstrip in Spain a few hours later, but it took another hour to get from the rural airstrip to Trent's condo.

When he opened the door for her and she stepped inside, she gasped. The place was amazing. Built in an old factory, the condo retained the original brick walls, but they'd been scrubbed to clean perfection. A row of four tall, thin windows brought in light that accented peach-colored club chairs across from a modern gray burlap sofa. The coffee table was a shiny wooden rectangle. Its open middle would have been the perfect place to stack magazines or books. But there were no magazines or books. Not in the open space of the table or strewn around. There wasn't a personal item anywhere.

"Let me guess. You don't come here often."

He tossed his keys on the long island of the spotless kitchen. Sturdy wood cabinets had been painted sage green. Shiny green, white and gray geometric-print tiles created the backsplash. Stainless-steel appliances completed the kitchen.

"No. I'm here all the time."

She glanced around. Even as particular as she was, she had magazines, books, pictures, scattered about.

"It's just all so…clean." Sanitary. As if he didn't have a personality. Or a family—

He had told her that he was distanced from his family.

The thought of not having pictures of Jake, Avery and Abby on her mantel or Seth, Harper and Crystal on the end table by her sofa squeezed her heart. The thought of not having her brothers and their families in her life or being in theirs almost brought tears to her eyes.

"I'm not one for having things lying around."

Okay. She'd give him that. But it had to be sad, difficult, having a mom but not being able to call her with questions or brothers and sisters-in-law to laugh with.

Before she could ask him about his family, he said, "Here's the plan. I'll contact my personal shopper. We'll have her send over some jeans, a few T-shirts and something nice to wear tonight so we can go out."

Not hardly. Her plan was for a soothing bubble bath. "*We* can go out?"

"For *dinner*. You do have to eat."

"Oh. Okay." She fought the urge to squeeze her eyes shut, dismayed with herself for jumping to conclusions. She was so uptight about Pierre that she kept assuming Trent was as bossy as her ex. She had to relax.

He picked up his phone, hit the screen three times and after a few seconds he said, "Claudine. I'm back in Barcelona. Unfortunately, it was an unexpected trip and I'll need clothes for at least another two days. Make it three."

He paused as Sabrina assumed the person on the other end of the call spoke. He laughed. "Yes, everything, including something nice to wear out to dinner tonight."

He paused again, chuckling. He clearly liked his personal shopper.

A sliver of jealousy wound through her, surprising her. First, she had no claim on Trent—didn't want one. Second, the woman he spoke with was in his employ. She laughed with her employees all the time.

"I'm traveling with a friend. She'll need three days' worth of clothes and something pretty for dinner." He caught Sabrina's gaze and grinned devilishly. "Yes. You know my taste. Get her what one of my dates would usually wear."

Sabrina's eyes widened. She'd seen his dates in sparkly little red dresses that clung to their bodies but looked okay because they were wafer-thin. She, on the other hand, had boobs and hips.

"I can't wear what your girlfriends wear!"

Trent ignored her. "About a size eight."

Shocked that he'd hit her size on the head, she nonetheless stormed over to him. "I'm not wearing something you'd get for one of your girlfriends!"

He clicked off the call. "Oh, sorry. You said that two seconds too late."

"No, I didn't! You deliberately hung up, so I couldn't change what you'd told her!"

He ambled over to the sofa. "Is that so bad?"

"Yes! Your dates are thin as paper! I have curves."

"Exactly. Curves that you never show off. You'll look great."

"I don't think so."

"I do. Besides, wouldn't it be fun to be someone different for a night?"

She shook her head. "I don't do things like pretend to be someone different." It had taken her too long to become the perfect McCallan daughter to step out of character.

"You just made my point. You *don't* do things like this, things that are fun just for the sake of having fun. You need to loosen up a bit. If you don't like the outfit, it won't matter. We're in a city where no one knows you. You can toss the dress when we get home."

Seeing she wasn't changing his mind, she marched to the Carrara marble island and grabbed his phone.

"What are you doing?"

"You think it's so fun to dress like someone else." She hit the redial button on his phone. "I'm calling your shopper and… Claudine? This is Sabrina McCallan. I'm Trent Sigmund's friend…the woman you're buying the dress for."

He sighed. "Seriously. I think you'll look great in something…"

Putting her hand over the phone she said, "Cheap? Sleazy?"

"Just a tad more sparkly."

She shook her head once, quickly, in disbelief. "Are you ashamed of me?"

He laughed. "Actually, I want to show you off."

Her breath stalled. He wanted to show her off—

She caught that thought before it could run away with itself. She was a McCallan. Her mother always said they had more dignity than to "show off." Still, she wasn't the one showing off. Trent wanted to show *her* off. Like someone who was important to him—

She'd never been important to anybody but her mom. She'd certainly never been important to a man. Her heart filled with warmth, but she fought it. She didn't need a man to show her off.

Still, one look at Trent's face and she knew she wasn't

changing his mind. But the craziest idea popped into her head. "And what if I want to show *you* off?"

He shrugged. "Have at it." He took the phone from her hands. "Claudine. I'm going to put Sabrina back on the line. Get me whatever she says."

He handed the phone back to her.

She looked from the top of his curly black hair, down the chest and flat abs she remembered from the morning, to his feet.

"I think Armani. A charcoal-gray suit with a pale blue shirt… I want it to be such a pale blue that it's almost white…and a silver print tie."

He made a gagging noise.

She said, "Thanks, Claudine," then also asked for a curling iron and hair-dryer before she hung up the phone. "Now we'll see who likes dressing like someone else."

He shook his head. "I don't hate suits. I just don't wear them often." He grinned. "This is going to be a fun night."

She sighed. "You really need to get out more."

They bummed around for most of the afternoon, eating lunch, walking under the leafy canopy created by the trees lining the streets of Barcelona. She marveled at the simple beauty of the city. She'd never been to Spain before, let alone walked the streets of one of its fabulous cities. It was easy to see that Trent spent a lot of time here because he knew the best restaurants, said hello to pass-ersby, was casually comfortable walking along.

When they returned to his condo around six, the purchases of Trent's personal shopper sat in two stacks of boxes and bags on the marble top of the kitchen island.

"Our clothes have arrived."

She strode over, running her hand along the first box.

Pink-and-white-striped with a black bow, it reminded her of coming home from school and discovering her mom had been shopping that day. It usually meant her dad was traveling and dinner that night would be happy.

Sensation after sensation poured through her. Relief. Joy. Expectation.

"Want to look at what's inside or take everything to the spare bedroom and try things on?"

"I think I want a few minutes to myself with the red spandex dress." A few minutes to get her heart to settle down and to savor the good memories flitting through her brain. She hadn't had the horrid childhood her brothers had, but a river of caution and fear had run through their Upper East Side penthouse. Good memories had been few and far between. When they came, she enjoyed the feelings they brought with them.

She took the bags and boxes to the spare room and began sorting through to see what was inside. Two pair of jeans and a pair of shorts—Barcelona was a tad warm—undergarments, and the smallest dress in recorded history.

Her memories forgotten, she marched back to the kitchen, waving the little blue dress. "I can't wear this."

"Have you tried it on?"

She sighed.

He opened the suit box. "Don't forget I'm stuck with this."

"It's a suit. You've worn them before."

"And you've worn dresses before." He shook his head. "Come on. Let's just have some fun tonight."

The seriousness in his brown eyes reminded her that his childhood might not have been filled with fear, but it had been filled with loneliness. So he wanted to have some fun? Couldn't she, for once, forget her mom's voice in her head and do something silly to make someone else happy? Someone whose childhood might have been sadder than hers?

Not wanting him to realize she was capitulating because she felt an unexpected connection to him, she gruffly said, "All right. But I'm tossing this sparkly little thing when we return tonight."

He shrugged. "Fine by me."

She huffed back to the bedroom where she showered, fixed her hair, applied makeup. When she couldn't put it off any longer, she shimmied into the blue dress and stared at herself in the mirror.

It wasn't god-awful.

Okay. Seriously. She went to the gym three times a week so though she wasn't waiflike, she had a nice figure. And the dress—damn his hide—looked good. She wouldn't want to be wearing it walking around with her mother, but she was with a friend.

A male friend who wanted to see her in a tight dress.

She shook her head. This was Ziggy…

No. Actually, she was with Trent. Adult. Sexy. Trent.

She slid into the tall silver shoes the shopper had also bought. Trent had said she made distinctions that didn't matter? Maybe thinking of him as a different guy was one of them?

Maybe she should go back to thinking of him as Ziggy—Seth's friend, not hers—to end all this confusion?

Sabrina came out of her bedroom, and Trent's mouth fell open. He'd known she'd look good. He assumed Claudine had bought the blue dress to match with what Sabrina had instructed her to get for him—

But wow. Blue was her color and she was born to wear the sparkly fabric that hugged her curves.

"I look like a hooker, Ziggy."

"No. You look like a woman who wants to have a fun night out on the town. And don't call me Ziggy." His voice softened with the familiarity he was feeling with her. "I like when you call me Trent."

He smiled at her and she weakly returned his smile. He couldn't imagine why a shift of names seemed to trouble her, so he turned in a half circle, showing off the Armani suit. "And how do I look?"

"Like a guy who forgot his tie."

He'd nixed the tie and had opened the top few buttons of his shirt in deference to the heat. But he also wasn't about to wear a suit dancing. And come hell or high water he was taking her dancing.

"Let's go."

She stayed right where she was. "If I'm going out in this, you're wearing your tie."

He relented. Not because she intimidated him but because he intended to get her on his side so that when he suggested dancing she'd happily agree. But he also had to acknowledge there was a certain boost a person got when wearing expensive clothes. He might like to fish. He might also be very at home in a small-town bar. But he was equally at home with power brokers.

Whether he liked admitting it, Sabrina was a sort of power broker. Smart and savvy, she could hold her own with the best of them. In a way, it was a coup that he'd gotten her to dress sexy.

Now he just had to come up with interesting dinner conversation that would win her over and put her in the mood to dance because if he was in Barcelona he was going to his favorite club.

But the second they were settled in one of Barcelona's beautiful restaurants and had ordered, she asked about his work.

"I buy stocks. I sell stocks. I buy bonds. I sell bonds. There's not much else to it."

"I know you think there's not much to what you do, but it's a skill. A gift." She looked at him over the salad the waiter sat in front of her. "Have you ever considered creating your own mutual fund?"

The horror of the thought almost made him choke. "Why would I do that?"

"I don't know. To contribute to society? To help other people?"

"Look, I have everything set up so that I do a reasonable amount of work and still have time for fun."

"I'm just saying you're the perfect person to create and manage a mutual fund."

She went on talking about business through the entire dinner. When dessert arrived, Trent felt four IQ points smarter, but not one iota relaxed.

He came to Barcelona to relax. She was ruining that.

"Do you always talk business?"

"No."

"Just with me, then?"

"It's the one thing we have in common." She shrugged. "My father always talked business at the dinner table with my brothers." She shrugged again. "It just seemed like the right thing to do."

Her past came into focus for Trent. "Let me get this straight. You talked business at the dinner table every night?"

"Not every night. My dad had business dinners some nights. When he was away, my mom would joke and play with us. But when my dad was around, we talked business."

"You think men only want to talk business?"

"Not just men. Women like to talk business, too."

"All the time?"

"Some of my most productive conversations are over lunch or dinner."

Knowing what he'd been told by Seth about their childhood and adding in this tidbit, even more of Sabrina's personality clicked for him. "Oh, honey."

"What?"

"We are so going dancing tonight."

He rose from the table, walked over and helped her with her chair. "Dancing?"

"I've seen you at charity balls. You love to dance."

And now that he thought about seeing her dancing, he realized he'd never seen her dancing with Pierre. Hell, he'd never seen Pierre.

"I do love to dance."

"Remember how much fun you had at the art show in Paris last year? The one where you could be Sally Mc-Millan because your family isn't as recognizable in Europe as they are in Manhattan?"

Sabrina's heart stopped. One of her brothers *had* told him. "All right, who do I shake silly? Seth or Jake? That alter ego is a secret."

"Seth mentioned it and accidentally." He winced. "He was telling me how good your work is and how proud he was of you last year in Paris when you could be Sally because you knew you wouldn't be recognized."

Unexpected warmth filled her. It surprised her that her brother bragged about her, but it surprised her even more that Trent remembered something from a year ago. Some years Pierre forgot her birthday. He never remembered her showings, and even if he did remember to come, he wouldn't be able to recall what had happened an entire year later.

"I do remember how much fun I had that weekend." There had been an after-party where she'd danced and danced with Avery and Harper.

He smiled. "Then let's go dance."

She nodded as his argument sank in. Just as in Paris the year before, no one in Barcelona would know her. Why not have fun the way she had in Paris? There'd be no one to tell her mom if she looked just the tiniest bit unladylike in the shiny blue dress—

Except she didn't feel unladylike.

She felt—

Actually, she felt young. Carefree—

A woman who was going to have a baby felt carefree?

She couldn't explain it. But the reminder that she was a soon-to-be-mom about to go dancing didn't make her unhappy. If anything, new joy filled her.

So, yeah. She was going dancing.

CHAPTER FOUR

TRENT DIRECTED HER out of the restaurant and into the city. They walked a few blocks and Sabrina began to hear and feel the pounding beat of the music pouring out of a building a block away.

The sound lured her down the street and by the time they entered the club, she wanted to dance. Really dance. Not just get on the floor and gyrate. She wanted to move. She wanted to stop being tense and forget about telling Pierre. Tomorrow would be soon enough to worry about Pierre.

Partly because she felt different tonight. Sexier. She knew it was the dress.

A dress *Trent* wanted her to wear.

The weirdest heat raced up her spine.

He led her to a booth that had four people sitting in the semicircle bench seat. He motioned to the people, who gaped at her, wide-eyed with interest.

"Sabrina, this is Mateo and Luciana and Valentina and Samuel. My friends. Guys, this is Sabrina, my friend Seth's sister."

Two of them said, *"Hola."*

Two said, *"Buenas noches."*

Trent faced her. "I met Luciana and Valentina clubbing a few years back. Eventually, Mateo and Samuel joined the group."

With the music blaring around them, Sabrina could barely hear him, so she knew his friends hadn't. She couldn't explain the goofy looks on their faces as she and Trent slid onto the bench seat with them.

"You are enjoying Barcelona?" Mateo asked, his English made smooth and sexy by his accent.

She nodded. She was enjoying Barcelona. "We took a walk this afternoon, under the canopy of trees. The city is breathtaking."

Luciana nodded. "It's a great place. There's always somewhere to go, something to do."

Sabrina tried not to stare at her. She was American.

Valentina said, "New York is like that."

Luciana shrugged. "Sometimes. I like it here better."

"You like it here better because it's warmer," Trent said with a laugh. He whipped off his tie and jacket and tossed them onto the bench seat. Then he took Sabrina's hand and pulled her off the seat. "I promised Sabrina we would dance."

He guided her to the crowded dance floor. When they stopped, Sabrina said, "Your friends seemed surprised to see you here tonight."

"No, I'd called them and told them I was coming, bringing a friend. I think they're surprised that you're so beautiful."

"You don't date beautiful women?"

He laughed. "So this is a date?"

"No!"

With a sigh, he relented. "They are surprised that someone who is an obligation, the sister of a friend who needs some assistance, is beautiful."

It was the second time he'd called her beautiful. Off-hand, casually, as if everyone knew. Or as if he couldn't stop noticing.

Her pulse sped up, and she stood there, staring at him. He laughed at what must have been a very odd expression on her face, but the music called to her. She felt like dancing again and at this point dancing was a much better idea than finishing their conversation.

She closed her eyes, pulled in a deep breath and let the music take her. Even if Trent had friends in Barcelona, no one knew *her*. She could dance like an idiot and tomorrow it wouldn't be in the paper.

So she let herself go. Let the beat take her arms and legs, let all the tension of the past two days ripple away. One song turned into another. Trent caught her hands and she opened her eyes. Lights flashed. Music blared. He twirled her around once, twice and she laughed. The third song rolled in on the heels of song two. She noticed Trent's friends were on the dance floor, squeezing in a few feet away. People around them twisted and turned, bodies moving to the beat. Trent laughed and waved, a signal that she was wandering a bit too far away from him and she slid back.

Beside them, a couple danced close. Keeping her hand on her partner's shoulder, the woman circled him before she pressed herself up against him and kissed him. One of her legs grazed up his hip and back down.

Sabrina's eyebrows rose. The room got hot. Trent grabbed her hands again but this time he pulled her out of the crowd and over to their table.

"I think we could both use some water."

As she slid into the booth Sabrina said, "You don't have to drink water because I can't have a beer."

He slid in beside her. "Funny. I'd have never taken you for a beer girl."

"I'm not. Usually I like Scotch, but beer is good on a hot day, at a barbecue, or dancing."

"I'm having trouble picturing you at a barbecue."

"Avery and Jake own a house in the country…close to the small town where she grew up. Jake loves to barbecue."

A waitress came over and Trent ordered water for them both. When she returned with two crystal glasses filled with water, he drank his without complaint or qualm.

She took a long gulp of hers.

"I notice you don't seem uncomfortable in the dress."

She glanced down at the form-fitting, sparkling blue garment. The symbol of her freedom in Europe.

"You haven't tugged the hem down once."

She hadn't.

She caught his gaze.

"You have the legs for a short dress."

Electricity shimmied through her. She closed her eyes and shook her head. It was the weirdest thing to know someone for ten years and not really get to know them until forced to spend two entire days with them.

But that wasn't the weirdest of the feelings floating through her right now. She liked him. She might not believe sparks flying and blood shimmering were a good reason to date someone, but tonight she realized the feeling did exist.

He made her blood shimmer. When he looked at her, her chest tightened. Knowing he'd chosen this dress for her, maybe because he wanted to see her looking sexy, sent her heart rate off the charts.

She had honestly thought the poets were wrong. But here she was. Feeling things she never believed existed.

She bounced from the table. "Let's dance some more."

Let's get out on the dance floor, where we can't talk

and I won't think about all these reactions that mean nothing.

She knew what love had gotten her mom. Heartbreak and fear. She didn't think she had any reason to fear Trent but giving in to these feelings would definitely cause heartbreak.

She slithered her way through the crowd to the dance floor. The pounding beat of the music urged her to move. Which was what she needed to do. Not to escape. Just not to think. Trent eased in beside her and before she knew it they were dancing beside the hot couple again.

The guy slid his hand up his girlfriend's neck and pulled her face toward him for an openmouthed kiss.

Sabrina watched, mesmerized. That would be how Trent would kiss. Sort of commanding with his hand hooking around her neck and pulling her close. But he'd also get right to the point with the openmouthed kiss.

She took a breath to clear her head of that thought, but as she did the music shifted again. A ballad replaced the pulsing beat. Trent slid his hand around her waist and took her hand. Before she could think to say no, she was in his arms.

It was so different than anything she'd ever experienced that she almost froze. She caught herself before she missed a step in the dance, but she couldn't stop feeling. Even the fabric of the suit she'd chosen for him was soft, sensual. His hands were slightly calloused. And when she looked into his eyes, she all but melted.

He was intelligent, sexy and happy.

And she was in his arms. Close enough to feel the movements of his body, to savor the feeling of his shoulder under her palm—

She swallowed hard. They were in Spain because she was on her way to see the father of her child. A guy she didn't want to marry because she didn't believe in marriage. She didn't believe in love.

And Trent, like her brothers, needed love to heal from the wounds of his lonely childhood. He might not know it, but as much of a planner, analyzer as she was, it was clear as day to Sabrina. She'd witnessed what had happened with Jake and Seth. They floated through life, unhappy, until the right woman helped them face their pain and let it go. *That* was what Trent needed. And maybe there'd be a third unicorn woman out there who could care for him the way Avery and Harper had healed Jake and Seth.

She eased out of his arms.

She wasn't that woman. She didn't believe in these squiggly feelings. And even if they existed, her mom had felt them for her dad and she'd married him and been miserable, afraid, for forty years.

No one, no feeling, was worth forty years of misery.

Trent saw the happiness drain out of Sabrina's blue-gray eyes. For a good two minutes he'd watched her changing, watched her interest pique and her breath stutter, indicating she was every bit as attracted to him as he was to her.

Then she'd stopped, frozen, and whatever had popped into her brain, it sucked every bit of happiness out of their moment…

He fought the disappointment that surged through him. Not just for himself, for her. These feelings might be good, but they were ill-timed. She carried another man's child. And though she thought Pierre wouldn't want anything to do with their baby, he might surprise her. Trent couldn't do anything about their attraction until that situation was settled. For the baby's sake, he hoped Pierre would want to marry her.

But if he didn't…

That was a question for tomorrow. Tonight, no matter how much he was enjoying this, enjoying *her*, giving in to their unlikely attraction wasn't right.

He stepped back. "I guess we're ready to go home."

She nodded.

They said goodbye to his friends, who were still all smiles. He was sure they were confused about Sabrina. They knew him well enough to know she was more than just his friend's baby sister, but his normal dates were tall and thin with wild hair and mischief in their eyes. Sabrina was serious. Beautiful but serious.

His feelings for Sabrina confused him, too.

Which was another reason to back off.

The return trip to his condo was made in total silence. In the lobby of his building, Sabrina gave him a sheepish smile.

"I'm just tired."

No. She'd figured all this out in her head, convinced herself they were wrong for each other and was back to her normal self.

Which was good. It *had to be good.* He didn't want to be the man responsible for keeping her baby from its father. Worse, he didn't want to be the fourth wheel in a relationship that should only have three: Sabrina, Pierre and their child. He'd already been the extra person in a family. He knew how painful and lonely it was.

They entered the elevator. The door swished closed and her perfume floated to him. He squeezed his eyes shut, trying to block it, but all that did was conjure visions of her dancing. Happily dancing. He hadn't seen her laughing at her brother's wedding, but she'd been happy tonight. Maybe because she'd been dancing with him?

He thanked God when the elevator doors opened. His thoughts were going in a very bad direction. Pride over showing a woman a good time was a normal male re-action. Especially a woman so beautiful. Especially a woman who had trusted him enough to wear the dress he'd chosen for her. And a woman who desperately needed a good time.

But that was all there could be to it.

They reached the door of his condo. He unlocked it and they stepped inside. She headed back to the extra room but pivoted to face him.

"Thank you."

Disarmed by her sincerity, he tossed his keys in the air and caught them one-handed. "For?"

"I could say stupid things like the dress or dinner or the fun time dancing, but that would be a cover. I needed to relax. You saw that. You helped me."

She said it as if no one had ever helped her before…

No. She said that as if no one had ever *seen* her before.

His heart contracted. No one had seen him most of his childhood. It had taken courage, genius and earning enough money to fund a small country before he'd felt seen, heard. Who would have thought a woman with two brothers who doted on her and a mother who thought the sun rose and set on her would feel alone?

He cleared his throat. "You're probably not going to believe this, but it really was my pleasure."

She smiled and caught his gaze with her big blue eyes. "Then maybe you should be thanking me."

He laughed because she expected him to. But a million thoughts raced through his brain. A million sensations bombarded his body. He hadn't felt this connection, this need, with anyone. Ever.

"I should." He paused for a breath. "Thank you. I really did have a great time." He wanted to kiss her so badly his chest ached with it. He wanted to show her she was beautiful and worthy of any man's attention. He longed for it with a desperation that surprised him.

But they weren't right for each other. And if they crossed a line and he hurt her, Seth would shake him silly…and he'd deserve it. But more than that, it would shift the focus of this trip. Maybe cause her to say no if Pierre wanted to expand their relationship because of their child.

He nudged his head in the direction of the hall, indicating she should go to her room. "Good night."

She nodded once. "Good night."

He tossed his jacket and tie to the kitchen island then sank into one of the two chairs in the living room. Using the remote hidden in the top of the wooden sofa table, he pressed a button that turned the huge mirror over the fireplace into a big-screen TV. He kept the volume down low enough not to disturb Sabrina and searched for something to watch.

It was going to be a long night.

Sabrina awakened the next morning feeling unexpectedly refreshed. She didn't know if it was too soon in her pregnancy for morning sickness, but so far, so good. No puking, no dizziness, no queasiness.

She showered and dressed in a pair of jeans and a pale blue T-shirt, but didn't slip her feet into shoes. Trent's condo was comfy. Homey. She padded barefoot to the main living area, telling herself she wasn't eager to see him. He was a fun guy. He had shown her a good time because that was who he was. She could have been as ugly as a muddy fence and he would have been a good host.

Because that was how she now saw him. Her host. Nothing more.

The night before, lying in bed, she'd convinced herself that everything between them was fine. There had

been no awkward moment when she was sure he wanted
to kiss her. Her pulse hadn't really skipped a beat when
he looked at her, and her heart hadn't nosedived when
she'd realized how good it felt to touch him. He was her
brother's friend, doing her a favor.

That was even how he'd explained her to his friends.

All those things she'd *thought* she'd experienced had to
have been one-sided. Otherwise, he would have kissed her.

Exactly.

She walked into the empty main area, hoping he stored
bottled water somewhere. "Trent?"

The place was eerily quiet. Kind of like her condo before she raced out for work each morning. Empty. Echoing the sounds of her movements back to her.

She peered around the kitchen island, down the long
row of sage-colored cabinets. "Trent?"

Well, she certainly wasn't going back to his bedroom
to ask about something as simple as a bottle of water.
She checked the refrigerator, found it empty and decided
she'd grab her purse and go out to look for a shop that
sold water...

Without the proper currency?

It was Monday. Surely, she could find a bank.

She was just about to return to her room to get her
purse when the condo door opened. Trent stepped inside, carrying a tray with two paper cups, the kind that
usually held coffee, and two bags.

"The two coffees are for me." He displayed a bag. "I
have water in here." He nudged his chin toward the second bag. "And bagels and cream cheese in here." He set
everything on the island. "Or, if you want, we can go
out for breakfast."

"You had me at cream cheese."

"Good. Because I'm starving, and we'd wait at least

twenty minutes for our food even if we went to one of the restaurants just down the street."

She rooted through the first bag and grabbed a water. After taking a long drink, she said, "Thanks. I didn't realize how thirsty I was."

"We danced a lot. I should have thought of that and had water in the fridge."

She might have relegated him to the role of host, but there was such a thing as being a demanding guest. A woman with proper manners would not do that.

"You don't have to wait on me. I'm fine."

"You're also my friend's little sister."

That reasoning was a good addition to her "host" theory for why he didn't want to act on the feelings that had pulsed between them the night before, and she pounced on it.

"Ah. Don't want to make Seth mad?"

He laughed as he walked around the center island, bent down and pulled out a toaster. "I've never been afraid of Seth."

She opened the bagels. "Really?"

He took two, split them and slipped them into the four-slot toaster. "Really. When we met, he was like a scared puppy. For all the lecturing your father had done, he hadn't taught Seth anything about the real world. Your brother knew how to do anything that involved money. He just didn't know how to get money."

Sabrina sat on one of the stools across the wide counter from Trent. "What does that mean?"

"Your brother's main source of income was an allowance. Anytime your dad withheld it, Seth went into a tailspin."

She leaned her elbows on the counter and her chin on her entwined fingers. "So what happened?"

"I was working as a waiter at a bistro and I got him a

job." He shook his head. "I still remember him standing there, watching everybody, as if absorbing everything. Then he picked up an apron and a pad and pencil and he went to work."

"That simple?"

"Oh, he dropped trays and spilled a drink on a guy's head—"

She gasped. "Spilled a drink on a guy's head!"

"In fairness, a customer in a hurry bumped into his elbow."

"Oh, that's funny!"

"You're not supposed to get *funny* from the story. You're supposed to see how hard he tried." Trent shook his head. "No, I think what you're supposed to see is that your brother didn't think himself too good for work. He was eager to make his own way."

"That's why we didn't see him for two years?"

"You didn't see him because he was tired of being humiliated and embarrassed by your dad. He'd have gone to see you or your mom in a heartbeat, but he wanted no part of your dad."

"He hadn't seen Dad in years when he passed."

Trent's voice softened. "Your dad hurt him a lot."

"I get that."

"And what about you?"

"What about me?"

"How did you fare with your dad?"

The bagels popped out of the toaster. As Trent pulled them from the little slots, Sabrina found knives in a drawer beside the sink and opened the cream cheese.

"My dad thought I was adorable. My mom capitalized on that. She taught me to be prim and proper." She took one of the bagels from Trent and began to slather it with cream cheese. "Very polite. Mannerly. It served me well."

Trent said, "Served you well?" before he took a bite of his bagel.

"As long as I never did anything wrong, he didn't yell at me or snipe at me or boss me around."

"Couldn't Seth and Jake have done that?"

"They weren't as cute."

He laughed. "I'm serious."

"So am I. I was an adorable child. Jake was all arms and legs and Seth didn't grow out of his baby weight until he was twenty. But also, they were guys. My dad wanted them to grow up tough and ruthless." She met his gaze. "As he was."

"And instead he turned them in the other direction."

"Jake was a maybe for a while. He might not have cheated or lied as our dad had but he was a hard-nosed businessman."

"Jake? The guy who melts every time Abby looks at him."

"It's why Avery didn't want to marry him. Why she was afraid to let him have a part in raising Abby. He didn't see anything but work, didn't care about anything but the McCallan legacy."

He finished the first half of his bagel. "Your family certainly has some tales."

"And we don't hide it. Hiding things was what my father did. So we're very open about our lives."

"Except Sally McMillan."

She snorted. "Sally's the exception. Otherwise, my work wouldn't be judged on its merit."

He grabbed the second half of his bagel. "I get it."

"Do you?"

"Well, as much as I can. I didn't grow up surrounded by maids and drivers. We didn't have to worry about the people who worked for us carrying gossip out to the street."

"There was more to it than that." She slowly spread cream cheese across the second half of her bagel. "My dad had a temper. We all just tried to stay out of his way."

He took a sip of coffee. "I'm sorry. I didn't mean to diminish what happened in your penthouse."

She shrugged. "You didn't. We all ended up fine. Even my mother."

"That's good."

She smiled and nodded but looking into his dark eyes, she remembered that everything from his not-so-happy family hadn't worked out. Oh, he had money and brains—genius—but he was alone.

"Anyway, the point of all of this was to explain that your brother and I grew very close while living together and working together. It started off as me and my friend Clark, then Clark brought in Seth. Then after a year or so Harper moved next door and Clark fell for her like a ton of bricks and spent all his spare time at her apartment. Then it was just me and Seth hanging out, working together, going to school. I taught Seth some street stuff. He taught me about investing and saving. And we both landed on our feet. I think of him as more than a friend. I think of him as a brother."

She considered that for a few seconds. "You think you owe him."

He bobbed his head in agreement. "Yes."

"He thinks he owes you and Clark."

"He owes Clark because none of us would have had a place to live if Clark hadn't come directly from the Midwest with enough money for a month's rent and a security deposit."

"But he owes you for the street smarts."

He laughed. "And he paid me back by teaching me things—and introducing me to the right people—after getting all three of us a job in an investment firm right out of university."

"Why didn't you throw in with Seth and Clark when they started their own investment firm?"

"They were conservative." He laughed devilishly. "I wanted to roll the dice."

"Lucky for you."

"Yes." He took another drink of coffee. "So what time do we leave for the ranch?"

She glanced down at her jeans and shirt. "I'm ready now."

He spread his hands accommodatingly. "So am I."

"Let's clean this up and we can head out."

"I'll clean up. You go get your things."

She rounded the island and pushed his hands aside when he reached for the bag of bagels. "Don't be silly. I can clean up."

He watched her make short order of tying the twist tie around the bagels and storing them in a drawer as he tucked the extra water into the fridge and wet a paper towel to wipe off the countertop.

Understanding wobbled through him. It was as if she went out of her way to let people know she wasn't pampered or spoiled. Seth and Jake hadn't had to do that because stories of their father's abuse had rippled into Manhattan's folklore. But Sabrina had been the adorable little girl. The one their father had doted on.

He supposed that was a good enough reason for her not to want to be thought of as spoiled—though compared to Seth and Jake she had been.

When everything was clean, she turned to go back to the extra room, but he stopped her. "Let's get all of our stuff and that way we can drive to the airstrip from Pierre's."

He didn't want to mention that when they got to Pierre's and she told the Frenchman about their baby, Pierre might want her to stay, and this way she'd have all her things. Trent was nothing more than a guy doing a favor for the sister of a friend. It would be good for her and Pierre to talk this out, maybe even needing a few days together to get through all of it, maybe deciding they wanted to make a commitment for the sake of their child.

But that didn't mean he had to like it.

In fact, he absolutely hated it. She rarely danced with Pierre. She never talked about Pierre making her happy.

And he was delivering Sabrina and her baby right to his door.

That was beginning to rankle.

CHAPTER FIVE

TRENT WAITED FOR her to get her things from the extra room and laughed when she came out lugging a suitcase bulging at the seams.

"We should stop and get you another bag. Or you could just leave some of the clothes behind with the blue sparkly dress."

She pretended great interest in searching through her purse. "Actually, I packed the blue dress."

That brought him up short. "Really?"

She met his gaze. "It grew on me."

Her eyes flickered the tiniest bit. A person who hadn't known what to look for would have missed it. He almost teased her about wanting the dress as a memento of a good time but stopped himself. He liked the idea of something he'd bought her hanging in her closet. He couldn't have her, but it was nice that they'd made a connection. Nice that she wanted to keep something he'd bought her.

He made a quick call to the doorman and when they stepped out onto the street, his shiny black Jaguar awaited them. The doorman opened the passenger-side door. She got in and Trent rounded the hood to get behind the wheel.

"I still say you should start a mutual fund."

Ah. On a long drive, the safest thing to talk about was business.

Punching the address of Pierre's house into the GPS, he said, "Not a chance."

"Maybe volunteer to be a mentor at my nonprofit."

He laughed.

"Maybe give just one lecture."

He almost said an automatic, "No," until he realized that getting involved with her business would keep them connected, keep him in her life. The scramble of his pulse at just the thought told him it was a bad idea. He was taking her to the father of her child, the man she should at least consider letting into her life, for her baby's sake. There was no place for him in that equation.

He pulled the car onto the street. "I'm a professional hider. Normal people don't know who I am. Bankers do. Investors do. But I can go to a coffee shop or restaurant without being recognized. I like it that way."

She said, "Humph," and settled back on her seat, but he could see the wheels of her brain were turning.

"You're not going to change my mind."

"You're so sure."

Keeping his attention on the road, he said, "Yep." He paused for a second then said, "Don't you like being Sally McMillan, getting away from your life?"

She cut him a look.

"That's my life all the time. Private. Secure. I can do anything I want—as long as I don't break the law—and no one cares."

The GPS took them out of Barcelona and onto a long stretch of road that wound through the country. The day was warm, the sun bright. Rays hit the leaves and grass and seemed to shimmer around them.

"Mind if I put the car's top down?"

She ran her hand down her loose hair. "Sure. It's not like I have a hairdo. Even if it tangles, I can brush it out. So I'm game."

He pulled off the road and lowered the top. In a few minutes they were cruising again, taking the advice of his GPS, with the wind in their hair. The noise of the air swirling around them precluded conversation, but there was something poetic about the silence. He liked peace and privacy. He loved the beauty of Spain and he felt like he was sharing that with Sabrina, a woman who seemed to use business—even the business of her art—so she didn't really have to experience life.

Shaking his head at the stupidity of his thoughts— he was neither a poet nor a philosopher—he cleared his head and focused on enjoying the drive. A little over an hour later, the GPS took them through a series of turns that led to their destination.

As he navigated a long lane framed on each side by wood fences that created a corral on both sides of the roadway, he watched Sabrina take it all in. Cattle, barns and outbuildings, all under the dome of a matchless blue sky.

He stopped in front of a pale brown stucco house and said nothing as she stared at the huge two-story structure. An etched-glass door, trimmed in dark brown wood with two glass globe lights standing sentinel, held her attention for at least a minute before she glanced over at him.

"Maybe he just rents the house?"

Trent shrugged. "Maybe." He hopped out of the car and eased around to the passenger side. Sabrina still hadn't moved. Heat shimmered around them in the stagnant air. The cattle were too far away to hear. If there was farm machinery working, the sounds of it also didn't reach the house. The dwelling had probably been located here for exactly that reason. To protect it from the sights, sounds and smells of the ranch.

It seemed Pierre was a tad craftier than everyone had given him credit for.

Trent opened the door. Sabrina delicately stepped out, but Trent suddenly envisioned her in the same jeans and T-shirt except wearing boots and a cowboy hat rather than sandals with her wild hair flowing around her. Would it even occur to her that she could fit here? Would it even occur to her that the prim and proper way her mom had raised her was to please a dad who had been dead for years…that she could be herself?

She passed her hand through her hair as if just remembering it had been tossed by the wind for over an hour. But rather than reach for a brush or comb, she glanced around again. Then shook her head and pointed at the steps leading to a porch with a dark brown railing.

"Let's go."

His heart sank. It was almost as if she'd seen what he'd seen. With her hair slightly messed and in blue jeans, she belonged here.

Would Pierre see that, too? Would the father of her baby see her in his home and realize she could fit?

Did Sabrina want Pierre to see her in his home and recognize that she belonged here…with him?

Sabrina took a silent breath, hoping to unscramble the confusion in her brain as she led Trent up the steps of Pierre's house. She saw dollar signs everywhere. The pristine grounds, the older home that had clearly been remodeled; the sheer expanse of land around her told her this was no winter retreat. This was a working ranch.

Still, she pasted a smile on her face before she rang the doorbell. As she waited for Pierre, she wished Trent wasn't with her because she had the oddest sense she was going to lambaste her ex for lying. Even if it was a lie by omission.

It so wasn't her. She didn't lambaste anybody. She stood up for her clients. She also stood her ground with her clients when they didn't like her advice. She could be tough, determined.

She simply didn't get into fights. She didn't lambaste people. She rarely even raised her voice. She let her facts and figures stand on their merit.

She didn't need to lambaste anybody.

She rang the bell again and looked around the ranch one more time.

A ranch might not be her style of living, but for heaven's sake, if Pierre owned this, he'd been seriously downplaying his net worth to her, getting her to pay his airfare to the US when he visited, letting her subtly pick up every check in every restaurant.

The insult of it resurrected an indignation she couldn't quash, as outrage over his dodging expenses sent a crackle of energy through her veins.

This time when she rang the bell, she hit it hard and let her finger rest on the button. The sound was so loud they could hear it on the porch.

"You might want to ease up on the bell, Skippy."

"He's not going to ignore me."

The door jerked open. A middle-aged woman with dark hair and huge dark eyes gaped at her as she rattled off something in Spanish.

Sabrina glanced at Trent who said, "She wants to know why you're holding on to the bell."

Sabrina yanked her finger away.

"Tell her I'm here to see Pierre."

He said something that Sabrina couldn't translate but which ended with Pierre.

The woman answered. Trent turned to Sabrina with a sigh. "He's not here."

Sabrina spun to face him. "What!"

"Pierre's not here. She's a maid just finishing her weekly work, about to go home for the day."

The maid said something else.

Trent smiled and nodded. *"Si."*

Sabrina said, *"Si?"*

"She asked if we'd like to come in for a cold drink."

Oh, she'd like to go in, all right. She'd like a bit of a look at Pierre's "winter" house to see what else he was hiding from her.

"Si. I'd like to come in."

The maid held open the door. Trent motioned for Sabrina to enter first. She stepped into a glamorous entryway with a huge chandelier and shiny black-and-white tiles arranged like a checkerboard.

The maid directed them to a room with the same flooring as the foyer. The far wall was a bank of windows that provided a stunning view of grass and trees growing against the backdrop of the mountains. A piano sat in front of the windows with a tall table, about bar height, against the wall by the door, but otherwise the room was empty.

Trent said, "Wow. I wonder how much it would take to get him to sell this place."

"Shut up."

He winced. "Sorry. I know you thought he was a struggling artist. And he might be." He brightened. "He could have inherited this ranch and be really grateful to his dead relative because he's not making enough from his art to support himself."

"Don't defend him."

The maid returned with a pitcher of something that looked like lemonade and two glasses.

Trent thanked her, then added another line that caused the dark-haired woman to nod and scamper away.

"What did you say to her?"

"I asked her to give us a few minutes."

"For what? To see how wealthy my struggling artist ex-boyfriend really is?"

"More like to let all this sink in."

"You mean the fact that he lied?"

He sniffed a laugh. "I thought you'd say something like he withheld information."

"You thought I'd defend him?"

"I thought you'd split hairs. It seems to be how you comfort yourself."

The maid returned, talking a mile a minute as she pointed at her phone.

Trent said, "Something's come up. She has to go. She said she shouldn't have let us in at all, but she recognized you from the picture on the piano and knew you must be a friend of Pierre's."

"The picture on the piano?" Sabrina walked over and found an eight-by-ten picture of herself—a candid shot, not something professional—framed in wood among a group of pictures. "Oh."

The simplicity of it made her breath catch.

"Don't go all mushy on the guy."

Her gaze snapped up. "All mushy?" She laughed. "No. Oh, no. I'm just a bit confused. Pierre's passionate, but not sentimental." She pointed at the group of pictures of people who had to be friends. "All this doesn't add up. He had money but never picked up a check."

"Because he was a cheapskate?" Trent suggested sarcastically.

She shook her head. "I think it was more about him maintaining an image. I thought he was a starving artist. Maybe he wanted to perpetuate that impression?"

"And now you're back to splitting hairs." He quickly downed his lemonade then angled his chin at the maid, who stood wringing her hands. "Let's go."

Sabrina headed toward the door, but the maid stopped them. Her dark eyes softened. She said something that ended in Italy.

Trent nodded and ushered Sabrina through the foyer and out the door. It wasn't until they were in the car that Sabrina said, "He's in Italy, right?"

"Yes."

"The man does travel."

Trent laughed as he started the engine. "She said if we go to his website, we'll see the address of the gallery where he has his showing."

She let all this new information about Pierre flow through her. Now that she'd wrangled her temper into submission, she reminded herself that they'd had a passionate but surface relationship. She could also understand why he'd withheld things. Neither had committed fully to the relationship. That was their deal.

"I don't blame you if you're angry."

"Actually, I'm not angry. I'm thinking. The bottom line is, Pierre hadn't told me everything about his life, even though I'd told him everything about mine."

He cut her the side eye. "Which is why you have a right to be mad."

"No. I told him everything about myself to explain why I didn't want anything from him but a nice, passionate fling. Part of the way he'd complied was to not tell me anything about himself."

He groaned. "Oh, my God. You've gone from splitting hairs to defending him."

"No. I'm understanding him."

Trent shook his head. "You are the strangest woman."

"No, I'm not. Lots of women are logical."

"Haven't you ever just wanted to let go?"

Had he missed the part where she'd kept her finger on Pierre's doorbell?

She glanced at him. With his attention fixed on the road, she could take a minute to study his perfect nose, high cheekbones, curly black hair. She had wanted to let go the night before. She had wanted to kiss Trent and just let whatever happened happen.

But being with someone like him was the opposite of how she'd spent her entire life. Protecting herself.

Trent Sigmund would entertain her, amuse her, treat her like a princess, make love like a desperate man one minute and a smitten man the next…and he'd disappear as quickly and easily as he'd entered her life. Because he didn't commit. The man didn't even have a picture in his Barcelona condo. And then she'd be hurt.

She had no feelings of pain because of Pierre. Sure, she'd been lonely. And seeing his extravagant home in Spain—and working ranch that probably netted him a boatload of cash every year—had been enough of a shock to boil her blood.

But she wasn't hurt.

Pierre did not have the power to hurt her because she'd kept her emotions out of their fling.

"Did you know my mom was crazy-mad in love with my dad?"

He stole a quick peek at her. "No."

"My dad blew into my mom's life like a hurricane. She wasn't wealthy, but she was beautiful, and she knew it. She'd thought that her beauty had gotten her the love of a wealthy, sophisticated man, and she felt like she'd won the lottery because he hadn't just been swept away by her. She'd been swept away by him. He spoiled her, ravaged her, bought her things, was good to her family."

"And when they got married, all that went away?"

"Yes. Except she still loved him."

"How could she love him after all the things he did to your brothers?"

She shrugged. "By the time he started bullying my brothers, her love had faded. But he threatened to use his money and power to take us away from her if she filed for divorce. She knew the only way she could protect us would be to stay married to him."

He shook his head. "Wow."

"That's what love does to people. That's the real result of letting go. And I will never—never *ever*—set myself up for any of that. Maybe, in a way, Pierre just proved himself to be like my dad, too."

Trent's eyes snapped to hers. "Did he hurt you?"

"No, but he did prove he can't be honest about money."

CHAPTER SIX

TRENT STARED AT her for a few seconds. They'd begun this journey with him not exactly rooting for Pierre, but at least hoping that she would let Pierre into their child's life. He still wanted her baby to know his dad, but he didn't agree that Pierre couldn't be honest about money. He thought the guy was a cheapskate.

But hearing her story about her parents, knowing she'd lived a difficult life when her dad was around, he suddenly understood why she wore stuffy suits and conservative cocktail dresses.

In a way, he also understood why the Sally McMillan pseudonym worked so well for her.

She was so afraid of life and love, afraid of getting close to someone, so afraid of getting hurt, that she downplayed her assets, dated a guy she knew she'd never fall for and wouldn't even consider being herself because she was protecting herself.

And he didn't blame her. He protected himself, too. His public appearances were few and far between—all so he could remain anonymous and be able to go to a restaurant or coffee shop without being mobbed.

He drove down the lane and turned to the right to make the return trip to the airstrip. "At least we packed and don't have to stop in Barcelona for our things."

She smiled.

His heart clenched. She might not be hurt but something was wrong.

"I just wanted to get this over with."

He nodded at her cell phone. "Google his website. Let's see where he is in Italy. We'll hop on the plane and be there in a few hours. Once you've spoken to him, I know a fabulous out-of-the-way restaurant. Family-owned. Mamma Isabella is still the main cook."

She started typing into her cell phone. "I love Italian food."

And he could share that with her. She couldn't drink, so he couldn't open a whole new world of wines to her. But she could eat. Mamma Isabella's spaghetti Bolognese was to-die-for. He paused. Mamma's spaghetti might be awe-inspiring but just the thought of her lasagna made his mouth water.

They'd eat outside on the restaurant patio so they could hear the night sounds and smell the earthy scents of the Tuscan air as the sun went down and the world quieted.

Then, tomorrow, if she'd let him, he'd fly her to Venice to show her the beauty of that city and take her for a ride on a gondola.

Excitement filled his chest. He'd taken a few of his female friends to Italy, Barcelona, Paris, but he'd never had this primal urge to experience one of those cities with them. Sabrina was hungry for experiences. Hungry for someone to see her. And he saw her. He knew who she was, what she wanted—

If she hadn't been in the car with him, he would have cursed. There would be nothing between himself and Sabrina. Even if SpongePierre CheapPants flat-out rejected her and their child, she didn't want a man in her life. For good reason. And he had his fears about being a stepfather, hurting her child the way his stepdad had unwittingly hurt him. It was crazy to long to show her the world he'd discovered because they couldn't share it.

"I've got his website."

His chest hollowed out. The thought of showing his world to her was the first personal excitement he'd felt in decades. And he'd talked himself out of it.

He took a quiet breath. Worked to put some excitement in his voice when he said, "Good."

"Clicking upcoming events."

He waited as her phone processed.

She frowned. "His announcement about Italy is in red."

He glanced over. "Red?"

Her fingers moved over her phone. "Oh. Italy is canceled."

"Oh."

Then why did he leave Spain?

Trent didn't ask the question aloud. Sabrina's emotions had been on enough of a roller coaster for one morning. But all kinds of things popped into his head. Like Pierre's Paris neighbor might have called him and warned him Sabrina was coming so he could hide from her.

The thought of it set his blood on fire. She might not have wanted anything permanent or serious with Pierre, but from everything Trent had seen of the guy, he was a louse.

"Here's something interesting."

He sure as hell hoped it explained Pierre's behavior, or when they finally did catch up with him, Trent wasn't sure he could be responsible for what he said or did to him.

"What?"

"There's a personal note from him explaining that his manager had overbooked him."

One of Trent's eyebrows rose. The guy was just full of excuses.

"There's an event in Ireland he does every year. A charity thing. It's not the same week every year so when his manager presented him with the opportunity for the Italy exhibit, he agreed, not knowing it coincided with the fund-raiser in Ireland. Something he's committed to supporting."

Trent tried not to give the guy credit for a soft heart toward the charity, but fairness forced him to.

Sabrina stopped reading.

He waited for her to say something. When thirty seconds went by with no response, he said, "So, Skippy, does this mean we're going to Ireland?"

"I guess."

Her lackluster response could have meant she was disappointed, or tired, or simply tired of chasing after SpongePierre.

"You know, you could send him an email."

She gaped at him. "To let him know he's going to be a father?"

"Yeah. I guess that is a little cold."

"He might not be the best person in the world, but I was raised better."

She certainly was.

She retrieved the information about the Ireland exhibit and he instructed her to forward it to his pilot.

It was dark before they landed at a private airstrip near Dublin. His assistant had contacted a rental car agency and a representative waited with the keys to a shiny black SUV. The man grinned and Trent smiled. His staff had been instructed to tip the man handsomely. Obviously, they'd listened.

After the copilot loaded their bags into the back of the SUV, Sabrina and Trent climbed in. They buckled up, Trent spoke the address of the hotel into his phone's GPS and the screen lit up with directions.

Sabrina gaped at the message. "We're an hour away from the hotel?"

He turned on the ignition and started the engine. "At least."

"Why do you use airstrips so far out of a city?"

He chuckled at the impatience in her voice. "Well, your brother Seth taught me that's the easiest way to sneak into town."

She crossed her arms on her chest, settled into her seat. "Sounds like Seth."

"Your brother Jake taught me that if you get a limo and a driver, you'll have an extra hour to work in the car as you are driven to the hotel."

"That's Jake."

"But I think it's the best way to see a country."

She turned to him, her face scrunched in confusion.

"Your entire family is on fast time. That's the part of the rat race I opted out of when I decided to go into business for myself."

"This has nothing to do with the rat race." She pointed outside her window. "It's dark."

She said the words as if he was daft.

He laughed. "Just think of the fun we'll have seeing Ireland on our return trip."

The moon suddenly appeared from behind a cloud. It didn't exactly bathe the area in golden light, but there was enough to see hills and trees.

The GPS gave him directions and they headed toward Dublin. When they finally arrived at their hotel, they stumbled in, exhausted and ready for bed. They registered for the rooms his assistant had booked, and each went their separate ways, agreeing to meet in the lobby for breakfast.

After a good night's sleep, he showered, dressed and took the elevator downstairs where a freshly scrubbed Sabrina—her long yellow hair in a ponytail—awaited him.

A hostess led them to a table and when she left, Sabrina said, "The event tonight is formal."

"Not exactly a blue sparkly dress affair?"

She busied herself unfolding her napkin. "No."

Okay. No joking around this morning. Not that he blamed her. This time they weren't popping into Pierre's apartment, arriving unannounced at his ranch or going to a city where he "might" have a showing. They'd seen the website. Tonight at eight o'clock, Pierre would be at a renovated castle in the countryside. He would show his art, donors would bid on the pieces, and the money would go to the charity sponsoring the event.

She would see him tonight.

So no jokes. No intrusion into her thoughts. This was her thing, not his. In fact, a smart escort might bow out, give her some time alone.

They ate their eggs and pancakes in near silence. When breakfast was finished, they left the restaurant, but he paused in the lobby. "I actually have a little bit of work to do this morning."

Hope lit her blue eyes. "You do?"

"Yes. But don't worry. I'll find a place to get a tux."

She glanced around the elegant lobby. "I should probably get a gown."

She looked so forlorn, so tired of chasing Pierre, he knew he had to do something to lift her mood. "I don't suppose you'd let me pick it out."

She laughed, then squeezed her eyes shut. "I think I better stick to my own style tonight."

He tucked his hands into his jeans pockets. "Okay."

She smiled slightly. He couldn't tell if she was relieved to be getting rid of him or glad to have gown-shopping to keep her occupied, so she didn't have to worry about what she'd say to Pierre.

"Okay."

Either way it didn't matter. She had things to do and despite the fact that he had to escort her to the showing that night, he didn't want to be in the way.

He especially didn't want to sway any of her decisions about Pierre. Though part of him questioned his judgment on that. He liked her. He was ridiculously attracted to her, and the side of him that went after goals like a bulldog desperately wanted to be let loose.

It wasn't like him to want something so badly and not go after it.

Sabrina returned to her room, did a little research on the internet and found the perfect boutique to purchase a gown for that evening.

She called for a taxi and was at the shop in forty minutes. Small, exclusive, the boutique had everything from the latest jeans to designer gowns. She had no desire to impress Pierre. She actually wanted to blend into the crowd, so she could ask for ten minutes alone with him, tell him he was about to be a dad, watch his face lose all its color and then tell him he could have as much or as little to do with his child as he decided.

She could probably do all that in jeans, but she didn't want to call any more attention to herself than she would draw when she asked for some private time with the star of the show.

Which meant she should probably wear pale blue. Most blondes did. It would be the best color to wear for blending.

A sales clerk came over, her smile light and pleasant. "How can I help you?"

"I need a gown." She winced. "For tonight."

"How close are you to a size?"

"Very. In the United States I wear an eight. No alterations required. I'm not sure what that translates to here."

The clerk waggled her fingers to direct Sabrina to a small sitting area in front of a dressing room. "I have three things that are absolutely stunning. You wait right here, and I'll bring them for you to try."

She returned five minutes later carrying the expected pale blue gown. Behind her was a younger woman holding a pink gown and a bright red one.

A sparkly red one.

She laughed. Then pressed her fingers to her lips.

The clerk said, "Is everything okay?"

"Yes. Fine. The red dress just reminded me of a friend of mine."

"We should try it first, then."

"No. We should try the blue one. It's the one I'll probably get. No sense wasting time."

The clerk helped her into the dressing room where she hung the pretty blue gown on a hook. Sabrina stepped out of her jeans and T-shirt and slid into the dress.

She felt nothing. She'd been wearing pale blue to please her dad since she was two and her hair had darkened from baby white to a soft yellow.

Still, looking like herself wasn't a bad thing. It was just a thing—

Or maybe she could try on the pink one?

She slipped out of the dressing room to tell the clerk she'd like to try the pink one. The clerk wasn't around but the pink and red gowns she'd chosen for Sabrina hung on a rack a discreet distance from the door. She could scoot over and grab another dress to try.

At the rack, she reached for the pink one but removing it from the hook revealed the sparkly red one.

It was so fun. So pretty. So open and honest. The construction indicated it would cling to her curves…but so what? In a few months she'd have a basketball for a stomach. Maybe she should take advantage of this opportunity to show off her still-flat tummy?

She slid the pink dress back to the hook and took the red one into the dressing room.

She swore she heard the sparkly dress laugh at her.

Okay. All right. It wasn't her usual style, but she'd had such fun in the blue clingy dress in Barcelona.

Was she saying Trent was right?

Hell, if she knew. She was pregnant and about to tell the father of her child he was going to be a dad. If she wanted to be a little—idiosyncratic—then she should let herself. She'd been in four countries in three days. If she wanted to wear red sparkles, so be it.

She slid the dress off the hanger and discovered it was backless. Devilishness slid through her. She stepped into the dress, slipping her arms into the long sleeves and then straightening the slim portion on her shoulders before facing the mirror.

Wow.

She grabbed her ponytail and twisted it into a knot at the top of her head, accenting her long neck, but also showing off her entire back.

Her entire back.

She looked like somebody else. Not like the little dress-up doll she'd been as a child. Not like the pulled-together businesswoman. Not like Sabrina McCallan, society woman, benefactor. Or even like Sabrina Mc-

Callan, aunt to Abby and Crystal and soon-to-be aunt to Jake and Avery's next baby.

She looked like…

She hesitated to say it…

But…

She looked like herself. Maybe for the first time ever, her real self. The self she knew she was deep down inside.

Studying her reflection, she swallowed hard.

Not because she was confused. Because she was over-whelmed. Had she really let other people rule her life so much that she wasn't herself?

Hadn't ever been herself?

She imagined walking up to Trent at the lobby of their elegant hotel, the red dress molded to her curves, her hair a waterfall of yellow curls caught so high that they barely reached her shoulders.

Would he be mesmerized?

Would he whistle?

She laughed. The jokester would whistle, and her face would redden, but she'd laugh. He always made her laugh. That was why she liked—

She snatched the dress off her shoulders, slid the sleeves down her arms and stepped out of the dress.

That was ridiculous.

She didn't like him. Well, she liked him as Seth's friend. And yes, she was noticing for the first time that he was so much more than what she'd thought. But the timing was all wrong.

And even if it wasn't…

Ultimately, he would hurt her or she would hurt him. He needed a wife like Avery or Harper. He needed a woman who didn't mistrust and fear emotions. He'd never said it. But she'd seen the magic the right woman worked with Jake and Seth and she was no one's right woman.

She took a breath, told herself to stop thinking about Trent as she put the red dress on the hanger again, shimmied her T-shirt over her head, wiggled into her jeans and stepped out of the dressing room.

The clerk raced in to meet her. "I'm so sorry! We got a customer, then another, then another."

Sabrina smiled. "It's okay."

"I see you tried the red one!"

"Yes, and it's lovely." Perfect. "But I'm going with the blue one."

She would have called herself a coward, but there was no point. In a way she was chickening out. But for good reason. This event wasn't about her and Trent. It was about her telling Pierre about their baby. She'd be crazy to muddy the waters with other emotions. Stupid emotions. Emotions she did not like or trust. Emotions she wasn't even sure she knew how to express or handle. She'd already shocked herself enough with seeing her real self in the red dress. She couldn't be throwing those other emotions into the mix.

In fact, for fifty cents she'd tell Trent to go home.

She *should* tell Trent to go home. She knew the place of the event, had something to wear, could get dinner on her own…and then face Pierre and catch a commercial flight home.

That was exactly what she should do.

Exactly what she *would* do.

She found a quick lunch and spent a few minutes idly walking the streets of Dublin, in love with the quaint shops and deciding to come back after she had her baby so she could visit a pub. She had a friend or two who would be happy to travel to Ireland with her, and she'd also decided to have a full-time nanny…that is if her mom didn't insist on coming along to help her with the baby. Her mom had turned out to be the most amazing grandmother. She wouldn't hesitate to allow her the opportunity to be a huge part of her baby's life.

Walking back to the hotel, seeing the shops, watching the tourists, picking out residents from the tourists, she suddenly understood why Trent liked to travel an hour through the countryside from the private airstrips he chose.

She would bet he was probably having a high time, walking Dublin's streets—that is if he wasn't in a tavern, convincing the locals he knew as much about soccer as they did.

The thought made her laugh, then pinched her chest with a longing so sharp she almost stopped walking. She would love to tour this city with him.

But she couldn't give him what he needed, and she wouldn't cheat him. What would have happened to her brothers if they'd settled for a woman who didn't know how to love?

She quickened her steps, got herself to the hotel and out of the temptation to see herself with Trent as quickly as she could. In her room she picked up her phone and tapped the contacts button to call him to let him out of his commitment to her, but also to get herself back to normal.

He didn't answer. She left a detailed message, explaining she had her gown, she'd eaten lunch, she was ready to face Pierre…

And he could fly back to New York now, rather than tagging along. She would check into commercial flights the very second she hung up from calling him. There wasn't even a reason to call her back.

She bit her lower lip. "And thanks. Not only do I appreciate the use of your plane, but you were a big help."

Well, that just sounded cold and impersonal.

"What I mean is I had fun in Barcelona. You helped

me keep my cool over Pierre's ranch. And I did see Spain and some of Ireland—even though it was dark."

She sighed. That just shifted it over to too personal.

She said a quick goodbye and hung up before she dropped her phone to a convenient chair and headed to the big bathroom of her luxury suite. She ran water in the tub and used some of the bubble bath available for guests. Twenty minutes later, relaxed and crinkly from the time in the water, she got out and wrapped herself in the big fluffy robe also provided by the hotel.

Tired, she sat on the bed, then lay down—just for a minute—then immediately fell asleep.

She woke with a start two hours later. Gasping, she realized she just barely had enough time to arrange for a car to pick her up before she showered and dressed.

She wasn't even sure she'd have time for dinner.

Which was fine. She'd had a big lunch. She raced into the shower to wash her hair and would have simply raced through getting dressed, except she picked up the curling iron to do her hair and remembered Barcelona.

Dancing and almost kissing.

She ignored the wave of attraction that tried to steal her breath, plugged in the curling iron and walked to the hotel room phone to call the concierge to see about getting a car to drive her to Pierre's event.

With those arrangements made, she returned to the bathroom and spent the next forty minutes styling her long, thick hair. She applied makeup, refusing to think of Barcelona, then stepped into the pretty blue gown.

But when she slid into the silver shoes bought by Claudine, Trent's personal shopper, she couldn't help thinking of him. About dancing. About watching the other couple kiss and wondering what it would be like to kiss Trent that way. About longing for it. About knowing—

with a woman's intuition that she'd always thought only a myth—that he'd wanted to kiss her, touch her, when they'd returned to his condo.

Her breath stalled as a confusing mix of yearning and self-doubt assaulted her. She told herself to stop thinking about things that couldn't be. But when she walked by her phone, still sitting on the Queen Anne chair, she looked down and saw there was a message.

Her heart sped up, but she forced it to slow down again. She'd called him and told him to go home. The polite thing to do would be to call her to say goodbye.

Might as well listen to it and get it over with.

She pressed the button to retrieve the message, but it wasn't Trent. It was her mom.

"Sweetie, where are you? I stopped by your apartment with cinnamon rolls the other morning and you weren't there. I figured you'd left for work early but when I went by today you weren't there again. I almost had your superintendent let me in to see if you were alive…but you know me. I'm not one to panic or butt in."

Sabrina laughed. Her mom panicked and butted in all the time.

"Call me."

She would. As soon as she talked to Pierre, the return trip to the hotel after the charity event would give her time to call her mom, when everything was settled.

Happy with her plan, she left her room, her essentials in the little silver evening bag Trent's shopper had bought for her.

Trent.

Sexy, smart, considerate Trent.

She checked her phone. He hadn't called her.

He had to have gotten her message. Maybe he didn't think a response was necessary? In fact, in part of her babbling message hadn't she told him it wasn't necessary for him to call back?

Wrestling with disappointment that she didn't want to feel, she headed for the elevator, got in and rode to the lobby. She turned to walk to the concierge desk but stopped dead in her tracks. There, chatting with the exuberant concierge was Trent.

Dressed in a tux.

His curly hair wasn't its usual wild and free. It had been cut and styled in a short arrangement that accented his sharp features, especially his dark eyes. He was cute, adorable, sexy, with his long, curly locks. With his short hair, he was devastating.

He looked up. Their eyes met and his were not happy.

CHAPTER SEVEN

SEEING SABRINA, TRENT sucked in a breath. She was so perfect it almost hurt to look at her. But he was also furious.

Call him and tell him to go home? Forget what he'd told her about Seth skinning him alive for dumping his baby sister in Europe?

His temper flashed at just the thought.

She sauntered over, the filmy skirt of her gown rippling. "Did you not get my message?"

His anger threatened to spill over. He took a second to stifle it before he said, "I am not dumping Seth's baby sister in Europe."

Though right at that moment she didn't look like anyone's baby sister. The skirt of the gown might have been full and flowing but the top cupped her breasts and lifted them like an invitation. Her long, silky curls kissed her shoulders.

He shook his head. Yelling at her or drooling over her wouldn't solve anything. "Your car is here."

She held his gaze with cautious blue eyes. "Okay."

He motioned to the door. "Let's go."

They headed to the revolving door. She started to speak but he cut her off. "Don't tell me I'm not coming or that you don't need me or that I can go home. I started this and I'm seeing it through."

Early-evening traffic filled the street, providing a cacophony of noise and confusion. Sabrina didn't argue when Trent climbed into the black sedan with her. The driver closed the car door before walking to the front and sliding behind the steering wheel.

They said nothing for the first ten minutes. He waited for an apology or even for her to start an innocuous conversation to get them beyond his anger. When she said nothing, the dam of his emotions broke.

"It kills me how you cannot understand that if I left you, Seth would be furious."

"Seth will be on his honeymoon."

He groaned. Always practical Sabrina would be the death of him. "He'll hear about this sometime and when he does all he'll see is that you were in a life crisis and I abandoned you."

"This isn't a crisis. It's a situation."

He gaped at her. "Does everything have to be so logical for you? Can you just once get mad? That man, Pierre—" he said the name with a disdain that rolled off his tongue like fiery darts "—didn't deserve the time he got with you."

No man really deserved her. She was soft and sweet. But hardened by a childhood with a father who expected her to be a perfect little doll. The man she finally let loose with, was honest with, had to be someone special. Someone who would see she deserved to be treated with kindness and love.

Not merely passion.

And right now the feelings he had for her were nothing but passion. He was angry, but she was gorgeous, sexy. He could picture every move of making love to her. He could almost see her reactions. Hear her coos and sighs of delight.

He scrubbed his hand across his mouth. It sounded as if he wanted to be that man. And he had to admit he liked the heat that raced through his veins when he thought about keeping her in his life, but that was wrong. He was a man made to be single, to enjoy life, to forge his own path. She was pregnant with another man's child, a woman who would need stability to bring order to her world right now.

And if both of those weren't enough, she was the sister of his best friend, which made her strictly hands-off.

"I know Pierre better than you do. I know how to approach this."

The reminder that she had to be hands-off stemmed his anger and shut down any fantasy he might have of being the man who brought love to her life. "Yes. Of course. I'm sorry. I shouldn't be butting in."

Obviously puzzled by his quick change of heart, she studied him for a few seconds before she said, "I get it. You're like Seth. You want to fix things."

He snorted. "Don't confuse me with your brother. I'm not a fixer. Seth is."

"He's like that from spending a lifetime trying to make everything run smoothly when our dad got home."

"I understand."

Sabrina did, too. She always had. But something about saying it out loud, after seeing herself in the red dress and realizing she was only now finding herself, caused puzzle pieces to shift and scatter and then come back together as a totally different picture.

That life of scrambling to please her dad was over.

Not just because he was gone, but because her brothers had moved on. Both were married now, creating their own families.

Her mother had moved on. She was the happiest grandmother on the planet.

And with the birth of her baby, *she* would move on.

She glanced out the window. Halfway between daylight and dark, the world shimmered with an eerie glow, but she could see trees and grass, a world outside the city on the way to a castle.

A castle. She was going to a castle.

A man on a bike rode the side of the narrow country road. Lights began to flicker on in houses.

The simplicity of it stalled her breath, made her smile. "Ireland is pretty."

"Just figuring that out?"

She was figuring out a lot of things. Like it had taken years and maybe even a pregnancy for her to shake off the sense that she still had to please everyone.

The inside of the car quieted. Lost in thought, she didn't say a word. Trent didn't, either. Finally, the driver turned onto a long lane and after a few minutes pulled the sedan up to the castle.

As she stepped out of the car, she saw that the sky had totally darkened. A blanket of stars twinkled overhead. She leaned back to see them fully, then breathed in a long draught of air. Like the cloudless sky, her brain had cleared. The weirdness of the time since her dad's death found meaning. She'd wanted to move on but had so many habits ingrained in her behavior that she'd felt like she was treading water. Now that she understood that, bits of her life finally made sense.

"Ready?"

Except him.

Trent's being in her life made no sense. She wasn't

even sure what he was doing here. Though he'd certainly stirred things up. Made her think. Maybe even helped her to realize it was okay to move on.

She glanced at him. With his shorter, slicked-back hair, his cheekbones were sharp, his dark eyes dominant, crystal-clear and focused. His full lips created a mouth just made for kissing.

The thought should have baffled her, but she'd thought about kissing him before, had wanted him to kiss her... still wanted him to kiss her. That was even more confusing than trying to figure out how to tell Pierre he was about to be a dad.

She straightened her spine. That was exactly why Trent was a distraction. A woman shouldn't be thinking about a new man until she totally settled things with the last one—

She stopped her thoughts. She couldn't lie to herself or let herself make up excuses. The truth of why she needed to stay away from Trent had nothing to do with Pierre. She'd never been attracted to a man this way before and it scared her. The hunger inched itself into her thoughts at the worst possible times. And it was wrong. Attracted to him or not, she couldn't give him what he needed.

She had to ignore everything she felt for him. "Let's go."

They walked up a cobblestone path to a huge gray stone castle. Spotlights in the grass surrounding the building highlighted turrets and stained glass. Two men in tuxedos stood by the enormous wooden doors. Obviously original, they'd been sanded and treated with a dark stain.

As Sabrina and Trent approached the doors, the two young men yanked on the handles and pulled them back, revealing the huge, well-lit foyer where men and women milled about, holding champagne flutes as they examined the paintings on view.

Sabrina gasped. "I can see why he didn't want to miss this."

Trent shrugged. "As parties go, it's a seven." He pointed to a huge picture of Pierre over a fireplace. "Or, if that's a picture of Pierre, maybe he likes the fact that these people seem to adore him."

She sniffed. The crowd parted, and Pierre walked out of a side room and into the group like a movie star making a grand entrance.

Trent shook his head. "If he just got here, we have to give him time to mingle."

"We? Don't think you're coming with me."

"You already told me that. But you should know that if I think things are getting ugly, I'll be in there so fast he won't get his next word out."

He took a champagne flute from a passing waiter. "Could you get a glass of water for the lady? And put it in a flute." As the waiter walked away, Trent said, "No point making it look obvious that you're not drinking."

She calmly said, "Thanks," but her insides churned. She'd dated Pierre for years, yet she hadn't known about his ranch, hadn't known about an event he did every year. When she saw the pretty girls approaching him, hanging on his every word, she knew why. He'd liked her, but he loved this attention.

That registered as a simple fact. She wasn't jealous or angry. She was finally seeing that she hadn't been paying much attention to who he really was—because he wasn't right for her and she'd always known it. She'd dated him for fun and he'd probably spent time with her for the same reason. Now she had to tell him he was going to be a father and she knew he'd be upset or angry. Or both. Their relationship had been free and easy, and creating a child was about as serious as it gets.

The waiter returned with her water. She and Trent walked around, looking at Pierre's paintings. She found the area in which she could bid on one of them or donate to the charity and she gave the assistant the appropriate information for a sizeable gift.

"Sabrina. How lovely to see you!"

At the sound of Pierre's voice, she turned—

Just in time to see Trent stiffen.

"Pierre, this is Trent Sigmund. Trent, this is Pierre." Tall, thin, wiry Pierre. Good-looking enough with his round eyes and black hair, but not really anything special. Not devastating like Trent.

Refusing to think that through, she caught Pierre's arm. "Is there somewhere you and I can talk privately?"

He glanced at Trent, clearly believing him to be her boyfriend or new lover. "Privately?"

Seeing no reason to disabuse him of a notion about something that was none of his business, she said, "Yes. I have something I need to tell you."

Though Pierre seemed unhappy about it, he pointed at the door to a room on the left. "Of course."

She went in ahead of him and he closed the door behind him. "What is this important thing you have to tell me?" He sauntered over and caught her upper arms, his smile warm and intimate. "If you're looking to get back together, I'm open to a discussion."

Revulsion rippled through her. Even assuming she had a new boyfriend, Pierre made a pass at her?

She stepped away from him. "No. It's not that kind of something." She took a breath. She was so far over him that sharing a child with him took on a new meaning. Something more objective. Something businesslike. "I'm pregnant."

His mouth fell open. "What?"

"I'm pregnant."

He stepped back. "I hope you're not here thinking we'll get married."

"No." She almost laughed at his narcissism, as if she'd gotten pregnant to trap him into marriage. Lord, the thought of a lifetime with him almost made her shudder.

"Oh, really? Why else would you fly across an ocean so soon after your brother's wedding?"

It took a few seconds to figure out what he meant. "Oh, you think I got all starry-eyed at the wedding?" She shook her head. "No."

"You'd better not." He walked even farther away from her. "Because we'd talked this through."

Her patience with him hit a wall. "You know what? Sometimes you behave like a real child. I've always known you filtered everything through the lens of your own benefit, but this is ridiculous." She stepped into his personal space. "I don't want anything from you. In fact, if you'd tell me you wanted nothing to do with our child I'd go home a happy woman. I'm perfectly capable of raising this baby alone... No. I *will* raise him or her alone. But for the baby's sake, you might want to be involved in her life. If not..." She shrugged. "I'll give her your name when she's eighteen and what happens from there will be up to you."

She turned and began walking out the door but spun around to face him again. "You should probably also grow up before your child turns eighteen." She almost turned to walk away again, but said, "And get my picture off your piano."

Pierre's faced whitened. "What? How did you know about…?"

"Nice ranch, by the way. I should bill you for about a billion dollars' worth of lunches and dinners…not to mention hotel rooms and airfare."

She pivoted and walked to the door, which she was sure Pierre had closed. Yet, here it was, open. She strode through, not bothering to close it for Pierre.

Her shoulders straightened. The long breath of air she took filled her lungs with something that felt a lot like freedom. Or empowerment.

She had been young when she began dating Pierre. She might have been smart, but she'd been sheltered, inexperienced…and maybe confused by her parents' relationship. She forgave herself for missing all the obvious signs that the guy was nothing but an egotistical spoiled brat. But she wasn't confused now. She felt strong, capable, intelligent—

Like a woman who was right where she was supposed to be, doing exactly what she was supposed to be doing.

Hiding along the side of the door, Trent had watched it all. Unable to bear the agony of waiting, he'd slid to the entry of the room where she and Pierre talked, turned the doorknob and jumped out of the way when the door opened on its own.

He'd heard every word and when she'd started to walk out, he'd slipped a few feet to the left and then gotten himself into the middle of the crowd looking at Pierre's paintings.

He'd stopped just in time to see her stride out, take a long breath and then grin.

She hadn't bested Pierre. There was no win or lose in this situation. There was only control and she had kept it. With or without Pierre, she intended to raise this baby properly.

She spotted Trent standing in the middle of the exhibit room and walked over.

Her blue eyes shone. Her grin…yes, a grin on sophisticated Sabrina McCallan…lit her face.

"Well, that was easy."

"I saw. Do you think he's going to want to have anything to do with your little boy or girl?"

"I don't know. But if he does, I'll set some ground rules, making him see the baby in New York, maybe even in my condo while I'm present until I determine what kind of influence he intends to have. And if he doesn't…" She shrugged.

Trent laughed. "You'll give your child his name and address when he turns eighteen and let it be up to the kid if he wants to know his dad." He laughed again. "That was perfect."

"No, that was fair."

He wanted to kiss her so bad he had a hard time controlling himself. Sabrina McCallan was strong, knew her mind, had been right about Pierre all along and would make a fantastic mother.

She glanced around at the people milling about the exhibit. "I'm ready to go."

"I'll have the valet tell your driver. But first—" He slid his hands to her waist and yanked her to him, planting his lips on hers out of sheer excitement.

But when his mouth pressed against the softness of hers, longing shivered through him, his common sense disappeared and instinct took over.

Kissing her was like his first taste of champagne, sweet and bubbly, but with a bite. That bite was his own need sliding through his blood. The scary thing was only a tiny bit of it was sexual. The need was more about the joy of sharing and connecting. To a man who made it a point to keep a safe distance to protect himself, tumbling head-first into an emotional connection was as sharp, as urgent, as anything sex could offer.

And also as frightening.

He tried to pull back, to save himself, to remind himself of everything at risk, but she caught his face and kept him right where he was, deepening the kiss by opening her mouth beneath his.

CHAPTER EIGHT

SABRINA GAVE HERSELF over to the kiss, curiosity urging her on. But when she realized what was happening, that this was Trent, the guy she'd wanted to kiss with a ferocity that confused her, she melted. Every cell in her body felt alive as if she'd awakened from a long sleep and was seeing morning for the first time.

She swiped her tongue along his, reveling in the sensations that spiraled through her as she linked the great, humble, determined, sexy guy she was getting to know to the man kissing her. The muscular shoulders beneath her trembling hands stiffened. Jumbled thoughts vied for attention.

She was just out of a bad relationship.

She was pregnant with *that* man's child.

Her parents had shown her the worst example of love imaginable. She'd seen firsthand what happened when two people who shouldn't have even become involved got married. Love was a plethora of intense emotions that caused people to make bad decisions. What she was feeling for Trent wasn't merely out of character; it was also out of control. Like speeding down a highway in a car so big your feet can't reach the brakes. Much like what her mother had described she'd felt for her father.

Trent made another move to pull back, but hesitated.

His warm lips moved ever so slowly, ever so gently, across hers again, building an ache in her chest. She wanted this so badly. Wanted *him* so badly. But this wasn't just about her, her fears, her troubles. She also knew *his* history, knew he needed a woman who was softer, more in touch with the emotions currently making her heart feel like it would explode.

She couldn't be the woman he needed, and to get involved with him would only muddy the waters of his life.

She pulled away, pretending great interest in straightening her skirt.

After a few seconds he said, "That was a surprise."

She wouldn't look at him. She might have finished the kiss, but he'd started it. How could he call his own action a surprise—?

Unless his feelings for her had overwhelmed him, as well?

It didn't matter. He needed—no, he *deserved*—more than she could give. She suddenly wondered about her competency as a mom. Emotionally deficient as she was, would she also be unable to give her child everything she needed?

She took a breath. Straightened her shoulders. Even in a bad situation, her mother had been the best mother in the world. She'd taught Sabrina everything she needed to know to assure that her child always felt loved, cherished, protected.

Trent watched her distance herself. He could have almost scripted the conversation in her head. She had a baby to care for. She didn't need a distraction.

That was fine. He knew all that, too. And he wasn't here to find a new lover. He was here to support her.

"I was proud of you back there."

She finished her imaginary straightening of her skirt. "Thanks. I felt empowered. Not doing what everybody would have told me I should do but doing what I knew was right."

Ah. And there it was. The reason she'd kissed him back, lured him into a deeper kiss when he would have ended it so much sooner. Standing up to Pierre, making a clear decision about her life, about her baby's life, had given her courage or confidence.

Which she would need to get through a pregnancy and raise a child.

A man who messed with that process would be as much of a narcissist as Pierre.

And Trent wasn't. He was a man in a weird situation. Attracted to a woman with a child on the way, when he was a guy who knew the realities, the difficulties, of step-parenting. Even people who tried often failed, and some of his scars from being left out still pinched sometimes. For the first seven years of his life, he and his mom had nearly been inseparable. Then she'd remarried and he'd gotten left behind.

The truth he'd always avoided crawled out from a far corner of his brain. If his mom hadn't remarried, he and his mom would have remained the team they'd become when his father died. Because she'd remarried, the older Trent had gotten, the more he'd understood that he couldn't begrudge his mom companionship, or more children, so he'd been the collateral damage.

He'd always looked at his genius, his success, as fate's way of making that up to him, and he accepted that and didn't reach for more. Actually, he'd never wanted more—hadn't wanted to test the waters of real love. He was okay with knowing he was an outsider, a loner.

Until that kiss.

He'd say he was a good kisser or she was a good kisser, except he knew the explanation wasn't quite that simple. It was more that *they* were a great combination.

But they were the wrong two people. Or maybe it was an accident that they clicked. Because they could not follow through on this. Not with her pregnant and him very aware of the troubles, the heartache, when a man couldn't accept a stepchild.

Their situation sucked. If she wasn't pregnant, they'd date, and he could analyze if their clicking meant something or not. As it was, his decision had to be made immediately. They couldn't test the waters. They couldn't play around and see if anything would become of what they felt.

He had to decide right now if he was willing to risk hurting her, risk her child's happiness. Or worse, risk the possibility that he could take away the opportunity of her and her child forming a great bond that would last a lifetime.

And right now the answer had to be no.

In the back of the car, returning to the hotel in Dublin, awkwardness ruled. A man could make up his mind that doing something was wrong, but that didn't mean a kiss won't haunt him.

After the strained first half hour of the forty-minute drive, his brain scurried to think of a neutral topic of conversation and all he could come up with was, "So how would one go about starting a mutual fund?"

His face hurt from holding back a wince. What was he doing? He had no intention of starting a mutual fund.

She faced him. "I'd probably let an investment firm do the heavy lifting on the setup." She shrugged. "Your name would carry the fund and you'd have to pick the stocks or bonds your company supported."

He held her gaze. She was dangerously smart and

very easy with her knowledge. Even the way she phrased things spoke of casual understanding of finances. He saw her father's influence. All those dinners where he'd grilled her brothers, she'd been paying attention.

"But I know you don't want to start one. You were tired of the silence in the car, groped for something to talk about and picked a topic you knew I couldn't resist."

In some ways he loved her honesty. In others, he wanted to run from it.

"I also noticed that you didn't ask about volunteering to mentor or lecture at my nonprofit. It's okay. I know that mentoring or lecturing for me would mean we'd see each other again. And I don't think either one of us wants that. Since Seth's wedding, we've been feeling something for each other." She sneaked a peek at him. "And we don't want to."

He'd been so gobsmacked over her admission that she'd felt something for him that he almost didn't hear the "And we don't want to."

When it sank in, he took a breath. He understood why he didn't want to. He didn't want to hurt her, to hurt Seth's little sister, or to hurt the relationship she would form with her child.

But all this time he'd leaned on the fact that she didn't believe in love to keep himself from taking what he wanted.

Now she was telling him she felt things for him? Making him want to forget all the reasons he had to stay away from her?

She might be brilliant about finances, but she knew nothing about shutting down an attraction. Because what she'd just said rippled through him like a challenge.

"Yeah. I'm not a very good risk for a ready-made family."

She shook her head. "Or maybe you are, and you just haven't found the right woman? Someone soft and sweet."

He would have snorted at that, except he remembered the way she'd kissed him. So hungry. So greedy. And he couldn't believe she didn't see herself as the right woman. But her expectant tone of voice, as if the strategist in her knew exactly what he needed, told him that she didn't see herself in that role.

Even after their powerful kiss should have clued her in that she really could be.

He rolled all that around in his mind and the only conclusion that made sense was that this might have been the first time she'd ever kissed someone she had genuine feelings for.

It humbled him.

And scared the hell out of him.

But if they talked about this any more, she'd be in his arms again that night and this time he wouldn't pull away.

"So I'd contact an investment firm—"

She laughed. "Don't want to talk about the attraction, huh?"

"Hell, no. *My best friend's baby sister?* We might be having some feelings but we both know they're wrong. I'm not a good candidate to be anybody's stepdad and if I hurt you, I'd lose my best friend. Now that you've talked to Pierre, we have, at best, twenty-four more hours together. Eight of those we'll be sleeping in separate rooms at the hotel. We can sleep on the plane or work on the plane. And once my driver drops you off at your condo in New York, we'll only see each other at parties Seth hosts. No one has to know any of this."

"So we've got what? Twenty more minutes of painful silence?"

"Not counting the hour-and-twenty-minute drive to the airstrip tomorrow morning." He shook his head. "Couldn't we talk about favorite TV shows?"

"I don't watch television."

"Good. Then I'll tell you about all my favorite TV shows."

He babbled on for ten minutes about everything from half-hour comedies to full-blown sagas on platforms he paid to access. To keep her brain from going in directions she didn't want to go, she paid close attention.

"So there are knights?"

"Yes."

"But it's present day?"

"Well, sort of. It's an alternate reality."

"Interesting."

"It is! It's interesting to think about how different life would be if one little thing in history hadn't happened or had happened differently."

Their gazes caught.

She didn't have to wonder why he'd stopped talking or where his thoughts had jumped because hers had tumbled in the same direction. What might have happened if they'd met under different circumstances? If she wasn't pregnant. If he wasn't someone who needed a woman more like Avery or Harper. Someone who knew how to love.

Because she didn't. Up until a few days ago, she hadn't even believed love existed.

Holding his gaze, she quietly said, "I wasn't talking about the show. I was talking about the fact that you're so enamored with television."

"Ah."

The car pulled up to the hotel. Trent opened the door, got out and extended his hand to help her.

"My brain likes to be busy. What does it hurt if it's rummaging around deciphering an industry or enjoying an alternate reality?"

She stepped out onto the sidewalk. "I guess none."

Still holding her hand, he led her into the well-lit lobby. Working to keep their attention on something that made no difference in either of their lives, he appeared to have forgotten he still held her hand.

But Sabrina hadn't. No one had ever done anything so simple, so romantic. Not that he'd taken her hand, but that the gesture had been natural as if his subconscious couldn't resist her.

They got into the elevator and rode first to the floor of her room. He walked her to her door and stopped. As if he just noticed he held her hand, he looked at their entwined fingers and then into her eyes.

The connection was so electric, it hurt to hold his gaze. His dark orbs kept secrets, made promises.

"You know I want to kiss you right now."

"Yes." Because she wanted him to kiss her, too. She wanted to pick up where they'd left off at the castle. Before they'd ruined it in the car by talking about reality—

Reality? That was three thousand miles away, across an ocean. Technically, they were alone in a hotel on another continent.

And as he'd said, no one needed to know about any of this.

If she looked at this the right way, that statement in the car was like an unspoken pact not to speak of anything that happened on this trip—

Including what happened right now.

The moment stretched out between them. A choice. Kiss him. Maybe even make love with him. And then—

And then...

Go home and pretend nothing had happened?

Have her face turn red every time they said hello at

one of Seth's parties? Feel awkward if they met at a coffee shop or passed on the street?

Or create a bond? Maybe fall in love the way her mom had and pine for him when he dropped her off at her condo tomorrow and then disappeared into the noise of Manhattan. After all, he was the one who'd said their feelings were wrong. Acting on the sexual attraction aspects would only confuse a time in her life that should be about the joy of pregnancy and preparing to become a mom.

She had a responsibility to the little life inside her. That was where her focus should be.

Turning away wasn't easy, but nothing about this situation was easy. That was why she avoided feelings. Getting hurt? Disappointing others? Those were things she didn't do.

So maybe not all the lessons she'd learned from dealing with her dad were useless?

She waved her key card across the lock to activate it. Turning the knob, she said, "Good night."

The door opened, and she stepped inside her room without a backward glance, her heart splintering with pain. The price of keeping her focus and her dignity was a wave of loneliness the likes of which she'd never felt before.

In bed an hour later, after a long bath, she wondered if he was thinking about her and knew he was. She had no idea what hummed between them, but if it was anything like the emotions that her mother had felt, it wasn't reliable.

And that was what she had to keep telling herself. She'd seen love firsthand and knew it frequently hurt people.

She forced her eyes closed. Quieted her mind. And eventually fell into a deep sleep. She had no dreams about Trent following her with a dog on a leash that kept getting tangled in the wheels of her twins' stroller. Her mind went totally blank, totally black.

Her phone woke her hours later. She answered with a groggy, "Hello."

"This is the front desk. The extra luggage ordered by Mr. Sigmund is being brought to your room now."

Instantly awake, she scooted up in bed. "Extra luggage?"

"He said something about a ball gown."

"Oh." A ball gown wouldn't fit into the carry-on she'd been stuffing with clothes for days. His remembering that, ordering the bigger case, could have caused her to swoon at his consideration, but they'd talked about this the night before. He'd said what they felt was wrong. And she'd cemented that belief when she'd walked away from a kiss, maybe even a one-night stand. She couldn't let her thoughts go backward.

"Thank you."

As soon as she'd disconnected the call, her phone rang again. Expecting it to be the concierge, she said, "Yes?"

"It's me. Trent. I take it you got the call about the extra suitcase?" Trent sounded like he'd been up and about for hours.

"Yes. Thank you."

"You're welcome. I bought a case big enough that you can store the gown and all the rest of your clothes and ditch the smaller case if you want, so you're just handling one bag, not dragging two. That was the good news. Here comes the bad. My new assistant only arranged for the rental car through last night. Apparently, an agent for the company picked it up this morning. My longtime assistant, Ashley, got us another one, but it won't be here until noon."

She sat up, coming to full alert. "Noon?"

"We should have left at seven."

"Seven?" She glanced at the clock. It was after nine. No wonder he sounded awake.

"I thought you'd want to get an early start."

"Then why'd you let me sleep in?"

"I was waiting for you to call me."

The wistfulness in his voice reminded her that he'd wanted to kiss her the night before, but she'd decided that anything, even something temporary between them, wasn't right, and she'd left him in the hall outside her door.

"I slept in." She licked her suddenly dry lips. "Give me ten minutes and I'll meet you in the lobby. We can eat breakfast in the hotel restaurant."

"I've had breakfast."

Oh. She almost said it but recognized that refusing a kiss the night before had set things in motion on his end, too. She'd drawn the line in the sand and he wouldn't argue, wouldn't even intrude on her day. He'd simply do what he'd set out to do: help his friend's sister. They'd found Pierre, she'd said her peace and now Trent would take her home.

"Why don't you have breakfast in your room and then a leisurely walk while we wait for the replacement rental?"

He didn't want to have breakfast with her or even hang out while they waited for their new rental car. Because she'd walked away from a kiss.

Or maybe after she'd walked away, he'd thought it through, the way she had, and realized even a one-night stand wouldn't work?

She didn't think that she'd hurt him or insulted him. He was too strong and too smart to get offended.

Unless he thought she hadn't liked their kiss…

That couldn't be true. She hadn't let him end it. She'd kept him where he was. Took what she wanted. Absorbed every wonderful sensation.

She suddenly wanted to tell him that. She wanted to put all her cards on the table and set things right. She didn't want him angry with her. She didn't want him distanced from her—

But wouldn't that just dredge up everything she'd settled when she walked away?

She swallowed down the need to set things right in favor of the hope that there was a woman out there who could help heal his wounds, the kind of woman her brothers had found.

"Okay. I'll call room service. Just let me know when the rental car gets here."

"Will do."

She didn't hear one iota of regret in his voice—

Of course not. Would he want her to know that she'd disappointed him? Big, strong, genius that he was, he wouldn't fail publicly. He would save his pride.

She disconnected the call and tossed the covers off the bed. She was done thinking about this.

The guy was sweet, kind, considerate, handsome…

He deserved a woman who could appreciate all that.

Trent disconnected the call and threw his cell phone to the sofa. He wasn't about to get angry with a new assistant who'd made a mistake, but he'd mapped all this out the night before. Get up at six, order breakfast from room service to eat while he read his usual newspapers, shower and dress and call Sabrina just before seven. That way she'd have time to get dressed while room service delivered her breakfast, but nothing else.

He'd planned topics for the drive to the airstrip.

Then he had a ton of things to read and evaluate on the plane.

Nothing about their time together would slip out of his control.

Because he'd finally figured out that *he* was the wild card. Sabrina was perfect Sabrina McCallan all the time. He was the one who kept losing hold of his emotions and doing things like kissing her or telling her he wanted to kiss her. He couldn't believe he'd done it. But when he'd made that backhanded comment about wondering how things could be different if just one thing had changed or if they'd met at a different time, her eyes had shifted, gone soft with yearning as if she'd applied the possibility to them and she wanted to know.

His mind started rolling through potential outcomes, and their odds weren't good for anything long-term, but for one totally inappropriate minute he'd believed they could have one night.

One night.

One blissful, perfect night that could live in their memories forever. As surely as he knew his first, middle and last names, he knew one night with her would stay with him for the rest of his life. And he wanted it.

He'd asked for the kiss, hadn't taken, knowing this had to be a mutual decision but she'd kept her cool and walked into her room.

After a restless night, he'd recognized she'd been correct. So he planned the rest of their time together down to the last minute.

Then his assistant had made a mistake—

He refused to let the late arrival of a rental throw him. He still had the conversation topics, still had the work that needed to be done. He would be a rock. He would not fall victim to the curiosity that constantly flitted through Sabrina's eyes. He would not see her as someone who'd never experienced real romance. He would hold his heart in check, refusing to let it soften over the longing that some-times quivered through her voice. Most of all, he would resist the temptation to be the guy who showed her the dif-ference between making love and being someone's lover.

That was what kept throwing him. She could say one thing with her mouth while her eyes told a totally dif-ferent story. Which meant he had to be so strong, she wouldn't even notice how hard he had to work at ignoring the curiosity, the yearning, she telegraphed with her eyes.

His personal assistant, Ashley, called an hour later. "I got confirmation that you'll have an SUV at noon."

"Thanks. And don't be too hard on Makenzie for get-ting the rental car information wrong. People make mis-takes."

Ashley laughed. "She didn't have her head in the game. She needs to learn to take things to their logical conclu-sion. If you needed a car to get from the airstrip to the hotel, you'll need it to get back to the airstrip. This wasn't one of those times she should have arranged to have your car picked up at the hotel."

"My schedule and my needs fluctuate so much when I travel that the person making the arrangements really has to pay attention. Think she's going to catch on?"

"She's smart. This mistake embarrassed her enough that she'll never do it again. Plus, we don't fire people. We give them a chance to grow into the job."

He chuckled. Ashley didn't miss a trick. Not even when he tested her. "Exactly. I'll see you next week."

"Going to the lake?"

"Maybe." Retreating to the lake wasn't a bad idea. He needed some time to himself, some time to get his pri-orities in line and his emotions in check. "The trip was a little jarring. I don't usually fly to three countries in four days. I may need to sit in one place an entire week to feel normal."

She laughed again. "Okay. See you *next* Monday."

He disconnected the call and shook his head. "A little jarring?" He should change his impression of Sabrina McCallan from class in Chanel to temptation in Chanel. But this wasn't about sex or his need. This was about her eyes. Her longing. Her curiosity. A curiosity she didn't want to satisfy. At least not with him.

He called her and told her their rental would arrive at noon and she said she'd be ready. Her formal, no-nonsense tone continued while they loaded their things into the SUV and for the first fifteen minutes of the drive.

That should have pleased him. As long as she was standoffish, he wouldn't make any slipups. But all he saw was a woman so curious about love and romance that she had to hide behind an overly polite facade.

Fine. Whatever.

He still refused to give in to temptation.

He internally screamed that at his hormones, which were absolutely positive he could lure her to him. Or at least show her a good time. Show her the way a woman should be treated. They'd both gotten sidetracked over everything that had happened the night before, and he'd forgotten that the last man she'd dated hadn't been kind to her. And he wouldn't fix that by ravaging her.

Sabrina's voice brought him out of his reverie. "Sky's getting dark."

They were far away from Dublin now, taking a country road that would lead to another country road and then another, which would ultimately get them to the super private airstrip where his jet sat.

"What's the weather supposed to be?"

"I don't know." She pulled out her phone. "I haven't looked at the weather in days. But I can check."

Using her thumbs, she hit apps and typed things and after a few seconds she cursed.

He stole a glance at her. "What?"

"I found something with radar and there's a band of thunderstorms coming our way."

He brushed it off. "Some rain."

"Lots of rain."

"We'll be fine."

CHAPTER NINE

SABRINA DIDN'T THINK SO.

"There are red bands in the streaks of yellow."

His brow puckered. "Red?"

"The guide says red means heavy rain. Like inches."

Three huge drops hit the windshield, then ten or twenty that turned into hundreds. Within minutes the rain was an onslaught so strong and so fast the sound of it drumming on the roof of the SUV was like thunder.

She scrambled to swipe down on the screen to read the rest of the information on the weather page. She gasped. "It's the tail end of a hurricane."

He gaped at her. "A hurricane?"

"More like a tropical storm now. They thought it was going to hit much farther north." She showed him her phone just as the wind whipped their rented SUV. The rain fell in thick sheets that prevented her from seeing the road. "This isn't good."

He drove the vehicle to the berm. "Let me have a look at that."

He took the phone, read the weather page and whistled. "Did you see the part about this being a slow-moving storm? This rain will last at least a day."

He tossed her phone back to her and pulled out his. He pressed two buttons then said, "We're in a huge storm here, Ashley. Something that was supposed to hit north of us but must have shifted. Look it up and tell us what we're dealing with."

"Give me a sec." A young woman's voice entered the interior of the SUV through the speaker. The *click, click, click* of computer keys followed it. "Ireland is getting the end of a hurricane." Another few clicks. "Wow. The predicted rainfall is not good. A couple of inches an hour. I hope you're still at the hotel."

The concern in Ashley's voice gave Sabrina a weird feeling. Not exactly jealousy. More like a recognition of how much Trent's assistant liked and respected him. The warmth flowing through her was pleasure that he'd found an employee who appreciated him. Then she realized an easygoing guy like Trent would surround himself with people with his same values. Picturing it, his personality and life came into sharp focus for her. He genuinely liked people. He really did want everyone to enjoy life.

"Actually, Ashley, we're in the middle of nowhere."

"Find shelter," Ashley said, the sound of the keys clicking punctuating her words. "Does Sabrina have an international phone?"

Surprised, Sabrina looked at him. He shrugged and said, "Yes."

"Use it to bring up General Maps. It will pick up your location on a satellite and find the nearest town."

Even as Trent said, "Great. Thanks," Sabrina brought up General Maps. Their location appeared on the screen, in the center of a map of the area.

"There's nothing for miles."

Trent said, "That's okay. I'll call you when we're settled, Ashley."

"Hey, I don't get to see how this turns out?"

"It's rain," Trent said, reassuring her. "We'll be fine."

The odd feeling hit Sabrina again. The connection between Trent and his assistant didn't sound romantic, but there was clearly affection there. And why not? Trent was a great guy. But hearing the concern in his assistant's voice was another proof of what she'd been learning about Trent in the past few days.

He wasn't just good-looking and rich. He was unique, wonderful.

Trent disconnected the call and turned to Sabrina. "We're going to have to continue moving until we find shelter."

"Okay." She nodded at her phone. "I can keep the maps program on-screen. If it comes up with something like a town or a farm or something, we'll know in time to look through the sheets of rain for it."

"That's the spirit." He blew his breath out on a sigh and pulled the gearshift into Drive.

"Let's go."

Ten nerve-racking minutes later, shelter appeared in the form of a castle at the top of a small hill.

Sabrina shook her head. "A castle? You've got to be kidding."

He peeked at her. "Beggars can't be choosers."

As if to reinforce his statement, the wind knocked at the big SUV again. Rain pummeled the windshield.

She pressed her hand to her stuttering heart. The castle hadn't come up on the maps app. But nothing had, and the rain had created rivers and ponds along the road and in the grass beside it. He was right. They had no choice but to check this out.

He turned to go up the hill. "Here's the plan. When I stop, you jump out and run for the door."

She nodded.

Trent drove to the top of the hill and stopped the vehicle. She punched her shoulder against her door. It popped open and she leaped out into the driving rain.

The castle's big wooden double doors were protected by a small overhang, but not enough to shelter her completely. Wind butted against her. Rain drenched her back.

She frantically searched for a doorbell. When she didn't find one, she grabbed the knocker and banged it against the wood.

No answer.

Trent raced up beside her, rolling their luggage behind him. She frowned, puzzled by his priorities.

"If we're going to be at the mercy of the owner of this castle, the least we can do is wear dry clothes."

Everything in their bags had been worn. That morning they'd put on the last of the outfits purchased for them by his personal shopper.

"All our clothes are dirty."

"Maybe the castle will have a washer?"

When no one answered after Sabrina's second knock, Trent set the suitcases on the stoop and banged the knocker against the door several times.

No one came.

He sucked in a breath. "Did you see a light when we drove up?"

Rain had soaked his shirt and dripped from his now-short hair. She couldn't help thinking of his assistant. What would it be like to work with this gorgeous man every day and not get a crush on him? She couldn't imagine it, until she realized Trent wouldn't flirt or make sexy talk with an employee. He'd create a safe environment for his workers.

Which meant every flirty word he'd said to her had been honest, genuine. He felt things for her that he didn't feel for other women. The thought filled her with equal parts of joy and confusion.

And an odd feeling of being special. But not in the way her mom and dad thought her special or the world thought her special. In a way that was more intimate. More real. She didn't have to jump through hoops for this man or be perfect. Lord knows she hadn't been anywhere near perfect. She'd been nervous about her pregnancy at the wedding, gotten angry about Pierre's ranch, told Pierre off, then walked out like queen of the world. A little too proud of herself.

And still he'd kissed her.

He'd said he couldn't help kissing her.

"If there's a light on, then we know someone's home but if there isn't, we're going to have to think outside the box."

She swallowed hard as the importance of Trent's feelings overwhelmed her. No pretense. No funny stuff. He just liked her.

Her. Exactly as she was.

She shook her head. "No. No light."

He leaned out of the small shelter and surveyed the castle, then popped back in. "I'm going to assume no one is home."

"Really? Just because of no light being on?"

"No. Because we can't stand out here forever. Besides—" He took a credit card from his wallet. "I've heard a lot of these castles are abandoned."

Breaking into a house wasn't what her brothers would do. It certainly wasn't what her mom would want her to do. Yet, there was something so elemental about it that her heart skipped a beat. The man was just so damned male.

She looked at the driving rain then back at him. "So

we're about to take refuge in a stone monstrosity that might be full of cobwebs?"

"You have a better idea?"

She considered telling him they should get back on the road, away from all the temptations that would dog them if they were alone in a house for God knew how long. But common sense and the pelting rain told her they'd never make it to the airstrip. Already the castle's grassy hill was shiny with water and puddles. The back roads they would take to the airstrip could get washed out, and if they did make it, they probably wouldn't be able to take off. They'd spend the next twenty-four hours in a cold, dark, dank hangar.

There was no good choice here.

"Get us inside."

He couldn't budge the lock of the thick wooden doors with his credit card, and he raced out into the storm, hoping to find another way in. After what seemed like hours of being bombarded by wind and rain, the front door opened.

Sabrina ducked inside, dragging her big suitcase. He grabbed his and yanked it in before he closed the door behind them.

Windows provided very little light but what furniture Sabrina could see was draped with dust covers.

"I don't see any cobwebs."

She glanced around cautiously. "Oh, I'm sure they're here."

He laughed. "You're going to have to look at this like an adventure." He disappeared into the darkness.

She heard a few clicks.

"Either the place doesn't have electricity, or the storm has already taken out the power."

She shivered as he walked over to her. Stuck in a scary

castle with a gorgeous, thoughtful, tempting man and no lights. No nothing, but each other.

He grabbed the handle of her suitcase. "Come on. Let's go upstairs and get out of these wet clothes."

The image that brought almost made her groan. She knew he wasn't propositioning her but that was how her silly brain took it.

Working to get her thoughts on track again, she said, "What if the owners were just out shopping and they come back?"

He sent her a patient look. "Seriously. People don't put dust covers on furniture when they go to the supermarket." He ran his finger along the newel post at the bottom of a curved stairway. "I'd say that's months' worth of dust, not days or even weeks. Months. This is probably somebody's country retreat."

She pulled in a shaky breath. It was dark, and she was cold and wet. She didn't feel like meeting an irate owner, too. But what he'd said made sense. Thick dust and covers on the furniture added up to a uninhabited house.

No, not a house. *A castle.*

If she hadn't been so cold, she might have laughed.

She started up the stairs, using her phone to light the way. Trent added his and the entire stairway came into view. Relieved, she did laugh.

"What's so funny?"

"We're in a castle."

"So? We were in a castle last night."

"But that one was renovated. This one might actually be abandoned."

"Maybe because it's haunted."

They reached the top of the stairs and found huge webs of dust arching from one side to the other in the second-floor hall. She winced. "No self-respecting ghost would stay in this castle."

"He would if this was his home hundreds of years ago and he'd died in a bloody battle to save it."

She groaned. "Now you're just trying to scare me."

"Let's see what's behind door number one."

Because he dragged the suitcases behind him, she opened the door and turned her phone light into the bedroom. A double bed, dresser and chair were draped in dust covers.

"Not very big."

She smirked. "Big enough for one of us."

"I think it might be smarter if we limited our messing things up to a room or two. Like one bedroom and the kitchen."

That brought more of those weird thoughts again. Snuggling together with the sound of the wind and rain outside their window. Kissing. Peeling off wet clothes.

He glanced around. "Right now I'd like to put on a dry shirt, take my phone light and investigate the place."

Thank God he'd interrupted those thoughts. She sucked in a breath. "If we both go, you'll have more light."

"Or we'll simply run down both phone batteries. I think we need to start conserving power."

Her eyes widened. "What are you saying?"

"That there's a possibility we'll be here more than one day. And if there's no electricity, there's no charging phones."

She breathed a sigh of relief. "I thought you were hinting we might need our phones to call for help."

He winced. "That, too."

Real fear sent shivers through her. "Oh."

"I could be dead wrong. But it's always better to be safe rather than sorry."

Of course! He was thinking ahead not out of fear but out of caution.

She felt ridiculous for being a ninny and blamed it on the darkness combined with the sound of the storm buffeting the castle. And the attraction that kept intruding itself into her thoughts.

"You're right."

He tossed their luggage to the bed. "I'm going to look for things like a generator or even a fireplace that works. But first I need to get out of this shirt."

She headed for the door, her phone lighting the way. "Okay."

"Where are you going?"

"Out. So you can change."

"Not if it means you have to use your phone. Take the dust cover off the chair or have a seat on the bed, then turn it off."

She sighed. "I'm just going out to the hall while you change."

"Why? You said yourself the house is totally dark. Besides, you've seen me without a shirt."

She had. That was what had started her confusion. Until that minute, he'd been Ziggy, her brother's wealthy but goofy friend. Now he was a sexy, adult male *Trent*.

She yanked off the dust cover, sat on the chair, then hit the button to turn off her phone and hoped it really was dark enough inside the castle that she wouldn't see him.

It was…but she heard him sniff loudly. "This is the shirt I changed into on the plane when we arrived in Paris. It still smells okay."

"At this point, I think body odor is the least of our worries."

"True." A few seconds passed as he probably wrestled into the shirt, then turned his phone toward her. "All right. I'm going to investigate the house. Do you want to come along or are you okay sitting here in the dark?"

"My clothes are wet too. I'll change while you're gone."

"Good thinking. Wish me luck. I'm hoping to find a generator."

After he left, she inched her way to the bed and found her suitcase. But Trent's sat open beside it on the dusty bed. She ran her hand along the folded clothes, marveling that he was so tidy, then at the feel in the fabrics. Denim, cotton and the silk of the shirt he'd worn with his tuxedo. As soon as she touched it, she felt every blissful second of the kiss they'd shared the night before, after she'd talked to Pierre.

She snatched her hand away. That was just stupid. Stupid. Stupid. She had never gone through a girlie phase and couldn't believe she was starting now.

Running her hand along clothes he'd worn, feeling things she could usually shut down, liking things about him she'd never looked for in a man before?

Was she nuts?

Hadn't she talked herself out of all this the night before?

She opened her suitcase and found the shirt she'd worn in Paris, along with a scarf to use as a shawl. The castle was old, and the darkness made it feel colder. She rummaged for something to dry her damp hair and pulled out one of the two pair of pajamas Trent's personal shopper had sent over for her when they were in Barcelona.

Thinking of Barcelona reminded her of dancing. Feeling young and free in the silly blue sparkly dress that she'd ended up liking. She remembered the couple dancing beside them, their sensuous kiss, remembered her guess that Trent would be a demanding kisser and got goose bumps.

No. She wasn't nuts. *He* was different. So different than Pierre. So different than most of the men she met that she was having trouble acclimating.

Satisfied with that explanation, she ran the pajama top along the bottom of her long hair, the part that had somehow gotten more rain, telling herself that her sound reasoning had her back to normal.

Ten minutes later he returned to the bedroom and flicked on the light.

Sabrina said, "You found a generator!"

"Nope. Breakers were off, which goes to prove that whoever lives here, doesn't live here full-time. Come on, let's go explore the kitchen. I don't expect to find much, but there might be some canned beans or soup."

They left the room and headed down the stairs. Though thick with dust, the corridor leading to the steps had wooden walls, painted white. Wood trim accented the high ceilings. Walnut steps, railing and newel post were brightened by white spindles in the stairway that matched the wood walls.

"Now that we can use our chargers, I can turn my phone back on."

He snorted. "Seriously? Are you one of those people who can't live without her phone?"

She walked down the final three steps, following him when he turned right to go through the huge foyer. With the space now lit, she could see the flagstone flooring, the high ceilings and long, thin walnut table that ran almost the entire length of the wall beneath the stairway. Looking at the ornate chandelier, with light poking through its dusty crystals, she imagined that in its prime, this entryway was amazing.

She sighed. "I like to Google things."

For that he paused and faced her. "Really?"

"Sure." She displayed her phone. "With this in my hand, I know everything or at least have access to it."

"You're pretty smart without that phone."

Pleasure washed through her at his compliment. "I know some things."

He turned and began walking again. "You know a lot of things."

"I should. Not only did I grow up with a dad who quizzed my brothers at the dinner table, but I mentor some very smart entrepreneurs."

They passed through a dusty sitting room. A cover draped a long, traditional sofa. The stone fireplace across from two wing chairs desperately needed repairs. The same was true for the fireplace in the equally dusty dining room, a long space with a table that seated thirty. She counted the high backs of chairs beneath another dust cover. Rough wood floors had been prettied up with area rugs that looked to be from the nineteen hundreds. Walls had been framed out and dry-walled or plastered, creating deep borders around the windows. Dusty pillows sat in the corners, making the wide sills look like reading nooks.

"I'll bet this place is fabulous when it's clean. It doesn't even look to need much remodeling."

"Remodeling?"

"I love to decorate."

"From the look of your condo, I'd say you're pretty good at it. So if that's what you like to do, how'd you decide to start a nonprofit that helps startups?"

She laughed. "I was thumbing my nose at my dad. He didn't see me as a businesswoman? Well, then I'd have a hand in running hundreds of businesses."

Stepping into an old-fashioned kitchen with wooden cabinets and a long wooden table, no island, no granite, just old-fashioned white appliances, Trent said, "That's brilliant."

"Once he saw what I could do, he asked me to join the family business, but I could envision him making me a vice president then never giving me any work. I'd be a showpiece…maybe a token woman." She shook her head. "I wouldn't have it. Besides, I don't bail on my friends."

He studied her face for a few seconds. "No. I don't think you do."

She sucked in a breath, said what had been on her mind awhile, "Obviously, you don't, either."

"So we have something in common?"

"I think we have a lot in common."

Silence stretched between them. Gazes locked, they studied each other as if waiting for the other to say something.

But she didn't know what to say. They were forming a bond, or maybe a friendship. It was so much sweeter, richer, than anything she'd ever felt for a man that longing billowed from her chest to her toes. She'd give anything to be able to test this, to try it. To see what it felt like to be with someone not out of convenience or for fun…but for real.

For real?

Real was what her mother had…a husband with a temper and three confused kids.

She did not want real… Did she?

CHAPTER TEN

SABRINA ALMOST GROANED when she realized she couldn't answer that question with a resounding, "No."

Seeming oblivious to her confusion, Trent walked to the cabinets, opened two and found only dishes. "We might have to eat the plates."

Glad they weren't staring in each other's eyes anymore, Sabrina opened a cabinet door. "Or we could go a day without food."

He turned on the tap. "There's water."

"Oh, I can shower!" She walked to a full-size door, opened it and displayed a pantry. "I see beans."

He laughed. "Good."

She walked into the closet-size room lined with shelves. "Chicken soup! I love chicken soup."

"Me, too. Now that we know there's food, let's finish our tour. I'd like to see the rest of this place."

"Seriously? You're willing to risk the dust?"

"Who cares about dust? Besides, you said you were going to shower."

It wasn't like they had a lot of other things to do, and occupying themselves with exploring the castle was a lot better than talking.

"Okay, let's go."

Because they'd entered the kitchen through the left,

they took the door on the right and found themselves in a butler's pantry. Two rows of cabinets were made from the same white wood that created the stairway walls. The same walnut stain that adorned the stair rail trimmed the cabinet doors.

"This is huge."

He looked around. "Everything needs to be painted."

She ran her finger through the dust of a countertop. "Or maybe just cleaned."

He opened the door at the end of the room.

Expecting to see another sitting room, she gasped when she saw the enormous dining hall. With ceilings as tall as the ones in the entryway, the same flagstone floors and a table long enough to seat a hundred, the room was the first of the space to really feel like it belonged in a castle.

Her voice echoed around her as she spoke. "This is fabulous." The stone fireplace was twice the size of those in the living room and sitting room. The high ceiling boasted wood beams stained the same walnut color as the stairway rail in the entryway and the trim of the cabinets in the butler's pantry. At least a forty-foot space sat empty beside the long table.

"I'm guessing that space is for dancing," Trent said. "I'll bet they host parties here."

"Balls," Sabrina said whimsically. "With women in flowing dresses and men in those ruffled shirts."

He laughed. "You might think you're pragmatic, but I still say you're a romantic."

She wished. Because if she were a romantic, she'd have kissed him the night before. She'd be laughing and flirting, not looking for dust so she'd have something to comment on. She'd be giving in to the longings that swept through her, acting on things she'd never believed in, when they shared a bed that night.

Her thoughts froze. What if she wasn't strong enough tonight to resist that pull? Would she toss away decades of common sense for a few hours of wonderful?

She cleared her throat. "You know… Now that we have lights, maybe we could commandeer a second bedroom."

He looked over at her and her heart jumped to her throat. No man had ever given her that look before. His full lips had thinned. His sharp eyes held her in place.

Okay. He clearly did not like her suggestion.

"I'm just saying that with light and electricity we can clean up after ourselves. Maybe even wash the sheets before we leave."

His head tilted as his eyes searched hers. "Sure. That makes sense."

Disappointment in herself rumbled through her and she almost cursed. She was such a coward. She should have said, "Hey, I really like you. But we're not right for each other and I think sleeping in the same bed would be just a bit too tempting."

That was what strong Sabrina McCallan would do. *Honesty* was her watchword. Not dodging things. But though Trent was probably the easiest man in the world to talk to, what she had to say wasn't simple or easy. Any time a man had tempted her before this, it was purely physical. She couldn't deny there was something more with Trent and if she explained it he would realize just how enticing he was to her.

And that would make her vulnerable…the way her mom had been.

Except Trent wasn't like her father. He wasn't harsh or demanding or even critical.

He was accepting, spontaneous, kind…

Double doors led outside, but rather than open them

to the rain, Trent went to the kitchen, found some cloths and washed a space for them to peer through.

Benches sat along a stone walk in what had probably once been a beautiful garden.

"I'll bet this was magnificent in its prime."

She peeked at him. "Makes me itch to get my hands on it and fix it up."

"And host a ball?"

She blew her breath out. "I wouldn't even have time to make a guest list, let alone remodel this place enough to invite friends, let alone host a ball."

She stopped, disgusted with herself. Trent wasn't anything like her dad, and avoiding the truth with him was shameful.

She squeezed her eyes shut, then popped them open and caught his gaze. "I don't want to think about remodeling this place because it will never happen. Spinning fantasies is a waste of time. Since I'm rolling with the truth here, I might as well also admit I don't want to sleep in the same bed with you because I like you."

His expression shifted but he said nothing.

"I think it's just a little too much like tempting fate for us to be that close."

One of his eyebrows rose. "Afraid you'll ravage me?"

"Don't belittle what I feel."

"Okay." His voice grew soft, serious. "I won't. Let's go upstairs and look for another room."

Her breathing stopped. She couldn't tell if it was from disappointment that he hadn't argued or relief that he hadn't argued. Anytime her mom disagreed with her dad he'd exploded—

But she'd already decided Trent wasn't like her father. Maybe his reaction to finding a second room was the true test of that?

They found a back stairway and ambled up. At the top were two large guest rooms, each with a private bath.

"Whoever owns this place, he was smart when he remodeled."

"Everything is rather convenient."

He strolled around the room and she watched for signs that he was angry and not letting it show.

"They probably cut out a bedroom or two to make the extra baths."

His genuine interest in the castle took away her concern about his anger. If he'd been angry, he'd pushed it aside. But she didn't think he'd been angry. He might not have liked her suggestion that they sleep in separate rooms, but he'd accepted it.

It wasn't as if she hadn't dealt with an even-tempered man before. She met lots of them at her nonprofit. She'd simply never been in a relationship with one.

Of course, Pierre had been her longstanding adult boyfriend. There'd been no reason to think of dating in years.

The final guest room was like the first two, but the third-floor master suite was enormous.

Trent peered around. "I'm guessing this is at least half the floor. I'm also guessing we're going to find a super-huge bathroom and walk-in closet."

"I'm thinking dressing room."

The master closet was a combination closet and dressing room. Everything was old, worn. But that didn't take away from the beauty of the space. She could almost see a husband and wife dressing, laughing and chatting with each other.

She shook her head to clear it of the image. "This is lovely." But the mood of the vision stayed with her. This was a house made with love. She could feel the happiness that even the dust and time couldn't bury.

Damn it. She loved this house. And she didn't understand her unexpected connection to something so far out of the realm of possibility. She wasn't a woman who spun fantasies, wished for fanciful things.

She was honest, sincere, hardworking...normal.

Or maybe not so normal if she couldn't even fathom being in a relationship with someone she didn't have to manage.

She turned to Trent, who was examining the craftsmanship of the dressing room built-ins.

"I think I'll take one of the smaller bedrooms. You can have the one our luggage is in."

He shrugged. "Doesn't matter to me. I can just as easily bring my suitcase to another room like yours."

There was that easygoing nature again. A guy who didn't have to compromise because he wasn't overly sensitive or demanding.

"Okay. Either way."

"I'll move my stuff later, after we eat." He paused. "Unless you're hungry now?"

"No. I'm fine." A thought hit her, and she politely said, "Unless you're hungry now?"

"Nope. I'm good for a few hours."

Silence spun out between them until she realized he was waiting for her to make a move. She strode out into the empty corridor. This is what she got for being honest: a stiff, formal atmosphere that seemed to suck the life out of everything. She shouldn't have told him why she didn't want to sleep with him. She should have let him draw his own conclusions...

But that didn't sit right, either. He'd been open, honest with her all along and she'd been open with him. It was only when sleeping in the same bed came into the picture that her reactions got muddled.

Not wanting this weird politeness to be the rest of their afternoon, she said, "Want to explore some more?"

He sniffed a laugh. "Dust phobia leaving?"

"It must be, because I'm suddenly curious to see if there's a dungeon or a tower where an old lord held women captive."

He hooted with laughter. "You have one hell of an imagination."

She almost told him about the Irish aristocracy she envisioned getting ready for a ball in the dressing room, but he'd only call her a romantic again. Just thinking about it made her heart hurt. Had she missed out because she wasn't a romantic? Did she not know how to deal with a normal man because she hadn't spun fantasies?

She couldn't even speculate. She simply knew she wanted her mind on something that didn't confuse her so much.

She pointed down a hall that veered off to the left. "I'll bet that leads to the back of the house and a stairway to a tower."

He snorted and motioned for her to go down the corridor.

They found four more bedrooms and a stairway that only led to a tower. She twirled around in a circle. Rain beat against a glass door, but she could see it led to a balcony.

"Well, what do you know? You don't just get your tower...you also get a balcony." He rubbed his elbow against the glass to clear it. "I'll bet you can see for miles up here."

"I'll bet this would make a great master bedroom."

He glanced around. "Why give up the perfect master suite that's already downstairs?"

"Then maybe I'd make this a reading room."

"Why not just let it be a tower?"

"Because it should be something special."

"A tower is pretty special."

She winced. "Sorry. I'm probably seeing this place in terms of remodeling because I have to do some remodeling in my condo and that's where my brain is focused. Everywhere I look I see a project."

He peered across the space at her. "Your ideas aren't bad."

"My ideas are spot-on." She turned in a circle again, taking in the space. "It's weird. I'm seeing the rooms, then seeing how I think they should be."

"Your brain is even busier than mine."

She shrugged. "Maybe. I never thought of it that way."

"Do you ever take a break?"

"That's what my paintings are about."

"Ah."

"What's that supposed to mean?"

"It means that you paint to relax, but then you monetize it."

She frowned. "I guess I do."

"Where do you vacation?"

She winced. "France."

"Oh, to see Pierre."

"You are really making me feel like a dull workaholic."

"Maybe you are a dull workaholic."

She gaped at him. "Seriously?"

His eyes fixed on the rain beyond the balcony, he said, "I'm not making fun or trying to tell you what to do with your life, but I'm noticing a serious lack of fun in everything you tell me."

"And I suppose your life's a real barrel of chuckles."

He faced her. "I fish. I travel. You met only four of

my Barcelona friends. I have a whole network of friends in Spain. I also take my staff on corporate retreats to places like Fiji."

"I do fun things."

He snickered. "Okay. Name some."

"Well, doing art showings is fun."

"We already established that that's an extension of your work."

She tossed her hands. "Stop! I'm starting to feel boring."

"You're not boring. Your job alone sounds incredibly interesting. You just don't know how to stop working." He took a few steps toward her. "I understand that you don't want to tempt fate while we're here."

She held back a grimace, realizing he'd barely reacted when she'd told him she didn't want to sleep with him because he'd been thinking it through.

"But there's a part of me that wonders why fate threw us together like this. Since we can't have a relationship, the only possible reason for it is that fate wants me to show you how to have fun."

She considered that and couldn't quite figure out what he was suggesting. "Here? In a tropical storm?"

"The end of a tropical storm. We're not stranded forever. The rain's got to stop sometime. We could be out of here tomorrow morning." He met her gaze. "Not enough time to do something we'd regret, but enough time to enjoy each other's company."

When he put it like that it sounded innocent...and maybe even a little bit wonderful. "How would we have this fun?"

"Well, we could dress for dinner."

"Dress for dinner?" She thought of the Irish people in the bedroom again. When she pictured them, they were always laughing. Happy with each other. Her heart pinched. She couldn't even imagine those kinds of feelings...

The squeeze of her heart intensified into longing. But longing was so untrustworthy. Not a feeling she'd indulged the few times it had appeared. "Put on our good clothes just because we can?"

"Shower, put on our good clothes, fix our hair and use up an hour or two of all the time we have on our hands. Then pretend to be lord and lady of the manor having dinner in the great hall."

Now he was going overboard. "Eat our warmed-up beans in the great hall? Seriously?" The vision in her head morphed again. She saw them sitting at the long table, eating beans, laughing...

Nothing sexy, nothing foolish. Just two people getting to know each other. Maybe appreciating each other?

Temptation sent tingles up her spine. Before she and Trent had headed to Paris to find Pierre, she'd scoffed at the concept of real relationships. She would have made fun of his idea of dressing up and being silly with each other. Now she didn't merely believe real relationships existed; she wanted a taste. Just a taste. One night of being herself, enjoying herself with a man she genuinely liked. A man she found so attractive she sometimes caught her breath just looking at him.

"All right. Fine." She headed out of the tower. "If I'm going to waste time, I might as well see if I can't do something Marie Antoinette-ish with my hair."

"Not Marie Antoinette. She's French. Think Irish lass."

She laughed and walked down the three flights of stairs and Trent followed her. He fully intended not to tempt fate. No sleeping together. But now that he'd taken romance out of the equation, when that longing he kept seeing flitted through her eyes, he just wanted to make her happy.

Stupid. Since in her own little McCallan way she was happy. Content. Wealthy, with a fulfilling career.

And he was Trent Sigmund. Newly rich. Sometimes crass. Friend of her brother.

When she made the turn to go to her bedroom, he kept going down the stairs, on his way to the kitchen. At the very least, he was not letting her eat beans out of a can.

He walked into the pantry and found a treasure trove of interesting food. Spam, something his mother liked to cook, and which could be good if prepared correctly. The ever-popular beans. The soup Sabrina had found. Canned corn. Canned beans. Canned peas. Some boxes of pasta that weren't past their use-by date.

He could make a really good goulash out of this.

He grinned and walked to the butler's pantry, looking for a stash of alcohol. There was none. But after searching through rooms, opening doors that might hide a bar, he finally found one. It contained nothing fancy like tequila for margaritas, but there was wine.

Wine and goulash.

It wasn't posh or classy, but it would be delicious.

He pulled two bottles of the wine from behind the bar and took them to the refrigerator, which he plugged in.

Because he only had to shave, shower and slip into his tux, he did some cleaning in the great room while the wine chilled and Sabrina took her time doing whatever it was that caused women to need two or three hours to dress.

The wind and rain that had been pounding the house slowed, indicating the storm was moving on. They probably would be leaving the next morning. He walked up the stairs to take a shower and put on his tux, thinking his plan was a good one. They'd have fun eating and dancing in the great room, then go to separate rooms, sleep for a few hours and leave in the morning.

Actually, her suggestion that they sleep in different rooms had made the plan perfect. He could satisfy the need to erase the longing from her pretty blue eyes without worry that he'd hurt her.

What could possibly go wrong?

CHAPTER ELEVEN

TRENT TOOK OFF his tux jacket to make the goulash and set the table in the great room. But when everything was ready, he slipped it on again and stood at the bottom of the stairway, just about to go up and check on Sabrina, when she suddenly appeared at the top. Wearing the pretty blue gown she'd worn to Pierre's showing, with her long hair wild and free, she walked down the steps.

"I thought about what you said about the Irish lass." She pointed at her head. "So, I washed my hair and let it dry naturally."

"It's perfect." *She* was perfect. "You look like you could be running in a glen."

She laughed. "So that's how this is going to be? We're getting in character and staying there?"

"Sure." He stuffed his hands in his trouser pockets, so he couldn't indulge the need to touch her. "If you're going to be stranded, it's best to be stranded somewhere entertaining." He smiled when she reached the bottom of the steps. "I found wine."

She grinned. "I'm pregnant. Can't drink wine, remember?"

He winced. "Sorry. I'll look for juice or we can drink water. I also found pasta and canned veggies and made goulash with macaroni, beans and corn."

"Sounds interesting."

He motioned for her to go to the great hall. "Oh, I forgot there's Spam, too."

She stopped walking, turned and frowned at him. "What the hell is Spam?"

"Canned meat that's pretty tasty if you ignore the fact that it's probably a zillion calories and loaded with cholesterol."

"I'm starving so I'd be willing to overlook that."

Temptation overwhelmed common sense and he took her hand and tucked it in the crook of his elbow to escort her to their dinner. "I was hoping you would. Sometimes Spam can be delicious."

"I'm going to take your word on that."

They entered the great room and she gasped. "Oh, my gosh! This is fabulous."

He'd dusted the table and chairs, swept the floor, set out good china and found glasses and candles, giving her the luxury she was accustomed to...even if the dinner was a sort of poor man's feast.

He pulled out the chair catty-cornered from his, and she sat, arranging her dress around her.

"Give me one minute. I'm pretty sure I saw a bottle of sparkling apple juice in the bar."

He raced off and sure enough there were two bottles. He grabbed one and headed back to the great room.

As he took the seat at the head of the table, an odd sense of rightness enveloped him. A peace he'd never felt.

He blamed that on the discomfort he'd always experienced as a child. Any time the family did anything fancy, he was the fifth wheel. Sabrina made him feel part of things.

Not wanting to examine that too deeply, he opened the apple juice and poured two glasses. "Sorry it's warm."

"I'm sure it's fine." She took hers and sipped delicately then closed her eyes. "It's excellent."

"The owner of this house has weird tastes. The wine I'd found was excellent, but he also had canned veggies and Spam."

"Maybe he has kids." She glanced around. "I can picture this house filled with kids."

So could he. "It would be the perfect weekend house if it had a pool."

"There might be a pool behind the gardens, something we couldn't see because of the overgrowth." She smiled. "My family has a house in Montauk. Our pool is pretty far back. Actually, it's a hike to the pool. If it rained hard enough, you wouldn't be able to see it from the kitchen." She laughed. "The ocean's such a long walk from the house that Avery wouldn't stay there."

He frowned. "Really? She doesn't like a good walk?"

"She wasn't married to Jake at the time she was supposed to stay there. In fact, they were sort of fighting. Mc-Callan Inc. was the biggest client of the law firm where Avery worked, and Jake was about to sue her to let him have a part in their baby's life. So the firm had to let her go because of conflict of interest."

He shook his head. "Your family does have its scandals."

"Without her job, she had to sell her condo and Jake suggested she live at our house in Montauk. But it was too big for her, too much house, too much furniture, too much everything and—" she changed her voice to mimic Avery "—too far from the ocean. So Jake made arrangements with Seth to let her stay in Seth's little cottage that was right on the beach." She smiled dreamily. "I think that's why she fell in love with him. He never forced our lifestyle on her. He found ways to make her happy."

Trent stared at her, seeing the romantic in her that she thought she kept hidden. He almost mentioned it again, but before he could, he saw her point about Jake and Avery. Jake didn't try to change the woman he loved because he loved her—exactly as she was.

In the same way Avery had stolen Jake's heart just as she was, Sabrina was stealing his. He wanted to please her, not change her. They might not have forever but he wanted to leave her with good memories.

This dinner was his one shot.

"You really look pretty tonight."

The compliment went straight to Sabrina's heart. Her face flushed, but before she had to fumble with a reply, Trent reached for her plate and poured a ladleful of goulash onto it.

It looked a little crazy, a little sloppy, not quite soup, but not quite solid, either, but it smelled delicious.

He filled his own plate then motioned for her to take a bite.

Trying not to be too obvious about her slight fear of Spam, she cautiously filled her spoon with pasta, vegetables and Spam and slid it into her mouth.

Flavor exploded on her tongue. The odd mix of vegetables and pasta and Spam bathed her taste buds. "Wow."

"Wow good or wow bad?"

"Good! It's delicious. It reminds me a bit of jambalaya."

"You've been to the South."

"My mother was a belle."

He thought about that, thought about dignified but generous Maureen, who hosted balls, gave away millions of dollars and loved Seth so fiercely Trent had been envious. "I can see it."

"It's why she fit so well into New York high society. Might have been slightly different rules, but it was the same game."

"My mother was a schoolteacher."

Her gaze jumped to his. "No kidding!"

"My dad—stepdad—was a dock worker. They could stretch a nickel better than anyone I've ever met." He smiled at the memories. "I learned to manage money from them."

Sabrina studied him. He'd learned how to manage money from his parents, obviously loved them from the look of affection that came to his face. Yet, he'd never clicked with his stepdad.

"It's why I know how to cook things like goulash."

A million questions assaulted her. She sorted through them before she carefully said, "Your family sounds nice." Not a question, more like an opening for him to talk.

"They are very nice. But they are solidly blue collar. Even the notion of expanding beyond their borough is uncomfortable for them. They like their block parties. They're active in their community. But that's kind of the point. They know who they are, like who they are."

"And you wanted more?"

"I wanted an education." He shrugged. "I didn't necessarily want to leave that life. I could live anywhere. I don't have a maid, just a cleaning service that comes in. I could keep my fancy cars in storage. No one has to know how much money I have." He laughed. "I could be the billionaire next door. But the truth is my family didn't want me around."

"That part sounds awful."

"It isn't when you realize that I hadn't fit for a while. I wasn't surprised when my stepdad turned down the house I'd bought for him and my mom." He paused, took a breath, then caught her gaze. "It made it official that I was out of sync with them."

"You make it sound so sterile. But I know it had to hurt."

"It did. Sometimes it still does. But everybody's supposed to grow up, to move on. I'm just the guy whose parents don't want him to come home for holidays."

Silence reigned as they ate a bite or two of goulash, took a sip or two of sparkling apple juice, then he laughed. "I'm making it sound horrible and it isn't. When I woke up the day after my stepdad turned down the house, I realized I could be whoever I wanted, do whatever I wanted."

She set down her spoon. "Make your own rules?"

"Why not? The old ones didn't work for me."

She sniffed. "The old ones don't really work for me, either."

"Then maybe you'd like to join me in the land where I decide what's good and bad, what's fun and what's not, and where I choose what I want to do and with whom."

"Not till after I hear some of the rules."

"Well, for one, you always have to be yourself...your real self."

She snorted. "I've been my mother's perfect daughter for so long I'm not really sure I know my real self."

"Maybe *this* is your real self."

She shook her head. "No. When I bought this gown, I tried on a red one I liked more."

"Really? Prettier than that?" He chuckled before he took a drink. "Because you look amazing in that one."

She took a sip of apple juice, letting his compliment sink into her soul. "The other was more beautiful. Red, with no back."

His brow wrinkled. "No back?"

"It was fantastic. It fit me the way the blue sparkly one

your shopper picked out fit. But it had long sleeves and a dramatic dip in the back that stopped at the very top of my butt. It was artistic and passionate and when I put it on…" She glanced down at her plate, then back up at him. "I felt it. That indefinable thing that clicks in your soul."

Confusion filled his dark eyes. "So why didn't you get it?"

"Because I have blond hair and blue eyes and wearing the color blue makes me into this physically perfect picture."

He only stared at her.

"Blondes wear blue. We look good in blue."

"It sounds like you have a snapshot in your head that you keep recreating."

Her eyes widened. "That's it exactly."

He leaned back in his chair. "When it comes to people, I know my stuff. I might have missed that my stepfather would eventually nudge me out of my own family, but I hadn't missed that he'd always been standoffish with me. And being attuned to that made me attuned to people in a different way, and that translated to picking up on things that make me a good investor. I can see when a CEO's bumpy marriage is going to cause him to lose focus for his company or when a board of directors is getting cocky, taking risks that might devalue their corporation."

"Makes sense." She swirled the liquid in her glass. "When I interview potential clients, I look for rough patches in their personal lives. That doesn't necessarily count them out. If the client is strong and motivated, I can teach them how to work around personal troubles, so they don't affect their business."

"Another thing we have in common." He poured more

apple juice into both of their glasses. "You should have bought the red dress."

She shook her head. "I was very close to it. But I wanted to blend in at Pierre's showing, not stand out. Trust me, in that red dress I would have stood out."

They finished their goulash, polished off the first bottle of sparkling juice and opened a second.

"We should probably wash these dishes."

Trent pushed back his chair. "We'll get them in the morning. Right now I thought we'd dance."

"Dance?"

He pointed to the great room's dance floor. "I want the full experience. We can pretend we're at a ball."

He walked to her chair and pulled it out for her.

"Or we could pretend we're the lord and lady of the house."

"At a ball?"

"Or alone." She pictured it. Her laughing Irish couple from the dressing room. The husband and wife who would own a castle like this. "With the kids tucked in bed and the servants in their quarters, they would dance."

And probably go upstairs and make love.

For the first time since Barcelona the idea didn't scare her. It felt like the perfect ending to a trip that had absolutely changed her.

He studied her as he slid his phone from his jacket pocket. "Why am I getting the feeling that you've thought this through?"

She shrugged. "Maybe I have."

He found his playlist, the one filled with slow, romantic songs, then held out his hand to her. He didn't remind her that she was supposed to be pragmatic, not a dreamer. He liked this side of her, sensed that he was with the real

Sabrina, the one who would have bought and worn the happy, artistic, sexy red dress.

Music filled the room. He led her to the dance floor and pulled her close. She melted into him and the sense of rightness he'd had at the beginning of the night drifted through him like the simple, easy notes of the song floating around them, creating a little world all their own.

He let himself soak up the feeling. He had lots of friends and girlfriends and employees who were friends. But he'd never had this closeness, this intimacy, with another person. He'd never wanted it. Never missed it. But holding her now, he knew that when they went back to their separate worlds this dance would haunt him. Make him wish he'd found the courage to let this relationship evolve to its natural conclusion.

"Do you ever think that some people aren't meant for forever?"

He leaned back, looked into her eyes. "What do you mean?"

"My parents soured me on marriage. Pretty soon I'm going to have a child to raise. That's going to limit everything I do." She shrugged. "I don't know what I'm saying."

He thought he did. At least a little. She might be a romantic, but she didn't think she'd get the happily-ever-after.

But why mention it now?

Unless…

"Are you saying you think we aren't made for forever?"

She held his gaze. "You wondered why fate had thrown us together. Well, there's a part of me that knows. I've loved everything about tonight, but more than that, I really like you."

"I like you, too." Her simple declaration sent need

rippling through him, and this time he didn't fight it. He dipped his head, kissed her slowly and thoroughly. "And?"

Her breath stuttered. "And aren't you just the tiniest bit curious about how this night should end?"

"I actually had a plan."

"You did?"

He spun them around once, then kissed her again. He hadn't taken his plan this far, but now that they were here, on the threshold of something amazing, the plan morphed, taking a wonderful turn. "I've decided to seduce you."

"Oh."

He kissed the lips forming the perfect, "Oh."

Drew the kiss out languidly.

Slowed their dance steps to almost none so he could enjoy her taste, the softening of her body against his, the yearning of his own body for hers.

When he pulled away she looked sleepy-eyed and happy. "Maybe we should share that room after all."

"Maybe we should."

CHAPTER TWELVE

CAUGHT IN THE spell of his dark eyes, Sabrina stood frozen. He broke their dance hold, took her hand and led her to the table where he blew out the candles, then to the door, the stairway and the bedroom. Arousal joined her awareness of how male he was, how lucky she was to have this just one night.

But everything was so perfect, the strangest feelings flitted through her. Thoughts of forever inched into her conscious, forming the realization that this wasn't just a man she wanted, this was a man she could trust.

She shoved those thoughts aside. She didn't want them intruding on her perfect night when she knew one night might be all they got together.

She stood on her tiptoes and kissed him until there was no reality around her but darkness and Trent.

When they woke together the next morning, he pulled her close and kissed her before he jumped out of bed to go to the room where he'd stored his suitcase to get his toothbrush.

With morning light streaming in through the open curtains, Sabrina knew she must have looked a fright, and while he was gone she ran into the private bath of her room to use her toothbrush and comb out the tangles of her hair.

But she stopped herself. She didn't hate her wild hair. She liked it. And, mysteriously, she looked like a woman Trent would date. Except she had a little more meat on her bones.

She combed her hair enough that it wasn't a mass of tangles and when he returned to the bedroom, wearing sweatpants but no shirt, she realized that with his now-short hair, he looked like the kind of guy she would date.

They'd always been these people. Just hidden under tons of misconceptions and a boatload of fears.

But why pick now to change…unless something about being together brought out the best in them?

He threw back the covers and patted the bed, indicating she should join him. She did. Willingly. Feeling a billion different things, the most confusing of which was the surety that this…being with him, wild hair, tight dresses, honest conversations…was her future. Her *destiny*.

If it hadn't felt so right, she might have argued with it.

And maybe she still should be careful, not let the happiness of making love to someone she truly loved cloud the truth. Especially since she'd told him the night before that she believed this was a one-time thing.

Still naked, she slid into bed and over to him. Something had happened the night before. Something wonderful.

And she wanted it.

Maybe she'd even fight for it—something so un-Sabrina-like she should have questioned it. But every time she tried, she would remember the night before and know with certainty she couldn't go back to being the person she'd been, but more than that she refused to go on without him.

He cuddled her against him and pulled the covers over them. He wasn't sure what had happened the night before but he wanted it.

He hadn't slept with a million women, but he'd slept with enough to know when something was special, perfect. He hoped Sabrina felt that, too, but if she hadn't, he had to figure out how to get her to see it.

Of course, he also realized he didn't have to do that today. Now that they'd found each other, they could date. He couldn't believe he'd thought that they couldn't. And he almost couldn't remember why he'd thought that.

The music of a mariachi band burst into the room. Leaning across him, Sabrina grabbed her phone from the bedside table and winced. "It's Jake."

"Your brother's ringtone is a mariachi band?"

She slid up in bed, dragging the sheet with her. "He likes to dance." She clicked her phone and said, "Hey, Jake."

Her brother's voice came through the speaker. "Where are you?"

"I'm in Dublin… Actually, outside Dublin."

"Dublin! What are you doing in Ireland? Mom's worried sick about you and it's no wonder. You're *not* home."

Sabrina laughed. "I'll be home tomorrow. I had something to do."

"What?"

She took a breath, glancing at Trent. He shrugged. Now that Pierre had been told there was no reason for secrecy anymore. He used that shrug to tell her he didn't see why she couldn't tell Jake about her baby.

"I had to tell Pierre that we were pregnant."

"What?" Jake's voice exploded from the phone.

Trent's eyebrows rose. Maybe he shouldn't have been so hasty in encouraging her to tell Jake.

"Look. It's all okay. I didn't want to tell anyone until I'd told Pierre and I told him two nights ago."

"That weasel is the father of your child?"

"He's the only guy I've been dating for the past four years. So, yes. He's the baby's father."

"Oh, hell."

"Don't worry. We're not going to do something foolish like get married. I told him that he could have as much or as little involvement with the baby as he wanted. But I also warned him that if he chooses to stay out of our child's life I'm giving our son or daughter his name when he or she reaches eighteen. What happens after that will be up to him or her."

Jake's voice softened. "You're really okay?"

She smiled at Trent. "I'm kind of excited. I've always wanted to be a mom. I know I'll get lots of support from you and Seth and Super Grandma." She gasped. "Hey, I haven't told Mom yet so just keep this between us."

"You know Avery will sense something and badger it out of me."

She laughed. "You can tell Avery. I'll tell Mom and Seth tomorrow."

"I'm glad you told me."

"I am, too." She glanced over at Trent again and she smiled. But he saw more than just her happiness. He'd experienced the closeness of the McCallan kids before, but hearing it firsthand tightened his chest. He couldn't imagine being this close to his half brother or sister, but he heard the sweetness of it in Sabrina's voice. He could tell she loved her brothers.

"So you're all by yourself in Dublin?"

"No." She looked at Trent again and he had the sense that this was something like a moment of truth. Would she tell her brother? And if she did, how would Jake react?

"Trent's with me."

His heart stuttered with relief.

"Trent?"

"I found out I was pregnant a few hours before Seth's wedding. Trent and I spent so much time together that day that I ended up telling him and he agreed to fly me to Paris, but Pierre wasn't there. So we went to Spain. Did you know Pierre has a huge working ranch?"

"The bastard."

"I know! He let us think he was a starving artist and all along he was... Well, maybe not rich, but at least solvent."

"He's a piece of work."

"Anyway, we found him in Dublin. I told him, and Trent and I headed for the airstrip, but we got caught in a rainstorm."

Jake's voice changed. "Rainstorm?"

"More like the end of a hurricane."

"Let me talk to Trent."

Sabrina handed her phone to Trent. "Jake wants to talk to you."

He fought an odd emotion that was sort of fear, but not normal fear, more like sheer panic that he'd have to explain his intentions to Sabrina's brother before he was even sure what Sabrina wanted.

As casual as possible, he took the phone and said, "Hey, Jake."

"If I'm on speaker, take me off."

"Okay." He clicked the button.

Jake said, "What's going on?"

"Exactly what Sabrina said. She needed help getting to Paris. I helped her. We'd be home right now except my assistant got the arrangements for a rental car wrong, then we drove right into this hurricane."

"Where are you?"

"We found an old castle. It looks like it was remodeled to be somebody's country house. I turned on the breaker, so we have electricity. But it almost doesn't matter now because I think we can leave for the airstrip this morning."

"Did you hear any of what happened with Pierre?"

Trent looked over at Sabrina and winked. "You should have heard her. She laid down the law."

Jake laughed. "That's my sister."

"Yep. You can be proud of her."

"And you're okay with all this?"

Okay with all this? He might have found the love of his life…

But now was neither the time nor the place to tell Jake that, especially since he didn't really know if Sabrina agreed with him.

She'd wanted one night. He'd given it to her. Now he greedily wanted more. He wanted everything.

"It was my pleasure to help her. You know I owe you and Seth more favors than I can repay."

"You don't owe us any favors—"

"Of course I do. But I would have helped Sabrina anyway."

"Okay."

"Want to talk to Sabrina again?"

"No. You two just be safe."

"We will."

Trent hung up the phone, a strange feeling tapping on his brain. Jake never questioned that he and Sabrina had been alone in a house overnight. He never warned Trent away from her. He'd bet his last dollar that Sabrina's brother hadn't pictured them naked in bed as they spoke with him.

"Your brother really trusts you."

Apparently following Trent's line of thinking, Sabrina said, "Or he trusts you."

He caught her gaze, weird feeling after weird feeling rippling through him. He couldn't forget what it felt like to hold her, to kiss her, to be kissed by her. Everything with her was different, more intense, more meaningful. He'd already decided he'd give his entire fortune for a chance to explore it.

And he had no idea what Sabrina was thinking.

There was only one way to find out.

Staring into her pretty blue eyes, he said, "Or he thinks we'd make a good match."

He waited. Their gazes locked. The longing he'd erased from her eyes had been replaced by caution.

Still, her voice was soft and breathy when she said, "Maybe."

His heart slammed into his ribs. If they pursued this, they'd be taking a hell of a chance. She was the baby sister of his friend. He had no idea how to be a good father…and she was pregnant.

Yet, it felt right.

Sabrina's phone burst out with a song Trent didn't recognize. His face must have registered his confusion because she said, "'Sunshine on My Shoulders.' My mom's a big John Denver fan."

He didn't know who John Denver was, so he only smiled, his thoughts going in and out and back and forth, his heart filled with something that felt a lot like hope… hope that wanted to spill over into joy.

"Hey, Mom."

As she listened to her mom talking, he almost stretched across the bed to nibble her shoulder, but he suddenly realized that she'd only been gone a few days, yet her mom had called twice. Her older brother had called once. If

Seth hadn't been on his honeymoon, Trent was sure he would have called, too.

She took a deep breath, made the *shhh* sound with a finger to her lips, then hit the speaker button on her phone, giving him the chance to hear her mom's call the way he had Jake's.

His hope rose again. Was her including him in the calls a sign that she saw this relationship as more than one night?

"Then Jake calls me and says you're fine but you're in Dublin. Dublin! What are you doing in Dublin?"

"I went to see Pierre."

Trent's gaze leaped to Sabrina's.

She closed her eyes, took a deep breath and said, "I'm going to have a baby, Mom."

"What!"

"It's okay. I told Pierre that he could have as much or as little contact with our child as he wants but we both were very clear about the fact that we don't want to get married."

Her mom said nothing.

"I've always planned to be a mom."

"Yes, you have."

Though Sabrina's mom answered, her tone was stiff, formal.

"Don't be upset because my baby isn't coming after a big church wedding. We know Avery's having another girl. Maybe I'll have a boy."

Silence.

"Remember how you fawned over Seth and Jake? Imagine another little boy to spoil."

A laugh drifted from the phone. "Little boys can be such fun."

"And I'll need help. Maybe you should come over

when I'm home and we can look at my spare room and see what we'd have to do to turn it into a nursery."

"We should hire a decorator."

Sabrina gave Trent a "watch this" expression. "I think you have good enough taste that you can do it without help."

Her mom laughed. "Are you buttering me up?"

"Maybe a little."

Maureen laughed again. "A baby."

"*Another* baby. You have Abby and Crystal, Avery's new little girl and now potentially a boy."

Maureen sighed. "We're blessed."

"Yes, we are."

Sabrina said, "Okay. I've got to go. You mull all that over and we'll talk when I get home. That should be tomorrow."

"How about if we have brunch together the day after?"

"That'd be great."

They said their goodbyes as Trent leaned against the headboard again. When she clicked off the call, he said, "Wow."

She laughed. "I wanted you to hear her panic because sometimes it's funny."

His heart warmed looking at her, seeing how much she loved her mother, remembering her affectionate conversation with Jake. Things he'd never had with his family. "You like to tease her."

"She's a hoot when she gets on a roll."

"I notice you didn't tell her about the hurricane."

"And have her hire mercenaries to try to rescue us?"

He chuckled. But he also realized she hadn't told her mom they were together. She'd told Jake, but not her mom.

"You really don't want her to worry."

"No. Not ever. We've had enough worry and pain in our lives."

That was when the closeness of the McCallan family came into sharp focus for Trent. Their father had been a tyrant. When he died, Jake found Avery and his life shifted enough that Sabrina, Seth and their mom began to relax. Abby was born. Then Seth found Harper, who brought Crystal into their lives. Seth took the shaky steps to becoming a father and for the first time, the clan McCallan became a normal family.

Now Sabrina was bringing another child into their happiness. And the family would grow even tighter.

Unless *he* somehow botched everything.

He knew nothing about being a dad. And if he hurt Sabrina, he would hurt Jake and Seth and Maureen. He'd ruin the peace they'd finally found.

Thinking back to the terrified boy he'd met when Clark brought Seth to live in their apartment all those years ago, Trent stiffened. Living with their dad had been awful. Seth had confided many times. Though the McCallan patriarch had been gone for years, this was the first Trent had realized how much the family had changed. How happy they were…

And he could ruin their peace.

If he knew he could fit, if he knew what he felt for Sabrina would be strong enough to endure his mistakes, he wouldn't hesitate.

But he was a misfit. He couldn't guarantee anything. Except maybe failure. For as much as he'd always said that his stepfather had never warmed up to him, there were two people in that equation. What if it hadn't been his stepfather's fault? What if it had been his fault? What if he didn't know how to connect, how to love?

After all, he'd never had a girlfriend that he'd stayed with longer than a few months.

And the price for failure here was Sabrina's happiness. The contentment she'd found in becoming a mom. The peace of her close family.

Sabrina slid down in the bed and half turned to nestle against him. He shifted away, rolling to get out of bed.

"Do you hear that?"

She lifted her head, paid attention. "I don't hear anything."

"That's just it. There's no drumming rain, no whipping wind. The rain stopped last night but now the wind is gone, too. I'm going to get dressed, maybe take the SUV up the road a few miles to check out the damage."

She shook her head. "We have all day."

"Not really."

Her face scrunched with confusion. "Trent?"

"Look, maybe we made a mistake last night."

"Two seconds before my brother called, you were on the verge of suggesting a relationship."

"Yeah. I was." Her boldness shamed him, but it was also her happiness—the hard-won happiness of her entire family—that made his decision. He stepped into the black pants from the tux he'd had on the night before, then faced her. "You and I have always been honest."

She held his gaze.

"So I'm going to continue that."

She nodded again, but her eyes clouded with confusion that almost did him in. His choice was to hurt her now or devastate her later.

"In the past forty years, your family hasn't had a lot of happiness."

Her face shifted. Her lips lifted into a warm smile and her eyes lit with joy. "We do now."

He sat on the edge of the bed. "Do you understand why?"

"I think my brothers finding love changed things."

"What if they'd picked the wrong mates?"

"If they hadn't married Avery and Harper?"

"If they'd married women who didn't fit into your family."

"They didn't."

"Pretend they did. Pretend they married someone your mom didn't like…" He stopped, slowly met her gaze. "Someone who wasn't a good mom to your mother's precious grandchildren."

"They're both great moms."

"But what if they weren't? What if they hurt your family dynamics?"

She searched his gaze before she said, "Like your stepdad."

"Yeah."

"What are you saying?"

"Your family is finally happy. Finally solid. It never dawned on me until I heard Jake's voice and your mom's voice just how fragile all this is for you."

"It's not fragile—"

"It is. You just don't see it."

She stiffened. "Because I'm not a romantic the way most women are?"

"No. Because you were right all along. A relationship between us is a bad idea. Not because one of us is bad or good…but because your whole life is going to change and so is your family's and I'm not the guy to take a chance with at this point."

She reached for him. "Trent—"

He caught her hand, kissed the palm. "This is about securing your family's happiness but it's also about me.

If we fail, and there's a good chance we will, your family isn't the only ones who will get hurt. I will, too."

Her eyes softened. "And you've already been hurt enough."

"Exactly." He said it softly, quietly, so angry with fate and himself and his upbringing and his shortcomings that he could have punched a wall, but he stayed calm, logical, because reason was the language she understood.

"And we've been together four days." He squeezed the hand he held. "A relationship is a fun thought. A wonderful possibility. But we haven't gotten in so deep that we know it will work, or that we can't back out before we make a mistake."

Sabrina stared at him. He was the most intuitive person she'd ever met yet he hadn't seen that it was already too late. Making love the night before had gotten her in too deep. She wouldn't have melted under his touch, given herself to him the way she had, as she never had with any other man, if she hadn't already fallen in love. She simply hadn't known it until they'd gone the whole way and her heart had lifted, and her soul had sighed with the relief of finally finding real love.

She slid away and took the sheet with her as she rose. "I get it."

"Do you?"

She nodded, pasted a smile on her face. "Sure. What we had was a one-night stand and all that. Besides—" she pointed at her belly "—I'm kind of going to be busy for the next nine months and eighteen years."

"Yeah." He returned her smile. "And you're going to make a great mom."

But she wouldn't make a great wife. She was so damaged that a man with his own problems couldn't take a chance on her. She wanted to kick herself for being fool-ish enough to romanticize what was happening between them when really it was nothing.

Her heart shattered into a million pieces. She knew better.

She'd always known the idea of real love was untrust-worthy.

But she'd been so sure. Not of herself…of him.

And he didn't want her.

Pain flooded her. Her chest ached. Her limbs felt like they wouldn't support her. "You know, I think I'll shower and dress while you check out the roads."

He rose from the bed. "Okay. I'll be back in twenty minutes."

She had to work to keep her voice from shivering when she said, "I'll be ready."

In the shower she tried to tell herself that it was better to be dumped after a one-night stand than to be married to someone for years before their true colors emerged. But it didn't stop the tears.

She'd trusted him. She'd fallen in love with him.

And he didn't want her.

When she was done dressing, she remembered the mess they'd made in the great room and cleared the table, tossed the burned-down candles, put the empty bottles in the trash.

She'd tried to do it clinically, tried to do it without re-membering what dancing with him felt like, without re-membering the slow, delectable kisses that she'd thought were filled with emotion. But everything came back to her…the emotion. The longing. The need. The fulfill-ment.

She forced herself to stop seeing herself and Trent and began imagining the Irish couple. She disappeared.

Trent disappeared. And the happy Irish man and woman with the kids filling the upstairs beds and the servants tucked away in the quarters were the man and woman who danced.

By the time Trent returned to tell her the roads were clear, she could pretend she was fine. But on the drive to the airstrip she texted her assistant to arrange to have a car pick her up at the airport in New York. She didn't talk to Trent on the flight and when the plane landed she walked directly to the McCallan limo that awaited her.

She didn't say goodbye.

She left him with his phone to his ear, back to doing the job that he loved.

CHAPTER THIRTEEN

Monday morning Trent awoke in his Upper East Side condo. Two stories, it boasted a commercial-grade kitchen, a wine room, a master suite fit for royalty and exclusive access to the roof. He filled a mug with coffee, threw a robe over his sweatpants and baggy T-shirt and climbed the two flights of stairs that took him to his haven.

Three conversation areas with outdoor sofas and chairs and glass stone fire pits sat on bright aqua area rugs. He walked to the edge, where a five-foot Plexiglas wall served as a barrier, leaned over to watch the sun rise...

And felt nothing.

Except anger with himself.

How could he have been so stupid as to seduce a woman who was off-limits? He had legendary self-control. He could analyze any situation and know—with absolute certainty—if it was good or bad, right or wrong, yet he'd forgotten important parts of the equation when adding his life to Sabrina's. She had a family, a real family who loved her. Family who would help her with her baby. Family who would give her baby the peace of belonging.

And he came with nothing. Except money. A little power. A lot of emptiness.

With a huff of anger, he turned from the spectacle in the sky and went back inside. There was no way he could take all this emotion to one of his lake houses. Being alone with this anger? With his self-recrimination? That wouldn't work.

What he needed to do was go into the office.

Talk to his staff.

Get back his sense of self.

And forget about soft blue eyes filled with longing... that he'd satisfied. Almost as if they were supposed to be together.

Calling himself an idiot, he gulped the coffee in his mug, jogged down the stairs to the master suite, showered, dressed and was in the back of his town car in under an hour. After a brief "Good morning" and an exchange about the beautiful end-of-August day, silence descended in the plush vehicle. He pulled his phone from his breast pocket and started reading newspapers.

Twenty minutes later he entered the building housing his offices, leaving the noise of Manhattan traffic behind. The ping of his private elevator announced his arrival at his office, so he wasn't surprised to see Ashley, a pretty twenty-seven-year-old in the process of getting her MBA, and Makenzie standing at attention, ready to work.

"Ladies," he greeted as he strode to his desk.

They scurried to follow him. "Good morning, Trent."

"I've texted a list of articles I want you to print out for me."

Makenzie looked confused. "Print out?"

He wasn't about to tell his staff that he was experimenting with different work habits to use his brain in a different way, so it wouldn't have time to slide over to Sabrina, to wonder where she was, what she was doing, if she was hurt or angry or both.

"Yes. Print out."

Makenzie looked about to argue, but Ashley gave her head a quick shake, a warning to the newbie she was training not to question the boss.

He rattled off a litany of instructions, watching Makenzie furiously taking notes as Ashley nodded.

But when Makenzie left the room, Ashley didn't follow her out. She closed the door behind her and turned to Trent.

"Are you okay?"

He didn't look up from his desk. "Why wouldn't I be?"

"Being stranded in a tropical storm and having to stay in someone else's house, waiting for roads to reopen, with a woman who is something of a stranger can't be fun."

But it had been fun. Some of the most fun of his life. He'd never felt more connected to another person. Never felt that complete.

"We considered ourselves lucky to find shelter and even luckier that it had canned food in a pantry."

"Canned food?"

"Peas, corn…" He shrugged. "Spam."

She laughed. "Spam?"

"I'll have you know I made a fantastic goulash."

Which Sabrina had loved. She hadn't laughed at his knowledge of the easy, low-cost meal. She never put on airs. She'd had the same empty ache in her soul that he had. Almost as if they'd been searching for each other.

Damn it! He had to stop thinking like that.

"Anyway, I have a lot of things to do today."

"I thought you were taking a week at the lake to unwind."

"My time in Ireland was my downtime. Now I need to work."

Ashley nodded and left, closing the door behind her.

He tossed his pen to his desk. If he let himself, he would remember every second of his time with Sabrina, every word she'd said, how different it had been to make love with her.

So he couldn't let himself.

But the second he forced away thoughts of Sabrina, emptiness filled him, along with the sense that the life he was so sure gave him purpose and meaning was actually a sham.

Sabrina pressed a button on her security pad and opened her condo door for her mother. Maureen walked in, her face glowing, her eyes shining. She caught Sabrina in a huge hug and squeezed so hard, Sabrina thought she'd break a rib.

"I'm so happy that you're going to be a mom."

"Me, too." She said the words brightly, but inside her heart was broken. Her soul shivered as if it had taken a beating and lost part of itself. "Would you like some coffee?"

Maureen held up a bag. "Yes. That would go very nicely with one of these cinnamon bagels. I know we'd talked about going to brunch but I'm too eager to get a crack at turning your guest room into a nursery."

When Sabrina had a bottle of water and her mom had a cup of coffee with refills in a silver service complete with cream and sugar, they walked to the sofa and chair.

Setting the silver tray on the coffee table, Maureen said, "So how are you feeling?"

"Good. Great, actually." She winced. "No morning sickness like Avery seems to get."

Her mother beamed. "Oh, lucky you!" She bit into her bagel and groaned with delight. "So good."

Sabrina swallowed the bite of bagel she'd taken. "The best in the city."

"So you're feeling okay…"

"Yes, but I need to be at the top of my game. An easy pregnancy will make it possible for me to get done all the things I have to do to be able to take time off work when the baby is born, as I create a nursery and playroom."

Finished with her bagel, Maureen rubbed her hands together. "No time like the present. Do you have a tape measure?"

"Yes." Sabrina walked to the kitchen island to get it. "Thanks, Mom. I really appreciate your help."

Especially when she was drowning in a loss so deep and so profound she wasn't sure she could decorate a box, let alone a nursery and playroom. But even as she had that thought, she realized Trent couldn't call his mom and ask for help. He couldn't call her to share his pride over his successes or even to wish her merry Christmas.

It hurt her heart to think about it, but she reminded herself that his awful past had limited his ability to have a real relationship as much as hers had. If anything, the terrible way they'd ended things had proven she'd been right all along. There was no such thing as real love.

She fought to keep her eyes from filling with tears. There might not be any such thing as real love but oh, how she'd wanted it to be real. Trent hadn't shown her a fairy tale. He'd shown her how two people who genuinely cared for each other could be good to each other. But that didn't mean it was without passion and romance. No man had ever made her feel giddy with delight or weak with longing. If she had one wish for the world it would be that those feelings could be sustained—

That people really could be connected.

That people really could care for each other forever.

That making love could be as warm and wonderful as what she'd felt with him.

That mornings after could be filled with love and laughter and a closeness that brought contentment and peace.

Until her family had called.

Though Trent had proven that those things exist, he'd also shown her that they couldn't be sustained and now she had to reenter the real world.

A little smarter.

A little stronger.

But a hell of a lot sadder.

She led her mom back to the second bedroom, her heart heavy. She might be pragmatic about what had happened, but it still hurt. If she hadn't arranged for her mom to help redecorate, she might not have gotten out of bed that morning. She might not have ever gotten out of bed at all.

She took the rest of the week off to scout wallpaper and flooring with her mom. After a long, lonely weekend, she arrived at her office on Monday morning to find the invitation to the annual fall charity ball had arrived while she was in Europe. She marked the RSVP as attending, told her assistant, Maria, to send it back and settled in her desk to work.

But thoughts of dancing in Barcelona came back to her like a punch in the stomach, followed by memories of dancing in the Irish castle's great room. If she closed her eyes she could feel Trent's arms around her.

Combing her fingers through her hair, she rose from her desk chair and turned to the view of Manhattan visible through the enormous window behind her work area.

She'd gotten herself to the point where she could keep her brain from thinking about Trent, or wishing things were different, but memories of little things invaded her thoughts all the time.

It might be because she'd found the blue sparkly dress in her luggage and couldn't quite get herself to donate it to charity. It might be because she'd begun leaving her hair natural because she really did like it that way.

No matter that Trent had hurt her, she'd found a piece of herself when she was with him. So when she returned to her desk to finish the mail and found the bill for the blue gown she'd bought in Dublin, she picked up her cell phone and dialed the number for the shop.

"I'm Sabrina McCallan. You probably don't remember me, but I bought a blue gown from you a little over a week ago. While I was there I tried on a red gown, too. I don't recall the designer, but it was a long-sleeved, form-fitting dress with no back."

The clerk said, "Ah. I know the dress you're talking about."

"I have a ball in two weeks. I'd like to wear that dress. Can I order it from you and have it shipped to New York?"

"Absolutely."

She gave the clerk her size and then full name and address for delivery. As sad and empty as she sometimes felt, she *had* found herself on that trip. That was the part of the experience she had to remember. She'd get the dress that made her feel like her real self to push forward another step.

She might forever mourn the loss of what she'd had with Trent, but she needed to move on, and what better way to help herself move on than by letting herself be the person she'd found that week.

Trent entered the Annual Fall Ball two weeks later, two steps behind Seth and Harper. He'd spoken with Seth a few times since returning from Ireland and Seth hadn't mentioned Sabrina. Apparently, she'd kept what had happened between them to herself.

He tapped Seth's shoulder and when Seth turned around to see him, he grinned. "Hey!" He clasped Trent's hand before bringing him in for the quick shoulder bump.

"Good to see you guys," he said to both Harper and Seth. "How's married life?"

Seth said, "Couldn't be better," and Harper laughed. "He's discovering that he likes cooking."

"Just stupid things like macaroni and cheese that Crystal likes."

"He's actually started texting helpful hints to Sabrina, though her baby won't be able to eat food like this for a good two years."

Seth laughed, and Trent's heart tumbled. He yearned to ask Seth how Sabrina was, if she'd been sick, if she was back to work...if she missed him, but he knew Seth would read into his eagerness and start making guesses. If Sabrina hadn't wanted her family to know something had happened while they were traveling, he didn't want to say the thing that tipped them off.

He also didn't want to seem like a lovestruck puppy. He was getting beyond what had happened between them. He really was. He'd actually hoped they'd see each other tonight, hold a decent conversation and maybe put a period at the end of the sentence of the story of them.

He drifted away from Seth and Harper and was drawn into a conversation with two bankers. He managed to get away from them to chat with a few real estate guys before he finally found his table. His seatmates were from two families with old money. He took the opportunity to pick the brain of the patriarchs—a person could never have too much knowledge about markets and industry—but a flash of red caught his eye.

He stopped talking and glanced over to see Sabrina, wearing a red gown, her hair down and a little wild.

She turned to take her seat at the McCallan table and he gasped. There was no back on the dress. It dropped to a spot just above her perfectly shaped bottom.

Memories of touching her, tasting her, assaulted him. If he'd been holding a fork, he would have dropped it. In the thirty seconds he stared at her, he knew why he was having so much trouble forgetting her… He didn't want to.

But looking at that dress, he realized it was *the* dress. Her declaration of independence dress. She was done following rules—

No. She was making her own rules.

The way he used to…

His gaze moved from her to her brother Seth and lovely Harper, to Jake and savvy Avery, to their mom… Maureen, a tower of strength.

Something shuffled through his mind so quickly he couldn't process it. He gave the entire family another once-over and realized what he'd seen…

They were fine. They were strong. Beside Avery, Jake looked invincible. Sitting next to Harper, Seth grinned in a way Trent had never seen before. Her red dress a symbol of her new sense of self, Sabrina glowed.

So did Maureen. She'd spent forty years in a bad marriage, protecting her children, but that was over.

No one would ever hurt this family again.

Not even him.

They'd fought for this life and they wouldn't let anyone or anything snatch it away from them again.

Realization brought him to his feet. *They* were fine.

Strong. Happy. *He* wasn't. The only thing keeping him from Sabrina was his fear that he would ruin the McCallans. Now that he knew he wouldn't, he saw the other side of his dread. The *reason* he'd drawn the conclusions he had.

Sabrina had faced down her demons on her trip to tell Pierre— No. Trent had forced her to face her demons when he hadn't faced his.

He didn't fully understand what had happened between him and his stepdad but he did know he couldn't have an honest relationship with anyone until he did.

He took a breath. He belonged with Sabrina. But not with the questions hanging over his head.

It was time to figure this out.

He rose, said his goodbyes and walked into the lobby of the grand hotel. He pulled out his phone to call his driver and in five minutes his car was at the entrance. The driver opened his door and once he was settled he gave him the address of his parents' home.

CHAPTER FOURTEEN

TRENT ARRIVED AT the two-story frame house. Trimmed hedges, a neat walkway to the front door and newly painted black trim against white siding said this was the home of a proud working-class family.

He headed up the walk to the black front door with the etched glass center panel. Though it was after ten o'clock at night, he rang the bell.

The door opened. His mother's jaw fell when she saw him, but he also noticed that her dark eyes lit with unguarded happiness.

She reached out to hug him. "Trent."

"Mom." He returned her hug, closing his eyes when emotion threatened to overwhelm him. They'd been a team for years after his father's death. He'd never been closer to another person. To have been away from her for three long years, suddenly seemed absurd.

He pulled back, opening his eyes, and saw his tall, slim stepfather. "Jim."

"Humph. Not Dad anymore?"

He wanted to remind Jim that he was the one who had run him off, refused a gift, made Trent feel he'd somehow wronged him, insulted him… That was after decades of being made to feel he didn't belong, didn't fit.

His mother wrung her hands and nervously said, "How about some cake and coffee?"

His stepfather scowled. "Don't be going to any trouble for him."

That was the attitude that had always made him feel less than, unwelcome. But today he saw it for what it was. Just as Sabrina had known Pierre was a narcissist, Trent finally saw his stepfather was a grouch. He might not have reached the heights of Jake, Seth and Sabrina's dad, but they were cut from the same cloth.

Today Trent simply wasn't going to be moved by him.

"Actually, Mom, I'd like a piece of cake." He smiled at her. "And some coffee."

"Coming right up!"

She scurried off and Trent didn't wait for his stepfather to invite him into the living room that had been part of the home his mom had owned when she married Jim. He slid by him, saying, "Why don't you and I have a bit of a talk while the coffee brews."

"What? You think you're going to put me down or make fun of me while your mom's out of the room?"

Seriously? For the first time in his life, Trent saw that his stepfather had some real issues. He slipped off his tux jacket and sat on the worn, but comfortable sofa.

"You know what, Jim? For decades you made me feel unwanted and tonight I finally see that maybe I shouldn't have accepted that."

His stepfather's mouth tightened.

"I was a kid. A little boy who needed a dad and you were…" He hesitated to say it, but if they were going to get this out in the open and deal with it, he had to say it. "You were jealous of me."

"I wasn't jealous of you. You were bad."

He shook his head. "No. I wasn't. I remember being

so excited to get a dad. I would have been anything, *done* anything you wanted. But you shut me down." He drew in a breath. "But none of that matters. I'm here to say the past is the past. You may not want to, but I think we should start over. I love my mother. I miss her and I miss Jamie and Pete, too. They're my family."

Jim squirmed a bit on his seat.

"And I want them back. You can join us when we have dinner or go to a show or even vacation together. Actually, I think it would be fun for all of us to rent a big house in Key West. We could hire someone to take us fishing. But if you want to stay home I've decided that's *your choice*."

Sounding old and tired, Jim said, "Your mother's not going to want to go on fancy vacations or to shows—"

"Of course I am." His mother strode into the living room, carrying a tray with three plates holding huge slices of chocolate cake, the coffeepot and three mugs. "I never did understand what happened when Trent bought us that house. Except that you said you didn't want it and Trent left without another word. I'd hoped it would iron itself out. Since it didn't I'm glad Trent's here, so we can fix it."

Jim rolled his eyes. "This is stupid." He strode to the stairway. "I'm going to bed."

Continuing with his decision to let Jim either join them or not, his choice, Trent said, "Good night, Jim."

He stopped, turned and shook his head as if realizing he might as well not fight this. "Good night."

It wasn't much, but it was a start. His mom handed Trent a piece of cake as Jim disappeared up the stairway.

"I think he's afraid of you."

Trent shook his head. "No. I think he's afraid of change."

"He's old-fashioned and he's proud."

Trent glanced around the tidy home. "He has a lot to

be proud of. I respect him and what you guys have. But he has nothing to fear from me." He took his mother's hand and squeezed it. "I just missed you."

"I missed you, too." She smiled at Trent. "And I'm so sorry. I always noticed things were different with you and Jim. I just didn't know how to handle it."

"We're fine, Mom. I think all of us hoped it would smooth out on its own. Because it didn't, we're fixing it now."

His new rules began to form in his head. "One night a month I can either visit here or take you to dinner and a show."

"That would be nice."

"Holidays I can come here until Sabrina and I get established."

"Who is Sabrina?"

He laughed. "Someone who might throw a ring back in my face if I get the proposal wrong."

His mother gasped. "You're getting married?"

"Not right away." He winced. "Technically, we haven't even dated but watching her handle a big problem that had come up in her life I suddenly realized I'd been running from mine." He shrugged. "And that's not who I am."

"No. You were never a runner. You always jumped right in and faced things."

"But I didn't know how to handle Jim."

"I think you do now."

"I think I do, too."

They ate cake and drank coffee and talked about anything and everything. He didn't say much more about Sabrina. He'd taken a huge leap involving her in his future when she might not want a damned thing to do with him and he didn't blame her.

But the woman with the problem had taught the man

who thought he didn't have any problems how to take a closer look and be a little more honest with himself.

She wasn't just a beautiful face with the great figure and a mind like a steel trap. She made him a better person and he wanted her in his life.

He just had to figure out the proposal she wouldn't be able to resist.

Sabrina McCallan stood by the huge double doors, looking at the castle outside Dublin, formal invitation in hand. The invite said the charity was having a showing of *her* paintings, but she hadn't realized it would be held at *the* castle where she and Trent had taken shelter from the rain—

And there were no cars for other guests. There was no line of limos dropping off dignitaries and society matrons. There was just her and the moonlight.

She'd checked into the charity and it was legitimate. They'd been thrilled she was planning to attend and were eager for the money from the showing—

Still, being here right now, it all seemed a bit odd.

As her driver maneuvered the big limo down the circular driveway to the road at the bottom of the hill, a case of nerves assaulted her. She opened her shiny black purse to get out her phone and call her car back, because the whole thing was beginning to feel like the first scene of a horror movie, but the double doors of the entry opened.

A man in tails greeted her. "Good evening, Ms. McCallan."

She took a breath. Would a serial killer go to this much trouble to get her alone?

Yes. Damn it.

"I'm sorry but I think there was some sort of mix-up here." Her phone in her hand, she stretched her thumb to call her driver.

The butler said, "Mr. Sigmund has been awaiting you."

She froze. Trent? She missed him in a way she'd never missed anyone because she'd let herself fall in love with him, and he'd rejected her. Now he'd lured her back to the castle where he'd hurt her?

The butler bowed at the waist, motioning for her to come inside. Though her first instinct was to reject Trent the way he'd rejected her, curiosity got the better of her.

She shouldn't be giving him the time of day. He'd hurt her more than anyone ever had. Not because leaving her had been so devastating but because until she'd met him she hadn't believed love existed. He'd shown her it did then took it all back. Leaving her alone, disillusioned and in the kind of emotional pain she'd managed to avoid for twenty-eight years.

As the butler led her through the first sitting room and into the more formal living room, she realized the place was clean.

Sparkling clean.

She glanced around, breathless with awe. Even in need of a good remodel the castle was amazing. A home. Not like the McCallan family's three-story condo where her mom hosted holidays or the mansion in Montauk, but a real home. With fires in the fireplaces and the scent of cinnamon as if someone had baked cookies.

A case of warm fuzzies overwhelmed her and she let them because they felt right. Something about this castle had always called to her.

"Sabrina…"

Trent walked over to her, his hands extended to take hers. His hair was short, the way he'd had it cut the last time they were in Dublin. He looked rich and powerful and sinfully sexy, but also warm and wonderful. Just the touch of his hands filled her heart with happiness.

But he'd also dumped her—

She pulled her hands from his and waved the engraved invitation. "I thought this was an exhibition. I called the charity, verified the facts."

"I gave them a ton of money to host this without hosting it. And it is an exhibition." He pointed to three of her paintings hanging on the wall to the right. "They just happen to be paintings that I own."

"You bought my paintings?"

"I would buy all of your paintings if it weren't so impractical and selfish." He glanced lovingly at a huge picture of a little blonde girl in a meadow. "I think that one's a self-portrait."

It was. But not in the conventional sense. She'd painted herself in a beautiful meadow, but alone. She'd always been surrounded by beauty, but she'd also been very much alone.

She suddenly realized this castle was the first place she hadn't felt alone, the first place she'd let herself be herself.

And he knew that.

"This whole deal feels kind of sleazy and cheap."

He arched a brow. "Let me assure you. It was not cheap."

"You know what I mean."

"I do." He turned and led her through the sitting room to a corridor she didn't remember to the great room. "But I knew it was going to take a grand gesture not just for you to hear me out, but to understand."

The table was set with the good china. Candles burned between the two catty-corner places.

The need to cry shivered through her. In the weeks that had passed, she'd barely let herself think about the night they'd spent here. And now here it was, recreated for her.

He lifted the lid off a silver bowl and the scent of his goulash floated out.

Tears filled her eyes, but she laughed. "What are you doing?"

"Apologizing." He stuffed his hands in his trouser pockets. "Explaining."

After the first week had gone by without a word from him, she'd dashed any hope that he might have acted hastily or made a mistake. She'd spent every day since then working to get over him. But one bowl of goulash, one sweet gesture, and she was butter.

"I let you go because I was afraid I would hurt the fragile peace your family had just established."

"So you said."

"But I saw your family at the charity ball a few weeks ago. I saw that you're all strong. Even your mom. And I thought it was a little vain of me to think I could hurt you."

"It was." But she had understood it. Even two years after her dad's death, she was still cautious, still afraid. It had taken four days with Trent for her to see she'd been living in a prison.

"Don't forget, I'd carried the guilt of ruining one family." He took a breath. "So I paid a visit to my mom and stepdad and realized I hadn't really ruined anything. My stepdad's a piece of work, frequently grouchy, but I think he's hiding a low self-esteem."

"Oh, yeah?"

He motioned for her to come to her seat and she did— slowly—as hope built inside her. A man who'd bought her paintings and arranged to meet her in the house where they'd fallen in love had to have something important to say.

He pulled out her chair and helped seat her, then took the chair across from the candles.

"You look lovely. Even if you are playing it safe with blue."

She laughed. "You didn't think I'd wear the backless dress to an event where I knew no one."

"I thought you were bold."

Her gaze jumped to his. "I am bold. I came to this castle only out of curiosity—" She stopped, cleared her throat. "I didn't even realize this was the castle we were forced to stay in."

"I bought this place."

Shocked, she glanced around. "You did?"

"For us. It was a matter of looking at public records to find the owner, but he wasn't willing to sell until I told him our story." He laughed. "Then he welcomed my offer with open arms. A few decades ago, he'd bought this castle for his new wife. They'd summered here with their four kids. When I told him you were pregnant, he knew we'd keep this house a real home. That's what he wanted. That's what I want."

Her throat tightened with the longing to weep, and she swallowed. He'd barely explained himself, but he almost didn't have to. The story of the castle owner was the most romantic thing she'd ever heard. And what she needed from him was the romance she'd always believed didn't exist.

Still, she wanted that last little bit of confirmation. "For us?"

"We've known each other forever without really knowing each other, so though I brought a ring—"

She gaped at him.

"If you don't want to take it, I'll understand. But no one has ever made me feel as wonderful as you do."

Emotion swelled in her chest, making it difficult to breathe, let alone think. She now knew romance was more than dancing and kissing. Honesty had brought them together. Only honesty would keep them together.

Her answer came straight from her heart. "No one's ever made me feel as wonderful as you make me feel, either."

"So we can take a few months or a few years." He shrugged. "Whatever we feel comfortable with before we get engaged."

Thoughts wound through her brain and eventually connected everything he was saying. "If that was a proposal you did a really poor job."

He laughed. "I chickened out."

"Why? You bought a castle! How can you chicken out at the best part? The part where you ask me to share it with you."

"Because the last time I saw you, you were still mad at me."

"The last time I saw you, you were naked. We were both naked. I could pick up right from that spot."

"You're not mad?"

"No. I understand. What happened between us happened fast. Now I see that you had some loose ends to tie."

He rose from his seat, sliding his hand into his jacket pocket and pulling out a black velvet ring box. Getting down on one knee, he opened the box and said, "Will you marry me?"

The tears she'd been fighting suddenly dried up. She pressed her lips together to stop a laugh before she said, "Yes."

Every crazy thing that had happened since the morning of Seth's wedding made sense.

After sliding the diamond on her finger, he took her hands and helped her to stand so he could kiss her.

"I feel like we're breaking about a thousand rules."

She laughed, lovingly looking at her diamond, then

into his eyes. "Some people aren't made for rules. I spent my entire life trying to keep my dad's rules. Now I would just like to live my life." She smiled. "With you."

"Amen to that."

He kissed her again.

Then a maid arrived followed by the butler. When Trent and Sabrina were seated again, the butler poured sparkling apple juice. The maid brought warm rolls and soft butter. Their duties accomplished, they scurried away.

She gave him a confused look. "A butler and maid?"

He buttered a roll. "You said kids would be sleeping upstairs and servants would be in their first-floor quarters."

She laughed. "You really pay attention."

"It's one of my best traits."

She wanted to tell him about the Irish couple she'd seen in her fantasies about this house but suddenly realized they were the couple. They'd always been the couple because she'd always known she and Trent belonged together.

That was when she realized there really might be such a thing as women's intuition. She felt it right now. They might not live in this castle full-time. It might be their summer retreat, but no matter where they lived they'd be happy. Forever.

EPILOGUE

A LITTLE OVER eight months later, Sabrina lay in a hospital bed with Trent holding her hand and her doctor telling her to push.

She did.

When the push was over, her mother wiped sweat from her brow. "That's great, sweetie."

Trent kissed her forehead. "Really great."

The doctor peered at her above the sheet draped over her legs. "Okay. We're ready for another push. Make this one a good one."

She took a long breath, focused her gaze on Trent's encouraging face and pushed with all her might.

The doctor laughed and looked at her over the sheet again. "We have a girl."

Her mother gasped. "A girl? I thought you said you were having a boy?"

The doctor handed the baby to a nurse who scurried away. "We need some more pushes."

Trent squeezed her hand. "You're good. Just a few more pushes and we'll get that little boy."

Her mother gaped at Trent. "What boy? Another baby? Twins?" She looked down at Sabrina. "You knew you were having twins and you kept that from me?"

She glanced at her mom. "I wanted at least one surprise from this pregnancy."

"Push, Sabrina! Now!"

She pushed again, and again, and a third time, really hard.

"And here's our boy."

Maureen leaned down, peering over the sheet as if needing to confirm the second child. "How does a woman hide the fact that she's having twins…and from her mother!"

Sabrina sighed. "Are you or are you not surprised?"

"I'm shocked."

Trent laughed and peeked down at Sabrina. "From the look on her face I'd say that's true."

The nurse walked over with their baby girl. She handed her to Sabrina, who laughed through her tears. "Oh, my gosh!" She caught Trent's gaze. "We have two of these."

He kissed her forehead. "I know."

"Are you sure we can handle this?"

"I don't see why not. We do have two cribs in the castle and another one on order for the condo."

His condo. He had more space for a nursery, a playroom and nanny's quarters. All that remodeling had been done weeks ago. Now they'd start planning their wedding.

The nurse brought over their son. She would have handed him to Trent, but Sabrina insisted on switching. "Babies need to bond first with their mom." She handed Trent the little girl, then took the boy from the nurse.

"Hello, Sebastian."

Maureen raced to the other side of the bed and looked over Trent's shoulder. "Oh, she's beautiful. So tiny." She caught Sabrina's gaze. "And you knew she was coming?"

Sabrina laughed. "Yes, Mom. Her name is Selena." She paused a beat then said, "Want to go out to the waiting room and tell Seth and Jake it was twins?"

Maureen clapped. "Oh, this'll be fun!"

She raced to the door but stopped and faced Trent. "Your parents got here, didn't they?"

He'd flown them to Key West for a fishing trip to celebrate his stepdad's retirement, not realizing Sabrina would go into labor early, and he'd had to send his jet back to retrieve them.

"They got here about two hours ago."

"Do they know about the twins?"

Trent stopped a laugh at her enthusiasm. Who would have ever thought the McCallan matriarch would love a good joke so much?

"Nope. Go have your fun."

She raced out of the room and Trent took his seat beside Sabrina's bed. "Are you okay?"

She cuddled Sebastian. "I'm so exhausted I could cry."

He laughed. "If what I'm told is true, we'd better get accustomed to that feeling."

Looking at her son, she smiled. "It'll be worth it."

He glanced at their little girl, already his in his eyes because he'd been with Sabrina since the day she'd discovered she was pregnant. "Yeah, it'll totally be worth it."

A round of laughter floated into the labor room from the hallway that led to the waiting room.

"I think your brothers like your joke."

"It wasn't a joke. It was a surprise. And every once in a while a family needs to be shaken up."

With a quick chuckle, he agreed. Once in a while, a family *did* need to be shaken up.

Since he'd met her, he'd reconciled with his family, bought a castle, remodeled his condo…become a dad and would soon be a husband.

Life didn't get any better than this.

* * * * *

RUST CREEK FALLS
CINDERELLA

MELISSA SENATE

Dedicated to
Marcia Book Adirim and Susan Litman.

Thank you for inviting me to Rust Creek Falls,
one of my favorite places to visit.

Chapter One

Any minute now, Lily Hunt's first blind date ever—
one of the six gorgeous Crawford brothers—was going
to walk through the door of the Maverick Manor hotel.
Lily waited in a club chair in the lobby's bar area by a
massive vase of wildflowers, her gaze going from the
window to the door every five seconds. She crossed
and uncrossed her legs. Folded and unfolded her hands.
Slouched and sat up straight, then slouched again. Tried
for a pleasant smile.

She also tried to get the better of her nerves, but she
still worried that her date would take one look at her,
pretend something suddenly came up, like a family emer-
gency or a bad cough, and hightail it out of there.

Oh, stop it, she ordered herself. Even though she really
did fear he might do exactly that. Lily, part-time cook,
part-time student, twenty-three-year-old tomboy who

lived in jeans and sneakers and had more hoodies than most teenage boys, was not the kind of woman who made a man think, *Ooh, I want to meet her.* That was more her good friend Sarah, who was gorgeous and so nice Lily didn't think it was fair. A month ago, Sarah had been the single mother of an adorable baby girl until she'd found herself falling for one of the Crawfords, ranchers from Texas who'd moved to Rust Creek Falls in July. Now she and Logan were *married.* And happily raising little Sophia together.

The Crawford brother Lily was meeting tonight? Knox. Tall, dark and dreamy like his brothers. She'd met some of the Crawford clan last month when they'd come to the Maverick Manor for dinner. Sarah had introduced Lily, and one brother was so drop-dead gorgeous she couldn't speak, which likely also contributed to why he hadn't glanced twice at her.

Confidence, girl! she pep-talked herself. Sarah had insisted on it earlier when she'd phoned to tell Lily to have a wonderful time and to call her after the date with every detail. And Vivienne Dalton, a wedding planner who'd been the one to fix up Lily with Knox, had also called to make sure she hadn't chickened out. (Yes, Lily had taken some serious convincing to accept the date in the first place.) Lily had assured Viv she was getting dressed and would be right on time at 7:00 p.m., classic date hour at the Maverick Manor. Viv had said, *Honey, I will give you only one piece of advice.* Lily had held her breath, waiting. Viv was gorgeous herself and married to Cole Dalton and ran her own successful business—a walking example of making things happen.

Be yourself, Viv had said.

That old yarn? Being herself hadn't exactly gotten

Lily very far. Granted, she had a great job as a cook at the Maverick Manor, the fanciest hotel in town. And people raved about her food, which had done more for her confidence than any appreciative glance from a guy ever could. Lily dreamed about having her own place—a small restaurant or a catering shop. Someday.

Today—tonight—was about her love life.

Two short-term relationships were all she had in that department.

She eyed the door. It was 7:00 p.m. on the nose. Lily had been there for five minutes, unfashionably early. She'd changed for the date in the women's locker room, stashing her work clothes in her locker and putting on her one good dress and one pair of heels and one pair of dangling earrings. She never wore makeup, but Sarah had suggested she try some tonight. So Lily had swiped on Maybelline mascara and sheer pinkish-red lipstick and felt like she was playing dress-up, but she supposed she was. She'd left her long red hair down instead of pulling it into a low ponytail the way she did every day.

Now 7:05 p.m. Knox Crawford was now late. Bad sign? Her stomach gave a little flop. The date clearly wasn't high enough on his priorities for him to be on time. Oh, cripes—now she sounded like her dad! Maybe she was getting antsy too early. *Calm down. Go with the flow. Sip your white wine.*

She took a sip…7:09 p.m.

Seven twelve. Humph.

Lily might not be Ms. Confidence when it came to men, but she would never let anyone treat her disrespectfully, and being almost fifteen minutes late for a date was bordering on rude. Right? Her last date was

six months ago (no interest on either side) so she wasn't
really up on date etiquette.

Seven fifteen.

"Lily!" came a female voice. "How lovely you look!
Job interview here at the Manor? Front desk?"

Trying not to sigh as she smiled up at Maren, a woman
she'd gone to high school with, Lily glanced down at her
royal blue boat-neck, cap-sleeve shift dress, a cotton car-
digan tied around her shoulders, and sandals with two-
inch stacked heels. It worked for church and weddings,
so she figured it would work for tonight.

"Actually, I have a date," Lily said, taking another sip
of wine. *Waiter, bring the bottle!*

Maren eyed her up and down. "Oh. Well, have fun!"
she said, tottering on her sexy high heels to the main
dining room.

Lily looked around the swanky lobby's bar area at the
women sitting with dates or out for drinks and appetizers
with girlfriends. Skinny jeans and strappy high-heeled
sandals. Form-fitting dresses. Slinky skirts. Everyone
looked great and evening-ready. And here she was in
her Sunday best.

Oh, Lily, get a clue already!

Seven eighteen. Her stomach flopped again, her heart
heading south. She was being stood up. First time she
actually "put herself out there," like her mom always
told her to do, and whammo: humiliated.

She could be plopped on her couch at home with
Dobby and Harry, her adorable dachshunds, eating left-
over linguini carbonara and garlic bread, and instead, she
was about to burst into tears. Whatever, she told herself.
She'd just go home, work on a recipe, watch a movie,
play with Dobby and Harry.

Just as her pep talk started making her feel better, her cell phone rang.

She didn't recognize the number but she was sure it was her date—or lack thereof. "Hello?"

"Lily, this is Knox Crawford. I'm so sorry I'm not there." There was some weird background noise as if he was covering the phone with his hand and talking to someone else beside him or something. Double humph. "Look, um, something came up and—"

Oh, did it? *Suuure.*

"And I'm really sorry but I can't make it," Knox said. "I—"

More weird background noise. Weird ocean-roar in the phone as if someone was definitely holding a hand over the speaker. Maybe he had his own female version of Davy Jones there with him. Selena Gomez or Charlize Theron, maybe.

"Hello?" a different male voice said. "Lily? This is Xander Crawford. My brother can't make it tonight, but I happen to be free for dinner and I'll be taking his place. See you in five minutes."

Uh, *what*?

"No, that's okay," she said, hoping her voice didn't sound as clogged to him as it did to her. *I am not a charity case!* The famed ire of the angry redhead? She was about to blow, people! "No worries. Bye!" She clicked End Call and stuffed her phone in her stupid little purse—she hated purses!—stood up, took another long sip of her wine, and stalked back into the kitchen, wondering how a person could feel angry and so sad at the same time.

Xander Crawford. Please. She'd seen him up close and personal and he was too good-looking, too sexy—

with a Texas drawl, to boot. She'd clam up and stammer or mumble or ramble, especially because of how weird this all was. And what was she? Someone to pity? The poor stood-up date? No thank you!

She was grateful her fellow cooks and her friend AnnaBeth, a waitress, were all so busy they didn't see her slip back into the break room. She opened her locker, and a photo of her dogs, one of her beautiful mother, and a restaurant review from the *Rust Creek Falls Gazette* that had raved about her filet mignon in mushroom pep-percorn sauce with roasted rosemary potatoes and sau-téed garlic-buttered asparagus reminded her who she was. Lily Hunt. She was meant to be creating magical recipes and figuring out how to get where she wanted to be in a year or two. Not trying to be something she wasn't: a woman who dated gorgeous, wealthy ranchers the entire town was vying for.

Yes, vying for. There were five Crawford brothers left and, according to Viv, their dad wanted to see them married and settled down, so he'd put the wedding plan-ner on the case to find them the right women. All the single ladies in town had put their names in the hat, and hell, why not Lily, tomboy and all? She was flattered Viv had even asked.

And now some stand-in Crawford was showing up, probably only to save the family name since they were new in town and didn't want their dating reps to be ru-ined. Yeah, no thanks.

"Well, Mama," Lily said, looking at Naomi Hunt's photo, her red hair all she'd inherited from her sophis-ticated mother. "I did put myself out there, but it didn't work this time. Maybe next." Not that she'd agree to an-other date anytime soon.

She changed back into her jeans and sneakers with a relieved *ahhh*, put on her T-shirt and tied her hoodie around her waist. She wiped off the lipstick and put her hair in a low ponytail, closed her locker and headed out the swinging door into the lobby.

Right into the muscular chest of Xander Crawford.

"I'm so sorry," Xander said to the young redhead he'd just barreled into. He'd been in such a hurry to catch Lily Hunt that he hadn't considered that the door into the kitchen might have someone coming through it from the other side. Luckily it hadn't been a waiter with a tray of entrées. "Are you okay?"

"I'm fine," she said, but her eyes were like saucers and her cheeks were flushed.

Maybe it was hot in the kitchen? "I'm looking for Lily Hunt. Do you know her? She works here as a cook. Is she still around?"

The redhead stared at him, and for a moment he swore she was shooting daggers out of those flashing green eyes. "*I'm* Lily Hunt. We met last month in the dining room. I was with my friend Sarah, who's married to your brother Logan."

Oh hell. Awkward.

"I'm bad with faces," he said, which was true. "I've met so many people since we moved to Montana that my head's still spinning."

Not to mention all the women who'd introduced themselves to him over the past month. Everywhere he went there seemed to be a smiling woman, offering her card—some of which smelled like perfume—and letting him know she'd "just love to have coffee or a drink or dinner anytime, hon." At first he'd wondered if women were that friendly in every town in the state of Montana. Until he'd realized *why* women were coming at him in droves. They were coming at all the single Crawfords—thanks to his dad. Maximilian Crawford had made a deal with a local wedding planner to get him them all hitched, and that wedding planner had apparently spoken to every single woman in Rust Creek Falls.

Why was that wedding planner so raring to go? Finding *all* the eligible women in town who might be interested in being set up with a Crawford brother?

Because Max had offered Viv Dalton one million bucks to get them all married.

One. Million. Dollars.

If he and his brother Logan hadn't witnessed the exchange with their own eyes and ears, Xander never would have believed it.

Anyway, Xander had a drawer full of scented cards and had not made a single call. His father shook his head a lot over it.

Still, he was surprised he didn't remember meeting Lily. She had the determined face of a young woman who was going places. He liked it. She had freckles, too. He'd always liked freckles.

He was aware he had a smile plastered on his face. Now she did, too.

"Uh, so," she said, "like I said on the phone, no worries. Let's just forget this ever happened, okay?"

He tilted his head. "What do you mean?"

"Your brother got cold feet about our blind date and canceled. You felt bad for whatever reason and took his place. You know who I don't want to be? The woman sitting across from the guy who gave up his evening to 'do the right thing.'"

"I always try to do the right thing," he said. "But trust me, dinner with a lovely woman is hardly a chore, Lily. I'd love to take you out to dinner if you're up for it."

Her expression changed from wary and pissed to surprised. She lifted her chin. "Well, when you put it like that." She flashed him a smile, a genuine smile that lit up her entire face. For a moment he couldn't pull his gaze off her.

"You're probably wondering why I'm wearing a hoodie and sneakers on a date," she said. "I just changed back into my work clothes. I could put the dress on again if you want to wait a few minutes."

"You look incredibly comfortable," he said, tugging at the collar of his button-down shirt. "Trust me, I'll take jeans and a T-shirt over a button-down and tie any day. Luckily, as a rancher, I'm not often forced into a tie."

She smiled that smile again. "Well, then, guess we're not eating here. Unwritten dress code. And to be honest, though I love the food at the Manor, I have it *all the time.*"

"Perk of the job, but I get it," he said. "Casual always works for me. I'm new around here, but I already know Ace in the Hole and Wings to Go pretty well. Either of those sound good?"

"Ooh, I'm craving chicken wings—in extra tangy barbecue sauce."

"Woman after my own heart," he said, gesturing toward the door.

She stared at him for a moment, then rushed outside as if she needed a gulp of air. "Uh, Wings to Go isn't very far." They started walking, Lily stopping to pet a tiny dog with huge amber eyes, then to look at a red bird on a branch. He liked that she noticed her environment—

and animals in particular. Xander's mind was always so crammed with this and that he'd walked straight into a fence post the other day. Two of his brothers had a good laugh over that one.

Once inside the small take-out shop, they ordered a heap of wings and four kinds of sauces. Lily got out her wallet, but he told her to put it away, that tonight was on him.

"Well, thank you very much," she said. "I appreciate that."

"My pleasure." He glanced out the window. "Given that it's such a gorgeous night, want to take our dinner to the park? We have a good hour of sunlight left."

"Perfect," she said with a smile. "And good thing my dachshunds aren't with us. Dobby and Harry would clear out the wings before we could unpack them. They'd even eat the celery on the side because it smells like chicken wings."

He laughed at the thought of two dachshunds attacking a piece of celery. He held the door open, and they exited into the breezy night air. She sure was easy to talk to, much more than he expected. Not that he'd expected anything since the only thing he'd known about Knox's date was her name. "I've always wanted dogs. Maybe one day."

On the way to the park, they chatted about dog breeds and Lily told him a funny story about a Great Dane named Queenie who'd fallen in love with Dobby but ignored Harry, who was jealous. He told her about the two hamsters his dad had finally let him get when he was nine, and how they were so in love with each other they ignored *him*. She cracked up for a good minute and he had to say, she had a great laugh.

Rust Creek Falls Park was just a few blocks away and not crowded, but there were plenty of people walking and biking and enjoying the beautiful night. Since they didn't have a blanket, they chose a picnic table and she sat across from him. For a moment they watched a little kid try to untangle the string of his kite. He looked like he might start bawling, but his mom came over and in moments the green turtle was aloft again. Xander swallowed, the tug of emotion always socking him in the stomach when he saw little kids with their moms. Big kids, too. He was always surprised at how the sight affected him. After all these years.

He turned his attention back to Lily and started opening the bags containing their wings. "My brothers and I love the food at the Maverick Manor. We're there for lunch and dinner pretty often. I'll bet you have something to do with that."

She popped open the containers of sauces. "Well, thanks. I hope so. I love cooking. And I love working at the Manor. I can try all kinds of interesting specials and the executive chef always says yes. Lamb tagine was last night's special and it was such a hit. Nothing makes me feel like a million bucks more than when someone compliments my food."

"I love how passionate you are about your work," he said. "Everyone should be that lucky."

"Are you?" she asked.

He dunked a wing in barbecue sauce. "Yes, ma'am. One hundred percent cowboy. A horse, endless acres, cattle, the workings of a ranch—it's what I was born to do."

She stared at him, her green eyes shining. "That's exactly how I feel—about cooking! That I was born to be in the kitchen, with my ingredients and a stove."

He held out his chicken wing and she clinked hers to his in a toast, and they both laughed.

Huh. Whodathought this night would work out so well? When he'd heard his brother Knox arguing with his dad earlier and then calling his date and canceling, he'd been livid. Not so much at his brother for not just sucking it up and going on the date, but at his father for being such a busybody. Knox might have gone on the blind date if he hadn't learned his dad had been responsible for it in the first place. Xander and Logan had told the other four brothers what their father was up to and to hide behind all large tumbleweeds if they saw Viv Dalton coming with her phone and notebook and clipboard, but Knox had thought the whole thing was a joke. Until Viv had apparently cornered him into going on a blind date with one Lily Hunt. He'd agreed and had apparently meant to cancel, then had put the whole thing out of his mind. Until his dad had said, "Knox, shouldn't you be getting ready for your date tonight?"

Knox's face: priceless. A combination of *Oh crud* and *Now what the hell am I gonna do?*

"What's so terrible about you going on a date?" Maximilian Crawford had said so innocently. "Some dinner, a glass of wine. Maybe a kiss if you like each other." The famous smile slid into place.

Knox had been *fuming.* "I always meant to politely cancel. I've been working so hard on the fence line the last couple days that I totally forgot about calling Viv to say forget it."

"Guess you're going then," Max had said with too much confidence.

Knox had shaken his head. "Every single woman in town is after us. Who wouldn't want to marry into a family with a patriarch who has a million dollars to throw around? No thanks."

"Well, it *is* a numbers game," their dad had said.

Knox had been exasperated. "I don't want to hurt my date's feelings, but I'm not a puppet. I'm canceling. Even at the eleventh hour. She'll just have to understand."

Would she, though? Getting canceled on when she was likely already waiting for Knox to show up?

So Xander had stepped in—surprising himself. He'd avoided Viv Dalton, the wedding planner behind the woman deluge, like the plague whenever he saw her headed toward him in town with that "ooh, there's a Crawford" look on her face. But c'mon. He couldn't just let Knox's date get stood up because his brother was so…stubborn.

And anyway, what was an hour and a half of his life on a date with a stranger? Some conversation, even stilted and awkward, was still always interesting, a study in people, of how things worked. Xander had been trying to figure out how people worked for as long as he could remember. So he could apply it to his own family history.

"Best. Wings. Ever!" Lily said, chomping on one liberally slathered in maple-chipotle sauce.

"Mmm, didn't try that sauce yet," he said, dabbing a wing in the little container. He took a bite. "Are we in Texas? These rival the best wings in Dallas."

"That's a mighty compliment. Do you miss home?"

"This is home now," he said, more gruffly than he'd meant. "We bought the Ambling A ranch and are fixing it up. We've done a lot of work already. It's coming along."

"So you and your five brothers moved here, right?" she asked, taking a drink of her lemonade.

"Yup. With our dad. The seven Crawford men. Been that way a long time."

Her eyes darted to his. "My father's a widow, too. I lost my mom when I was eight. God, I miss her."

Oh hell, she'd misunderstood about his mother and he didn't want to get into the correction. "Sorry to hear that."

"I'm sorry about your mom," she said.

Well, now he had to. "Don't be. She's not dead, just gone. She took off on my dad and six little boys—my youngest brother, Wilder, was just a baby. When I let myself think about it, I can hardly believe it. Six young sons. And you just walk away."

He shook his head, then grabbed another wing before his thoughts could steal his appetite. These wings were too good to let that happen.

Change the subject, Xander. "So what else do we have in common?" he asked, swiping a wing in pineapple-teriyaki sauce. "You have five brothers, too?"

She smiled. "Three, actually. All older. So you can guess how they treat me. We all live together in the house I grew up in—the four of us and my dad."

"Protective older brothers. That's nice. Princess for a day for life, am I right?"

She snorted, which he didn't expect. "*Exsqueeze me?* Princess? My brothers treat me like I'm one of them. I don't think they know I'm a girl, actually. I'm like the youngest brother."

He laughed, imagining the four Hunts racing around the woods, playing tag, trying to catch frogs, swinging off ropes into rivers.

"They do appreciate that I cook for them, though," she said. "And I do so because they're hopeless. I told my brother Ryan that I was teaching him to cook and that he should heat up a can of stewed tomatoes, and I swear on the Bible that he put an unopened can of tomatoes in a pot and turned on the burner and asked, 'How long should it cook?'"

Xander cracked up. "That's bad."

"Oh, yeah. He's better now. He can even crack an egg into a bowl without sloshing half on the counter or floor. It's all great practice for me for one day owning my own business—either a restaurant or a catering shop. I'm also studying for a business degree online—just part-time. But I want to learn how to start and run a successful business. I'm covering all the bases."

"Wow, impressive!" he said. "You're what, twenty-two?" She looked young. Very young. Too young for him, certainly.

"Twenty-three."

"I've got seven years on you, kid," he said. "And I'll tell you, following your passion is where it's at. I'm a big believer in that."

She sobered for a moment; he wasn't sure why, but then those green eyes of hers lit up again. "Me, too."

They spent the next twenty minutes talking about everything from the differences between Texas and Montana cattle and terrain, where to get the best coffee in Rust Creek Falls (she was partial to Daisy's Donuts but he loved the strong brew at the Gold Rush Diner), the wonders and pitfalls of having many brothers, and her favorite foods for each meal (omelet, chicken salad sandwich on a very fresh baguette, any kind of pasta with any kind of sauce). They talked about steak for ten minutes and then steak fries, thick and crispy, seasoned just right and dipped in quality ketchup.

The wings were suddenly gone but he could talk to her for hours more. They laughed, traded stories, watched the dog walkers, and she told him funny stories about Dobby and Harry. He loved the way the waning sun lit up her red hair and he felt so close to her that he leaned across the table, about to take both her hands to give them a squeeze. He truly felt as if he'd made a real friend here tonight.

But when he leaned, Lily leaned.

Her face—toward his.

He darted back.

She'd thought he was going to kiss her?

He cleared his throat, glancing at his watch. "It's almost nine? How did *that* happen?" He tried for a good-natured smile, but who the hell knew what his expression really looked like. Xander had never been able to hide how he felt. And how he felt right now was seriously awkward.

He liked Lily. A lot. But did he like her *that way*? He didn't think so. She was a kid! Twenty-three to his thirty. Just starting out. And she was the furthest thing from the women he usually dated. Perfume. Long red nails. Slinky outfits and high heels. Sleek hair. And okay, big breasts and lush hips. He liked a woman with curves. Lily was…cute but not exactly his usual type. Not that he could really tell under her loose jeans and the hoodie around her waist obscuring much of her body.

All he knew was that he liked her. A lot.

As a friend.

"Yikes," she said, that plastered smile from when they

first met on her face again. She jumped up. "Dobby and Harry are going to wonder where I am."

He collected their containers and stuffed them back in the bag, his stomach twisting with the knowledge that he'd made things uncomfortable. *Never lean toward a woman*, he reminded himself, *unless you're leaning for a kiss.*

"I live pretty close to the park, so I'll just jog home," she said quickly, tossing him an even more forced smile. "I'm dressed for it," she added. "Thanks for dinner!" she called, and ran off.

I'll drive you, he wanted to call out to her, but she was too fast. He watched her reach the corner, hoping she'd turn back and wave so he could see her freckles and bright eyes again, but she didn't.

Hell if he didn't want to see her again. Soon.

Chapter Two

The Ambling A was a sight for the ole sore eyes. Sore brain, really. Xander had thought about Lily all the way home, half wanting to call her to make sure she'd gotten home all right, half not because she might read into it.

Which made him feel like a jerk again, flattering himself.

But the way she'd leaned in for that kiss…

He would *not* lead her on.

He parked his new silver pickup and got out, the sprawling dark wood ranch house, which literally looked like it was made from Lincoln Logs, making him smile. He loved this place—the house, the land, the hard work to get the ranch the way they wanted. Xander headed in, never knowing who'd be home. Hunter, the second-oldest Crawford (Xander was third born), lived in a cabin on the property. A widower since the birth of his daughter,

Hunter and his six-year-old, Wren, needed their own space, but the girl still had five uncles to dote on her. Logan, the eldest, had recently moved to town now that he was married with a baby to raise, but he worked on the ranch, as they all did, so it was almost like he'd never left.

The place sure had changed since the day they'd arrived. They'd mended fences for miles, repaired outbuildings, cleaned out barns, burned ditches and worked on the main house itself when they had the time and energy. A month later, it was looking good but they had a ways to go.

He came through the front door into the big house with its wide front hall and grand staircase leading up to a gallery-style landing on the second floor. He saw his dad and three of his brothers up there, going over blueprints, which meant his dad had proposed a change—again—and his sons were trying to talk him out of it. There was many a midnight argument taking place at the Ambling A. When they heard the door close behind him, they all came downstairs.

"Well, well, if isn't the knight in shining armor," Wilder, the youngest of the brothers, said with a grin.

Xander made a face at Wilder and shook his head, hoping they'd go back to talking blueprints. "Lily is hardly a damsel in distress. She's very focused on what she wants. She can definitely take care of herself." The more he thought about her, about what they'd talked about, her plans, her dreams, the more impressed he was.

Logan smiled. "Sounds like the date switch was a date *match*. Knox's loss."

Knox wasn't around. He probably had left to get away from their matchmaking father.

"So? *Was* it a love match?" Finn asked. "When's your next date?"

Twenty-nine-year-old Finn was the dreamer of the group. He could keep dreaming on this one, because another date wasn't going to happen.

Lily was too young. And Xander was too jaded. She'd barely lived, and he was already cynical about love and guarded.

Xander rolled his eyes. "Get real. She's twenty-three. C'mon. And very nice."

"Ah, he used the kiss-of-death word. *Nice,*" Wilder said. "Nothing gonna happen there."

That settled for the Crawford men, they turned their attention back to the blueprints. Xander scowled as they ducked their heads over the plans, gabbing away as if they didn't just dismiss a lovely, smart, determined young woman as "nice."

Oh, wait. He was the one who'd called her that.

But his brothers had stamped her forehead with the word, which meant she wasn't hot or sexy or desirable. All without even laying eyes on her.

They'd written her off.

And so did you. You're the one who put her in the friend zone in the first place.

His dad came in from the kitchen with a beer. "Ah, Xander, you're back from the date! Have you already set up a second one?"

"You don't even know if we had anything in common, Dad," Xander said. "Maybe we weren't attracted to each other."

"I just have a feeling," Max Crawford said with a smile and a tip of his beer at his son. That *feeling* should tell his father otherwise.

"I think we're just meant to be friends, Dad," Xander said.

"Meaning she's not his type," Wilder threw in. "Xander likes his women with big hair, big breasts, big hips and big giggles. All play, no talk."

His brothers cracked up.

Xander supposed he deserved that. He did like curvy blondes who didn't delve too deeply and liked to watch rodeos and have sex without expecting much in return other than a nice night out and a call once in a while. But one of those curvy blondes had managed to get inside him and surprise him, and he'd fallen hard, only to find her in bed with his best friend. The betrayal still stung. All these miles away from Texas.

Max shook his head. "You boys should give 'not your types' a chance. You'd be surprised what your supposed type turns out to be."

Logan raised an eyebrow. "If I remember correctly, Dad—and I do—it was *you* who told me that a single mother of a baby was *not* the woman for me. And she is."

"Told you you'd be surprised what your type is," Max said with a grin.

Logan threw a rolled-up napkin at his dad and shook his head with a laugh. But last month, Xander had caught wind of some of his father's arguments with Logan about dating a single mother. Max had hinted that if the relationship didn't work out, there would be *three* sad hearts—including a child who didn't ask to get dragged into the muck. Xander had known his father had to be thinking of his ex-wife and how she'd abandoned them all. Times like that, he forgave his dad for being such a busybody.

Still, Xander *was* sticking to his type, but this time,

there was no way any woman was getting inside. These days, he was only interested in a good time and he always made that clear.

Except that hadn't been clear to Lily Hunt. Oh hell. She'd thought she was going on a date in good faith, that had gotten all messed up, and then he'd stepped in to save the night—and had ended up making it worse. He shook his head at himself. Now he really did want to call her and doubly apologize, but how would *that* sound?

Uh, hi, Lily, sorry for making your night go from bad to worse when you actually thought I was leaning in a for kiss.

Getting stood up by Knox might have been more fun.

He sighed.

But maybe Lily was just out for a good time herself? Could it be? She seemed a little too focused and serious-minded for that, though. Still, with her life so set on track, perhaps she just wanted a nice night out and some laughs. It was possible.

He tried to imagine Lily Hunt, with her freckles and big dreams and flashing green eyes, so full of life, out for a good time, giggling and whispering about what she was going to do to him while raking her nails up his thigh. Frankly, he couldn't. First of all, her nails had been bitten to the quick. And honestly, he didn't want to think of her in any way but as a new friend.

"Well, I need to do some research on the cattle we want to add to the Ambling A," Xander said. "See y'all in the morning." He took the steps two at the time, wanting to get away from this conversation.

Lily wasn't his type. Plain and simple. And even if she were, he wouldn't be interested in a relationship. Not anymore. Besides, he had the ranch to concentrate on and a new state to discover, not to mention a new hometown to get to know. That was enough.

Just let the night go, he told himself.

Upstairs in his bedroom, he sat at his desk and opened his laptop, fully intending to research local cattle sales. But he found himself going to the website for the Maverick Manor and looking at their lunch menu—just in case he wanted to drop in tomorrow after a hard morning's work.

"French dip au jus on crusty French bread and a side of hand-cut steak fries" was one of tomorrow's lunch specials. He'd just eaten and his mouth was already watering for that meal. Yeah, maybe he'd go to the Manor for lunch and even pop into the kitchen to say hi to Lily.

That was what friends did, right? Popped in? Visited? Said a quick hello? He'd do that and leave. That would make things good between them, get rid of all that awkwardness from tonight. They could truly be friends. Everyone could always use another friend.

But damn if he wasn't sitting there, staring at the list of the Maverick Manor's decadent desserts and thinking about feeding Lily succulent strawberries, watching her mouth take the juicy red fruit.

What the hell? The woman wasn't his type! They were just going to be buddies.

He clicked over to the cattle sale site, forcing his mind onto steers and heifers and far from strawberries and twenty-three-year-old Lily Hunt.

"Ooh, Lily, that hot Crawford cowboy was just seated at table three," whispered AnnaBeth Bellows, a waitress at the Maverick Manor and Lily's good friend. Lily had told AnnaBeth about her date with Xander so Lily knew the hot cowboy had to be him.

She almost gasped yet kept her focus on her broiled shrimp, caramelizing just so in garlic, olive oil and sea salt. She added a hint of cayenne in the last few seconds, and plated it the moment she knew it was done. Sixth sense.

According to Mark, table eight's waiter, the group was from New Orleans originally even though they lived in Kalispell now. Lily always had the waiters find out where her diners were from so she could add a tiny taste of home to their dishes. It was just a little thing Lily did that her diners seemed to appreciate, even if they didn't know why they reacted so strongly, so emotionally to their food. The other cooks thought it was a lot to deal with, but Lily enjoyed the whole process. Food was special. Food was your family. Food was home in a good way, the best way, and could remind people of wonderful memories. Sometimes sad memories, too. But evoking those feelings seemed to have a good impact on her diners and on her. So she continued the tradition.

She placed the gorgeous shrimp, a deep, rich bronze, with its side of seasoned vegetables on the waiter's station and raced to the Out door to the dining room. She peered through the little round window on the door, looking for the sexy cowboy.

Yes, there he was. Sitting by himself, thank God, and not with a date set up by Viv Dalton, which was her immediate fear when AnnaBeth had whispered that he was here.

Of course, he could be waiting on a date.

"Dining alone," AnnaBeth said with a smile.

Lily couldn't help grinning back, her heart flip-flopping. "Could a man *be* more gorgeous?"

"Yes—my boyfriend," AnnaBeth said, "even if Petey-pie has a receding hairline and a bit of a belly. He's hot to me."

Lily laughed. "And Pete's the greatest guy ever, too." Yes, indeed, Lily should aspire to a wonderful guy like AnnaBeth's "Petey-pie." Kind. Loyal. Full of integrity. Brought her little gifts for no reason. Called her Anna-Beauty all the time. Making Lily wistful.

Lily bit her lip. "Okay, why is Xander here after that awkward moment from hell last night on our not-a-date?"

"The *almost* kiss," AnnaBeth suggested, watching for the other two cooks plating, which meant she'd have to rush off to pick up. "I'm telling you, Xander was just caught off guard. He wasn't even expecting to have a date last night, right? But then he did, a wings picnic, and he fell madly in love with you but didn't expect to and now he's here to ask you out again."

Lily laughed. "I love you, AnnaBeth. Seriously. Everyone needs one of you. But life is not a Christmas movie. Even though I wish it were."

"Listen, my friend. You have to make your own magic. Just like you do with your food."

Lily watched Xander close the menu. She wondered what he'd decided on.

"Ah, time to take the cowboy's order," AnnaBeth said. "Back in a flash."

Lily watched them until she noticed her boss, Gwendolyn, eyeing her and then staring at her empty cooking station. She darted to her stove, working on another batch of au jus for today's French dip special.

In a minute, AnnaBeth was back with Xander's order. The special.

She smiled and began working on it and four more for other tables. But to table three's sauce she added just a hint of sweet, smoky barbecue sauce, a flavor that would take Xander Crawford back to Texas where he'd lived his whole life until a month ago.

Could he be here to see her? If he wasn't interested in her—and he sure hadn't seemed to be last night with that not-kiss thing—wouldn't he *avoid* where she worked?

But then she thought of him and the reaction he must get from women, and she was flooded with doubts. There was no way Lily of the hoodie and sneakers would be Xander Crawford's type. When she was young and girls at school would make fun of her for being a tomboy, her mother would always say, *You're exactly as you should be—yourself.* That had always made Lily feel better. And maybe Xander *liked* a down-to-earth woman with flour on her cheek and smelling of onions and caramelized shrimp and peppercorns.

Anything was possible. *That* was the name of the game.

She smiled at the thought, adding a pinch of garam masala to table twelve's sauce since they were honeymooners who'd just returned from India. For table fourteen, visitors from Maine, she added a dash of Bell's Seasoning, a famed New England blend of rosemary, sage, oregano and other spices.

Lily worked on five more entrées, her apron splattered, her mind moving so fast she could barely think about Xander in the dining room, eating her food right now. Was he enjoying it? Did it hit the spot? Did it bring a little bit of Texas to Montana today?

"Five-minute break if you need it," Gwendolyn called

out to her. "Your tables are all freshly served so you're clear."

"Ah, great," she said, grabbing her water bottle and taking a big swig, staring out the long, narrow window at the Montana wilderness at the back of the Manor.

"I just had the best French dip sandwich of my life," a deep voice said from behind her, and she almost jumped.

Xander! Standing right there.

"Craziest thing," he said. "I took two bites and started thinking about the ranch I grew up on in Dallas, my dad teaching me and Hunter how to ride a two-wheeler. I was a little mad at my dad earlier, and now I'm full of good memories, so he's back out of the doghouse."

"You can't be in here," she whispered, trying to hide her grin. She shooed him out the back door, the breezy August air so refreshing on her face. "So you loved the French dip?"

"Beyond loved it. It tasted like…home. I know *this* is home now, but that sandwich reminded me of Texas in a good way. And I left behind some things I'd like to forget."

Huh. Like what? she wondered. A bad relationship? His heart?

"It's a little trick my mother taught me when I was young," she said, making herself keep her mind on the conversation. "My maternal grandparents moved to Montana from Louisiana, and my grandmother would add just a dash of creole seasoning to everything she cooked here because it reminded her of the bayou. My mama was a little girl when they left the South, and she never forgot that taste, so she taught me about it. Now I try to add a little taste of home in all my orders. It's easy for the waiters to get a personal tidbit about where they're from or have just been."

He stared at her for a moment, his dark eyes unreadable. What was he thinking? "You're not an everyday person, Lily Hunt."

She wasn't sure how to take that. "Uh, thank you?"

He smiled. "I mean that in the best way possible. I'm not sure I've ever met someone like you. You have a bit of the leprechaun in you."

She narrowed her eyes at him. "Aren't leprechauns supposed to be the worst kind of mischievous?"

"Magical. That's what I meant. You've got a bit of magic in you." His voice held a note of reverence, and she was so startled by it, so overwhelmed, that she couldn't speak.

"I have to have another French dip," he said. "For the road. It was so good I feel like I should get seven to go for my brothers and dad. In fact, can you take that order?"

She grinned. "Absolutely."

"Good. Maybe they'll get off my case about last night's date and stop asking me all kinds of questions. I tried to tell them we're just friends, that it wasn't really a *date* date, since you were fixed up with Knox. But you know how brothers are."

Her heart sank to her stomach, so she wasn't capable of speech at the moment. All she could manage was a deep everlasting sigh of doom.

Why had she let herself believe a nutty fantasy that this man, six foot two, body of Adonis, face of a movie star, a man who could have any woman in this town, would go for the tomboy with red hair who smelled like onions? Why? Was she that delusional?

I love how passionate you are, he'd said more than once in the very short time they'd known each other.

She wasn't delusional. She *was* passionate about life—and love, even if she'd never experienced it. She sure knew what incredible heart-pounding lust felt like, though. Because she felt it right now. With Xander Crawford.

This is what it feels like to fall in love. And it was impossible to stop, like a speeding train, even if the object of her affection just told her "it wasn't a *date* date" and they were "just friends."

Just friends.

Get back to earth, she told herself. *Go make his seven French dips to go.*

"Well, back to work!" she said too brightly, and dashed inside, then realized she'd left him high and dry in the back and he'd have to find his way around to the front of the hotel to return to the dining room.

He'll manage, she thought as she got back to her station to prepare his order. She saw him sneak and dart through the kitchen, her heart leaping at the quick sight of him. Sigh, sigh, sigh.

"Lily, you're amazing," her boss said. "*Seven* French dips to go for table three?" Gwendolyn was beaming at her, so at least she had big love at work if not in her personal life.

Forget Xander Crawford and focus on where you want to be next year: owning your own catering shop or little café, whisking your customers away to home.

Sure. As if she could forget Xander for a second.

Chapter Three

"**A**m I right?" Xander asked his brothers and father as they sat on the backyard patio of the Ambling A, gobbling up their French dips. "Is this incredibly delicious or what?"

The Crawfords were so busy eating they barely stopped long enough to agree. Knox held up his beer at Xander. Hunter said he wanted two more.

"I'll tell you what *I'm* right about," his father said, taking a huge bite of his sandwich. "That you went to Maverick Manor for lunch just so you could see the pretty chef again. Admit it."

"Yeah, admit it," Finn said with a grin.

What was that old line? No good deed went unpunished? No way would he ever bring these gossips a good lunch again! "I went because I was *hungry*. So how's the roof on the barn coming, Logan?" he asked his eldest brother, hoping the others would shut the hell up.

"Logan, tell Xander instead how wonderful married life is," his dad said. "Someone special to come home to at the end of a long, hard day."

Oh, brother. Literally.

Logan laughed, finishing the rest of his French dip and taking a sip of his beer. "First, that *was* damned good. Compliments to your chef, Xan."

"She is not *my* chef!" Xander shouted.

Six Crawfords laughed. One stewed in his chair.

"Second, Dad is right," Logan said. "Finding Sarah changed my life. Nothing beats coming home to her every night, waking up to her every morning. And raising that cherub Sophia with her? I feel like the luckiest guy in the world."

Huh. Xander eyed his brother. He was dead serious, heart-on-his-sleeve earnest.

"All of you are going to be that lucky, too," the Crawford patriarch said. "You know, I had to be both mother and father to you boys. I didn't always get it right. I guess I want just to see you all settled down and happy. I want you to have everything you deserve. All the happiness."

Logan put a hand on his dad's shoulder.

"To happiness," Finn said, raising his beer. "I'm into it."

"Even Knox can't *not* toast to that," Hunter said.

Xander eyed the always-intense Crawford brother. Knox raised his beer again with a bit of a scowl. Knox had thanked him for going out with Lily in his place, then had grimaced when Max Crawford said, "Now that you're over being stubborn about it, there are a hundred more single beauties out there, Knox, ole boy."

"First of all, I'm still not going out with anyone," Knox had said. "Secondly, there probably aren't a *hun-*

dred people in this town, Dad," he'd added, and had made himself scarce until he smelled the French dips.

Rust Creek Falls was tiny, less than a thousand residents, but nine hundred fifty of those had to be single women. Or at least that was how it had felt ever since Max Crawford had announced—erroneously!—that his six sons were looking for wives.

"Xander, you should probably make a reservation at the Manor for dinner now, just in case," Max said with a grin. "Find out if your chef is working first, though."

Xander got up, tossing his wrappers in the trash can. "I think I hear one of the calves calling for me." He headed for the barn, the too-familiar sound of his brothers' laughter trailing him.

His chef. Hardly!

"Mmm, mmm," he heard his dad say as he rounded the barn. "This roast beef takes me right back to Texas. Coulda ordered it from Joey's Roadhouse, am I right?"

Xander smiled. *Told you.* He'd been taken by surprise as bits and pieces of memories had popped into his mind while eating at the restaurant. Just flickers that he thought he'd forgotten: Logan threatening a bully on his behalf. Knox telling their dad off when he thought their dad was being unfair with Xander about something. The constant runs to the grocery store for milk since six growing boys could finish a gallon after one cold-cereal breakfast. Christmas after Christmas, each boy picking a brother's name from the Santa hat to buy for, the three years in a row that he got Hunter.

His mother in a yellow apron.

Now it was *his* turn to scowl. He didn't often think about his mom. He didn't remember much about her, just maybe the thought of her. There were few pictures of

Sheila Crawford in the family photo albums; he had no idea what his dad had done with the rest of them. Max had probably stored them up in the attic, leaving just a few for the boys to have some idea what their mother had looked like. Logan, Xander and Hunter remembered her the most but even they had been too young to hold a picture of her in their minds. Somehow, Xander did remember the yellow apron. And long brown hair.

A calf gave out a mini moo and he shook his head to clear his mind. All this thinking of home and his family's ribbing him about "his chef" nicely contradicted each other. Thinking about his mother reminded him that marriage didn't work out. That even the people you could count on to love you, by birthright, could leave. Just walk away without looking back. Between that and finding his girlfriend and best friend in bed, he gave a big "yeah right" to happily-ever-after.

"Yoo hoo! Anyone home?" a very female, high-pitched voice called out.

Xander came out of the barn to find an attractive, curvy blonde, just his type, he had to admit, smiling at him as she walked over from her car. "Hi, can I help you?"

"I'm so sure you can, honey," she said, her voice lowering an octave. "I'm Vanessa and I was hoping to hire one of you tall, strong, strapping cowboys to teach me how to ride a horse. I'm a town gal, so no horse or land of my own."

Xander knew there were plenty of horse farms and ranches in the area that offered riding lessons. The Ambling A wasn't one of them.

He had a feeling this woman was here for a cowboy and had zero interest in horses, if her very high heels and short dress were any indication. But any woman in the market for a Crawford was looking for a wedding ring. So despite the fact that Vanessa was his type to a T, he'd have to sit this one out.

"Ah. We don't offer riding lessons, but perhaps one of my brothers can give you the rundown on who does."

"I'd be happy to hear it from you," she said, puckering her glossy red lips a bit.

"I'm not really one of the eligible Crawfords," he said.

She frowned. "I don't see a ring. Unless you're spoken for."

Lily's face flashed into his mind. His chef. That was weird. "Well, I do seem to be seeing someone, unexpectedly," he added, for no godly reason. Then realized that was why Lily had popped into his brain. She was his way out!

"For goodness' sake, why didn't you say so and save me the trouble of flirting?" She fluffed her hair. "Any of your *eligible* brothers around?"

He smiled and mentally shook his head. A woman who knew she wanted. Had to give her credit for the chutzpah. "Let me see if Finn knows about riding lessons. Be right back."

"Finn? I do like that name," she said, peering around.

"Hang on a sec."

He went around the back of the sprawling ranch house to find the Crawfords just finishing up. "Finn, there's a woman here to see you."

Finn perked right up. That was a line he liked. "Say no more," he said before dashing around the house.

Xander smiled. That was easy. He went back into the barn and got down to work, ignoring the giggles coming from Vanessa as Finn flirted.

A flash of freckles and determined green eyes came to mind again. He should let Lily know his family loved the French dip, too, right? She'd probably appreciate hearing that. He could stop by the Manor and say it loud enough for her boss to hear; who couldn't use a gold star at work from a happy customer?

Yeah. He'd stop by and let her know. A good friend would do that, and he had a feeling that was exactly what he and Lily were going to be: good friends. That was it. Sorry, Matchmaking Dad.

The Hunt house was a big white colonial not far from the center of town. Xander glanced up at the second-floor windows, wondering which room was Lily's. He had a vision of himself standing out here at night, tossing pebbles at her window to get her to come out as if they were in high school or something.

Something about this very young woman had him all discombobulated.

He shook his head to clear it and rang the buzzer on the side of the blue door. He liked the color; it was a deep-sea blue that might be interesting for the barns at the Ambling A.

An auburn-haired guy in his midtwenties opened the door. One of Lily's three brothers, he presumed. He had on a pristine Kalispell Police Academy uniform, including a cap.

"Hey, you're one of those Crawfords," the guy said, his hazel eyes intense on Xander.

"I am. Xander Crawford, specifically. I haven't broken any laws, have I? I haven't been to Kalispell yet."

The guy scrunched up in his face in confusion, then glanced down at his uniform. "Oh, this. I'm on my way

to school. Not a cop yet, but I will be in a few months."
He eyed Xander, then looked behind him into the house,
then turned back. "Got a minute?" he asked. "I was hoping to run into one of you, but I'm rarely in town during
the day." He extended his hand. "Andrew Hunt."

Okay, now Xander was confused. "Pleasure to meet
you," he said. "So what can I—we—do for you?"

"I'm wondering about your overflow," Andrew said,
stepping out onto the porch and shutting the door.

"Overflow?" Xander repeated.

"I heard your father's trying to get his sons married
off and offered a wedding planner five million bucks to
get the job done. A buddy told me that since then, all the
places he goes in town to meet women have dried up.
Even at Ace in the Hole, our place to play darts and always meet a few ladies, even if we already know them,
there was *no one* there last Saturday night. Just a bunch
of guys. Man, it was depressing."

"*One* million," Xander corrected—quite unnecessarily,
but still. "And I see the problem."

"So, I was thinking, if you're on one of your dates and
it doesn't work out, maybe you could mention that you
know a great guy in the police academy and set something up for after six, any night."

Wait, now *Xander* was a matchmaker? Good Lord.
"Look, Andrew, I—"

"I know, I know. But listen. I'm about to have my act
totally together. I'm ready to settle down. And the playing field has been decimated. Your faults, dude."

Xander had to give him that. "I see your point."

"I'm just saying, if you want to mention my name
and availability to any lovely lady you're not interested
in, I'd appreciate it."

"I'm not interested in *anyone*," Xander said—quickly. "This is my dad's thing. Not mine."

"Well, just think of me, leaping over walls at the academy and studying for my procedure quiz, a forty-five minute commute each way, all with the intended goal of serving and protecting our communities one day."

Xander sighed. "I'll see what I can do. What's your type?"

"Nice," Andrew said. "I like nice. My last girlfriend? Not so nice. Pretty, but ooh boy."

Xander laughed. "Got it. Nice." He shook his head at that one. "I'll keep this between us."

"Oh, no need," Andrew said. "I've got the family on it, too, but they're no help. You'd think having a sister a couple years younger would mean lots of introductions and dates, but nope. Lily's either in the kitchen here or in the kitchen at the Maverick Manor or hunched over her laptop taking her online class. Thanks, Lily." He smiled.

"Speaking of Lily, I'm actually here to see her."

Andrew tilted his head. "Really? Why?"

Xander stared at him. "We're friends."

"Oh. Yeah, I figured you two couldn't be dating. I mean, she's *super* single, but I can't even imagine her throwing her name into the hat to land some rich cowboy. No offense."

"None taken," Xander said with a smile. He could imagine how Lily had her hands full with this crew if the other three Hunts were anything like Andrew.

"So you're on board?" Andrew asked. "With the overflow?"

"Sure," Xander assured him.

"Awesome." Andrew tipped his Kalispell Police Academy cap at Xander, then threw open the door. "Lily!" he bellowed. "Someone's here to see you!" He headed past Xander to the driveway. "Later, dude," he added amiably, jogging down to his car.

Wondering what he'd just gotten himself into, Xander watched Andrew drive off.

"Be right there!" he heard Lily call from somewhere in the house.

It was crazy, but the sound of that voice? His heart skipped a beat.

How many times had she told Andrew not to scream from one room to another? Lily was in the kitchen, working on a vegan entrée she hoped to introduce as an option at the Manor so that all their guests were covered, and she'd heard Andrew's loud voice as though he were standing right beside her.

She took off her apron and washed her hands, figuring her visitor was Sarah, whom she'd texted to mention that Xander had come in for lunch earlier and had barged right into the kitchen to see her. She'd asked if that could possibly mean he did like her *that way*, even when all signs pointed to a friendship only.

Sarah had said men often didn't know how they felt and figured it out as they went along or sometimes in one fell swoop. If *she* liked Xander *that way*, Sarah had texted, then she should go for it.

But it wasn't Sarah in the hallway. It was Xander.

What on earth was he doing here?

And looking so incredibly gorgeous. She'd never seen him in his cowboy clothes. Dark jeans. Brown boots. A navy T-shirt. And a brown Stetson held against his stomach. *Be still, my idiot heart*, she thought. His slightly long hair curled a bit at the nape of his neck, and his dark brown eyes were on her. The man was too good-looking.

Dobby and Harry were sitting on either side of him, staring up at him. Dobby was sniffing his cowboy boot. Harry was giving him the once-over.

Xander knelt down and gave each dog a pat, earning wagging cinnamon-colored tails. "Well, you must be the famous Dobby and Harry I've heard so much about. And even though you look identical, I bet you're Dobby and you're Harry."

"Name tags give it away every time," Lily said with a grin. "They can never get away with switching places like most twins."

He gave them both another pat and stood up. "I stopped by Maverick Manor to pay compliments to the chef from six other appreciative ranchers, and your friend AnnaBeth said you'd finished your shift, so I thought I'd stop by here and tell you."

Okay, granted, Lily's house was pretty close to Maverick Manor. She could walk there if her very old car broke down. But still, he went out of his way to go see her at the restaurant. Then out of his way again to "stop by" her house?

He liked her. Whether he knew it or not. Her stomach flipped—in a good way—and she had to stop herself from smiling like a lunatic.

Thank God for friends like Sarah who understood men! Crawford men, in particular.

"Something smells amazing," he said, sniffing the air.

Okay, she loved when he complimented her cooking skills. "I'm working on a tofu dish for a vegan option at the Manor."

"In cattle country? Well, if you can make tofu smell

that good, I imagine it'll be a hit. I'd pay a million bucks for a Lily Hunt hamburger."

She laughed. "You're going to give me a big head."

"Hey, maybe you could give me a cooking lesson sometime. I'd pay you well for your time." He named a crazy figure.

"Seriously? That much for one lesson?"

"Seriously. But I want to learn to make all my favorites. Teach me how to make that French dip. Teach me how to make fettuccini carbonara, which I crave every other day. Teach me how to make a pizza from scratch without burning the crust."

Teach me how not to fall in love with you, she thought. She was practically a goner.

"Lily, any more of that par-something thingie left?" a male voice shouted from upstairs. Ryan, the brother closest in age to her.

Lily smiled and shook her head. "Parfait!" she called back, even though she'd never stop her brothers from yelling from room to room if she did it, too. "And no, you four attacked it and there was none left for me."

"Sorry!" Ryan shouted back. "If you make more, make like five extra!"

"I see I'm not the only one who can't resist your cooking," Xander said. "Maybe I could observe as you make the tofu dish. Get a handle on the inner workings of a kitchen before we set up a formal lesson."

Xander Crawford wanted to watch her make tofu? "Who cooks for you guys now?" she asked.

"We take turns burning food. Logan's all right on the grill, but he moved out. We order in, pick up and go out *a lot*."

She laughed. "Well, follow me, then." She turned to

the dogs. "Dobby and Harry, feel free to go back to snoozing in your sun patch." The dogs waited a beat to see if the newcomer had a treat or rawhide chew for them, and since he didn't pull anything out of his pocket, they lost interest and walked back to their big cushy bed by the window and curled up.

"That's the life," Xander said, smiling as he followed Lily through the living room, past the dining room and into the kitchen.

She'd never been so aware of someone following her into another room before. He was so tall, so built, so *male* that she almost melted into a puddle on the floor. She was very used to being surrounded by testosterone. But this was something entirely different.

Especially so close up. Because the kitchen wasn't all that big and Xander was right beside her at the stove, his thigh almost touching hers.

Could she handle the heat? That was the question.

Xander was standing so close to Lily he could smell her shampoo—the scent a combination of flowers and suntan lotion. She wore green cargo pants, a white T-shirt covered by a red apron that read Try It, You'll Like It, and weird orange rubber shoes. Her long red hair was in a messy bun on top of her head with what looked like a chopstick securing it.

His awareness of her clobbered him over the head. He used to argue with his brothers over whether a man could be friends with a woman he found sexually attractive, and some said yes and some said no way because the sexual element would always be there and that meant there was more than friendship at work. Xander believed a man could absolutely be friends with a woman.

Since when was he sexually attracted to Lily, anyway? Just because he was noticing every little thing about her? The orange rubber shoes were hard to miss. Right? He was here to learn about tofu, something he knew absolutely nothing about.

And something he had absolutely no interest in, too. *You didn't even know she was making tofu until you were inside the house. You came here on pretense.*

This was getting confusing. But an undeniable fact was that he was in this kitchen because he wanted to be around Lily. Listening to her. Talking to her. Looking at her.

He suddenly pictured her naked, coming out of the shower, all that lush red hair wet around her shoulders, water still beaded on her breasts and trailing down her stomach and into her navel. Every nerve ending went haywire and he shivered.

"Caught a chill?" she asked, glancing at him as she browned the little pieces of tofu in a fry pan. "I hate that. This morning I was making pancakes, fifty of them for the bottomless pits I call my brothers and father, and I suddenly got a chill even though I was standing right in front of a gas flame in August. Crazy."

He was hardly chilled. Nope, not at all.

Now she was talking about sesame oil and how to make the tofu crispy for the stir-fry. She was saying something about cornstarch and pepper, but he'd stopped hearing her words and focused instead on her face and body.

Granted, she wasn't curvy. Or big-breasted. Or remotely his usual type. But there was just something about her. He must be losing his mind because he thought it was the freckles. Or the green eyes. Or the wide smile.

Or the way she talked so animatedly about the difference between a wok and a sauté pan.

"Going to make tofu stir-fry for your family tonight?" she asked him, holding out a piece of the brown crispy not-meat on a wooden spoon. She brought it up to his mouth, and he looked at her, then slid his lips around it.

She flushed.

He flushed.

He leaned closer.

She…backed away. As if she'd been there, done that, and had lived to tell the tale.

"I, uh, you…have sesame oil on your cheek," he rushed to say, leaning a bit closer to dab it away. He forced himself not to lick it off his finger.

Saved. He hadn't been about to kiss her. No sir.

He had to get out of this kitchen, this enclosed space, with this woman. She was his buddy, that was all. Even if he *were* attracted to her, she was too young and had big dreams that she should focus on. He was a grumbly, stomped-on, love-sucks guy who wasn't getting over it anytime soon. She needed the male version of herself. A guy as great as she was.

Not that he wanted to think of her with *any* guy.

Oh hell. He needed to go find a Vanessa type and forget about this green-eyed, freckled, curveless chef who had him all discombobulated. Yes. That was what he needed. An airhead who wouldn't make him think, wouldn't challenge him, wouldn't stab a dagger through his chest.

"Appreciate the lesson," he said. "The Crawfords might not be ready for tofu, but I might surprise them one day."

"So how do you want to schedule the cooking lesson?" she asked, stirring the pan.

"Let me check my calendar," he said. "I'm pretty busy right now. In fact, I'd better get going. Later, buddy."

He didn't miss her face falling.

Buddy.

Cripes, Xander. You always go that step too far. Why had he added that unnecessary zinger?

Because now they both knew—for sure. They were friends. That was it.

He smiled awkwardly and then headed out the kitchen door as if the place were on fire.

Chapter Four

Buddy.

Buddy!

Every time she heard that word—in Xander's sexy voice—echoing in her head, she alternated between disappointment and *oh hell no!* She was not going to be buddy-zoned by Xander Crawford when she'd lain awake all night imagining the kiss that might have taken place in her kitchen yesterday.

The kiss that did not happen but could have. He would have swept her up into his arms like in a movie and carried her up to her bedroom—no, scratch that. He would have carried her into his silver pickup, raced her back to the Ambling A and his bedroom, and they'd have spent the afternoon making mad, passionate love and coming up with silly names for their new relationship. Xanlil. Lilxan.

Not exactly flowing off the tongue. Their "celeb" name sounded like a prescription medication.

She smiled, then sighed inwardly as she carried the tray of drinks and treats while Sarah Crawford wheeled her baby stroller over to a table way in the back of Daisy's Donuts. They were going to talk shop—translation: *men*— so they needed to be away from pricked-up ears in the small town. Luckily, there were only a handful of people sitting in the shop, mostly teenagers who couldn't care less about Lily's love life, so she planned to tell Sarah everything.

Not that there was much to tell. But she did need advice. And Sarah was not only way more experienced at relationships, she was married to a Crawford.

Sarah parked the stroller and smiled at her sleeping little Sophia, the seven-month-old beauty so sweet in her pink-and-white-striped pajamas, I Love Daddy in glittery print across the front. The pj's were a gift from Daddy himself, Xander's eldest brother, Logan, who loved Sophie as if she were his own flesh and blood. To him, she clearly was. Lily's faith in everything was always restored whenever she thought about Sarah and Logan's love story.

Two days had passed since their second awkward moment involving leaning toward each other, and Xander Crawford hadn't shown his face in the dining room of Maverick Manor or made arrangements for his pricey cooking lesson. He was clearly avoiding her. Of course, Lily could text him about the lesson, push things a little. But she was not going to chase a man who was making it clear he wasn't interested.

Blast. That was the thing. He did seem interested— to a point. And then he backed off. She wasn't getting just-friend vibes from the guy. Or maybe she just didn't know enough about men and relationships to understand what was going on here.

Maybe nothing was going on.

Please, Lordy, don't let me be one of those delusional creatures who thinks this and that when there's no there *there!*

Lily took a bite of her lemon-custard donut and sips of the refreshing iced tea, the sugary goodness that was always able to do its own restorative work on her mind and heart. Temporarily for the moment, anyway. As Sarah sipped her iced latte, Lily filled in her friend on all things Xander.

Sarah picked up her frosted cruller. "Yup, I know that advance-and-retreat well. I went through it with a Crawford brother myself. I'm telling you, Lil, it takes men a while sometimes to see what's in front of their gorgeous faces."

Lily eyed Sarah's beautiful wedding ring. "I don't know. I have all kinds of crazy feelings for Xander. *All* kinds. I think he's incredibly hot. So sexy. And he's smart. Funny. Laughs at my jokes. He loves dogs. He's passionate about his work and helping his family restore the Ambling A. Did I mention he's so hot I can barely look at him sometimes?"

"Oh, trust me, I know that well, too. The man is interested, Lily. I wouldn't say it if I didn't think it was true. Sounds to me like maybe he didn't plan on getting involved with someone, though."

"But he has a highly skilled wedding planner setting up dates for him—for all the single Crawfords," Lily pointed out.

"Ugh, that," Sarah said with a grimace. "Has Xander gone on any?"

"I don't know. I hate the thought of him being fixed up with anyone." She took a grumpy bite of her donut, even the delicious sugary confection not making her feel better this time around.

"Well, worry not, my dear. You said he asked you to give him a cooking lesson, right?"

"Right…" Lily prompted, confused by where her friend was going.

"You'll be confined to one room for a few hours, working on a few recipes together—then testing them out. A lot can happen in a few hours." She nodded sagely and took another bite of her cruller, sliding a glance at baby Sophia, who continued to snooze through Lily's man troubles.

Hey, at least she had man troubles. In the past year, she'd had one bad date. That was it.

Why? Because she was shy around men? Because she was a tomboy?

She glanced down at her jeans and blah blue T-shirt with Billy's Bait Shop and an illustration of a worm on a line. Then she looked at Sarah. A new mother. And what was Sarah wearing? A cute sundress and flat metallic sandals. Her friend looked so pretty and pulled together. What was Lily's excuse for dressing like one of her brothers?

Oh God. This shirt *was* her brother's. Ryan's.

You are hopeless, Lily Hunt. This wasn't her or her style. She'd always wanted to tag along with her older brothers and so she dressed like them to play rough like them, and it had just become her look. Huh. Maybe she needed to go shopping. And beg Sarah to come with her and play stylist.

And what? Skinny jeans and a tighter, more feminine top would suddenly make Xander Crawford fall for her? Nope. Didn't work that way. Whatever made Xander so…ambivalent about her had nothing to do with her look. She thought, anyway.

Why was this so confusing?

"Lily, if something is between you two," Sarah added, "it'll happen. Trust me."

Hope bloomed in Lily's heart. She thought about the way they'd almost kissed in her kitchen two days ago. "You are absolutely right."

The thought of something happening between her and Xander—like being in bed with him—almost had her blushing. "I might have to get a little bold." Same with her cooking. Same with working on her business degree. Same with anything she wanted. She had to put herself out there, climb out on a limb and make stuff happen.

Sarah grinned. "Indeed you might. Go for it."

The next time she saw Xander, she *would*.

She needed a new look. She needed new *moxie*. And she felt it roaring up inside her.

Xander decided that if Viv Dalton was going to set him up on dates, he might as well have some control over whom he was fixed up with. Since he'd arrived in Rust Creek Falls, he'd made excuses every time the woman had approached him. He'd see her coming toward him in town, notebook in hand, one hand in a wave, a determined gleam in her eye, and he'd tap his watch and turn in the opposite direction. Now he'd actually arranged a meeting with Viv and sat across from her in her office, watching her big smile fade with every word he said. Viv was a few years younger than him, tall and slender with blond hair in a fancy twist. Her eyes were narrowed on him as though she couldn't quite believe what she was hearing.

He'd been at it for a good five minutes. "She doesn't need to be very bright," Xander went on. "Chatty is fine, but let's keep it to small talk."

"Uh, got it," Viv said, barely able to hide the "you've got to be kidding me" expression on her face as she took notes. "So let's see if I've got this straight, Xander." She peered at her notebook. "You're looking for a peroxide blonde who knows her way around a curling iron, wears makeup and high heels, and has a 'great giggle'? Great laugh I've heard before. Great giggle is a new one."

"Look, my dad wants you to set me and my brothers up on dates that might lead to something serious. So shouldn't I let you know what I'm looking for in a woman?"

"But you're not actually looking for *anything*, Xander. If I may be so blunt."

Touché. "What I'm not looking for is to get serious," he explained. "I think it's important that you know that. I don't want to hurt anyone, disappoint anyone, lead on anyone. I'm looking to have a good time—that's it. And I know what I like."

The way Xander saw it, he could do himself and Andrew Hunt a favor. Anyone Viv set him up with who was too nice or too interesting or actually had him sharing details of his life the way Lily had within ten minutes would find her name and number passed on to Andrew.

Viv sat back in her chair and clasped her hands in her lap. "I heard that instead of Knox, *you* ended up going out with Lily Hunt. How'd that go? I'm assuming not

well, since Lily is the opposite of everything you described as your perfect woman to not be serious about."

Green eyes and freckles and orange rubber shoes
came to mind. Tofu. Dachshunds named Dobby and
Harry. Suntan lotion and flowery scented hair.

He wondered what kissing Lily would be like. Passionate, he was sure of that. Lily approached everything
with zing. Kissing her would be like having all of her.
And if kissing her would knock him out, he could only
imagine what seeing her naked would do to him. Where
else did she have freckles?

"Xander?"

He blinked and realized Viv Dalton was staring at
him. Waiting for a response. Oh God. He'd been fantasizing about Lily Hunt. What was happening here exactly?

He cleared his throat and sat up straight. "Lily is a
very nice person."

"Ah, nice," she said with a nod.

He frowned. "Well, she *is* nice. She's great. Smart,
full of life, passionate about her job, has big goals and
dreams, loves her family, dotes on those little sausage
dogs. Did I mention she's going to give me a cooking
lesson?"

Viv eyed him, scanned her notes and then leaned forward. "Tell you what, Xander. I'll see who might fit the
bill and text you if the right gal comes to mind."

"Perfect," he said, getting up. "No pressure. I like
no pressure."

"No pressure," she agreed, standing and shaking his
hand. "Good luck with the cooking class."

Was it his imagination or was there a slight gleeful-
ness in her tone?

He wished he'd scheduled that cooking lesson for right

now. He wanted to be with Lily, talking to her, looking at her, making a mess in the kitchen with her. But hadn't he met with Viv specifically to set up dates with his type in order to push Lily from his mind? Yes, he'd done exactly that and now he wanted the opposite.

All those things he'd said to Viv about Lily were true. So of course he wanted to be around her. He liked her, plain and simple. Maybe the cooking thing was too much. Too…intimate. Yeah, it kind of was. He could put that off for a while until he understood just what he was feeling for Lily Hunt.

That settled, he decided to go pay her a visit, see if her dogs needed walking since she was so busy with school and her job at the Manor. A friend would absolutely do this.

During the next week, Lily counted five times that Xander Crawford had found a reason to "stop by." *Five* times.

Early in the week, he'd appeared at the back door of the kitchen of the Maverick Manor and offered to take Dobby and Harry for a walk since it was an "incredibly gorgeous summer day" and she was cooped up at work. That sure was thoughtful. His visit had coincided with her fifteen-minute break, so they'd stood outside in the back and chatted about the day's specials, which included homemade spicy onion rings, and how onions did not make him cry like other people, and how he preferred sautéed onions to raw on his burgers. He'd started to go, then had turned back and said he wouldn't able to schedule that cooking lesson for at least a week since he was very busy with work "and stuff" at the Ambling A. Disappointment had lodged so heavily in her chest that she'd been surprised she hadn't tipped over. Then, off he'd gone, her brother Ryan reporting fifteen minutes later that "the tall dude came by and took out the dogs and good thing because I forgot to, sorry."

The next day, Xander had texted her a hello and she'd responded with a frazzled emoji and mentioned she was stuck on a school assignment about business expenditures, and a half hour later, there he was, showing her a few pages of the financials from the Ambling A, and two hours later, everything made sense. Up in her bedroom, he'd spent two hours going over economics and finance—that had to mean *something*. She'd had to force herself to concentrate on the topic and not on the fact that Xander Crawford was sitting on the edge of her bed. She'd done a lot of fantasizing about Xander in that very bed.

The next afternoon, he'd needed a "woman's opinion on which tie he should wear to a rancher's association meeting since he was thinking of running for the board—or maybe not."

Sarah had squealed over that one when Lily texted her about it. The man is crazy about you!

Except he never "leaned" toward her again. Not the next two times he'd dropped in at the Manor—once in the kitchen to rave about the grilled tuna lunch special, or when he'd appeared right before quitting time last night because he thought she might like some company walking home. She certainly did. They'd sat on her porch, watching Dobby and Harry run around the fenced yard. He'd commented on the crescent moon and the Big Dipper, and she'd almost rested her head on his shoulder. That was how natural being with him was. How comfortable she was with him.

That he liked her wasn't in question. But he didn't look at her the way she was sure she looked at him. He looked at her the way she looked at the two male cooks at Maverick Manor. Like friends.

So...what gives?

Being buddies with a man who made you fantasize about taking off his shirt and undoing his belt was a first for Lily. She lost her train of thought midsentence when she was around him or he popped into her mind—which was constantly.

"Lily! I need your help!" came the very loud voice of her brother Andrew from the direction of his bedroom.

She sighed and put down her Economics 101 textbook. She was focusing more on a tall, dark and hot cowboy than on the difference between classical economics and Keynesian economics, anyway.

She headed two doors down to Andrew's room. She coughed as a cloud of men's body spray greeted her. Waving the air in front of her, Lily said, "Wherever you're going tonight, you're gonna need to stand outside for a good twenty minutes to let all that dissipate."

Andrew, who was all dressed up—for him, anyway, since he was either in his police academy uniform or a T-shirt and sweats—eyed his reflection in the bureau mirror as he brushed his short hair. He added a dollop of gel. "No way, sis. According to the bottle, I smell like mountain energy." He took in a deep breath and smiled. "Heidi will love it."

"Who's Heidi?"

"My date for tonight. We're going to the Maverick Manor. You working tonight? Please say yes. I need you to do that thing you do with people's food so that tonight is extra magical."

Lily laughed. "I'm not working tonight, sorry. But I'm sure your date will absolutely love you. Where'd you meet her?"

"I haven't yet. It's a blind date. Thanks to Xander. I owe the guy. He set us up."

Lily gaped at her middle brother. "Xander? How'd that happen? I didn't even know you two knew each other."

Andrew glanced at her in the mirror, then used his fingers to slightly push up the front of his hair. "We met the other day when he came to the house. I asked him if he'd talk me up to any of his dates that didn't work out, and he called me a couple days ago and said he'd met a great young woman and thought we might like each other, so he gave her my number and she called. How awesome is that?"

Yeah, awesome. Xander was going on dates. And passing on the ones who didn't warrant a second date to her brother. She wondered how many Xander *hadn't* passed on.

"Should I wear black shoes or cowboy boots?" he asked.

She glanced at his feet. "Either."

"Oh, big help!" he said. "Thanks."

The thing was, she really didn't know. She wasn't exactly a fashionista. And she hadn't exactly gone on a lot of dates to know what guys wore. Xander had been wearing expensive-looking black shoes on their not-a-date, but his pants were dressier than Andrew's dark gray chinos. "Go for the shoes," she suggested.

He nodded. "I think so, too. The Maverick Manor isn't exactly the Ace in the Hole."

She dropped down on the edge of his bed. "So…what did Xander tell you about Heidi?"

"Just that she was very nice and he thought I'd like her."

"Nice?" she repeated.

"Nice. That was my one request."

Huh. That was a surprise. "I thought guys wanted pretty and hot and fun."

"Some guys, I guess. I'd be happy with all that. But what's the point of hot if she's a royal PITA?"

Lily laughed. "Good point."

Andrew put on his black shoes, glanced at himself one more time in the mirror, said "Wish me luck" and then raced downstairs before she could say another word.

She wondered why the date with nice Heidi hadn't worked out with Xander. Duh, she realized. Because Heidi was nice. And Xander obviously didn't go for nice. A man like Xander Crawford, who could have any woman in town, would want hot. Maybe nice, too, but hot.

Exactly what *she* wasn't.

She groaned.

Whatevs! she screeched at herself. Hot wouldn't get her her own gourmet café or catering shop, now would it? Hard work would. Brains would.

She sighed and trudged back to her room. As she flopped onto her bed next to her econ textbook, her heart sank so low she thought she might crash through the bed onto the floor.

Her phone pinged with a text.

From Xander.

She almost didn't want to read it. How had she gotten his small attentions all week so wrong? She'd really thought there was something brewing between them. But they really and truly were "just friends."

She stayed flopped on her back and read the text.

This might be too short notice, but I'd like to hire you to cook a special dinner for my dad and brothers on Saturday night. We finished repairing a tough line of fence and I'd like to celebrate with a family party. I'm thinking 7:00 p.m. for dinner. We're all pretty much meat-and-potatoes kind of guys, but I'll leave the details up to you.

Saturday night. Two days from now. Hell yeah, she was available. But what was the point? To fall even harder for a man who wasn't remotely interested?

Still, they *were* friends. And he was asking for her help. In fact, he was offering her another paying gig— and if she wanted to take two courses next semester, she could use the extra money.

I'm in! she texted back ever so breezily when she felt exactly the opposite. And thanks, she added.

Thank YOU, was his response.

If only there was a magic spice or ingredient she could add to the food to make Xander Crawford fall for her.

Okay, she couldn't help it. C'mon, how could she? Of course Lily found an excuse to hustle over to the Maverick Manor to check out this Heidi who was too nice for Xander Crawford. She was sure Heidi would be a plain-Jane type like her. Then she'd know that it wasn't her so much as her look that didn't attract Xander, and maybe she'd feel better.

It's not you, it's me. It's not me, it's you. Who the hell knew?

Big sunhat pulled down low, red hair tucked up under, Lily dashed into the Manor and stood behind the giant vase of wildflowers. She glanced around the lobby for her brother. No sign of him. She was glad there was no sign of Xander, either—on a date with another woman.

She dashed into the kitchen and peered through the Out door into the dining room.

There. Table eleven by the window. Her brother was smiling and chatting. And facing him was…America's Next Top Model.

Or close to it.

What? This was Xander's "it didn't work out but she's nice"? Heidi was tall and busty, Lily noted, wearing a pretty yellow sundress with a flounce near her knees. She had on high-heeled sandals. And if Lily wasn't mistaken, sparkly baby blue toenails. She also had long honey-brown hair in perfect beachy waves.

Lily watched as Heidi laughed at something her brother said and reached over and touched his arm. Andrew could not look happier.

If this woman wasn't Xander Crawford's type, then who was? Certainly not Lily Hunt.

It was time to give up on him. Cook his family dinner for the celebration, teach him to cook those three favorite dishes, make some money for her future and then move on.

"Lily? Someone called you?" her boss, Gwendolyn, said, rushing over to her. "Great! If you could whip up three filets, subbing the baked for the rice pilaf, that would be great."

Before Lily could say a word, Gwen, wearing her frantic expression, was heading over to Jesse Gold's station, but the cook was nowhere to be found. Gwen flipped a filet mignon and poured béarnaise sauce on it, letting the flames sear it. "Jesse was turning green and almost fell over, so I sent him home. We're booked tonight, so even me pitching in here won't be enough."

"I'm on it," Lily said, whipping off her hat and declaring the filet done and plating it.

This was good, actually. Being so busy would keep her from thinking about Xander and his horde of dates. Beautiful dates.

"Hey, Lily!" AnnaBeth said with a smile as she came in from the dining room. "Your brother's here on a hot date. He's having the filet special, she's having the lemon sole. Oh, and she's from South Dakota, by the way. Gonna work your magic on her fish? Is South Dakota famous for anything?"

Lily immediately thought of chislic, like shish kebabs but without the vegetables. Just delicious little chunks of salted meat on tiny skewers. They hadn't ordered appetizers, but she'd make up a small dish of chislic for them from a filet mignon that Gwen said had ended up searing too long when Jesse had been distracted by not feeling well.

She worked fast and had a little plate ready in no time. "Here," she told AnnaBeth. "You can tell table eleven this is compliments of the chef."

"Ooh, that looks delicious," AnnaBeth said.

Lily smiled and got back to work, starting on Heidi's sole now that her brother's filet was at the rare mark. By the time the sole was done, the steak would be perfectly medium.

"Uh, Lily?" AnnaBeth said, rushing over with the plate of chislic. It was untouched. "Your brother's date took one look at this and said 'Excuse me,' and ran out of the dining room. I think she might be in the restroom."

"Oh no. The dish upset her?"

AnnaBeth bit her lip. "I think so."

Lily plated the entrées and then dashed to the window on the door, AnnaBeth on her heels. Her brother looked worried. He kept glancing toward the arched doorway that led into the lobby.

Oh God. Had she ruined their date? Had "home" brought up bad memories for Heidi?

She had to get back to her station and work on her orders. She had another waitress with four tables that had recently been seated, and she needed to be on point.

They raced back over to Lily's station, AnnaBeth putting the two dishes on the elegant serving tray. "I'll try to find out what's happening."

Lily didn't add her special ingredients to the next three tables of orders she'd received from Holly, the other waitress in Lily's section. Maybe she should mind her own business. She shouldn't even be here at all. Now thanks to her nosy ways, she'd wrecked her brother's date when it had clearly been going very well.

She made two of the special pasta entrées, got three more filets going and two more lemon soles, forcing herself to focus on her work and not her urge to rush back to the little window to see if anyone was still at her brother's table.

AnnaBeth came back into the kitchen with her empty tray.

"Is the food just sitting out on the table getting cold?" Lily asked.

AnnaBeth smiled. "Nope. In fact, come take a look."

Lily's eyes widened and she rushed back over to the window. Her brother and Heidi now sat side by side at the round table instead of across from each other. Heidi was holding up a piece of her lemon sole to her brother's mouth, and he took the bite. Heidi then picked up her napkin and dabbed Andrew's lips, and then they both laughed and held each other's gazes.

She had no idea what had happened, but she was glad it had!

Lily's phone pinged with a text. Probably Xander canceling on hiring her for the party.

She glanced at her phone on the counter. No—the text was from Andrew. Her brother had practically typed a novel.

Heidi's freshening up in the restroom so just a YEEHA! that you ended up working tonight and made that little SD appetizer for her! Turns out her mom died last year and always used to make chislic every Sunday for family dinner. She got all emotional and excused herself but I found her in the lobby and told her about Mom passing and how Dad still makes her crawdaddy mac and cheese and corn bread every Sunday for us, even though his corn bread is awful, and how we feel her with us. We talked about our moms for a while and then it was like we'd known each other forever. We're going out again tomorrow night! You rock, Lil. Don't know how you do it but I'm glad you do.

Huh. She sent back a heart emoji, her own heart bursting with happiness for him and for herself, since she hadn't ruined his night after all. Au contraire.

At least one Hunt's love life was going in the right direction.

Chapter Five

Xander had exhausted his excuses for checking to see if Lily "needed help" during the past hour that she'd been in Ambling A's kitchen. She'd let him help make the béarnaise sauce for the filet mignon, which had smelled amazing, and also peel potatoes, which he'd found less fun, and then she'd shooed him out to be with his family.

Something was different between them, he thought. She was being kind of…distant. Treating him as if he were a client instead of… Instead of what? Someone she was close to?

A friend?

Why couldn't he seem to get a grip on where he was with Lily? He should be happy she was treating him like a client instead of a crush—if that was what he should call it. In the past week, hadn't he gone out with three women, one set up by Viv Dalton, two who'd asked him out in town, to restore order to his head?

And despite making it clear to Viv that she should set him up with only airheads who giggled, she'd arranged a date with a perfectly nice, intelligent, interesting woman named Heidi whose family had moved to Montana from South Dakota last year. They'd had a lot to talk about, and she'd looked a little surprised when he'd said at the end of the date that he was going to be honest and tell her he wasn't looking for a relationship with anyone and that he knew a great guy who was, if she was interested. Heidi said she trusted his opinion, and voilà, she and Lily Hunt's brother Andrew were on date number three right now, third night in a row.

The other two women he'd gone out with had been more his type. One giggled even when she'd backed her car—she'd insisted on driving since she had a little two-seater she liked zipping around in—into the sheriff's SUV. Then she giggled as the sheriff, who didn't look remotely amused, gave her a Breathalyzer test. They hadn't had an ounce of alcohol to drink at that point, but afterward, Xander could have used a few bottles of whiskey to get through the next hour of dinner. He'd turned down her suggestion of a nightcap in her condo, seen her safely home and then walked back two miles toward town, where luckily his brother Wilder had been passing by in his truck and given him a ride back to the ranch. Man, had Wilder had a good laugh all the way home.

Xander had wanted to cancel the next night's date, but then he remembered how he'd refused to let Lily get canceled on, so he'd forced himself out with Dede, who was the cheerleading coach for the high school and had a bad habit of screaming "Whooooo!" whenever she was excited about something, holding her arms straight up in the air and shaking imaginary pom-poms. She wasn't an airhead at all, it turned out, and luckily, she'd ended the date early, sobbing that she'd only asked him out to make her ex jealous and they'd walked right past the guy in the restaurant she'd known he'd be eating in with his family and he hadn't even blinked.

Dating and relationships sure were hell.

"Go on," Lily said now, making shooing motions with her hands. "I'm fine in here. It's my habitat, remember?"

He nodded and smiled but wanted to stick around. Find out what she'd been up to the past few nights since he hadn't gotten a chance to pop in on her. But her focus was on the heap of steaks and potatoes and asparagus smelling so incredible.

Go, he ordered himself, everything in him resisting leaving the room. "Holler if you get lonesome in here by yourself."

"The kitchen is the one place I never feel lonely," she said, locking eyes with him.

He held her gaze, something—hell if he knew what—spinning up inside him. He couldn't move his feet, couldn't look away.

But then she was shaking the pan with the asparagus, and turning down the burners on the steaks, and he took one last good look at her profile, the freckles on her nose and cheeks, before slipping out, his chest heavy.

The laughter and loud chatter in the living room grabbed his attention as he headed in, the Crawfords all congregated for the party to celebrate another piece of the Ambling A coming together, becoming home.

Hunter sat with his six-year-old daughter, Wren, on his lap, her long blond hair in two of the most crooked braids Xander had ever seen. Hunter had been mother and father to his sweet little girl since Wren was born, and Xander had to hand it to him for doing such a great job. He braided hair and packed day-camp lunches, and stayed up all night when Wren was sick or had bad dreams. The guy had a lot on his shoulders. Sometimes Xander wondered how *he'd* do as a father—not that he had any plans to become one anytime soon.

It was crazy how even when you picked the right woman, as Hunter had done with his late wife, your whole life could go belly-up. It was a sober reminder that Xander was 100 percent correct not to get serious about a woman.

Sharing the big couch with Hunter and Wren were Logan and Sarah, Sarah playing some kind of clapping game with her adored niece. Finn was deep in conversation with Wilder in the two club chairs across from the love seat where Xander sat with Knox, who was deep in thought—as usual. Meanwhile, his father sat in his space-age recliner with features that turned on lights and the television, and massaged his back and neck.

"Well, Crawfords," Max said with a drawn-out shake of his head, "I must say I'm disappointed to see that there's only one lovely woman joining us for dinner to-night. By this point, I expected at least half of you to be seriously involved."

"Can we not alk-tay about this in front of En-Wray," Hunter muttered through gritted teeth, nodding his head at his six-year-old daughter.

"I know pig latin, Daddy," Wren said with a grin.

Xander laughed. "And there are *three* lovely women at the table tonight, so there's your quota, Dad. Sarah, baby Sophia and Wren."

His father's gaze moved from Logan's wife and baby to Hunter's little girl, and he grinned. "I stand corrected. But still!"

"Don't you mean *four*?" Sarah asked. "Isn't Lily joining us for dinner?" She glanced around at faces but lingered on Xander's.

"Of course she is," Max said, slapping his knee. "That talented chef did all the hard work—she should get to sit down and relax and enjoy her own masterpiece."

"I agree," Sarah said with a smile. "In fact, I'll go put a place setting out for her. Be right back."

Seat her next to me, Xander wanted to tell Sarah, but of course he couldn't. He watched her dash into the kitchen.

Five long minutes later, Lily came out of the kitchen holding a platter of steaks that smelled so good everyone went silent for a moment. Sarah was right behind her with a tray of big bowls holding roasted potatoes and asparagus. Xander hopped up and asked if he could help bring anything out, but Lily smiled and said this was everything.

Then she glanced around and looked kind of uncomfortable and said, "Sorry that I'm not exactly dressed for a dinner party. I really just expected to be in the kitchen, not joining you."

"What?" Max said, eyeing her. "You look just like the rest of us. One of the boys."

Oh, Dad, Xander thought. *Enough with the asides.*

Lily bit her lip and awkwardly smiled, shifting a glance to Sarah, who was casually dressed but not quite to the degree Lily was. Lily wore a red scoop-neck T-shirt with a white apron over it, loose jeans and blue sneakers, her red hair back in a ponytail.

Luckily everyone else was focused on the aroma and platters and trooped into the huge dining room, Max taking his place at the head of the long farmhouse table. Xander took a seat down at the other end to avoid any marriage-oriented conversation his father might start up. Logan and Sarah sat across from him, baby Sophia sleeping in her carrier on the hutch along the far wall.

Lily took a seat right beside him.

"First, a toast," Max said, raising his wineglass. "To the Ambling A and all the hard work you boys have put into turning this place into a home. I couldn't be prouder of you. I'll include myself in there, since I'm out there busting these old bones every day, too."

They all laughed and raised their glasses, clinking.

"And thank you to Lily, our chef for the evening, for this amazing dinner," Max added.

There was more clinking.

"My pleasure," Lily said. "Well, everyone, bon appétit!"

Platters and bowls were passed around, everyone commenting on how good everything looked.

"Oh, and Lily," Max said, "I have to apologize for my son Knox and all that brouhaha with your date. But it looks like things worked out just fine. I mean, here you are, sitting next to Xander at a family dinner." He winked and loaded his plate with potatoes.

"Really, Dad?" Knox said with a shake of his head. "And no need to do my apologizing for me. I spoke to Lily privately in the kitchen right after she arrived."

Xander had noticed Knox go into the kitchen and come out a couple minutes later. He'd figured his brother was making amends.

Lily's cheeks were as red as her T-shirt. "Xander and I are just friends."

"Just friends," Xander seconded.

"Ah, so we can talk about all the dates you went on this past week," Wilder said. "Any work out?"

"Come on, Xan," his father said. "Tell me you have one *second* date."

Was it his imagination or was Lily pushing her potatoes around on her plate, her expression both grim and forced pleasant?

"Let's leave Xander's private life to himself," Sarah said. "You boys. Seriously!"

"Yeah, let's listen to Sarah," Xander agreed, wanting to hug her.

"Fine, fine," Max said. "Now, Lily, I hear you have three brothers, so you're used to all this testosterone."

Lily laughed. "Definitely."

The conversation thankfully turned to stories about the Hunt brothers and the Crawford brothers, both matched for mischief.

"Oh, Lily," Hunter said. "I'm really sorry but Wren and I won't be able to make your kids' cooking class tomorrow afternoon. I forgot I promised a friend I'd help him move. Wren was really looking forward to it."

"Aww," Wren said, looking pretty sad. "Now I won't know how to make tacos."

"Well, I'll be hosting more kids' classes," Lily assured her. "The next one is for kids a bit older than you, Wren, but I'll have another one for your age group in September. That's just a month away."

Xander recalled Lily mentioning she taught cooking classes at the town rec center, but he hadn't known Hunter and Wren signed up. "Why don't I take my niece to the class?" he said. "I'm free tomorrow afternoon. And then I get to spend some time with my favorite six-year-old."

And Lily, he thought.

"Yay!" Wren said. "I want to learn how to make tacos! I love tacos!"

"Perfect," Hunter said. "Thanks, bro."

Xander nodded back.

Lily sent him an awkward smile. Why was everything like that between them? Awkward and hesitant? Something was up. But what?

"Lily, I don't know where you learned to cook like this," Max said, "but thank God you did. Amazing."

There were murmurs of agreement and the conversation turned to favorite meals, then Lily brought out dessert, which were mini chocolate tarts, and suddenly dinner was over, and Lily was in the kitchen again.

Xander grabbed a few empty platters and took them into the kitchen, hoping no one would do the same. Lily stood at the sink, scraping pans.

"We'll clean up, Lily," he said. "Don't even worry about all this."

She whirled around with a grin. "Really? First the cook gets invited to dinner and now I don't have to wash pots and load the dishwasher? I'm not usually this lucky."

"Trust me, you especially deserve not to clean up with my dad getting all personal like that. Sorry."

"No worries. I'm well used to dads and brothers ribbing on me." She put the pans in soapy water to soak. "So…sorry the dating isn't working out. Though I guess that's good for my brother. I think Andrew is totally in love."

"Glad to hear it." He wanted to tell her he wasn't dating to find a serious girlfriend, let alone a wife. But was he supposed to blurt out the truth: that he was speed dating to remind him what he was and wasn't looking for?

Not looking for: Real. Serious. Even close to forever.

Looking for: A hot kiss or two. More if the woman was looking for the same and nothing else.

The reality was that Lily Hunt in her T-shirt and ponytail and blue sneakers, with sauce stains on her shoulder, was keeping him up at night by just being *herself.*

Lord. Was he falling for Lily? That was impossible, right? She was seven years his junior and looked like any number of his buddies' kid sisters in her hoodies and jeans.

He wasn't falling for her. He just liked her. That was all. When was the last time he'd met someone and developed a real bond, a real friendship? A long time ago. He just forgot what it felt like, and it was confusing because it had happened with a woman.

Hadn't he said women and men could be friends? Yes, they could.

Case in point: him and Lily.

"Well, we'll see how the dating goes this week," he said. "Viv has three more set up for me and that's just the first half of the week."

Her face fell. Just for a second. But he caught it. She had feelings for him—he knew that. And it was better not to play with her. He was telling the truth about the dates, and she should know so that she wouldn't hang any hopes on him.

If he hurt her, disappointed her, made her think something more could go on when it couldn't…he'd never forgive himself.

She was so young. She had her entire life ahead of

her. Practically all her twenties. And big dreams to fuel her. She didn't need some cynical guy already in the next decade of life.

She gave him a tight smile. "Good luck, then." She darted past him into the living room with him trailing her, said good-night and thank you to everyone, and then beelined for the door. Xander almost wished car trouble on her so he could drive her home, but her little silver car started right up.

Leaving him staring out at the red taillights disappearing down the drive.

"Jeez, just admit you've got a thing for her," Logan whispered as he came up behind him.

"What?" he said. "Of course I don't. She's twenty-three, for God's sake. I'm *thirty*." And he was done with caring about a woman, with thinking about the future beyond a couple days. He saw where that had gotten him.

"Whatever you say, bro," Logan said with a smile and a head shake. "In due time. In due time."

"Meaning?"

Logan laughed and looked over toward the living room, where his wife sat on the sofa, lifting their baby up and down and kissing her on the cheek.

"Now you have me married with a baby?" He huffed away to get a beer, Logan's laughter trailing him.

By the time Lily pulled into her driveway, she'd burst into tears three times and had five text messages waiting for her from Sarah.

Told you he has feelings for you! her friend wrote. Taking over for Hunter at the kiddie cooking class? She added a few heart emojis and a chef hat emoji and Lily burst into tears again.

I'll believe it if he ever kisses me, she typed back. Until then, I'm operating under the assumption that he likes me as a friend.

Three dates set up this week. All before Wednesday!

She headed inside the house to find her dad home alone, Dobby and Harry beside him on the couch, a bowl of popcorn on the other side of him. He was watching a *Law & Order* marathon on cable. He took one look at her expression and put the popcorn on the coffee table and patted the space where it had been.

"Come watch, Lil. Did you know identical twins have the same DNA and one could be convicted for the crime his twin actually committed?"

"I don't think I ever thought about it before, Dad," she said, plopping beside him. Dobby came over and settled in her lap, and she stroked his soft ears.

"Everything go okay at the Crawfords'?" he asked.

The food: yes. The company: yes. Her heart: no. "Yeah," she said, unable to disguise the weariness in her tone.

"You like that tall one with the brown hair, don't you?" her father said.

She stared at her Dad. "They're *all* tall with brown hair. But how'd you know?"

He pointed the remote at the TV and shut it off, then turned to her. "Because you're my baby girl. And trust me, I never forget that. You might think I treat you like one of your brothers, but that's because I've always tried to treat you all the same. But you're the only female in the house, Lil, and you might think you hide your emotions like we try to, but you're bad at it."

Lily laughed, but tears stung her eyes. "I'm falling in love with someone who thinks of me as a friend."

"I wouldn't be too sure," her dad said. "Sometimes it just takes a while for us lugheads to know our own minds. Did I ever tell you how I thought of your mom as just a friend when we first met?"

"What? No way. You always said it was love at first sight."

"More like love at third sight," he said with a smile. "Your mom was so pretty and sparkling I didn't think I had a chance. So I didn't even give her a romantic thought in my mind. But then I got to know her and fell in love whether I liked it or not."

Lily laughed again. "You fell in love against your will?"

"Sort of. I didn't think she'd ever return my feelings. But she did."

Lily always loved hearing about when her mom and dad met. "Well, I don't think that's going to happen here. I look like a boy with long hair."

"Xander may see much more than that," her father said. "As I always say—don't rule anything out till you know for absolute sure you should."

Dobby licked her hand, which still had the faintest residue of filet mignon no matter how much she'd scrubbed.

"Thanks, Dad," she said, leaning her head on his shoulder.

He gave her shoulder a pat and then put *Law & Order* back on, the identical twin—who hadn't even known he had an identical twin—insisting he was innocent.

She wasn't in the mood for TV right now but she needed something to take her mind off Xander Crawford and her lack of a love life. Plus, it was nice to spend time with her dad. Real time. She'd opened up tonight and she hadn't done that in a long time. Sometimes Lily felt like she was changing every few seconds, new experiences hitting her left and right.

Dobby licked her hand again, and she hugged him to her, the warm little dog like a soothing balm.

After the show, Lily hugged her dad, too, and thanked him for listening—and for the good advice—then headed upstairs. She took a long, hot shower, changed into her comfiest pj's, and then got into bed, tossing and turning for what felt like hours, but when morning came, she felt well rested. Talking to her dad had definitely helped.

Don't rule anything out till you know for absolute sure you should.

Xander had pretty much confirmed she should rule him out when he mentioned his dating schedule. Right?

But he'd also made a point of seeing her later today by taking his niece to her cooking class. *Duh, because you're friends.*

She would never get to the bottom of this at this point.

She stood in front of her bureau, staring at herself in the mirror. On the dresser was a photograph of her mother—beautiful, sophisticated Naomi Hunt. She wore a sleeveless dress, dangling earrings, her hair wavy and loose around her shoulders. She'd lost her mom when she was eight, and her dad and brothers had raised her. She'd wanted to be just like Andrew, Ryan and Bobby, and so she'd never worn dresses or pink or played with dolls. And it had probably been a little easier on her dad not to have to learn to braid her hair or take her clothes shopping or paint her toenails, so he'd let her be.

And now this was what she looked like: one of her brothers. Except even her brothers had more style than she did.

Maybe it was time to change her look—just a little. Wear something besides T-shirts and jeans all the time. Learn to put on mascara without looking like a raccoon. She didn't even own perfume.

She wondered if Xander would be attracted to her if she was a little more girlie. But the problem with that was then it would bother her that artifice had gotten his attention instead of the real her.

She flopped herself down on her bed. How she wished her mama was here to talk with about this stuff.

Not that her father hadn't done a great job last night, she thought with a smile.

She heard one of the dogs scratching at the door and she opened it, and Dobby and Harry jumped on the end of her bed and curled up with their satisfied little sighs.

"We'll see," she told them. "Lots to think about. Maybe I'll even talk it over with you two."

Dobby eyed her, but Harry was already snoring.

Chapter Six

Most Sunday afternoons, Lily taught a cooking class for kids. For the summer, she also offered two workshops for older kids, which met for an hour every week on her three days off. Today was a one-day seminar for five- to eight-year-olds, which a parent or caregiver needed to attend, as well. She adored working with the young cooks.

She scanned the registration list. She had six students—her maximum so that she'd be able to give them all attention—including Wren Crawford. As the kids and their adults arrived in the rec center kitchen, Lily forced herself to stop thinking about Xander and to focus on the class. So far, everyone was here except for the Crawford duo. There were two dads, one with a daughter, one with a son. And three moms, two with daughters and one with a son. Lily checked them all off on her list, kneeling down to say hi to each of her students and handing them their special orange apron that they would take home at the end of class and could decorate with fabric markers.

She couldn't help but notice how nicely dressed two of the three women were. Granted, one was in a T-shirt and jeans like Lily, but the other two looked so polished, one in a flippy cotton skirt and ruffly tank, the other in a blue sundress.

Lily glanced at her jeans and blah sneakers. Granted, she was about to get salsa all over herself, but wasn't that what an apron was for? Ina Garten and Nigella Lawson didn't wear T-shirts to cook in. Why should Lily?

You're not one of the Hunt boys, she told herself. *You're you. Lily. And you've never really figured out what expressing that means—aside from cooking.*

She sure liked Layla Carew's pale blue cotton sundress with the embroidered hem. The woman looked pretty and comfortable and summery. Who said Lily couldn't wear something like that?

No one.

"Is this it?" Layla asked suddenly, looking around. "I thought Hunter Crawford signed up for this class."

"I thought so, too," Monica Natowky added. Monica—wearing the flippy skirt and lots of bangles on her bare, toned arms.

Lily sighed inwardly, her gaze going to their ring fingers. Empty!

Were they here for the kids' class? Or to land a Crawford?

She glanced at the third woman's finger: gold band. And what had Darby Feena come to the kids' cooking class wearing? A T-shirt and jeans. Normal, appropriate wear for the activity!

Still, it would be nice to not always be mistaken for a

nanny or a student herself. When Layla had first arrived, she'd gone up to Monica to introduce herself, thinking *Monica* was the teacher.

Ugh. Lily had no time to be thinking about her wardrobe issues. She had a class to get started.

Right then, Xander came in, holding Wren's hand, and Lily wanted to tell him to drop off Wren and leave. Who did he and his brothers think they were? Their single status and gorgeousness were causing a scene all over town, making women act like idiots. Including her. Please!

And boy, did he live up to every bit of that gorgeousness. He wore dark jeans and a green henley shirt, his shoulders so broad and his hips so slim. Lordy, Lily could look at him all day.

"Hi, Hunter," Layla trilled with a toss of her blond curls behind her shoulders. "I'm Layla and this little nugget is Mia."

Lily was about to introduce Xander and Wren to the group when Monica practically knocked her out of the way to rush over to shake his hand.

"Hunter, it's *so* nice to meet you. I'm Monica, and this is my darling nephew, Jasper. Jasper wants to be a rancher someday, too. Don't you, Jasper?"

"Yup," the cute little boy in the Western shirt and cowboy hat said.

Xander looked at both of them as if they were from Mars. "I'm not Hunter. Sorry."

Their gazes went right to *his* ring finger.

"Oh, no apologies necessary!" Monica said. "You must be one of this li'l angel's *uncles*, then."

Oh, brother. Had these two women *really* found out that Hunter Crawford had registered for the course with his daughter and signed up for that reason? Xander gave her a sheepish kind of smile as if he was so innocent. Humph!

Lily broke up this display of ick by announcing it was time to get class started. Monica frowned and darted back to her space. Each student and adult shared one table where Lily had set up bowls of precut veggies. In the first row there was an empty table next to one of the dads; Xander chose that spot instead of the free table beside Monica and in front of Layla. She could practically hear them sigh with disappointment.

"Welcome!" she said in her loud, kid-friendly voice. She stood behind a table full of bowls and her electric hot plates. "I'm Lily Hunt, your cooking teacher for today. Guess what we're making?"

"Tacos!" lots of happy voices shouted.

"That's right. We're making vegetarian tacos. Who knows what vegetarian means?"

A little boy raised his hand, and Lily called on him.

"It means a food that isn't meat!" the boy said.

"Right!" Lily said. "Now, I love beef tacos. And chicken tacos. And salmon tacos. But today we'll make vegetarian tacos with delicious black beans, cheese, salsa, lettuce and tomatoes!"

"Yay!" a few of the more exuberant kids shouted.

"Okay, kids!" Lily began. "I've already cut up the tomatoes because using knives can be really dangerous and only adults should use sharp knives. But I want each of you to come up to my table and point out a tomato from my bowl of whole vegetables. I'll give you a hint what a tomato looks like. It's red. And round."

"I see it!" a girl shouted.

Six pairs of little legs went running over to Lily's

table, each pointing at a plump tomato in Lily's big bowl and then taking a small bowl of cut tomatoes.

"Okay, now you can go back to your seats," Lily said. She explained where tomatoes came from, and that they were actually considered a fruit *and* a vegetable. There were lots of animated questions about vines and seeds, and then Lily asked each student to take their big measuring cup and scoop out a half cup of the cut-up tomatoes. Lily demonstrated where to find the markers on the cups, then instructed the adults to show them closer up.

"I love tomatoes!" Wren said, jumping up and down, her blond pigtails flying. "I know how much a half cup is. My daddy lets me help cook!"

"That's awesome, Wren!" Lily said.

Xander shot her a smile, and Lily's knees gave a slight shake.

She headed over to the tables to high-five kids as they measured out the tomatoes, trying not to look at Xander. She kept her attention on the class, sending each student back to her teacher's table to choose a head of lettuce, and after a mini lesson on lettuce, the kids got to shred theirs by hand (after washing up!) and add their half cup of lettuce to their bowls. Lily gave a little talk on cheese next, having the kids taste three different kinds and learning why some cheeses complemented certain foods. Finally it was time to heat the beans, and Lily told them all about where beans came from. For ease of the class, she'd opened up several cans of Goya black beans and the kids gathered around the low table where she had a hot plate, having each kid add a pinch of the various spices. Then the students added diced tomatoes and spices to a bowl for the salsa, some of which ended up on their aprons and in their hair. Finally, it was time to learn about taco shells, and after those were heated up, everyone was excited to build their tacos with their bowl of ingredients.

"Wow," Xander said from the first row. "I had no idea tacos were so educational. I really learned quite a bit."

"Me, too," Monica trilled. "I make the best tacos, don't I, Jasper? We should invite Xander and Wren over to have them this week."

"Wren's a *girl*!" Jasper said very earnestly.

"Boys can be friends with girls, you know!" Wren shouted over her shoulder.

"Well, in any case," Monica said, "we'd love to have you over. Tuesday night?"

Was this woman really asking Xander out right here, in a children's cooking class, in front of everyone? Including his six-year-old niece? Good God.

"I appreciate the invitation," Xander told her, his voice awkward to Lily's ears, "but I'm afraid my schedule is crazy the next few months."

At least he hadn't said yes. But still!

"Ah, well, if you find yourself with a free night, just look me up. Monica Natowsky."

He gave her a tight smile and turned his attention to the taco shell that Wren was filling with her bounty.

"I can't wait to eat this!" Wren said. "Can I take a bite?" she asked Lily.

"Let's wait till everyone's tacos are assembled, because that would be extra polite, right?" Lily said.

"Right!" Wren said, looking around.

"Okay! Looks like everyone is ready. Bite!" Lily said.

The crunching was music to her ears. There was a round of *mmm*s and *this is so good* and a few *I love this class*es.

And then after cleanup and a quick Q&A, Lily dismissed the class, already missing them as the adorable little students left. Monica and Layla were among the last to leave, wistfully looking at Xander, who was deep in conversation with one of the dads.

"Uncle Xander, can I go play in the playground with Molly?" Wren asked.

"I'll watch them," the girl's dad said.

Xander smiled. "Sure, go ahead. I'll be there in a few minutes. I'm just going to say thank you to Ms. Hunt."

Wren wrapped her arms around Lily's hips, surprising her quite happily, then ran out with her friend, Molly's dad right behind them.

And now suddenly it was just Lily and Xander.

"I meant it—I had a blast," he said. "You have a real gift for teaching kids."

"Thanks. That means a lot to me. I really love working with children of all ages."

"Did you know you had a tiny fleck of cheese on your cheek?" he asked, stepping closer and reaching out his hand.

"No, actually," she whispered, her belly tightening. "I did not."

He dusted off the cheese, his brown eyes on hers, serious, intense. And unless she was delusional, which she might be, there was desire in those depths.

He leaned in.

And dammit, even if he'd discovered a black bean in her hair and was leaning close to flick that off, she was leaning in, too.

But this time, he kissed her. His hands were on her face, drawing her closer, his lips firm and soft and tender and passionate all at the same time.

Oh, my.

Yessssss!

Kissing Xander was everything she'd fantasized about—day and night—since their date in Rust Creek Falls Park.

He opened his eyes and stepped back, looking at her, his expression changing. She still saw that unexpected desire, but something else seemed to be shoving its way in. She had the feeling the kiss had taken him by surprise. That he wasn't even sure he'd meant to do it.

Nooo! Desire good. Confusion not good.

"That was some kiss," she whispered, because that was the only voice she had at the moment. "I liked it. A lot."

Sarah would be proud. So would Lily's mother. *State your intent. Stake your claim. Put yourself out there!*

There would be no take-backsies here. Not of that kiss, which she still felt burning her lips.

His smile was warm as he reached out his hand and touched her cheek. The way a man did when he cared about a woman he had just kissed passionately.

Yesss!

"I need to be honest, Lily."

Oh, cripes, she thought, her heart plummeting. *No, don't be!*

"I don't know what the hell I'm doing," he said, taking a step back and leaning against the table. "There seems to be something between us, but as I've said, I'm not looking for a relationship. I'm not looking to start something."

Jeez. Did he have to be *that* honest? Of course she wanted the truth, hard as it was to hear, but couldn't he leave her a little room to hope?

"I got burned bad right before I left Dallas," he said, running a hand through his dark hair. "I went to my girlfriend's condo to surprise her with an engagement ring, to tell her I'd stay in Texas for her instead of moving to Montana with my family. I found her in bed with my best friend—a lifelong buddy I *thought* was my best friend. I told them both to go to hell. A few days later, I left the state with my family, so that helped, but the burn... That followed me, Lily."

She reached out a hand to his arm. "I understand." Her heart ached for him, for how painful that must have been. The shock and betrayal. The loss of two people who'd meant a lot to him. Suddenly, his push-and-pull made sense.

He stared at her for a minute and it seemed like he almost wished she'd been less compassionate. As in maybe he was hoping she'd say: *Well, then don't go around kissing women you don't intend to start something with,* so that he could argue and she could huff away. Giving *him* the out.

She wouldn't ever say that. Granted, she had very little experience when it came to romance and love, but she knew how even a minor rejection had hurt. She could only imagine how hurt Xander had been and the number it had done on his head—and heart. He felt something for her, but he didn't want to *go there*.

"Well," he said, taking another step back. "I'd better go check on Wren."

She wanted him to stay, for them to keep talking—openly and honestly. But she could tell he needed some space, and his niece was waiting for him outside. "Tell her she gets an A-plus for today."

But not you, because you're keeping me at arm's length and you've got long arms.

He hurried out, the door closing behind him.

Lily touched her mouth, the feel of his lips still lingering. Now what? He'd kissed her. A real kiss. Then told her he wasn't interested in more.

Listen when someone tells you something! That would be the wise thing. But her heart was in full control of her right now, and it wanted Xander Crawford.

And Lily Hunt had never been one to *not* go for what she wanted.

After dropping Wren off with Sarah and Logan for the rest of the afternoon, Xander headed to the cattle barn. He needed to do some hard labor, some serious mucking, to get his mind unstuck. Right now, his brain was on a loop about how good it had felt to finally kiss Lily, to do what he'd been thinking about for weeks now. But then his head had come to a hard stop as if it had hit the brakes itself. He didn't know what he thought. Felt. Wanted.

He pulled on plastic gloves and grabbed a rake and headed into the back stalls. A few minutes in, he knew he was right to take on this chore instead of an afternoon off as had been the plan. His mind was already clearing.

Now all he could think about was how young Lily was. Just starting out in life. And he felt so world-weary and cynical. His trust level was nil. And that diamond ring he'd bought back in Dallas? He'd marched right back to the jeweler, needing that black velvet box out of his hands and life immediately, and thankfully, the shop had taken it back, refunding every pricey cent. That had felt good, at least. But if anyone had ever told Xander that one day he'd fall in love and plan a surprise engagement, only to end up returning the ring the next morning, he would have said they were nuts.

He heard footsteps and the humming of a Frank Sinatra song, which meant it was his dad who'd entered the barn.

Xander poked his head out of the stall to find Max Crawford pulling on a pair of black heavy-duty plastic gloves like Xander had on and then grabbing a rake, too.

"Hey, thought you had the day off," Max said. "I'm on mucking duty today."

"I know, but I could use some hard labor, so here I am."

"Fine with me," Max said. "My least favorite job on the chore chart." He and his rake went into the next stall, the strains of "Fly Me to the Moon" drifting in the air. "Interesting that you need to muck out stalls after taking Lily's cooking class. Almost like that woman has you all topsy-turvy."

He sighed and rested his chin on the top of the rake. "I guess she does. I didn't move to Montana looking for a relationship, Dad. The opposite, in fact."

"I know you had a bad breakup in Dallas, Xander. But that shouldn't hold you back from finding happiness again."

"You haven't," he said, then wished he could take it back.

But he couldn't; it was out there, hanging over the edges of their side-by-side stalls.

Hell, maybe it was good to finally have this conversation. His dad hadn't remarried, hadn't gotten serious with a woman Xander's entire life.

Because his wife walking out on him, on their family, had been unbearable.

"Sorry," Xander said, feeling like a heel. "That's your business and I have no right—"

"Yes, you do," Max said. "You have every right. If I'm going to push a determined wedding planner on you and your brothers, you have a right to know why I don't practice what I preach."

Xander came out of the stall and stood in the doorway of his dad's. His father was tall and imposing but somehow looked so...vulnerable.

"I just want you boys to be happy. To have what I didn't. I might have given up on happiness for myself but hell if I'm gonna stand by and watch what that taught you boys. You need love. Partners. Family. That's what makes the world go round, Xan. Bitterness just makes it come to a screeching halt."

Xander nodded, and then walked into the stall and embraced his dad, Max stiffening with clear surprise at first, and then hugging him back. "I know. Believe me."

He headed back into his stall and started mucking away. And for the next couple of hours, he and his dad worked in silence, Xander's mind clearer but no answers on the horizon.

Chapter Seven

Communication from Xander Crawford following The Kiss:

Sunday night, a text: Thanks again for the fun and informative cooking class today. Wren had a great time.

Response: My pleasure.

Monday morning: I woke up craving lobster rolls for some reason. On the specials menu at MM?

Response: No, sorry.

Monday night: Lobster rolls tomorrow?

Response: No, sorry.

Later Monday night: Jeez, I thought I had an in with the chef.

No response.

Tuesday morning: Just checking in.

Response: Smiley face emoji. Super busy—have a great day!

The old Lily might have raced over to Kalispell Monday morning to buy lobster and all the fixings for lobster rolls. Eager to please. Like a puppy. The old Lily might also have kept the text conversation going on Tuesday by asking open-ended questions.

But a new Lily had taken root inside her—every day, with every satisfied diner at the Maverick Manor, every "great job, Lily" from her boss, every decent grade on her schoolwork, every time she understood a difficult business concept. Add to it these new feelings for a man—the first time she'd truly fallen in love—and Lily felt different in her bones. Like a woman instead of a kid.

On Wednesday afternoon, Lily bit into her cruller at Daisy's Donuts, Sarah Crawford sipping her iced latte while baby Sophia napped in her stroller at their table by the window. She filled in Sarah on the big kiss and the conversation that followed—not the details of what Xander had shared about his ex, but just the gist that he had a big closed sign over his heart.

Sarah's eyes lit up. "This kiss says everything!"

"I want to hope so. But he told me he's not looking to start anything. *That* actually says everything."

"He's a cowboy who's been kicked in the head by unexpected love," Sarah said. "He needs time to reclaim his own mind. And when he does, watch out, Lily."

Lily laughed. "I love your optimism. But I won't hold my breath." She bit her lip, thinking about that kiss. Sometimes she could still feel the imprint of his lips. "You know what? I'm not even going to think about it. Xander needs to figure out how he feels, right? I think I should just take a step back. Kind of like I was doing with my responses to his texts."

Sarah took a bite of her chocolate cider donut. "I have

to say that the way you responded to those messages sure kept them coming. I love the 'Just checking in.'" She laughed. "Poor guy."

Lily smiled. "I like this newer, wiser me. I'm not sitting around endlessly thinking about him and his deal. I'm focusing on work, school and my future. Which I hope includes him, of course," she admitted.

"I have faith," Sarah said with a big nod.

Lily sipped her own iced latte and couldn't help but notice again how nice Sarah looked—for just coffee out with a friend. Sarah wore pale pink capri pants, a white tank top with a ruffled hem around the V-neck, and adorable multicolored leather sandals that wrapped around her ankles three times. She was the sleep-deprived mother of a baby and yet she wore a little makeup and earrings and she smelled like a hint of perfume—not baby spit-up. She looked this way because she wanted to. It truly had to be that simple.

"I want a makeover," Lily said.

Sarah's eyes lit up. "Ooh!"

"I want to look like *me*—the me I've never explored because I was too busy wanting to fit in with my brothers and be accepted by them. I want my outside to match all the changes I've made on the inside. I'm going for my dreams."

"Including the six-foot-two-inch one?" her friend asked.

Lily smiled, then bit her lip. "Crazy thing is, Sarah— he likes me *this* way. Salsa on my cheek, onion-scented hands, loose jeans, no makeup, no style. He likes me as I am." The truth of it practically knocked the breath out of her. The way he looked at her—even on that first nondate in the park—was proof. The kiss was proof.

Xander Crawford likes me, she thought, a rush of happiness swelling in her belly. *He's attracted to* me.

"Okay, now I'm going to cry," Sarah said, tearing up. "I know exactly what you mean."

"But wanting this makeover is for *me*. About *me*. I want to find out who I am if I let myself really go for it. So will you help me?"

"Is right now too soon?" Sarah asked with a grin. "I wish I didn't have my dentist appointment in fifteen minutes or we could take off for Kalispell now and hit the shops and salon."

"Need me to babysit?" Lily asked.

"Actually, I have a sitter all lined up who should arrive any minute now."

"Oh, well next time, call me," Lily said. "I love taking care of Sophia." She looked at the beautiful sleeping baby, her bow lips quirking.

One day, I want a Sophia of my own, she thought—for the first time. She sucked in a breath as a sense of absolute wonder overtook her. She'd never really thought about getting married or having children; she'd always figured she would, but the notion had always seemed a few years down the road. Several years.

Lily bit her lip again as she wondered if falling in love with Xander Crawford had anything to do with her sudden baby fever.

"How about tomorrow morning for the makeover?" Sarah asked. "Ooh, Lily—you can debut your new look at the dance Saturday night!"

"I wasn't planning on going," she said, thinking about the Rust Creek Falls Summer Sunset Dance, held every year in a different location. The whole town always turned up, apparently—well, except her, and no one had ever asked her to the dance, not that she couldn't have gone with a girlfriend. Dances had never been her thing. Starting with semiformals in middle school and working up to the senior prom, which she hadn't gone to, either.

"I know for a fact Xander will be there," Sarah said, wriggling her eyebrows. "All the Crawfords are going."

"Oh, great," Lily said. "I can watch Xander dance with every single beauty in town. Wonderful way to pass the time."

"Want to know a secret?" Sarah asked. "But you can't tell Xander I told you."

Lily leaned closer. "Scout's honor." She held up three fingers.

"Logan confided in me that Xander actually told Viv Dalton to only set him up with women he'd have nothing in common with. Viv reported him to Max, their dad, who was asking for a status report and why Xander wasn't engaged yet." Sarah laughed. "That man. Seriously."

"Nothing in common with?" Lily repeated. "Why bother, then?"

"Want to know Logan's theory?"

Lily leaned closer again.

"Logan thinks his brother is trying to just get his dad off his back—by dating at all—and only agreeing to dates with women he won't fall for because he's already fallen for someone and can't deal."

Lily's eyes widened. "That's some theory."

"With a lot of truth to it. Doesn't that sound about right?"

"I'm hardly used to flattering myself, Sarah. The man kissed me. Once. That doesn't mean anything."

"We'll see," Sarah said with a devious grin. "So tomorrow—girlie day in Kalispell?"

"I have to be at work at four. Otherwise I'm free."

Sarah actually clapped with excitement. "Can't wait."

Huh. The *new* new Lily at the Summer Sunset Dance. With Xander in attendance. Could be very interesting.

"There's my adorable niece," came a very familiar masculine voice.

"Did I mention my sitter is Xander and that I asked him to meet me here?" Sarah asked with yet another devilish grin as she stood up. "How nice that both of you are in the same place at the same time and will have to communicate in person. You might even ask him to the dance Saturday night," she whispered.

Ooh, Sarah was good—Lily had to hand it to her. Even if she wanted to bop her friend over the head with the rest of her cruller.

Sarah then leaned over the stroller to give Sophia a kiss on the forehead. "Be good for Uncle Xander and Auntie Lily," she whispered.

Lily's eyes widened. Auntie Lily. Uncle Xander.

Technically, Lily had always been Auntie Lily, before Sarah had even married into the Crawford family.

"Xander, thank you so much for babysitting!" Sarah said. "Lucky for me I ran into you at the Ambling A this morning just when I was fretting over needing care at the last minute. Turns out I could have asked Lily since she has the afternoon off."

Yup, Sarah was *good*.

He smiled, giving Lily a nod but keeping his attention on Sarah. "My pleasure, really. Least I can do since you'll be stuck in a dentist's chair." He turned to Lily. "Nice to see you," he said awkwardly.

"You, too," she said.

Sarah gave her a quick hug, gave Xander a quick rundown on what to expect—which was Sophia sleeping for the next hour—thanked him again and then dashed out.

"So you're free right now?" Xander said. "Want to help me babysit? I'd do anything for my sister-in-law, but if Sophia wakes up, I have no idea what to do. Logan gave me a few lessons over the past few months in how to hold her, but I'm not even good at *that*."

Lily laughed. "Consider me at your service."

He blushed slightly, and maybe she shouldn't have said that. Of course, she hadn't meant anything flirty by it, but hell, she was the new her and maybe she *had*.

Xander tried not to stare at Lily, but he could barely drag his eyes off her. The past few days he'd thought of little else besides that incredible kiss in the rec center kitchen. And he needed to concentrate when he was working at the Ambling A. Yesterday he'd almost knocked himself out by stepping on a rake he hadn't noticed lying across the barn floor. This morning, his brother Finn had apparently said "Earth to Xander" three times before he realized someone was asking him something out by a pasture fence.

So when he'd run into Sarah, who'd looked frantic about a dentist appointment and needing someone to watch Sophia, he'd volunteered. Babies slept a lot, right? He figured he'd park his keister in Daisy's for the hour and a half, drink three or four caffeinated beverages, give the stroller a gentle rock if Sophia got fussy, and have a little time to himself to get his head clear.

He was having to do that a lot lately.

And here, right in front of him, was the woman keeping his head in the clouds.

A little wail came from the stroller, a tiny fist jutting out in complaint.

"Someone woke up on the wrong side of the stroller this afternoon," Xander said with a smile. He unbuckled the harness and carefully scooped out Sophia, holding her the way Logan had taught him and rubbing her back. Hey, this was as easy as he thought it would be.

Until Sophia started screeching.

"Thought I was getting the knack of this," Xander said, frowning. "Guess not."

Sophia's cheeks were red and she started waving her tiny fists.

"It's me. Uncle Xan," he said, rocking her side to side and bouncing her in his arms. "Peekaboo!"

"Waaah!" Sophia screamed.

"What am I doing wrong?" Xander asked.

"Sometimes a baby just gets fussy and needs a new face," Lily said. "Want me to try?"

"Waah!"

"Please," he said, handing Sophia over.

Lily took the baby, rubbing her back and cooing to her. Sophia seemed to like that. She was still flailing her arms but her cheeks were less red. "There, there," she whispered, rubbing her back some more.

Sophia stopped crying.

"Lucky you were here. Or Eva would have kicked me and Sophia out," he said, sending a rueful smile over to the donut shop manager behind the counter.

"How'd you get so good with babies?" Xander asked. "You're the baby of your family."

"I've always babysat. Since I was twelve. And before I started offering cooking classes to supplement my income, I worked part-time at a day care in the infant room."

"I've done group-brother babysitting so that Logan and Sarah could get some time to themselves, and among the five of us, we did pretty well, thanks to Hunter, who knows what he's doing. I thought I had this."

Lily laughed. "I can just picture you Crawford brothers hovering around a tiny baby, trying to figure her out."

"We're pretty clueless, but hey, we do love our niece."

"She's one lucky little girl to have such doting uncles." She gazed at Sophia, giving her another bounce and letting her stretch her legs. The baby seemed much happier. "Well, I've got the next couple hours free, so I'm happy to help. Why don't we head to my house and change her and give her a bottle if she's hungry, then take her for a walk?"

He liked the idea on two counts. He'd have a pro with him just in case and he'd get to spend time with Lily. "Sounds good. And thanks."

Sophia did not want to go back in the stroller, so Lily held her while Xander wheeled the stroller out of Daisy's Donuts.

"Hi, Xander!" trilled a feminine voice.

Lily glanced up to see a pretty woman with long dark hair and an amazing body smiling at Xander as she approached the shop. The brunette gave Lily a quick assessing glance, seemingly decided she was no competition and turned her megawatt smile back to the hot rancher.

Xander nodded politely and kept walking, the woman's sexy smile turning into a sulky frown.

"Get that a lot, huh?" she asked as they headed up North Broomtail Road.

Who'd think it would be such a drag to have attractive women throwing themselves at you? But it was.

"Thanks to my dad, yes," he said. "First there are the women who are looking to meet Mr. Right, and my dad created his own dating service with six men. Now five. Then there are the women who heard a rumor that my dad promised Viv Dalton a million bucks to get us all married, and they figure there's big money in the family. So, double whammy."

Lily smiled. "Don't forget the women who simply like the idea of going on a date with an interesting cowboy newcomer. That was me, you know. When Viv asked if I wanted to be set up with Knox, I wasn't thinking about marriage or a million dollars. I was just thinking it sounded like fun. A rancher from Texas? With five brothers? I'd bet we'd have a lot to talk about."

"Touché," he said. "But women like you are few and far between."

"I don't know about that, Xander. I think women and men—everyone—just want what their heart desires."

"That's a nice way of putting it," he said.

"People are just people, Xander. Not everyone is for everyone—that's the thing to know. Everything else is none of our business."

"Meaning?"

"Let's use your family as an example. Knox clearly wasn't the guy for me. If he was, he'd have gone on the date. But he didn't so we didn't get the opportunity to see if there was something there. You stepped in, and we hit it off. Knox and his reasons for canceling are not my concern or my business. What matters is who I *do* connect with. Not who I don't and the reasons why."

"You learned this in Economics 101?" he asked.

Lily laughed. "I've been doing a lot of thinking lately about what draws people together and pulls them apart. Why some people work and some don't. Half is chemistry and half is timing."

"I'll buy that. And if the timing is wrong?"

"Then that chemistry goes to waste. All that connection, interest, fun, desire, sharing, talking, laughing—buh-bye."

He glanced at her. "That seems like a shame."

"Yup, sure does."

For a twenty-three-year-old newbie at life, she sure was smart about human interaction, he thought. Maybe too smart.

They arrived at Lily's house, Sophia still content and surveying the world—or Rust Creek Falls—from Lily's arms. As they headed in, Xander hoped he'd run into Andrew so he could find out how things were going with Heidi. The two had gone out a bunch of times already. And they were a good example of what Lily was talking about. Xander hadn't been the guy for Heidi, but one suggestion of Andrew Hunt and voilà—they were practically engaged.

Chemistry and timing. If you had both, you had everything.

He and Lily had chemistry, but the timing? Not so good.

The Hunt house turned out be empty. Everyone was still at work, so Lily suggested they hang out in the living room and let Sophia crawl around the big soft rug. But first, Lily took her in the bathroom to change her, and strange as it was, he missed the two of them when they were gone, even for the two minutes it took Lily to return with a smiling Sophia in her arms.

They both lay down on opposite sides of the rug to create a pen of sorts for Sophia, making peekaboo faces to get her to crawl to them. Sophia shrieked with delight every time Xander revealed his face. He laughed, having too good a time playing house with Lily and Sophia.

Way too good a time.

As Sophia crawled all over Lily, the beautiful redhead making exaggerated faces at the baby and blowing raspberries on her belly, he was completely transfixed.

He could see himself coming home to Lily and their baby.

Whoa, he thought, bolting upright. Where had *that* come from?

"So how many kids do you want?" Lily asked. "Someday, I mean."

"Honestly, I've never really thought about that. I like the idea of a big family like I had, older siblings, younger siblings. Always someone around."

"I don't know about the younger siblings, but I liked growing up in a big family, too. I always envisioned four kids at least."

"Four little redheads," he said with a grin. "And freckles across their noses."

She touched a hand to her nose. "These were the bane of my existence when I was a teenager. I've gotten used to them."

"I like freckles." *I like your freckles. I like everything about you.*

The smile that lit up her face almost did him in. He watched her lift Sophia into her arms and hoist her high in the air. *Focus on the baby, not the woman. You're babysitting. That's all that's going on here.*

His father had set some crazy roller coaster on high

speed and so, Xander had met Lily Hunt in the first place. Otherwise, he wouldn't know her. He'd be working the Ambling A, focusing on renovating the ranch, his new family home—his new life. Falling for a woman who could destroy him with a snap of her fingers? No, thank you. Not again. He might have feelings for Lily, but hell if he'd let them go deeper than he already had.

To reinforce that, he let himself think about something he'd forced from his mind six weeks ago.

Britney in bed with Chase. The woman he'd been about to propose to. And his lifelong best friend.

We're so sorry. We didn't mean for it to happen. We're in love, Xander. This isn't just some affair.

Yeah, that made it better.

He felt himself tightening up, the walls closing in. Good. Because he felt like himself again. Like the man he'd been the past six weeks. Keeping to himself. Working hard.

Ping.

The sound shook him out of his bad memories, and he leaned his head back, sucking in a breath.

Lily had received a text, and as Sophia crawled over to him, Lily grabbed her phone. "Sarah's all done." Lily texted something back. "She'll be by to pick up Sophia in a few minutes."

Good. He needed to get out of here. Breathe some open air.

Relief flooded him when Sarah arrived. Lily settled the baby back in her stroller, and there it was again, that tug of his heart as he watched her. He was barely aware of the small talk he made about what a good baby Sophia was, how Lily had saved the day with her mad baby skills. The door closed behind Sarah, and then it was just the two of them.

Leave. Head to the door. Go.

But he was rooted to the floor. He wanted out. He wanted to stay. He didn't know what the hell he wanted.

"Thanks for helping out," he said. Awkwardly, with his hands in his pockets. "I guess I'll go now."

"Any time," she said.

And still he didn't move.

They stared at each other for a moment, both just... standing there.

"You know, you never did get your cooking lesson, Xander. If you have time now, I could show you how to make a delicious bacon and cheese omelet, which is exactly what I'm craving this second."

You should leave. This woman has mystical, magical powers over you.

Which was clearly why he *couldn't* leave. And besides, he was hungry.

"That does sound really good." He followed her into the kitchen, dying to pull her into his arms and kiss her again.

But she now had a carton of eggs in her hands, and had instructed him to crack five in a bowl. He was so focused on her face, her freckles, her lips that he hadn't heard half of what she'd said in the past few minutes.

He took the carton and got busy cracking, getting only two little bits of shell in, which Lily scooped out with a spoon.

"Anyone home?" a male voice shouted from the front door.

Good thing, too. Because he'd been about to lean in

again. Close. Despite everything he'd been feeling just ten minutes ago.

"Sounds like Andrew," Lily said. "In the kitchen," she called back.

"What else is new?" Andrew said as he came sauntering in with Heidi right behind him. He smiled. "Ah, *this* is new," he said at the sight of Xander. "Or is it?" he asked with a grin.

"Xander and I are friends," Lily said, cutting her flashing green eyes at her brother.

"Got it," Andrew repeated with a little too much mirth in his voice. "You're just friends."

"Xander," Heidi said with a warm smile, "did I ever thank you for fixing me up with Andrew? I've meant to."

"I'm glad it worked out," Xander said.

"It's worked out and then some," Andrew said, dipping Heidi and giving her a dramatic kiss.

Heidi laughed and swatted him. "I'll tell ya," she said to Xander and Lily, "over the past few months I must have gone on thirty dates. I thought maybe I was just too picky or that I'd never find my guy. And then out of nowhere, a date very strangely fixes me up with another date—and he's the one. You just never know. Life is crazy."

"I love that," Lily said. "And I agree. You just never know. Being open, saying yes—that's how you find what you really need."

"Exactly," Heidi said.

Again, he thought about what Lily had said about chemistry and timing. Heidi could have so easily told him no way, that she didn't need a blah date setting her up with her next blah date. But she'd been open to possibilities, and now it looked like she and Andrew were headed somewhere serious.

Possibilities. Exactly what he didn't want to explore. For damned good reasons.

"So I'm giving Xander a cooking lesson on the art of omelets," Lily told her brother and Heidi. "Bacon and cheese. If you guys are hungry, stick around and you could join us."

"I love bacon," Andrew said. "So I guess this is our first double date, Lily."

"Just *friends*, remember?" Lily said.

Did "just friends" want to kiss her the way he'd imagined doing so a second ago? No.

"I'm going to try not to burn the bacon," Xander said to change the subject. He grabbed the package from the counter and used a knife to slit open the side.

"Well, we'll be in the living room," Andrew said. "Sorry in advance about all the PDA you might be forced to witness."

He got another swat from Heidi for that, and then Xander was once again alone with Lily in the kitchen.

"They're very sweet," Lily said. "I'm so happy for my brother. His life is really coming together. Now if you could just get Bobby and Ryan hooked up, they'll be out of my hair, too."

He laughed. "Sorry, but I told Viv I'm done with the fix-ups. So I won't have any referrals to make."

She stared at him. "Oh?"

He nodded, using the tongs to lay the bacon in the big square fry pan. *I thought I could stop thinking about you by dating women I'd never really be interested in. But nothing makes me stop thinking about you.*

Silencing that inner voice, he barked at himself, *Get*

*your mind back on the cooking lesson. Get control of
your own head, man.*

"So you were saying I can pan-fry bacon or bake it
in the oven?" he asked. "I think my dad bakes it. Half
the time it's burned."

"That might be a temperature issue. And keeping it
in too long. With bacon, you have to keep a steady eye.
I like frying because the smell fills the air faster and I
like how the oil jumps in the pan. I know, I'm crazy."

He smiled. "It's fun getting your wrist singed by splat-
ters of burning oil?"

She laughed. "I've been through it all, cooking wise.
I can take a little heat."

*Can you? You're twenty-three. So young. So innocent.
So...idealistic.*

Her idealism was one of the reasons he admired her
so much.

God, he wanted to kiss her.

She started talking about cooking temperatures, but
he missed everything she said. Her long red hair, despite
being pulled back into a ponytail, made him want to run
his hands through it. He wanted to kiss every freckle
dotting her nose and cheeks.

"Smells good!" Andrew called from the living room.

Xander had barely been aware the bacon was frying.
He made himself pay attention as she showed him how
to scramble the eggs, which of course he knew, how to
let the omelet set and cook at the same time, when to
add the cheese and bacon and when to fold it. They had
two pans going, two omelets in each, and suddenly they
were ready and smelled amazing. The ones he was responsible for looked a little lopsided, but still delicious.

"We'll eat these," he said. "My first diners can have yours."

She laughed, and again he wanted to pull her against him and just hug her, hold her.

He didn't know how long he was going to be able to contain his feelings for her. If he even should at this point. Maybe they could just see what was between them. Maybe it wouldn't last, they could get each other out of their system, and he could go back to being Not Getting Involved Xander.

"Going to the dance at Sunshine Farm on Saturday night?" he asked as she showed him how to slide the omelet onto a plate.

He suddenly imagined them pressed chest to chest, her arms draped around his neck, his around her waist as they swayed to a slow country ballad. The warm, breezy summer air blowing back her long red hair...

She added a handful of grapes to each plate. "I was just talking to Sarah about it today. The Rust Creek Falls Summer Sunset Dance. Sounds fun. Will you be there?"

"I think all the Crawfords are going, so yes. I'll show my face but I don't know how long I'll stay."

"Well, I'll definitely see you there, then. You'll save me a dance before you rush off into the night?"

"I will," he said, dragging his eyes off her and onto the plates.

It was almost like a date. But not quite. He'd see how it felt, dancing with Lily. Thinking of her as his. A slow ease into giving in to his feelings for her.

It was a start, right?

Chapter Eight

Kalispell was the nearest big town to Rust Creek Falls, a forty-five minute drive but worth it for the access to shops where Lily could look through clothing racks and jewelry displays, and maybe even get her makeup done at a beauty counter. She'd been going to Bee's Beauty Parlor, which was right next door to two of her favorite places—Daisy's Donuts and Wings to Go—ever since her dad realized her hair would need trimming every few months and that his attempts were woefully uneven. Lily had even called Bee's to make an appointment for a real haircut, but they were booked solid because of the dance. Luckily Sarah had gotten recommendations for salons in Kalispell and now Lily was sitting in a huge swivel chair in Hair Genie, a trendy-looking salon in the center of town, Sarah standing beside her.

"So what do you have in mind?" her stylist, Ember

(Lily had no idea if that was her real name or not), a chic young woman all in black, asked as she assessed Lily's hair, running her fingers through it, picking up strands and examining the ends. "Very healthy. You can do anything with this thick, straight, silky texture."

Lily looked at Ember's gorgeous mane, which was exactly what she wanted hers to look like. "I love *your* hairstyle. Would that work on me?"

Ember smiled and nodded. "Absolutely. I just have some simple long layers. Keeps it easy for me to pin up so it doesn't get in my way when I'm working, but the layers give the thick, straight texture a lot of oomph and swing."

"That's perfect for you, Lily," Sarah said, standing on the other side of her and looking at her reflection. "Lily's a chef," she told Ember.

"Then it's vital to keep the front layers very long so they don't fall in your face," Ember said. "Plus, you can dress up the cut or keep it casual—just like with fashion. Let it air-dry or a quick blow-dry for a casual look. Use a heated styling brush or curling iron and you can do amazing beachy waves."

"Perfect. I put myself in your hands," she told Ember. Then she grinned at Sarah. "I'm so excited!"

"Me, too," Sarah said. "Okay, I'm gonna go read magazines—something I never get to do."

Lily looked at the shiny silver scissors in Ember's hand and felt like this moment marked the culmination of everything she'd worked so hard for the past year. Working toward her degree in business. Quitting the Gold Rush Diner for a swanky restaurant like the Maverick Manor and getting promoted to line cook (she had been a prep cook her first six months, but the few times she'd filled in for a cook had caught her boss's attention). Making plans, even if they were just in her head at this point, for having her own place someday, whether a small restaurant or her own catering shop or even both. Her look would now catch up with the woman she'd become on the inside.

She closed her eyes, wanting her haircut to be a surprise.

Twenty-five minutes later, Ember announced she was all done and that it was time to unveil the new Lily Hunt. Sarah came running over and Lily heard her gasp.

She opened her eyes.

Wow. "I love it!" Lily shrieked. Her hair was still long, the layers starting at her shoulders and flipping back a bit to blend in with the rest of her hair. Ember had her move her head from side to side like she was in a shampoo commercial.

"You look amazing!" Sarah said. "It's gorgeous! Chic and stylish but still casual at the same time. It's perfect!"

Lily shot out of her chair and threw her arms around Ember.

The stylist laughed. "I love getting that reaction. See you in six weeks for a trim. Or since you live a bit of a distance, you can just have a local salon keep up the trims, and come to me if you want to make another change. I am your hair genie," she added with a grin and bow.

"Squee!" Lily shouted as she and Sarah left the salon. She couldn't stop touching her hair and shaking it. "I'm going to make you sick after a while, Sarah."

"I completely get your excitement," her friend said. "Ooh, let's check out that clothing shop." She pointed across the street at On Trend, a boutique. "Look at that pretty dress in the window."

Lily was already staring at it. It was a knee-length sundress, a pale pink with spaghetti straps. Sexy and playful. And perfect for the dance.

They linked arms and dashed across the street and into the shop.

Lily found the dress in her size and slung it over her arm, then Sarah directed her to the racks of jeans, wagging her finger when Lily looked at a pair of her usual type of jeans.

"Try these," Sarah said, picking up a pair of dark-wash skinny jeans. "And these. And these."

A saleswoman gathered what they'd chosen so far and hung the items in a dressing room. Sarah came over with armloads of tops and sweaters and pants. Lily had an armful of her own.

Ten minutes later, Lily was in the dressing room. She started with the pale pink dress.

She took off her T-shirt and shorts and slid the dress over her head, the soft fabric lovely against her skin. It fit perfectly, neither tight nor loose. She stood back and looked at herself, tears poking her eyes.

Yes. Yes, yes, yes. This is me.

She stepped out of the dressing room and Sarah literally clapped.

"It's beautiful! It fits you so well! Oh, Lily!"

Lily stared at herself in the floor mirror. "I always shied away from pinks because of my hair, but something about the light pink works. Have I ever worn spaghetti straps? I don't think so."

"You look amazing," Sarah said.

"Want to try these cute shoes with it?" the salesclerk

asked, holding out a pair of silver ballet flats with a pointy toe.

The shoes looked great with the dress and were shockingly comfortable for not being sneakers or the clogs Lily usually wore to work.

A half hour later, Lily brought her "yes" pile to the counter, her gaze drawn to the intimates section. "Maybe a couple of sexy bras and matching undies would round out the plain white cotton and little purple flowers on my current collection."

"Definitely," Sarah said with a grin.

Two lace bras, one a blush color, one black, and two matching pairs of underwear joined the stack on the counter. She was getting the dress, two pairs of skinny jeans, two pairs of slim capris, one black pencil skirt, three tops with cute details and two pretty cardigans. Plus three pairs of shoes—the silver ballet flats, a pair of charcoal leather heels that she could actually walk in and strappy sandals. All the pieces worked together so that she'd have outfits. She couldn't wait to move her current wardrobe of loose, boring jeans and T-shirts to the back of her closet.

Next they stopped in a cosmetics shop, a saleswoman giving her a tutorial on a natural and an evening look. When the woman capped the pink-red lipstick and Lily looked in the mirror at her makeover, she gasped again.

"Whoa. I've never worn this much makeup. But it doesn't look like I'm playing dress-up. It just looks like an enhanced me."

"Exactly," the woman said. "You look very elegant."

"Me, elegant," Lily repeated. "First time anyone's ever called me that!"

Sarah grinned. "Welcome, Enhanced Lily!"

Lily laughed, peering at herself in the mirror, still unable to believe she could look like this if she wanted. "I wonder if Xander will even notice."

Sarah's eyes probably popped. "What? Are you serious?"

Lily sighed. "I don't think what I look like is the issue."

"Well, if the T-shirt and jeans Lily has that man all wrung inside out," Sarah said, "imagine what the sexy Lily is gonna do to him!"

Huh. She hadn't thought of it like that before.

Lily grinned.

"Yes, you're going," Max Crawford bellowed at Knox in the family room at the Ambling A on Saturday afternoon. "And you're going," he said, pointing at Hunter. "And you're going." This was directed at Finn. "The kvetching around here—over a casual summer dance. Give me a break! You're all going and that's that!"

"Well, I guess we're going," Wilder said on a chuckle.

"No one wondered if *you* were going," Knox said to Wilder, a guy who'd always lived up his name. "Of course you're going."

"Damned straight I am," Wilder confirmed. "At least thirty women asked me to save them a dance."

Little did those women know that Wilder was about as interested in marriage as Xander was.

"Ditto," Finn said.

Now *there* was the single women of Rust Creek Falls's best chance of Viv Dalton's "dating service" ending with a walk down the aisle. The dreamer of the family, Finn was always falling in love. Out of love just as fast and hard, but then back in love—with the same enthusiasm. Xander didn't get it.

"Just thirty?" Hunter asked. "Try at least a hundred here."

"Once again," Knox said, "I doubt there are a hundred single women in this town."

"Feels like it, thanks to dear old Dad," Hunter pointed out.

Knox gave a firm nod. "That's the truth."

Logan rolled his eyes. "Oh, you poor, poor guys. Going to a social event where you'll dance with women and have some good food and meet new people."

"Oh, shut up," Xander said. "Once you settled down with Sarah, you were able to walk along the streets of this town in peace again. You have no idea what we go through." He grinned and held up a palm for a high five from Wilder, sitting next to him on the sofa.

Logan threw a pillow at him, and Xander's gaze caught on his brother's wedding ring. Xander sure hadn't seen that coming—the marriage—but Logan had surprised them all. Not only had he fallen crazy in love but with a single mother of a baby. Watching his older brother become a father to little Sophia sometimes stopped Xander in his tracks, stole his breath. Because it was so unexpected? Because it made Xander wonder about himself and whether he'd have a family of his own someday? A wife, a baby? Despite all his head-shaking to the contrary, the thought of a wife and child had been creeping into Xander's head lately.

Like at Lily's house. When they were babysitting Sophia. When he was watching Lily with his niece. All sorts of insane ideas flew through his mind.

Eh, he thought. One Crawford brother out of six did

not mean they were all headed in the direction Logan had gone. He glanced at his brother, who always looked happy these days. Content. Purposeful.

Logan had the lightest hair of the six Crawfords—that *had* to have something to do with it. The darker-haired brothers would remain single the way they were supposed to.

While Finn and Wilder got in an arm-wrestling match, Knox and Logan betting on the winner, and Hunter confirming with his sitter what time she'd be over to watch Wren, Xander took the opportunity to slip away unnoticed. He headed up to his bedroom and shut the door on the voices and laughter in the family room.

Two hours until the dance. Xander moved over to the window overlooking the front of the house, the pastures and fields, the cattle just standing there calming him down. He had no idea what he was so revved up about, anyway.

Because he thought of tonight as a date of sorts? It wouldn't be, not really. It was just a casual dance, being held outdoors at Sunshine Farm, which Eva and Luke Stockton had turned into a guest ranch last year. Sure, he'd dance with Lily once, maybe twice. He'd probably stay for a half hour and then leave.

He'd lost track of how many women asked *him* to save them a dance. Except for one. The only one that mattered. Lily. Which meant maybe he should dance with a lot of women. He might have Lily Hunt on the brain but he didn't want to.

You followed your heart once before, and you got slammed in the gut with a sharp right hook. Punched in the head, too. Knocked out. That was how it still felt.

Britney and Chase were married now. Just like that.

They'd flown to Vegas, figuring their families and friends would stop giving them a hard time about their sudden union and how they'd betrayed "that poor Xander" if they proved they were the real deal. So they'd taken a road trip and married in a chapel in some fancy hotel.

Xander knew this because Chase had written him; how he got his address in Montana, Xander had no clue. But Chase had sent a letter, a real letter, not an email, again saying he was sorry about what happened, that he'd mourn the end of their friendship for the rest of his life, but that he found the right woman, the only woman, and though it killed him that she was his best friend's woman, Britney was his life.

The letter had arrived a couple weeks after Xander had moved to Montana with his family. At the time, he'd quickly read it and almost ripped it up, but then shoved it back in the envelope and stashed it in his top dresser drawer under a pile of socks, where things went to die. Like the one photo he had of his mother. Like a photo of him, Britney and Chase at a carnival photo booth.

Xander went to his dresser and stuck his hand under a bunch of rolled socks until he found the photo. Britney, long blond hair everywhere, Chase with his military-short cut and Xander, with his long dark hair. In one of the four little black-and-white photos, Britney was laughing uproariously at something Chase said while Xander laughed, too. Now that he thought about it, their romance had probably started that day.

Interesting that Xander had held on to the photo. He had no idea why he had—and didn't want to think about it right now. Back under the socks it went, the dresser door shoved shut.

He moved over to his bed and dropped down on it, his gaze landing on his bedside table, on the old diary lying there. Xander had almost forgotten about the diary entirely. He and his brothers had been replacing the rotted floorboards in this room, which Xander had wanted because it faced the front yard and he always liked to face forward, when they found something buried. A jewel-encrusted diary with the letter *A* on the front. *A* for the Ambling A? The ranch had come with the name, and they'd all liked it, liked the unknown history that was behind it, so they'd kept it. Plus, they were ambling men themselves, weren't they?

The diary was worn with time and age—and locked. Someone had buried this diary under the floorboard and had either forgotten about it or passed away. The Ambling A had been a vacant mess for decades until the Crawfords bought the property and started renovating, so who knew how long the diary had been buried under the floor. Or why. Xander had thought about trying to pick the lock, to see if there was anything interesting in the diary about the Ambling A, ranch secrets or a clue to whose diary it was, but a simple attempt to get the lock open hadn't worked and then he just lost interest in the old journal. He wasn't one to write down his thoughts and feelings, though maybe it would help.

Dear Diary,

I found the woman I was about to propose to in bed with my best friend. People suck. Love sucks. Forget the whole damned thing.

Yup, that was how his diary would start. Then maybe he'd get to something like this:

Dear Diary,

There's a redhead named Lily who has me all be-

witched. She's not my type. At all. Except for the fact that I can't stop thinking about her or imagining myself in bed with her. So does that make her my type? I guess it does.

Xander gave a rueful chuckle and stood up. He was losing his mind.

While he was pulling out a shirt, he envisioned himself dancing with Lily under the stars, in the moonlight, his woman in his arms.

His woman? He was *definitely* losing his mind.

Chapter Nine

"*What?*" Andrew Hunt said on a croak.

Lily, halfway down the stairs of her house, almost took her phone out of her new little beaded cross-body purse so that she could snap a photo of her brother's face and his priceless expression. *Surprised* didn't begin to capture it as he stood in the foyer.

Or Bobby's. Or Ryan's. Or her father's.

"*What?*" Andrew repeated, his mouth still dropped open, jaw to the floor.

"Lily?" Ryan asked, peering closer at her as he came out of the kitchen with a beer.

"That's not Lily," Bobby, right behind Ryan, said with a firm shake of his head. "Who are you and what have you done with our baby sister?"

"Oh, my God, that is definitely Lily," her father said, one hand over his mouth, another over his heart.

Oh, brother—literally. She sucked in a breath and finished walking down the stairs, the four Hunts staring at her, mouths still agape.

"I mean, Lily, I've seen you in a dress a time or two," Andrew said, "but this isn't just you in a dress. This is…"

"Lily as a nominee at the Academy Awards," Bobby said. "Wow," he added.

"Fairy Godmother up in your room or something?" Ryan asked, the Hunt green eyes completely confused.

"Can't a girl doll up a little for a dance?" she asked innocently, moving over to the large mirror above a console table in the hallway. She checked her appearance for a stray bit of mascara or something in her teeth.

But nope—she was camera ready.

She'd gone with the pale pink sundress with the spaghetti straps, the hem ending in a swish just above her knees. She wore the pretty earrings she'd bought in Kalispell, silver filigree hoops, and three delicate silver bangles on her left arm. The ballet slippers, which kept the outfit casual and simple, were perfect for an outdoor dance at Sunshine Farm. Makeup, including the famous "smoky" eye Sarah had taught her to do, a sweep of mascara, pink-red lipstick, her layered hair all shiny, bouncy and loose, and a spritz of a perfume sample she'd gotten in the boutique—and she was all ready to go.

Oh, and the blush-colored lace bra and panties underneath it all.

She took a final glance at herself in the mirror, gave her hair a fluff and turned toward the Hunts, who were still all staring at her.

"Uh, *what*?" Andrew asked again.

Lily laughed and faux-bopped him on the arm. "You guys know I've been making a lot of positive changes lately. Working on my business degree, upping my game with my recipes and cooking techniques at the Maverick Manor, really thinking about my future plans, saying yes to experiences I normally wouldn't." She didn't add that those yeses included one to Viv Dalton when she'd asked if Lily wanted to throw her name into the Crawford brothers dating pool. But it was a great example of how she'd gone from *Nah, but thanks* to *Why not?* "So I wanted a new look to reflect who I feel like on the inside. I'm not the scrappy tomboy chasing after you guys in the woods with an insect net anymore."

"Well, you'll always be that girl," her dad said. "But you're this woman, too."

Aww, her father had tears in his eyes. Now he was going to make Lily cry and she would mess up her mascara. She'd practiced applying it four times last night until she got it right, somewhere between natural and enhanced.

"You look flipping amazing, Lil," Andrew said.

"Beautiful," Bobby agreed with a bow.

"You know I like to rib you," Ryan added, "but I have to agree. Wow."

She grinned, thrilled with the response. "Thanks, guys. That means a lot. I'm all dressed up with somewhere to go." *Yes, I am! And look out, Xander.* She couldn't wait for his reaction.

Andrew glanced at his watch. "Speaking of the dance, I need to go pick up Heidi. See you all there."

"Want a ride, Lil?" Ryan asked. "I didn't even think you were going or I would have asked earlier. Bobby and I are picking up a couple friends, then heading over."

"I'll take my car," she said. "But thanks." The Hunt brothers headed out, and Lily breathed a sigh of relief, glad to not be under the microscope any longer.

"Should *I* go?" her father asked. "Dances aren't usually my thing, but…"

Lily felt her eyes widen. "You should!"

"Well, if you're going and look like a princess, I could certainly put on a nice shirt and comb this rat's nest on my head and sway to a country tune or two. Say hello to some people."

Lily's heart leaped. "Go change," she said with a smile. "Maybe your blue shirt with the Western yoke and the gray pants? Or even a pair of dark jeans?"

His eyes lit up. "Back in a jiff," he said, taking the stairs at a dash.

Lots of changes happening in the Hunt household, she thought with a smile. Her. Andrew in a serious relationship with Heidi. Bobby and Ryan in business together with their auto-mechanic shop. And now her dad, who'd dated here and there over the years but never let anything serious develop, was going to a town dance when he never had before.

Five minutes later, her dad was back downstairs, in the Western shirt and jeans Lily had suggested, and his good cowboy boots. He'd combed his hair and even added a little bit of his aftershave.

"You look great, Dad," she whispered, trying to avoid crying.

He nodded, dusting off imaginary lint from his shirt. "*We* look like a million bucks. Shall we?" he said, holding out his arm.

Lily grinned and wrapped her arm around her father's, her heart about to burst.

Xander saw her hair first. And just a swath of it because she was surrounded by people. He'd been on the lookout for Lily since he'd arrived at the dance about fifteen minutes ago, but there had been no sign of her. Now he'd caught a glimpse of that unmistakable red hair, those lush fiery tresses. There was something different about it, the bit he could see. Sleek and...sexy.

He moved closer, craning his neck around Henry Peterman, who was six foot four, built like a linebacker and blocking his vision. He went around Henry, and stopped dead in his tracks.

Whoa.

It was Lily—he was sure of it. But she looked nothing like the Lily he'd known for the past few weeks.

Damn, she cleaned up well.

Henry was saying something to her, and he saw Lily smile politely and respond, then step back. Another guy took Henry's place. Then another.

"Sorry, but I promised my first dance to someone," he heard Lily say.

That was his cue. He sure as hell *hoped* so, anyway.

"Lily?" he said strangely in the form of a question. Whoa, whoa, whoa. "You look beyond beautiful."

She smiled, those gorgeous green eyes all lit up. "Thanks. I needed a change."

"This is some change," he said. "Stunning." He stared at her, completely tongue-tied all of a sudden and unable to think of another thing to say. "Uh, I could go get us some punch. Nice night," he added. *Smooth, Xander. You're great at conversation.*

"I'd rather dance," she said, holding out her hand.

Her soft, pretty hand. She wore sparkly blue nail polish, silver bracelets jangling on her arm. He took her hand and led her over to the dance area, which was pretty crowded. The band was playing an old Shania Twain song he'd always loved, a slow one.

He barely heard the whispers around them as she slid her arms around his neck. *Is that Lily Hunt? Oh, my God, that's Lily. Holy buffalo, did you see Lily Hunt?*

"Guess I'll be getting that a lot tonight," she said, her eyes only on him.

They were practically chest to chest. So close he could see every individual freckle across her nose.

His hands were on her waist, on the soft, silky fabric of her dress. "Pretty in pink," he said. "Isn't that a movie?"

She smiled. "I've seen it at least ten times," she said, tightening her arms around his neck. She glanced around, then looked back at him. "It really is such a gorgeous night. I've heard that this dance is the town's way of saying goodbye to summer every year. I'm definitely not ready to see summer go."

"Me, either." He'd associated Lily with summer since he'd met her at the beginning of August, their first date, if it could really be called that, on a wings-and-sauce picnic in the park.

"And I love all the white lights strung in the trees," she said, staring up at the lights. "So festive and pretty."

"Like you," he said. He hoped to God he wasn't blushing because his cheeks sure were burning.

She laughed. "You're not used to seeing me like this."

"No. I could get used to it, though. I think. You looked great the way I met you. And you look great now."

She stopped swaying and stared at him, her expression…wistful. "That means a lot to me. Thank you."

They continued dancing, his throat going so dry at being this close to her, holding her, breathing in the delicious, sexy scent she wore, that he needed some punch or he'd pass out.

"How about that punch now?" he asked.

"I'd love some."

He headed past throngs of people, most of whom he recognized now from town and the rancher association meeting he and his family had attended. Logan and Sarah were slow dancing at the edge of the dance area, Andrew and Heidi making out as they swayed not too far away.

Xander said hello to Luke and Eva Stockton, who owned Sunshine Farm and had turned it into this gorgeous guest ranch with a welcoming main house and cabins dotting the property. He saw a couple of his brothers talking to Nate Crawford, who owned the Maverick Manor, and his family, distant relatives of Xander's clan. A bunch of attractive women crossed his path with smiles and "save me a dance, will you, cowboy?" Yes, two had actually said exactly that. He finally made it to the punch and downed a cup, then poured two more and headed back over to where he'd left Lily.

Except she wasn't there.

He should have known better than to leave her alone! Of course she'd been surrounded by men the minute he'd left and was probably now dancing with someone.

The thought turned his stomach.

His gaze ran over the dance area. He saw Wilder with his arms around a pretty brunette. Finn was talking more than he was dancing with a blonde. Max Crawford was chatting up two women who looked to be his age by the buffet table. The Jones brothers—millionaire cowboys who'd moved to town over the past couple of years from Tulsa, Oklahoma—were dancing with their wives, and

Xander made a note to meet one or two of them tonight since they'd also come to Montana from out of state.

Finally, he caught a swish of the red hair. He craned his neck around two women who were looking longingly at Hunter as he was deep in conversation with their nearest ranch neighbor, and yes, there Lily was. Dancing.

With Knox.

What?

It wasn't a slow song, so his brother didn't have his arms around her. And Lily's arms were up in the air at the moment as she laughed at something Sarah, dancing next to her with Logan, said.

Now Knox was whispering something in her ear. Lily laughed and touched Knox's arm.

A red-hot burst of anger swelled in his gut. Knox had had his chance to date Lily and had opted out. *So move along, buddy.*

He marched over with the two cups of punch, someone's elbow almost knocking them out of his hands. "Hey, Lily," he said with a fast glare at his brother. "I have our punch."

"Oh, great!" Lily said. "I'm so thirsty! All this dancing."

"None for me?" Knox asked with too much amusement.

Xander narrowed his eyes at his brother.

Knox chuckled at what had to be the murderous expression on Xander's face. "I was just apologizing again to Lily for how I acted a few weeks ago. The date that wasn't. I was telling her all about Dad's master plan to get us all hitched and how the whole idea made me nuts after I'd already agreed on a date."

"I completely understand," Lily said. "And besides,

I got to meet Xander," she added, those beautiful green eyes looking straight into his.

"I'll go say hi to Nate," Knox said. "Thanks for the dance, Lily." He smiled and walked away, sending an infuriating wink at Xander.

Lily took one of the cups of punch and held it up. "A toast."

He raised his, as well. "To?"

"To change," she said, holding his gaze.

Dammit. She had him there. Change, progress, forward movement made the world go around. Stagnancy was a slow death. Case in point: Xander moving to Montana. He might have stayed back in Dallas, stewing in his bitterness. Instead, he'd opted for an entirely new state, a new life, and he'd met Lily. A woman he couldn't stop thinking about.

"Change is good," he agreed.

They clinked cups and he watched her drink, tossing back her head, her long, creamy neck so kissable-looking.

"Thanks for this," she said. They put the cups down on a tray of empties on a table, then headed toward the buffet, where there were light appetizers and tiny sandwiches.

"Must be hard to eat anyone else's food but yours when you're the best cook in town," he said, popping a mini quiche in his mouth.

She laughed. "That is some serious high praise. Thank you. But I'm hardly the best. All the cooks at the Manor are amazing. And Sarah and I had lunch in Kalispell that blew me away. I had no idea vegetable soup could be that good."

"Maybe we could go check out one of the restaurants

in Kalispell sometime," he said. "I'd love some Thai food. Or really good Italian."

"Are you asking me on a date, Xander Crawford?" she asked. "Or are we just friends?"

He felt his cheeks burn. "I… We're…" He gnawed the inside of his cheek. "I'll go get us more punch. Be right back."

The minute he left he realized that by the time he got back, she'd likely be dancing with someone else. *That is what you get, idiot*, he chastised himself. *"I… We're." Stammer, stammer, stammer. Jeez. What the hell was that?*

But he had no idea what he meant it as. Date. Friends. He just knew he wanted her to himself.

He hurried over the five feet to the punch bowl, filled two cups and yup, when he got back, Lily was dancing with some guy in a straw cowboy hat. He had a good inch on Xander, too, which bugged him.

At least it wasn't a slow dance.

The song ended and he saw Lily smile at her partner and dash away—right toward him.

"Why do I keep leaving you by your lonesome?" he asked.

"Because you have to torture yourself before you accept that there is something going on between us, Xander Crawford."

"Say how you really feel," he said with a smile.

"Hey, this is the new me. The real me. We're at a dance on a beautiful summer night. I'm in this pretty pink dress. You have on that gorgeous brown Stetson. My favorite Dierks Bentley song is playing right now. Seems like just the place to see what's what."

He handed her the punch, feeling like he'd been

socked in the stomach. She was 100 percent right. They downed the drinks, tossed the cups and hit the dance floor.

The moment her hands slid around his neck, he knew he wasn't letting her go again, wasn't letting her out of his sight.

"So what's this about an old diary you and your brothers found buried in your bedroom?" she asked, looking up at him. "I overheard Logan and Sarah talking about it. You guys found it under the floorboards?"

"Funny, I was just thinking about the diary earlier tonight. It's on my bedside table—locked. I tried to get it open with a letter opener, but I need something smaller. Plus, should I really be opening it? I don't know."

"Whose is it?" she asked, her hands both hot and cool on his neck.

He shrugged. "No idea. Someone must have hidden it under the floorboard to keep it from prying eyes and either forgot it when they moved or wanted it buried forever. I really don't know. There's a letter *A* on the cover of it. It's jewel-encrusted and was probably all fancy and expensive when it was new."

"An old jewel-encrusted locked diary!" Lily said. "Something so romantic about that! I wonder whose it could be."

"Don't mean to eavesdrop," Nate Crawford said from behind Lily. A tall, good-looking man around forty, Nate was dancing with his wife, Callie. "If it looks really old and has an A on the cover, it probably belongs to someone in the Abernathy family—that's where the Ambling A ranch originally got its name. The Abernathys left town a generation ago, though."

"Wow," Lily said after Nate and Callie excused themselves to the buffet table. "It would be great if you could get it back to an Abernathy. Imagine the family stories written in the diary."

"Or family secrets," Xander said.

"Those, too. Still would be so wonderful to return it."

He nodded. "I'll ask around about the Abernathys."

The song changed, a slow one this time, and Xander found himself pulling Lily a bit closer.

"If that's okay," he whispered.

"Oh, it's more than okay."

He breathed in the flowery scent of her hair. He could stand here holding her forever.

"Cutting in," said Henry, the huge linebacker of a cowboy. He practically knocked Xander out of the way to get to Lily.

"Her dance card is full, sorry," Xander snapped.

Lily stared at Xander, crossing her arms over her chest.

"Say what now?" Henry asked, looking confused.

"Lily promised all her dances to *me*," Xander explained.

Now Lily's stare turned into a glare—at Xander.

Henry shrugged. "Oh. You two are a couple? I didn't know. Sorry." He left, walking up to a pretty blonde standing at the edge of the dance area.

Yeah, that's right.

"I didn't get a chance to tell Henry that he misunderstood," Lily said, raising an eyebrow.

"Misunderstood what?" he asked, not liking where this was headed.

"That we're a couple. We're just *friends*. Isn't that what you keep saying? Of course that means I can't promise *all* my dances to a buddy, Xander. You understand, right?"

Grrr. "I… We…"

Now there was merriment in those flashing green eyes. "That didn't work out too well for you before."

She was right. It didn't. And he was done with all that. Lily. His Lily.

He tipped up her chin and kissed her. Hard and soft. Passionately. One hand stayed at her waist as the other went into those lush red strands.

And dammit, there was that parade clanging in his head again. Cymbals. Marching band. Someone singing hallelujah.

They were *a lot* more than just friends.

"Well, I guess he wasn't mistaken," Lily whispered.

Chapter Ten

Ooh la la, Lily thought, wrapped in Xander's arms, his soft, warm lips on hers. *Make this kiss last forever.*

"Can a guy cut in?"

She peeled open one eye to see Xander glaring at a cowboy in a white cowboy boots. "Sorry, but we're kissing here," Xander said.

"Yeah, I know," the guy said, wriggling his eyebrows.

"Ew?" Lily said, grimacing at the creep.

Xander made a fist. "Want to know *this*?"

"Possessive dudes are out," the guy said, shaking his head as he walked away.

A beautiful breeze swept through Lily's hair just then, and the creep was forgotten. All she saw was Xander's handsome face and his dark eyes. All she felt were stirrings she'd never experienced before. All she wanted was to be alone with him.

"Maybe we should go kiss somewhere more private," she whispered.

"In total agreement," he whispered back.

He took her hand and led her along the edges of the crowd, craning his neck for a good spot where they could be alone. But everywhere they looked, people or couples had taken over, even on the far side of the barn, where a pair of teenagers was making out, both of them giggling as she and Xander popped their heads around and said, "Sorry."

"There's always the Ambling A," Lily said. Boldly. Very boldly.

Those dark eyes of his locked on hers. He knew exactly what she meant.

And she did mean that. She wanted to be alone with Xander Crawford. In his bedroom. In his bed.

"It's closer than my house," she rushed to add. "And who knows when my dad might head home. Your father looks like he's having too good a time to leave anytime soon." She nodded her head over to the buffet table, where Max Crawford held court with four women.

"Nice to see him getting out and enjoying himself," Xander said. He seemed almost grateful for the reprieve in their conversation. The change of subject.

Because they both knew if they made love tonight, there would be no turning back.

"My dad, too," she said. Peter Hunt was pouring a cup of punch for a woman Lily recognized from the circulation desk at the library. *Good for you, Dad*, she thought with a smile.

Oh, wait, she thought. She'd given her dad a ride here so she needed to tell him she was leaving for a bit. He had a key to her car so could just drive himself home if need be.

For a bit? Hopefully they'd be gone for hours.

She pulled out her phone and sent her dad at text: Going for a ride with Xander. He'll drop me home so feel free to take my car home.

He sent back a kiss and heart emoji, then a smiley face. Have fun. And yes—too much fun.

Oh, Dad, she thought with a smile as she put her phone away. Always so supportive.

"So," Xander said. "The Ambling A."

She nodded. Twice.

He took her hand and led her to where a zillion cars and pickups were parked. "I wisely parked in a place where I could get out easily," he said as he opened the door of his silver truck for her. "I thought I'd be leaving in a half hour. Alone."

"Surprises are great, aren't they?"

"This one sure is," he whispered so low that she wasn't entirely sure he'd said that, but thought he had.

They headed out toward the ranch, the radio playing low, the windows halfway open to let in the warm and breezy summer night air. In ten minutes they were at the Ambling A, not a car in sight.

"It's our lucky night, for sure," he said. "No prying eyes." He helped her out of the truck and took her hand, leading her into the house.

She'd been here recently, cooked in the kitchen, eaten at the dining room table, talked and laughed with all the Crawfords, and now the house felt comfortable and familiar and dear. He gestured toward the stairs, and up they went.

Oh God, oh God, oh God. Suddenly a dream she'd had

for three weeks was about to come true and she could hardly believe it.

The overhead light was off in Xander's bedroom, just the table lamp casting a soft glow over the bed with its blue-and-white quilt and four pillows.

Xander closed the door behind him—and locked it. "Finally. A little privacy. A lot of privacy, I amend."

She smiled. "I'm not used to all that attention. I'm not sure if I liked it or not, to be honest." Debuting her new look at the dance was half fun, half the opposite of fun. At first, the reaction had been welcome. But when guys started buzzing around her just because she suddenly looked "hot," to use the word one cowboy had whispered in her ear as he'd walked past, Lily had had enough.

"I didn't have this 'Cinderella' night so that I could dance with fifty guys or have more dates than all you Crawfords combined," Lily said. "I just wanted my outside to reflect my inside."

"I think I know what you mean. I've always seen you, Lily Hunt. No matter what clothes you're wearing or if you smell like flowers or garlic, I see you. And I've always admired that person."

She stepped toward him until she had him backed against the door, her arms snaking around his neck. "I know. Even when things got awkward on that first date, I *knew*. I caught you by surprise, Xander Crawford."

He grinned. "You sure as hell did. Kapow!" he added, faux-punching himself in the jaw with his right hand, which he then slid around her waist.

She leaned up on her tiptoes to lift her face toward his and he met her in a kiss that almost had her knees wobbling. Good thing he picked her up in his arms, never breaking that kiss, and carried her to the bed.

She was on Xander's bed. Oh God. Oh God. Oh God. Yesssss!

A thousand butterflies let loose in her stomach just then.

Lily wasn't a virgin—but her two short-term relationships, where both guys had been as fumbling as she was, hadn't exactly taught her the art of sex. When she was nineteen and had decided to finally lose her virginity to her first real boyfriend, she'd summoned the courage to ask a close girlfriend how you knew what to do. Her friend had told her she wouldn't have to think about it at all, that desire would lead the way, and she could respond in any way that felt right and natural. Lily had thought that was good advice and it had actually made her feel more equipped. Her first time, she'd felt more anticipation than desire and the experience hadn't exactly been all that comfortable. With the second relationship, the guy was so shy that she had to lead the way. So nothing remotely like TV or movie sex had ever happened in her life.

She had a good feeling that Xander knew what he was doing.

He lay beside her on the bed, on his side, his hands caressing her hair, her face, her back. And then he was kissing her again, and she closed her eyes, almost unable to process all the emotions swirling inside her. She moved closer against him, kissing him with equal passion. There was too much clothing between them, she thought, her hands in his thick, wavy dark hair.

"A little help with the zipper?" she asked as she sat up, glancing at him.

The grin he gave her made her laugh. "My pleasure," he said, kneeling behind her.

He unzipped. Then he slowly moved the spaghetti straps off her shoulders. He kissed the sides of her neck, her collarbone, and she shimmied out of the dress, never so grateful for having bought new undergarments.

"Ooh, that's sexy," he said, taking in the blush-colored lace demi bra and matching bikini panties. "You're sexy."

Lily Hunt, sexy. No one had ever said *that* before.

She went for his belt buckle, and again, the happy surprise on his gorgeous face emboldened her even more.

"I've always said, you're a woman who knows what she wants and goes for it," he said as he kicked off his jeans and she unbuttoned his shirt.

And kissed her way down his chest.

Who *was* this woman?

One of the best parts of tonight was that she knew it wasn't the makeover giving her confidence. It was the way Xander Crawford made her *feel*. The real Lily had truly come out of her shell, every last bit of her.

In less than a minute, they were both naked. Lily felt his gaze on her, and she didn't feel exposed or shy or awkward. She only felt desire. And desirable.

Xander reached into his bedside table drawer and out came a little square foil packet.

And then he was kissing her again, his hands everywhere, his lips everywhere. The moment they became one, Lily gasped and lost all ability to think beyond how incredibly good she felt, how happy she was.

How in love.

Lily's eyes fluttered open, and she almost pulled the quilt over her head to go back to sleep when she remembered: this wasn't her bed. And she wasn't alone.

A smile spread across her face as she turned her head

slightly to the right to see if she'd dreamed the whole thing.

Because it had been a dream. Wow.

But nope, Xander Crawford was right there, fast asleep. He didn't snore, either.

She watched his chest rise and fall, rise and fall, mesmerized by his pecs and the dark swirls of hair. She wished she could stay in this bed all day—all the days of her life—but she had to sneak out before a whole bunch of Crawfords woke up and caught her creeping down the stairs.

She gave Xander one last look, drank in every gorgeous bit of him, then picked up her pink dress and slipped it on, put on her shoes, found her little beaded purse and slung that over her torso. She wanted to kiss Xander goodbye but didn't want to wake him, so she tiptoed to the door and pulled it open as gently as she could.

Lily peered out left and right. The coast was clear. She dashed down the stairs and was almost at the bottom when she realized she'd ridden here with Xander.

Which meant she was going back upstairs. Very quietly. She'd have to wake Xander, after all.

Which she was now looking forward to.

Unless things would be weird? Awkward? The morning after with its bright light? She turned around and took the first step back up, suddenly not wanting to move too quickly.

What if Xander regretted their night together?

She was barely on the fourth step up when the front door to the Ambling A opened and Lily froze, her back to it. She had no idea who it was who'd come in.

Someone who'd also had a good time at the dance, clearly.

"That red hair can mean only one woman," the male voice said. "Hey, Lily. How are ya?"

She tried to force the embarrassed grimace off her face and turned around. It was Wilder, Xander's youngest brother. He looked a bit rumpled but otherwise as handsome as all the Crawfords were with his slightly long brown hair and the piercing dark eyes.

"I'm well," she said, then rolled her eyes at herself. Could she sound more stiff? "I'm doing just great. How are *you*? Have a good time at the dance?" The questions rushed out of her mouth to put the focus back on him.

"Oh, yeah," he drawled. "Almost too good a time." He took off his cowboy boots and left them by the door. "So you're in the same clothes you were in last night, but you're just getting here?" he asked.

Thank you, Lord! Because she was on her way up the stairs, Wilder must have thought she'd just gotten here.

"Long story," she said, figuring Wilder Crawford was not really interested in her love life.

"Let me guess. You had too much of the spiked version of the punch, fell asleep under a tree, woke up with leaves in your hair, then remembered you promised your buddy Xander you'd give him a cooking lesson and so here you are."

Um, no. She wanted to tell him she wasn't the kind of person who passed out under trees at parties, but she wanted to run with the idea that she hadn't just tried to sneak out of the house after spending the most amazing night of her life here.

"Well, I see I made you blush, and honestly, Lily? Don't worry about it. If you knew *half* the crazy times my brothers and I have had, then you'd really have something to blush about. And I'm not even talking about the women coming and going. Ask Xander to tell you the story of the time he had three dates in one night. People say I'm the wild Crawford who lives up to my name? Xander has us all beat for notches on the bedpost. Including here in Rust Creek Falls. He's not even the tallest of us. Personally, I don't get it…"

Her stomach dropped.

What?

As Wilder went on about how much each Crawford could bench-press, Lily tuned him out, suddenly wishing she hadn't given him the impression that she and Xander were "just friends."

Now instead of being embarrassed at getting caught, she wanted to run away. Maybe bawl.

"Well, I'll go wake Xander. Bye!" she croaked out and dashed up the stairs.

"If you're making pancakes, make at least ten for me!" he called up.

Oh God. Did everyone hear that? Had Wilder woken up the whole house?

She raced into Xander's room, shutting and locking the door behind her, her heart beating so loud she was sure it was what woke Xander.

"You've got too many clothes on," he said, propping up in bed. "You've *got* clothes on."

Calm down, Lily. Don't go all just-how-many-women-have-been-in-this-bed *on him. Everything that happened before last night was the past.* Last night was a new beginning for them both.

Right?

She could feel the exact spot her heart was bruised. Dead center. Was she another "notch on the bedpost" as Wilder had unwittingly put it?

Back in high school, the guys had had a brief sickening game they'd dubbed "least likely." Whoever got the most girls they were least likely to kiss to kiss them, won. Won what, Lily didn't know. Unearned respect from the idiots, she guessed.

That week, ten guys, most from the football team, had asked Lily if she wanted to take a walk—with a gleam in their eyes. The first time, she'd been so bewildered that one of the hottest, most popular guys in school had sort of asked her out that she'd said yes, without any idea if she actually liked him or not. Turns out they had nothing much to say on their ten-minute walk, but all he'd been after was a kiss on the lips. Once he got it, he'd said, *Booya!* And run back toward the school. The next morning, Lily had heard a group of cheerleaders talking about the bet and how skater dudes were suddenly asking them out—as if.

Lily had said no to the next nine guys who'd "asked her out."

And had had a hard time trusting in a man being attracted to her *for* her ever since.

But with Xander, she knew he was. She knew it and believed it the way she knew her own name.

So forget the past. Everything is about now. Now, now, now.

Never mind that *now*, she felt very unsure of herself. No. Not of herself. Of *them*.

"Wait," Xander said, frowning. "Were you about to leave?"

"I actually did leave but got halfway downstairs when I remembered I didn't drive here. So I'm stranded."

He grinned. "Guess that means you'll have to come back to bed." He held up the side of the quilt.

"I ran into Wilder on the stairs," she said, arms across her chest. "At first I thought he caught me doing the famous walk of shame, but turns out he thinks we're just friends, so he gave me an earful about the women who've come and gone from this very room since you've been in Rust Creek Falls."

"Wilder talks too much," he said, shaking his head.

"You were supposed to say 'fake news.'"

His expression softened as he realized he'd confirmed her worst fears.

"I won't lie to you, Lily. I've had a couple of very short-term…experiences. Just the first couple weeks after I moved here and felt really overwhelmed by everything."

Her arms fell to her sides and felt like they weighed a hundred pounds each. Like her heart right now.

"I was so upset about what happened back in Dallas," he continued, reaching for his pants. "I wanted to forget and so I went out a lot those first couple weeks. Not even here in town, but in the surrounding towns to be more anonymous."

"You're my third lover," she blurted out. Then immediately wished she could take it back. She dropped down on the edge of the bed, facing away from him. "The first guy? There was no second time. I think we both just wanted to get our virginities over with and it wasn't exactly a spiritual experience." She sighed. "The second guy and I lasted a few weeks but we didn't have any chemistry except when it came to discussing pastry— we met in a baking class." She stood up, then dropped back down. "My point is that I don't have much experience in any of this. And you clearly do."

"Well, I've got seven years on you," he said, getting up

and pulling on his jeans. "I'm thirty years old. Friends of mine have been long married with two kids by my age."

She turned to face him, stunned silent for a moment by the sight of the morning light hitting the muscled planes of his chest. Just hours ago, her hands had explored every millimeter of that chest. His entire body.

And now...everything was wrong.

And everything hurt.

He walked around his bed to his dresser and pulled a blue T-shirt out of a drawer. "One of the reasons why I was so hesitant about us," he said, putting on the shirt, "was because I know what getting emotionally involved leads to."

Dammit. Was he going to do this? Had she actually set this conversation in motion? Oh God.

No. Wait one minute. She was not about to blame herself for talking about reality. The truth. If he wanted to revert back to the guy who hid from life—and love— well, that wasn't her fault.

It just happened to hurt like hell.

Crud.

Had she really thought her night with Xander was going somewhere? That he'd suddenly be over his past and trust in the world again?

Yes, she had thought so.

Maybe because she was as young and experienced at life as he'd said she was.

"I thought there was more between us," she said. "Was I wrong?"

He held her gaze for a second, then turned away, his attention out the window. "You weren't wrong, Lily. But I guess this conversation just brought up all the reminders that—"

He stopped and sat down on the edge of the bed, running a hand through his hair.

"Reminders that...?" she prompted.

"That I'm jaded and bitter. And you're young and hopeful and idealistic and have your whole beautiful life ahead of you."

"That's total bunk, Xander Crawford. You're just scared spitless that you feel more for me than you intended. And so you're pushing me away."

"Lily—"

But again, he stopped talking.

"When you find someone truly special, you don't let them go, Xander. Do you realize how rare it is?"

"Is it?" he asked.

"Oh, so I'm just a dime a dozen?" She glared at him, grateful the anger was edging out the hurt. No, wait. There the hurt was. Punching back for control.

At least the anger was keeping her from crying. That she'd do in private.

"This wasn't how I envisioned the morning going," he said, standing up. "Not at all. I thought we'd make love three more times, then I'd sneak you into the shower with me, and then whisk you off to the Gold Rush for scrambled eggs and home fries and bacon and a lot of coffee and then we'd go back to my place for a repeat. That's what I thought this morning would be."

Now she did feel like crying. "I wanted that morning, too, Xander. I still want it."

"But you want a lot more than that, don't you?" he said gently.

"Hell yeah."

"I'm sorry, Lily. I messed up by kissing you in the first

place because I just couldn't resist you. And now I've made this huge mess of things. I'm very sorry."

"You're sorry for sleeping with me?" she said, her voice sounding more like a screech. This time, the anger had knocked out the hurt with a solid left jab. "How dare you!"

"Lily, no, I—"

"I need a ride home. And I'd like that ride to be *silent*."

He let out a harsh sigh and headed for the door.

Tears pricked the backs of her eyes.

Lily raced down the stairs, dimly aware of laughter coming from the direction of the kitchen. She could hear a couple of voices. She had to get out of there before anyone saw her—especially now that this really was just another notch on Xander's bedpost.

She tried hard to keep the tears from falling, but down they came. Lily flung open the door and ran out, zooming for Xander's truck. She got in, wiping away her tears. *Take a deep breath. Do. Not. Let. Him. See. You. Cry.*

By the time he got in the driver's seat, she was composed.

Do not think about last night. How you kissed at the dance. How you two drove to the Ambling A with all those feelings, romance in the air, love in the air, all your hopes coming true...

She wanted to blame it on herself for falling for Xander when he told her by his actions alone on their first date that he was going to smash her heart to smithereens.

She wanted to blame it on that blasted Wilder Crawford—and her unfortunate timing of running into him—for telling her stuff she had no business knowing. Or wanting to know.

But the blame for her feeling like she'd just been

kicked and Xander's probably feeling like hell? That was on Xander himself—and his stubbornness.

But as he started the truck and pulled out, something occurred to Lily. Something the old Lily would have thought of immediately. The new Lily had too much confidence, though, so the news flash hadn't seeped into her consciousness until now.

Maybe it had nothing to do with Xander living in the past and being stubborn.

Maybe he just didn't love her back.

Chapter Eleven

Xander pulled up in front of Lily's house, Dobby and Harry sitting outside on the porch, Harry on his back on the mat, taking in the brilliant sunshine of late August. Xander wanted to run up and rub that furry little belly, feel Harry's soft-as-silk floppy ears, talk to her dad, ask her brothers how things were going at the auto mechanic business, where they'd fixed his brother Finn's brake issue the other day. He even wanted to hang out with Andrew and hear how things were with Heidi. Xander's first fix-up.

At least he brought love to someone. Two someones.

Please don't rush out of the truck until I get to say something, he thought, but couldn't make himself speak the words. He didn't know *what* he wanted to say.

I'm sorry didn't cut it. There was so much more to say but he couldn't put words to it.

He turned off the ignition and turned to face her. "Lily."

But nothing else came out of his mouth.

She waited. She tilted her head. Waited some more. Then she said, "Everything between us led to last night, Xander. And last night was something beautiful. Personally, I think you're crazy for turning your back on it. But if that's your choice, I guess I have to respect that." She cleared her throat and reached for the door.

"Last night *was* beautiful," he said.

"And?" she prompted.

"And…maybe it's better we cool it now rather than someone gets run over by a Mack truck down the road."

"You're the only one driving that truck, Xander," she said—between gritted teeth. Then she got out of the car and stalked to the door in her pink dress, the dogs jumping up to greet her.

He watched her pet both of them and bury her face in their fur, then hurry inside, the dogs behind her.

The door closed and he felt so bereft.

He felt *something* for her, that was not in doubt.

He started the truck and drove toward the Ambling A. A hard day's work would help set his mind at ease by taking his brain off Lily completely. But by the time he got to the ranch, his mind was a jumble. Memories of last night, of what it was like to make love to Lily, to be one with her, how complete he'd felt, kept jabbing at him.

He didn't want to feel complete, though. That was the damn problem. He'd felt complete in Dallas with Britney to the point that he was going to propose.

And wham. Knocked upside the head and left for dead.

A little dramatic, but that was how it felt.

He needed a walk, and the now overcast morning suited his mood. He'd survey the miles of fence line out past the barn, see if any part of it needed repair. He wrapped a tool kit around his hips, then headed out on foot to the fence, a good mile away. As he neared it, he could see his brother Knox with his tools, working on a long gap in the wiring.

"Guess we had the same idea for this morning," Xander said.

Knox glanced up. "Glad you're here. I could use a hand." Knox used a tool to stretch the wire, and Xander wrapped the wire around and around the next section to secure it. "I was riding fence when I noticed it." He glanced for Xander's horse. "You walked all the way out here?"

"A lot on my mind," Xander said.

"Yeah, ditto. But after working so hard there's no way I'd want to hoof it back, so I brought the trusty steed." He nodded up at the beautiful brown mare.

"Still mad at me for dancing with your chef?" Knox asked. But Xander could tell his brother wasn't kidding.

"Yes, actually. Dammit." He sighed and ran a hand through his hair. "Not dammit that you danced with her. Dammit that she *is* 'my chef' and I'm screwing it up. I really care about Lily. I more than care about her. I just don't *want* to. If that makes any sense."

"Unfortunately, it does. All part of our legacy."

Their legacy. The six of them rarely talked about their upbringing, and he figured that was what Knox was referring to.

"With our family past, who the hell wouldn't be wary of love and marriage and all that stuff?" Knox asked, not looking up.

Xander didn't know all that much about their mother, but she'd been considerably younger than their father, jumping into the marriage not long after they'd started dating. And he knew that Sheila Crawford had left Max and their six young children for another man—and never looked back.

If his mother had been able to do that, anyone could. Britney sure had.

So why wouldn't Lily? When she had her whole life ahead of her at just twenty-three?

She was probably right when she'd said, in so many words, that the past was running his life, that it had too tight a grip on him. But right now, that grip was stronger than hers.

"You'll figure it out," Knox said, shaking him out of his thoughts.

"Meaning?"

Knox tightened the final piece of wire. "Either Lily will win out or the family legacy will. Logan got lucky. Maybe you will, too."

Huh. He hadn't really thought of it that way before. But he knew luck had nothing to do with Logan settling down with Sarah and baby Sophia. *Love* had won out.

For some crazy reason, he felt a little better than he had when he'd first walked out here. Maybe because he forgot that love *could* win.

Lily was glad she'd had to work today. One of today's specials was the Aegean pizza she'd introduced to the menu, an immediate hit, and she'd made at least thirty of them since the Manor had opened for lunch. She had her eye on the six in her oven as she sliced chicken and chopped garlic and green peppers for the next batch, trying to not pop all the delicious feta cheese in her mouth before she ran out. Her waiters had reported on where her diners were from, but she couldn't exactly add barbecue sauce or cayenne pepper or roasted chestnut shavings to the Aegean pizza without ruining it, so she kept her special additions to the other entrées. She'd made several big pots of minestrone soup, adding a bit of this and that to it to bring her diners a bit of home. Five tables had ordered servings of the soup to go, so that had brought a smile.

And she wasn't feeling much like smiling today.

When she left for the day and arrived home, she didn't even bother going upstairs to relax or take a bath to soothe her weary muscles and mind. She hit the kitchen. She had a few clients around town who loved her cooking at the Manor and hired her to make special-occasion meals or texted her that they were ill and could she drop off what they were craving. This evening, she was making split pea soup with carrots and tiny bits of ham for Monty Parster, her seventy-five-year-old widowed client who had a cold. Monty was usually robust and volunteered in the library, putting away books that had been returned, and Lily adored him. She'd make him a pot of his favorite feel-better soup on the house.

"And this is the living room," she heard her dad suddenly say, along with two sets of footsteps. One with a definite heel.

"Why do I smell something amazing?" a woman's voice asked.

Oooh, did her dad have a date over?

"That must be my daughter, Lily. She's a chef at the Maverick Manor. Best cook in the county, maybe even the state. Or the country!"

"Well, whatever she's making certainly smells like it," the woman said.

Lily liked her already.

"Lil?" Peter Hunt asked as he poked his head inside the kitchen.

"Hi, Dad," she said with a smile, stirring the pea soup as it simmered. It *did* smell good.

He pushed open the door, and behind him was an attractive woman around his age with shoulder-length dark hair and warm hazel eyes. "Lil, this Charlotte McKown. We met at the dance last night."

Lily extended her hand. "It's so nice to meet you. The dance was wonderful. I must have eaten ten of those little ham-and-cheese quiches."

"Me, too," Charlotte said. "And a little too many of the mini raspberry cheesecakes."

Lily laughed. "Yup, same here."

As her dad escorted Charlotte to the powder room so she could freshen up before their dinner at the Manor, Lily gave the soup a taste and declared it done and perfect. She shut off the burner just as her dad came back into the kitchen, a big smile on his face.

"Our first date was breakfast at the Gold Rush Diner," he whispered. "We were so full of French toast and pancakes and bacon that we skipped lunch."

"So this is an all-day date?" Lily asked with a grin. "Dad, I'm thrilled."

"We have a lot to talk about. She's widowed, too. And has four grown kids just like me. She takes Pilates and does yoga and volunteers in the clinic. She's a great person."

"Sure sounds like it," Lily said.

They could hear the powder room door opening, so her dad kissed her on the cheek and dashed out.

Lily laughed. Her dad sure seemed to be falling in love.

Next would be Ryan and Bobby. They'd probably each met someone at the dance, too.

Oh well, she thought. At least most of the Hunts were happy. She carefully poured the soup into a big container, put a lid on it, grabbed some crackers and sourdough bread and then headed out to her car.

A few minutes later, she was in Mr. Parster's little Cape Cod–style house. He sat in a recliner with a cro-cheted throw over him, a box of tissues beside him. Lily prepared a tray with the soup, which was still piping hot, and the crackers and bread, and a glass of lemon water, and brought it out to him, placing it on a table that wheeled right over his lap.

"Ah, my favorite split pea," he said. "Did I ever tell you that you make it just like my wife did?"

She smiled. "You gave me her recipe. It's my favor-ite version, too. I make it for the Manor, too, and it's al-ways a hit."

He took a spoonful. "Ahhh," he said. "So good. And trust me, it's you, not the recipe. My second-oldest daughter made this for me the last time I was sick, and I tell you, it was terrible! Something was just missing. Not that I told her that!"

Lily smiled. She adored Mr. Parster.

He took another spoonful, then nibbled on a piece of the sourdough bread, which Lily had made herself as well yesterday. "I'm sure that hoity-toity Maverick Manor pays you a fortune, but you could be making a killing by going into business for yourself as a personal chef. I'd hire you to make every meal for me. Good thing I actually like to cook myself or I'd go bankrupt. Oh, speaking of, will you be teaching another cooking class for seniors? I'm interested in Asian cooking."

"Wait," she said. "You think I could make a living as a personal chef? Here in Rust Creek Falls?"

"Are you kidding? You'd rake it in. Those who are sick. Single parents. Working parents. Dolt bachelors who never learned to crack an egg. Special occasions. Parties. Work events. Trust me, everyone knows when Lily Hunt is working at the Manor and they go those days."

"Really?" she asked. Mr. Parster was a bit of a busybody who was on at least five town boards, so it was possible he was in the know.

"I don't go around blowing smoke," he said. "Anyway, just an idea." He ate two more spoonfuls. "Heavenly. How do you get these carrots so soft and delicious?"

She laughed. "I'm very happy you love the soup. And thank you for the compliment. Well, the rest of the soup is in the fridge with reheating instructions. Want me to stick around? Make you some tea?"

"Nah," he said. "My other daughter is coming with a German chocolate cake. She's a much better cook than Karly. Don't tell her I said that."

Lily laughed. "Sworn to secrecy."

As she headed out to her car, she couldn't stop thinking about what he'd said. Personal chef? She'd thought about having her own restaurant one day, something small to start, to learn the business and grow as a chef. Or her own catering shop for events. But being a personal chef hadn't really occurred to her. Made-to-order dishes for individuals and families? And businesses and events, too? Hmm. A more personal touch.

She could have her own business doing what she loved.

She could even turn her little gift for reminding people of their best memories and home into her work.

Lily's Home Cookin'.

Her heart leaped and pulse sped up. Yes! She would start her own home-based food business as a personal chef. She could offer meal-prep kits and ready-made dishes and make herself available for parties and events. She could be all things to all stomachs!

Lily's Home Cookin'.

This time, when tears pricked her eyes it was because she was overcome with joy. Her mother would be proud of her. She knew it.

She drove home, thinking about the business plan she'd need to create. Using what she'd learned in school, doing some more research online and really homing in on what she envisioned for her business, Lily could even approach the bank about a small business loan. She wouldn't need incredible overhead to start, but she'd need decent padding for the ingredients she'd need, cookware, containers and labels, advertising, an accountant and her own space.

Yes. It was time to find her own home, a condo or small house with a good-sized, modern kitchen. Her dad would understand and he'd also be proud of her.

All that settled in her mind, she turned on the radio, planning to sing along at the top of her lungs to her favorite station, but there was a commercial on. Of course.

"Northwest Montana's Best Chef Contest this weekend in Kalispell," the radio host was saying. "Deadline to enter is tonight at midnight. See details online at NW Montana's Best Chef Contest dot com. Good luck, local cooks! Ten thousand big ones would even get me to enter—if I could cook a burger without charring it to death."

One of her favorite songs came on, but Lily snapped off the radio. *Ten thousand dollars?*

Ten. Thousand. Dollars.

More than enough money to get her business off the ground, pay first and last month's rent on her own place and have some cushion for emergencies.

She had to enter that contest. She had to *win* that contest!

Lily pulled into the driveway and rushed inside, dashing upstairs to her desk and opening her laptop. She typed the name of the contest into the search engine, and there it was. According to the site, the first round was an elimination event on Friday night—all hopefuls would make the same dish, based on the same recipe and the same ingredients. The top ten entrants would move on to round two. Three finalists would be chosen to move on and after the next round, one winner would be named. And awarded ten grand and the right to call herself Northwest Montana's Best Chef. *Note*, she read. *All entrants must bring an assistant who will aid only with prep, help fetch ingredients, cookware, utensils and plates during the competition, and help with time management.*

Wait—*what?*

An assistant?

She raced out of her room into Andrew's. Not home. Neither were Bobby or Ryan. She texted all three.

Busy this weekend? I need an assistant for a cooking contest in Kalispell.

Within fifteen minutes, she had a "no can do" from them all. Andrew had a special orientation at the academy. Bobby and Ryan were booked solid at the auto-mechanic shop. And she already knew her dad had two special dates planned with Charlotte because he'd texted her so while she'd been in the powder room during their dinner out.

Sarah had a baby—no way could Lily, or would Lily, even ask her. Two other very busy girlfriends were also not likely to be available.

There *was* one other person she could ask. He might be free. And willing.

But if he said yes, could she really bear spending the weekend with him? Her heart would break a tiny bit more every time she looked at him.

She *had* to enter the contest—and win.

Which meant picking up the phone and calling Xander Crawford.

Chapter Twelve

Lily grabbed her phone, sucking in a deep breath. She punched in his number and brought the phone to her ear, her heart beating a mile a minute.

"Lily?" he asked. "Everything okay?"

"Everything's fine. I just need a favor. A big favor."

"My answer is yes," he said.

She flopped down on her bed, eyebrow raised. "You don't even know what the favor is."

"Don't need to, Lil. I'd do anything for you."

Tears stung her eyes. This time, not from joy. But from the bittersweet poke at knowing how much he cared about her—and how she'd never have him the way she wanted.

I'd do anything for you—except be in love with you or lie to you about it.

The cooking contest, she reminded herself. She had

to think only of that. "Does 'anything' include being my assistant for the weekend at the Northwest Montana's Best Chef Contest? We'd leave Friday night and return Saturday night. I know you probably can't do it—it's last minute and practically all weekend and—"

"How many aprons should I pack?" he asked. "Do I own an apron? Do I get to wear a chef's hat?"

She almost burst into tears. She had to cover her mouth with her hand and squeeze her eyes shut. That was how touched she was that he was going to help her.

"I'll bring the aprons," she managed to say. "And yes on the chef hat."

"Count me in, then," he said.

She could barely catch her breath. "Thank you, Xander. You have no idea how much this means to me to enter the contest." She told him all about her business plan, the idea for Lily's Home Cookin' and how the ten thousand would get her started and then some.

"I always said you'd run the world someday, Lil. I'm happy to help you. And honestly, any time you need something, I'm here for you. I'd do anything for you," he repeated.

Except be in love with me. Except be with me. Except commit to me.

At least she had her weekend assistant. And she knew she could trust him to work hard and fast. The time they'd spent in the kitchen at the kids' cooking class and his few cooking lessons gave him a good familiarity.

Now she'd just have to get through the weekend with total focus on the three dishes they would make instead of on the man she loved.

She could do that. She *would* do that.

"Are you free now to discuss what I'll be doing?" he asked. "I could be over in fifteen minutes."

Wait—he wanted to come over?

"You could explain to me what you'll be cooking and what I'll need to do to help, how the contest works. I don't want to be the one who ruins the whole thing for you by chopping something in the wrong dimensions."

Lily smiled. "Well, there's a website with a ton of information. But sure, why don't you come over, and we'll go over it, and work out a plan based on what I know. The actual dishes I'll be making are a surprise."

"Oh, *that's* always helpful in a competition," he said. "Right?"

"Be right over, Lil," he said.

She held the phone on her heart for the next few minutes, unable to get up, unable to think.

She could barely get through knowing the man she loved was coming over to talk about the contest. How in the heck would she get through a weekend that promised to be incredibly high stress as it was?

She just would. You *want it*, you *make it happen*. Wasn't that her motto? Sure, sometimes it *didn't* happen, à la Xander Crawford.

But it had to this weekend with the ten thousand bucks. It just had to.

A weekend away with Lily? Yes.

Helping Lily with something very important to her? Yes.

She'd get her assistant and he'd get his friend back. Win-win.

He drove over to her house, greeted by Dobby and

Harry, who ran out for their vigorous pet-downs, Lily standing in the doorway.

She wasn't in the pink dress but she still didn't look like the Lily he'd always known.

She wore very sexy jeans that molded to her body. A V-neck tank top that showed her curves. And sandals that revealed sparkly green toenails. Her gorgeous red hair was sleek and shiny and loose around her shoulders.

She looked too hot.

And man, he thought she'd looked hot before this change.

With the dogs at his shins, he headed in, trying not to stare at Lily.

"I can't thank you enough, Xander," she said. "I know we left things kind of awkward, so…just thank you."

He nodded. "Happy to help." He followed her up to her room, and she shut the door behind them. He sat down at her desk chair; she grabbed her laptop and sat cross-legged on the bed.

The bed, of course, brought back memories of the last time he saw her on a bed. In bed. Under his covers.

"So what's my role?" he asked. *Stop looking at her legs. Stop looking at her hair. Stop looking at her.*

She told him what the site said about the assistant's role. "So, you can chop veggies, gather ingredients, get me a sauté pan, and you can say, 'Lily, you have a half hour left.' But you can't do any actual cooking."

"Well, that's good because I'm pretty bad at it."

"I recall you making excellent omelets," she said. "Even Andrew remarked on how good it was."

"Nice try, Lil. But *we* took the ones that I made. They had the good ones *you* made. Remember?"

"You did a great job turning the bacon with the tongs

and getting the cheese out of the fridge," she said with a grin. "And that's pretty much your role at the competition."

He raised an eyebrow. "Except I don't know a sauté pan from a colander."

"Good point. Let's hit the kitchen and I'll give you a tutorial. You can even take notes."

He actually pulled a tiny notebook with a little pen in the spiral from his back pocket. "Of course I'll take notes. I've gotta help you win."

She got up from the bed, her gaze on him, and it took everything in him not to reach for her, to say he was sorry, that he had no idea what he was doing.

But she'd already opened the door and was waiting for him.

In the kitchen, she knelt down in front of a cabinet and pulled out a bunch of pots and pans. She put them all on the counter. "Which do you think is a sauté pan? You'd cook fish in it or chicken or make an omelet."

"Probably this one," he said, pointing at one with shallow sides. "I think."

"Correct!"

"Soup or chili or spaghetti pot?" she asked.

"I'd think it would have to be pretty high to be a spaghetti pot, and I know when my dad makes chili, it's always in some huge pot." He pointed to the pot he thought would be right.

"Correct again!" she said. "A-plus so far."

They went through all the pots and pans, then moved on to the cooking utensils, covering everything from spatulas to colanders to food processors.

"Catch!" she said, tossing a green pepper at him. "Get ready to slice, dice and chop."

He caught it after it bounced against his chest. "Catch!" he said, tossing it back.

She got it in one hand. "Catch!" she said, turning around and tossing it behind her.

"Ha, got it!" He laughed, tossing it up in the air and catching it with his left hand. "Who knew you could have so much fun with food?"

She grinned. "I did."

"You're going to win the contest. I know it."

She smiled, then sobered fast. "You really believe in me."

"Sure do. I've had your French dip. That's all I need to know."

Lily laughed and he realized how much he'd missed that beautiful sound. He wished he could always make her happy. "Well," she said, clearing her throat. "Time for the cutting lessons."

For the next hour, she showed him how to slice thin and thick, how to dice, how to peel and separate garlic cloves.

They'd been in the kitchen for three hours when she let out a giant yawn.

"Someone needs to get her cooking contest rest," he said. "What time are we leaving tomorrow?"

"I need to be there no later than six."

"I'll drive. Pick you up at four forty-five just to be safe. Better to be a half hour early than a few minutes late."

She wrapped her arms around him and kissed his cheek, and again he wanted to pull her against him and never let her go.

"Thank you so much, Xander. You are a true friend."

Friend. Buddy. Nice. Just friends. The words echoed in his head.

They were going away for the weekend. Together. Staying—he assumed—in the same room. Or was he just hoping they were?

"I guess I should book a room for myself?" he asked as he washed his hands in the sink.

"I already did. We have two single rooms but the guy taking the reservations said they were among the last rooms available. So phew."

His heart sank.

You can't have it both ways, man, he reminded himself.

Late that night, after a practice dinner on her family that they all raved about, and another half hour lying on her bed staring up at the ceiling, and another half hour going over the contest website for every detail, Lily decided to start packing. She set her suitcase on her bed and opened it, wondering what to take—for the competition *and* a weekend away with the man she was madly in love with.

For the competition, she'd wear her new jeans and tank tops and bring two light cardigans, plus her trusty lucky clogs, which were comfortable and nonslip and made her feel grounded.

For the weekend away with Xander, she'd bring the sexy underwear (because why not? Even if he never saw it, she'd know it was there) and the sleeveless little black dress and strappy sandals.

Hell yeah. You never knew.

She grabbed her phone and texted Sarah: Entering a

weekend-cooking competition in Kalispell. Guess who my assistant is?

OMG. No way.

As friends. But hopeful.

Me too! Wow! Good luck on both fronts!

Just after she sent back a smiley face emoji, someone knocked on her door. At her "come in!" her brother Andrew poked his head in.

"Got a minute?" he asked.

"Sure."

He came in and sat down on her desk chair. "I just wanted to say thanks, Lil. Everything is because of you."

She put down her phone and stared at Andrew. "What's because of me?"

"Me being really happy. Having Heidi in my life. Dad dating for the first time in forever. I think he's in love."

Lily smiled. "Dad does seem really happy. I met Charlotte. She seems great. But how is either relationship my doing? I didn't introduce you to Heidi or Dad to Charlotte."

"Still it's *because* of you. When I watched you enroll in school for business administration, it spurred me to really think about what I wanted for my future—and I enrolled in the police academy. Then you made pals with a Crawford, and I got the cojones to ask him if he'd pass my name and number to any date he thought would work out. And I met Heidi. You said you were going to the annual dance that you never went to and Dad goes and falls in love. It's all thanks to you. You made really positive changes in your life and now we're doing that, too."

Her heart pinged. "Andrew, you're gonna make me cry."

"Mark my words—Ryan and Bobby will be engaged by Christmas."

Lily wondered if either of them had met someone special at the dance. Both were a little more private than Andrew, who'd always worn his heart right on the ole sleeve. She had seen her other two brothers talking to a couple different women through the night, so maybe they had. The dance seemed to be magical for all the Hunts.

She recalled watching Andrew dip Heidi during a slow song and kiss her. She'd even snapped a photo, which she'd surprise him with one day. "And what about you?" she asked, wiggling her eyebrows.

She could see his cheeks flush and a big dopey smile light his face. "I've already been looking at rings. Maybe you could help me pick one out? I want to propose on her birthday in October."

"Awww! Andrew! I'm happy for you! And of course I'll help you ring shop!" She gave him a big hug.

Now all she had to do was get her own love life in order. And she had a whole weekend to work on it.

Chapter Thirteen

The Northwest Montana's Best Chef Contest was being held in the Kalispell Luxury Lodge, which was a bit on the outskirts of town. The sprawling one-story guest ranch had an enormous hunter-green peaked roof with the name of the hotel across it. It wasn't as luxe as the Maverick Manor, but there were wide planked floors covered with gorgeous rugs, leather love seats and armchairs in sitting areas, and pots of flowers everywhere. On the other side of the hotel reception desk, two women sat at a registration table for the contest. There were at least thirty people in line, mostly in rows of two. The chefs and their assistants.

"Yikes, I hope being in line by the deadline counts," Lily said to Xander. It was only five thirty so she was sure they'd make it to the table by six.

The guy in front of her, wearing a bright purple apron, turned around and said, "It does—I asked!"

"Phew," Lily said. "Thanks."

Xander slung his arm around her, and she felt instantly cheered. They'd chatted nonstop on the way to Kalispell, a forty-five-minute drive, and she wondered if both of them were filling in any potential silences before they could happen. Maybe he'd figured she'd use the time to talk about what had happened between the night of the dance and the next morning. But she was not going to bring that up.

This weekend would speak for itself.

She just had to let it.

He seemed to sense she was a little nervous about what to expect from tonight's elimination round, so while they waited in line he stayed mostly silent, though his arm was a constant comfort around her shoulder.

The line moved quickly, since there were two people handling the check-ins. Finally, Lily was up.

"Hi, I'm Lily Hunt for the competition," she said to the blonde on the left.

As the woman handed her a form to sign, a name tag to fill out and instructions to report to the Sagebrush Ballroom down the hall, someone tapped her on the shoulder.

"Lily!" a male voice said with faux cheer.

She knew that voice.

She turned around. Ugh. It was him. The bane of her existence at the Gold Rush Diner in Rust Creek Falls, where she'd worked for a year as a short-order cook before daring to apply for a line cook job at the Manor. Kyle Kendrick. What a jerk. Luckily, his reputation preceded him because when he tried to get a job at Maverick Manor, her boss, Gwen, had apparently said: "You should watch who you insult while walking down the street. My husband and I were coming toward you and you told him to stop hogging the sidewalk with his 'beer gut.' I almost punched you out myself, but he stopped me."

Kyle was slightly built and not very tall and had a fake-angelic look because of his wavy, light blond hair and blue eyes, which probably saved him from getting beat up as often as he might have. Though she had seen him come to work with a few bruised cheeks.

He was still at the Gold Rush. The only reason he'd lasted there so long was because he was good at his job. Not only good, but fast. She wondered if anyone from the Manor was here for the competition. She hadn't seen any of them, but they might have checked in earlier.

"I plan to win this thing, Hunt," Kyle said, a pretty blonde woman checking her phone beside him. "I want to open a bar and grill focusing on my signature steak-burger. People at the Gold Rush tell me they prefer mine to yours at the Maverick Manor. And for less than a third of the price."

Well whoop-de-do. "I wish you luck," she said. "See you inside." She took Xander's arm, and they headed to the Sagebrush Ballroom. *Please let me be stationed far away from him*, she said in a little prayer.

"My brothers and I had steakburgers the other day at the Gold Rush," Xander said. "And I happened to hear a waitress yelling at someone named Kyle to watch his language, so I know he was there. The steakburger didn't come *close* to yours."

"I knew I liked you," she said with a grin.

She'd almost said *I knew I loved you*. Almost. Thank the universe she'd caught herself.

They entered the Sagebrush Ballroom and got on an-other line, this one much shorter. There were hundreds of chairs, most full, set up at a good distance from several rows of tables where ten people stood making something on what looked like hot plates. Three more people with clipboards were walking among the tables, taking bites of something, then jotting something down on their clipboards.

Oh gosh. This had to be the elimination round. Hotplate cooking? And what were they making? From the smell of it, could be grilled cheese.

She watched a different man with a clipboard and headphones hand the woman in front of her a number, then direct her to take a seat. Then it was Lily's turn.

"You're number two hundred forty-six," the man said to Lily. He wore a name tag that read Hal. "You can take a seat and wait for the grouping with your number to be called."

Lily's eyes practically bugged out. "Did you say two hundred forty-six? That's a lot of entrants."

"Tell me about it," he said. "Our judges' stomachs are getting seriously full. But the deadline to register here at the hotel just passed, so there shouldn't be too many more of you. Good luck," he added before gesturing for her and Xander to take seats.

"Suddenly I'm not as sure of myself," Lily whispered to Xander. "There could be three hundred people entering, who all think they have what it takes to win."

"Yes, but only you truly do," Xander said, slinging that strong, comforting arm over her shoulder again.

She smiled and shook her head. "I'm glad you're here," she whispered.

"You've got this."

Lately, Lily felt like she could do anything. But when Xander was by her side, she *knew* she could.

"Numbers two forty through two fifty, please appear in a line at the first table. Chefs only—no assistants."

"Gulp. I'm on my own," she said, standing up.

"Like I said, you've got this." He kissed her hand and she almost gasped. "For good luck," he added.

She wouldn't mind a *real* good-luck kiss—on the lips—but she'd settle for the hand. *For now,* she thought with a devilish smile.

She hurried up to the table with the nine others on their way. Ugh again! Kyle Kendrick was right in front of her. Of all the times to arrive, she had to pick the same time he had?

"Hope your grilled cheese doesn't burn," he said, barely turning around.

"Oh, yours, too," she said, rolling her eyes.

Interestingly, while the line formed, staff were scrubbing at the hot plates to get rid of any former cooking residue. At least she wouldn't be dealing with a burned-on mess from her predecessor.

The ten of them were directed to enter the rows of tables and to stand behind the hot plate with their number beside it. Kyle was two forty and the first in his row. Lily was first in her row at the table adjacent.

The man with the clipboard appeared. "Welcome to the elimination round! I'm Hal and your emcee for the competition. Because we have so many entrants, this seemed the best way to narrow down the field to the top ten chefs. Good luck to all of you!"

Lily eyed Xander, who had moved to the front row, close to where she stood. She smiled at him, and he flashed her a thumbs-up.

"You will each make the perfect grilled cheese with the simplest of ingredients," Hal continued. "White bread. American cheese and half a cup of butter. A staffer will now hand out your ingredients."

Next to the hot plate was a butter knife, a plastic spatula and a salad-type plate. A young woman handed Lily a small tray containing two slices of bread, the butter and two slices of yellow American cheese.

Once the ten hopefuls had their ingredients, the man with the clipboard continued. "You have fifteen minutes to make the perfect grilled cheese, which will then be voted on by our three judges. Ready, set, turn on your hot plates!"

Lily pressed the little red on button. She could feel the hot plate warming up.

Hal looked at his watch. "Three, two, one, and begin!"

Lily dropped some butter on the hot plate, then slathered both sides of the bread, every speck, with the remaining butter. Because she couldn't control the temperature of the hot plate the way she could a burner at home, she decided to put one slice of cheese on each piece of bread and start that way. Once the cheese started melting, she flipped one onto the other, gave a gentle press with the spatula, then flipped, then flipped again. When the outside of the bread was golden brown and the cheese looking perfectly gooey, she turned off the hot plate and slid the grilled cheese onto the plate.

"One minute remaining!" the man with the clipboard said.

Lily flipped the sandwich over on the plate, then cut it, hoping she'd timed it right and the cheese was sufficiently gooey in the center. Yes—looked like it was!

She glanced over at Xander, who was at nodding at her with a smile. *Looks Lily Hunt good*, he mouthed, and she grinned.

A judge began on each section of the table. A blonde woman cut a piece of Lily's sandwich, her expression giving nothing away. She took another bite, then jotted down something on her clipboard. The two other judges did the same.

Their group was then dismissed.

Lily rushed over to Xander. "I have no idea how I did. Hot plate grilled cheese isn't exactly my specialty."

"Probably why they chose that method—because the best chefs will know how to make an incredible grilled cheese with very limited resources. And I'm sure yours will be among the top ten."

She dropped down on the chair beside him, watching the next group go. The smell of burning cheese soon filled the air, but the good AC system and fans took care of it. The poor chef responsible started to cry, then shut off her hot plate and stormed off.

"Well, that's one less cook to worry about," Xander whispered. "And who knows how many others stalked off before the results were announced."

Lily fidgeted in her seat for the next half hour, till it was over and Hal announced that the judges would have their results within minutes.

"Gulp," Lily said, grabbing Xander's hand and squeezing it.

He kissed her cheek and she felt so comforted that she just leaned her head against his shoulder.

"Okay, entrants!" Hal called out. "Thank you all for coming and making your grilled cheese for us! We know that all of you are great chefs, but alas, only ten can move on to the next round. And so, in no particular order, here are the names of our final ten contestants!"

Lily squeezed Xander's hand harder.

Hal had named eight chefs so far—five women and three men, including that horrid Kyle Kendrick, who'd let out a "Yeah, baby!"

Please, please, please, she prayed silently. *Pleeeeeze!*

"Our ninth contestant is Lily Hunt."

Lily's mouth dropped open just as Xander pulled her into a hug.

"You did it!" he said, kissing the top of her head. "You rock!"

She barely heard the name of the tenth contestant. All she knew was that Xander's arms were around her and she'd made it into the next round.

Right now, life couldn't get better.

"I'm sorry, but I only see a reservation for Lily Hunt," the woman at the hotel reception desk said. "A single. There's no reservation for Xander Crawford—and we're booked for the competition. There's a hotel two miles away you could try."

Two miles away from Lily? No, Xander thought.

"Surely you have *one* extra room somewhere in the hotel for a hardworking rancher assisting the best chef in Montana," Xander said, turning on the charm. He *could* when it was necessary.

"Northwest, but thank you," Lily said.

Xander put his arm around her shoulder. "All of Montana. The country, probably."

The woman behind the reception desk had an "aww" look on her face, but it didn't seem to help the cause. "Sorry. As I said, we're booked solid. There's just one reservation for your party."

Lily frowned. "But I was told we'd have two single rooms. Adjoining."

"I'm sorry, miss. There's nothing I can do."

"I can check into the other hotel," Xander told Lily. "No biggie."

Lily shook her head. "No way. We'll bunk together."

"You sure?" he asked. Innocently. As if he hadn't been hoping she'd say exactly that. Sharing a room with Lily tonight? Just what he wanted.

Sometimes a guy needed time to think while the object of his confusion was right there.

"Of course." She leaned toward the woman behind the desk. "Please tell me the bed is at least a full size and not a twin?"

"It's a full," she assured her with a smile.

Xander nodded at Lily. "Well, there you go. Room for us both." Except Xander was six foot two and a hundred eighty pounds. He hadn't slept in a full-size bed since middle school.

Once they were registered—and Xander insisted on handing over his credit card—they went to the elevator. Lily was quiet on the ride up, probably a little uncomfortable about sharing a room after all that had happened between them—and not happened—so he held both their bags and let her have her thoughts.

"You're sure you're okay with sharing a room?" he asked as he led the way to a door marked 521. "I can be back and forth in a flash. Two miles is nothing."

The truth? Two miles was forever when it came to being near Lily. He could barely stand being away from her back home.

"It's fine," she said. "We're…whatever we are. I can handle one night. You'll just stay far on your side of the bed."

"Scout's honor," he said, holding up the three-fingered symbol.

Unless neither of them would be able to resist the other and a twin bed would have suited just fine, he thought.

The room was tiny. Barely enough space for the bed, which sure looked small, a dresser with a TV over it, a desk and chair in the corner, and a small bathroom but a jetted tub. He'd definitely take advantage of that.

While Lily unpacked her bag, he opened up the curtains. They did have a view of the mountains. Way off in the distance, but they were majestic and beautiful. He could stare at mountain peaks all day.

"So, what should we do tonight?" she asked. "There's a restaurant in the hotel or we could go explore Kalispell. There are some great restaurants."

"Let's explore," he said.

She smiled. "Just give me five minutes to change."

He was wearing a button-down shirt and his nice jeans, so thought he'd just stay in that. He went over to the full-length mirror on the wall by the bathroom and gave his hair a tousle, smoothed his shirt and then went back over to the window to look at the mountains of Glacier National Park.

"All ready," Lily said, coming out of the bathroom.

He turned toward her and gaped. Holy cannoli.

Humina, humina, humina.

She wore a sleeveless black minidress with a V-neck, a delicate gold necklace dangling in just the hint of cleavage. *Sexy* did not begin to describe how she looked. Her gorgeous red hair was sleek past her shoulders, and her slightly shimmery red lips beckoned him close.

All of a sudden he realized he was standing a foot in front of her. Staring.

"You surprise me constantly," he whispered. "There are so many facets to you and I love them all."

"Do you?" she whispered back.

He'd tripped a bit on the word *love* once it had left his mouth. But he'd meant it and nodded. "You're amazing, Lily Hunt."

She smiled and now it was her eyes that were shimmering. "You always know what to say. It's what I love about *you*."

"Well, I don't say what I don't mean."

She squeezed his hand and then headed for the door as if she needed to escape this conversation, and he understood why. He was confusing. He was confusing her. And he hated that about himself. His words, his actions very clearly said something about how he felt about Lily. But he seemed to be ruled by a very stubborn brain that had called a halt to letting him really feel all that she engendered in him.

They left the hotel and drove to downtown Kalispell, a very different town than Rust Creek Falls. Home barely had five hundred residents. Kalispell around twenty thousand. The streets were bustling with tourists and residents, heading into the many shops and restaurants.

Xander parked in a public lot, and they started toward the main drag. "Thai?" he suggested, pointing across the street. "Italian? Japanese?"

"You know what I'm dying for? Barbecue. Or chili. Something that sticks to your ribs."

"Say no more. My brother Hunter told me about a new American place that has both. Montana Hots, it's called." He did a search on his phone. "Just four blocks up."

She smiled and wrapped her arm around his. "Gorgeous night. It's fun getting out of Rust Creek Falls, though I love it there. All these people and the different shops and eateries. Sure is exciting."

"I agree," he said, opening the door to Montana Hots. The place was pretty big so there wasn't a wait. They decided on a table outside with huge planters of flowers creating a barrier to the next restaurant.

Lily ordered Grandma Cheyenne's Blue-Ribbon Chili. Xander went for the ribs, which came with way too many sides, but he never passed up garlic mashed potatoes and coleslaw.

"I wonder if one day I'll have a place like this," she said once the waitress left. "I always thought I'd have a restaurant of my own. But I'll tell ya, when my client, Mr. Parster, said I should be cooking for the town as a personal chef, something just lit up inside me like a firecracker. I instantly knew that's what I want to do right now. Have my own business, cook to order, develop a clientele. Maybe five years down the road, I'll seriously think about a restaurant."

The waitress returned with their drinks, two spiked lemonades.

"You can definitely count on seven hungry Crawfords being on that client list," he said. "So if I want a rib eye steak and roast potatoes delivered to my home, all I have to do is text you?"

"Yup. I'll do meals on call, but I'm also planning a meal kit business. I provide the ingredients, all wrapped up, and cooking instructions, so there's no shopping or measuring necessary. An easy-to-make meal for two or four or six. I'll have a rotating menu. I'll also have a menu for all dietary plans. Gluten free, vegan, vegetarian, low-carb, you name it. Lily's Home Cookin'. That's what I'm naming my business."

"Lily's Home Cookin'. I could have that every day. And most likely will."

She held up her lemonade with a smile, and he clinked their glasses.

Suddenly he pictured himself sitting at a table in a house, their house, about to gobble up whatever incredible dish his Best Chef in Montana had dreamed up.

Their house.

Sometimes, when he thought of him and Lily that way, in a fantasy way, he didn't get all tied up in knots over the reality. Sometimes, it just felt right.

Their entrées were served, his ribs incredible and Lily's chili, which she held up to his mouth in a big spoonful, equally delicious. They talked about their own grandmas' chili, though in Xander's case, it was Grandpa's chili that everyone in the family lined up for when they got together. They talked about her hopes for Lily's Home Cookin', and then Lily said something that had him practically choking on his garlic mashed potatoes.

"I think in about six months, once my business is in a good groove, I'll be able to focus on my personal life. I've really ignored it for far too long."

He paused, his fork hovering in midair. "Your personal life? What do you mean?"

"Well, my love life. I might be young, Xander, but I'm an old soul. I think, anyway. I'm ready to settle down. Find my guy. The man I'm meant to be with forever."

He swallowed, the dry lump going down hard.

"I may even ask Viv Dalton to set me up." She smiled and took a spoonful of her chili, then tore off some corn bread.

How could she eat at a time like this?

When she was talking about finding a husband. Another man. Not him.

He was not ready to let her go.

But he wasn't ready for anything else, either.

Cripes.

Luckily, she changed the subject to corn bread and how her dad always made it on Sundays. "Even when we all realized I was a really good cook, he still insisted on making the Sunday corn bread the way my mom used to. I love that."

"Is it any good?" Xander asked, then finished off the last rib.

"I love my dad like crazy, but no. It's terrible! I'm not even quite sure what he keeps forgetting. Maybe a different ingredient every time."

He smiled. "Corn bread is like French fries and pizza. Even bad, it's good."

Lily laughed, that sound he loved. And the thought of some other guy hearing that melodic, happy laugh for the rest of his life was like a punch to his gut.

Dinner over, they decided on dessert somewhere else, and found a make-your-own frozen yogurt shop full of customers. Xander made a bizarre pistachio, mocha-chip concoction, with a zillion toppings, while Lily went for the strawberry shortcake fro-yo with multicolored sprinkles. They walked and ate, people watching, window-shopping, oohing and ahhing over cute dogs of all sizes in a pet store display.

And then they were done with their desserts and it was getting late, so they headed back to the hotel since they needed to be in the hotel kitchen at 7:00 a.m. Apparently, the Luxury Lodge had three kitchens, and for the weekend, the competition would be using the small one designed specifically for room service.

Lily was quiet in the elevator up to the fifth floor. Because she was thinking about tomorrow?

Or tonight?

Probably both. He slid the card key into the slot on the door, and they headed inside, his gaze landing on the small bed. They would be sharing that tonight.

"Well, I'll just go change into my pj's," Lily said.

He swallowed. Would her pj's be as sexy as her little black dress?

She dashed into the bathroom with some garments in her hand and her tote bag. A few minutes later she emerged in navy blue gym shorts and a fitted white T-shirt.

Yes, her pj's were as sexy as her black dress.

Her hair was in a topknot, and he could barely take his eyes off her long neck. There were freckles on her neck.

"Your turn," she said, slipping into bed, sliding to the very edge. He was surprised she didn't fall between the bed and the wall.

He grabbed a pair of basketball shorts and a T-shirt, changed in the bathroom and came out to find Lily with the blanket pulled up to her chin. He slid beside her, trying to not brush against her, but the bed was pretty small. Lying next to her without touching her was going to make for a hell of a long, sleepless night.

"Good night," she whispered.

He turned to face her. "Good night. Good luck tomorrow."

She smiled, the slight illumination from the moonlight that spilled in through the filmy section of curtains lighting her beautiful face, the freckles he loved so much. "You're my good-luck charm."

"Glad to be," he said.

She closed her eyes and then turned to face the wall, so he turned to face the windows, knowing he'd get zero sleep.

Chapter Fourteen

Lily must have been so tired and stressed about the competition and about sharing a room with Xander that she'd fallen right asleep. How she'd managed that, she had no idea. But the next time her eyes opened, it was morning, her cell phone alarm buzzing at 5:45 a.m.

Xander was on the floor, bare-chested, doing crunches. Of course he was.

"Morning, sleepyhead," he said. "You're gonna knock 'em dead this morning."

"God, please don't let me poison a judge," she said, her eyes widened.

He smiled. "Lil, it's an expression."

Deep breath, girl, she told herself. "I'm just so nervous. I have to win. I have to."

"You will. Believe it and it shall be so."

She laughed. "Who said that?"

"I forget. Yul Brynner in some movie?"

She cracked up and shook her head. "Last one in the shower is a rotten egg!"

"Are you inviting me to shower with you?" he asked, standing up. All six foot two of him. Bare-chested.

"Absolutely not." Though she'd love it. But no way. She was not letting anything about their not-romance get in the way of making it into the next round.

He grinned. "Go ahead. Ladies first."

She grabbed some stuff from the closet and her tote bag and shut the bathroom door behind her. The hot shower did her worlds of good, soothing her muscles, cramped from trying not to brush up against Hottie when he'd first slid in bed beside her last night.

She got dressed in her new skinny jeans, her lucky red T-shirt with the Daisy's Donuts logo on it, and her trusty clogs, and then took three deep breaths. She dried her hair with the weak blow-dryer on the wall, then emerged to find Xander doing push-ups.

Hot. Hot. Hot. He got up and headed in the bathroom with his clothes, and was out within ten minutes, dressed casually and looking gorgeous.

The lobby offered a continental breakfast for guests, and though Lily could barely eat right now, they stopped there. With a strong cup of hazelnut caffeine in her and half a blueberry muffin, she was good to go when they hit the kitchen at six fifty.

As she and Xander entered the kitchen where the contest would be held all day, there were murmurs that it would be like *The Great British Baking Show*, where they'd be given the ingredients and a recipe, and would have to make the same thing.

"You're all going down," Kyle Kendrick said with a toss of his blond bangs.

"In your dreams, blondie," a woman with very long dark hair said.

Hal, the emcee with the ever-present clipboard, came in. "Okay, contestants and assistants. Each of you was given a number when you entered the kitchen. Please stand at the station that has your number on the cupboard."

Lily was number five—which had always been one of her favorite numbers. Her birthday was on the fifteenth. And she'd been hired at the Maverick Manor on May 25 of the previous year. Lots of good fives in her life.

She'd met Xander on August 6, but it was close.

The kitchen had ten stations, each with its own four-burner stove, oven, stainless steel counter space, mini fridge, sink and cupboards. She and Xander stood at the counter, which faced the front of the kitchen, where Hal stood with his clipboard and headset.

"This morning, you will make a perfect Western omelet. Seven of you will be eliminated. Three of you will move on to the final round this afternoon. In the drawer of your counter you will find a recipe for the omelet. You will find all the ingredients and utensils you need in your station, along with a full spice rack. You will have twenty minutes to make your perfect Western omelet. Oh—and I will answer your burning question: yes, you may alter the recipe to suit yourself. Of course, that may get you in trouble or it may put you in the lead. Who knows?" he added with a devilish grin. "Assistants, you may take one minute to familiarize yourself with the cupboards while the cooks peruse the recipe. Ready, set, go!"

While Lily pulled open the drawer and took out

the recipe, Xander opened the cupboards and the mini fridge. The recipe was basic. She'd definitely enhance it. This was about being the best—not being safe.

This morning at the continental breakfast buffet, she happened to overhear two of the contestants talking about the judges. Two were married and from New Orleans originally; they'd gotten married there on a Mississippi riverboat cruise, which made her think they probably had good associations with their hometown. Perhaps a little taste of home in her Western omelet would give her a slight edge with them, and be just delicious enough to sway the third judge. Lily had no idea where he was from.

"Contestants! You have twenty minutes. Starting in… three, two, one, cook!"

"Okay, what do you need?" Xander asked her.

"I need a medium sauté pan and a spatula. I'll grab the ingredients."

In moments, the right pan and the perfect spatula were on the counter. Lily got the burner to the right level, added butter to the pan and began beating five eggs. She added a small amount of milk, then beat the mixture some more.

"Xander, I need you to finely dice one onion, one green pepper and one yellow pepper. Put all your love for beautiful vegetables into your work. Meanwhile, I'll dice the ham."

"Got it!" Xander said, rushing to the pantry. "All my love for onion and peppers coming up." He pulled out the ingredients, got out a chopping board and began dicing away. "Love you, onion that I'm cutting with a really sharp knife. Chop, chop, chop."

"Um, could you keep it down over there?" snapped

the guy at the station to their left. He was in his forties and wore a neon-green apron that said I Can Explain It to You but I Can't Understand It for You. How nice. "I'm trying to concentrate."

"I can talk *and* concentrate," Xander told him. "But I'll try to lower my voice."

"Gee, thanks," the guy said.

Lily smiled at Xander and rolled her eyes, then continued dicing the ham. She added it to the pan, giving it a stir.

"Done," Xander said, bringing over his chopping board.

He slid the very nicely diced vegetables in the pan, and Lily sautéed them in the butter, waiting until they softened. Hmm, the onions and peppers and ham smelled heavenly. Of course, the entire kitchen smelled amazing.

"You stupid buffoon!" the woman at the station to the right of Lily screamed. At her assistant—who was red in the face. "How could you drop the eggs? We only had five!" The woman turned to Hal with the clipboard. "Hal, I can get more eggs, right? My idiot sister dropped ours and they're all over the floor."

"Sorry," Hal said. "No more eggs in your fridge, no omelet, so that disqualifies you. Please pack up and leave the kitchen. You are *not* Northwest Montana's Best Chef."

The woman was seething. "And this is not *Top Chef*!" she yelled, then stalked off, her poor sister trailing.

"Sorry," the sister said meekly, and ran off after the former contestant.

"Ooh, that's too bad," Xander said. "Thanksgiving sure won't be fun for them this year."

"Right?" Lily said, shaking her head.

"And then there were nine!" Kyle Kendrick called out.

Jerk.

"Ten minutes, Lil," Xander said.

She nodded and flashed him a thumbs-up, then Lily added the eggs to the pan, debating whether to add a little cheese. There were four kinds in the fridge, but a true Western omelet, a purist one, didn't have cheese. She'd skip it.

"Four minutes, Lily," Xander said.

"Four minutes left!" the assistant behind their station bellowed.

"Oh hell!" someone shouted. "The omelet's stuck to the pan!"

"I am so gonna win," said Kyle Kendrick. "No one makes an omelet like I do. No to the one!"

"Yes, chef!" his assistant said. She happened to be the pretty blonde Lily had seen draped over Kyle last night in the lobby as she and Xander returned from Kalispell.

Lily rolled her eyes so hard that Xander cracked up.

"Find that funny, do you?" Kyle said, glaring at him. "You'll see."

Now it was Xander's turn to roll his eyes.

"Eyes on your own paper, kids," Xander whispered.

Lily laughed and high-fived him.

"Two minutes, chef!" Kyle's blonde said.

"Two minutes, Lil," Xander said, getting a glare from Kyle.

She loved that he was having a good time. Competitions could seriously stress out some people, but Xander rolled with it, doing a very careful and good job.

Just before she flipped the omelet she added a hint of tabasco sauce and a dash of cayenne pepper across the omelet to bring that little taste of New Orleans. The omelet looked absolutely divine, if she did say so herself.

"Can I eat that?" Xander asked.

"If there's any left over," she said, giving her shoulders a shimmy. She waited until the bottom of the omelet was the perfect shade, then flipped the sides onto each other.

Done.

She plated, added a sprinkle of kosher salt and a little pepper—and waited.

"Time!" Hal called. "The judges will now begin their rounds. Please provide three forks."

Xander handed Lily three forks, which she placed on three folded napkins next to the plates.

The female judge came over and studied the omelet and then made some notations. She took a bite, then another, looked at Lily, and made a notation, then moved on.

When her husband, one of the two male judges, took a bite, Lily swore he closed his eyes with a tiny sigh, but that might have been her fantasy. He made his notes. The third judge took three bites, always a good sign, and jotted his comments.

"My goodness!" said the female judge to a contestant two rows behind Lily. "How much salt did you add?"

Lily heard crying. She felt so sorry for whichever contestant it was that she didn't even turn around. Xander didn't, either. He just squeezed her hand.

"That's two down!" Kyle announced. "Eight of us left."

"Jerk," Xander whispered.

After conferring with the three judges, Hal stepped forward. "And the three contestants moving into round two are..."

Lily held her breath.

* * *

Xander tried to remember the last time he'd prayed. When he was a kid, around four or five. He'd wait at the window for his mother to come back, but she never did. So he started praying every night, since someone at school had told him that was how you got stuff you wanted.

His mother had never come back.

He prayed now—to the universe, to nature, to the big man upstairs. *Let Lily's name be called, please!*

"Kyle Kendrick!" Hal announced.

Crud, Xander thought.

"Boo-yah!" Kyle said, fist-pumping his way up and down the aisle. "Where do the winners stand?" he asked.

"You can stay at your station for now," Hal said. With the teensiest note of disdain, unless that was wishful thinking. Probably was.

"Kerry Atalini!" Hal called next.

There were six contestants left. Xander took Lily's hand and held it, and he wondered if she could feel him praying beside her. He was thinking that hard.

She closed her eyes, too.

"And our third and final contestant moving on to the final round—Lily Hunt!"

Her eyes popped open. Xander picked her up and whirled her around, then kissed her solidly on the mouth.

"You did it!" Xander whispered in her ear. "And this afternoon, you will beat both other contestants and win the ten grand!"

She threw her arms around him and hugged him and he held her tight. He was so proud of her. So proud *for* her.

"Contestants, we will reconvene at noon on the dot

in this kitchen for the final round. Only one of you will be named Northwest Montana's Best Chef!"

"Sorry, Lily, but it's going to be *me*," Kyle said, sauntering by her with his assistant trailing him on her high heels. How she puttered around the station in those three-inch things was beyond him.

Xander ignored him. "Any idea what the final-round meal is?" he asked Lily as they left the kitchen and headed for the elevator.

"No clue. But I feel ready for anything. Thank you so much for being a great assistant, Xander."

"You taught me everything I know," he said, batting his eyes.

She gave him a playful sock on the arm. "Seriously. Thank you."

"You are very welcome."

The moment they got into the room, Lily said she wanted to take another shower and get the smell of peppers and onions out of her hair and skin. When he heard the water turn on, he wished he was in that shower stall with her. Washing her beautiful body. Lathering up her hair. Making soapy love to her.

He parked himself on the desk chair, his attention on the bathroom door. On the water running. He had Lily on the brain. Every part of him craved her, wanted her.

The water stopped. The bathroom door opened. Lily came out, her hair damp, her body wrapped in a small white towel.

She stared at him as she walked over, then straddled him on the chair.

Ooh boy.

Hadn't he said she was full of surprises?

"One of us has too many clothes on," she whispered.

"Yeah, *you*." He slowly undid the towel, reveling in every gorgeous naked bit of her.

She undid his belt buckle. Then the snap of his jeans. The zipper came down. He picked her up in his arms and carried her to the bed, grabbing a condom from his wallet—he always kept one in there, but he'd brought five for this weekend. Wishful thinking. And good thing he had.

Then they were under the covers, a tangle of arms and legs and hungry lips.

Once again, she rocked his world. That was no longer a surprise.

"I love you," she whispered as she climaxed, and Xander froze. Just for a second.

But Lily must have felt it because she pulled back a bit, looking at him. "I shouldn't have said that. I didn't mean to say it—it just burst out of my mouth."

"Lily, I…"

"Oh, that again," she said, the look of disappointment so pronounced that he tried to force the words but they still wouldn't come.

Did he love her? All signs pointed to yes, but then why couldn't he say so? Why couldn't he even say so to himself?

He heard her sigh. "I should really be focusing on the next round," she said. "I'd better get dressed and go in search of some strong coffee. I don't know what came over me, why I jumped your bones. Let's forget the whole thing. I'm just running on competition adrenaline. This. Never. Happened." He'd come to know her so well that he could see she was hiding her misery behind a plastered-on fake smile.

"Lily, I—"

But she'd grabbed some clothes from the closet and shut herself in the bathroom.

When she emerged, he was dressed, too, and hoping they could talk, but again, he was tongue-tied. Stuck, really. That was how he felt: stuck. In what, by what, he wasn't sure.

"I'll see you at eleven fifty in the kitchen," she said, grabbed her tote bag and rushed out of the room.

Xander might not know if he loved her, but he sure felt like he hated himself at that moment.

Lily sat in the lobby, sipping her second excellent cappuccino, trying not to think of the humiliation she'd just endured.

I love you.

I...don't. Sorry.

Fine, he hadn't said that. But the "Lily, I..." followed by nothing said as much.

She knew this already. Why had she jumped his bones? Why had she blurted out the true depth of her feelings for him?

Because you love him. And you're not hiding anymore. This is me. I'm a passionate person who loves hard and if I feel it, I'm gonna express it.

Tears stung her eyes and she blinked them back.

She'd tried to be so tough last night, telling him she was looking forward to finding her guy and settling down soon. She'd been hoping to make him realize she wasn't going to be around forever, that some other man would snap her right up.

But he hadn't even reacted. And so she'd changed the subject and tried to move on from thinking about romance to just focusing on the contest.

But the high of making it to the final round was so profound that she'd felt like Wonder Woman for a while there, floating up to their room in a haze of happiness and pride. She'd been named a finalist with Xander beside her, Xander helping her. That made it all the more sweet.

And in the shower, all she could think of was how badly she wanted him in there with her. She'd planned her little daylight seduction right then and there. And she went for it.

So had he.

Until she'd come out with the *I love you.*

Cripes.

"Hi, Lily!" said a female voice.

It was Kerry, the other contestant besides Kyle in the final round. Kerry was in her late twenties or early thirties with dark pixie-cut hair and black framed eyeglasses. She had a tattoo of a pink cupcake on her shoulder. Lily recalled that her assistant was a woman who looked a lot like her, her sister probably. "How amazing is this?" Kerry said. "Almost three hundred entrants, and it's down to three of us. I can't even believe it."

"I know. I can't, either. I came here hoping and praying but not expecting."

Kerry smiled. "Ditto. Although I think what's-his-name expects to win."

"Ugh," Lily said. "He's from my hometown. He's good but he's not exactly the nicest guy."

"Well, then I hope it's one of us. Ladies unite!" she said with a grin. "What do you plan to do with the money if you win?"

Lily explained about Lily's Home Cookin' and hoping to get that business off the ground without having to take out a loan.

"What a great idea!" Kerry said. "I love it. I live an hour from here in the opposite direction or I'd definitely order me some Lily's Home Cookin'."

Lily grinned. Kerry was a sweetheart. "So how about you? What are your plans?"

"I really want to open a small casual café where moms can bring their kids and the little ones can run around. I'll have a train set on a table, and dolls and trucks and Legos and blocks. A reading nook. I love to cook but my real love is baking, so I'll have amazing pastries and maybe offer some light kid fare, like grilled cheese. I know I do that really well."

Lily laughed, recalling their elimination round entrée. "Right? Do you have a child?"

"Samantha," Kerry said, a wistful look coming over her face. "She's two and a half and the love of my life. Her dad took off on me, but left me with the best part of himself, so hey, I'm happy. My mom's watching her for me while I'm here."

"Aww, that's really great. My assistant is the love of my life but he just thinks of me as a friend."

Kerry gave Lily a "you're crazy" expression. "Uh, I saw with my own eyes how that incredibly hot guy looks at you, talks to you and acts around you. He's a man in love. Trust me."

Sarah seemed to think so, too. Why was Xander the only one who didn't see it? "Well, he doesn't want to be, unfortunately."

"Ah, good thing is that you can't stop progress. He'll come around." She glanced at her watch. "It's eleven thirty. I'm gonna go freshen up for the big moment."

Can't stop progress. Hadn't Lily herself said that recently?

"See you soon," Lily said. "Thank you, Kerry. And good luck."

"To you, too, sweetie," Kerry said.

Lily finished her cappuccino, staring out the window, wondering if it could be true, that you really *couldn't* stop progress. Thing was, *was* there progress with Xander when he kept taking a giant step backward?

Sigh.

The final round was a chili cook-off.

Lily seemed really excited about that, all signs of her earlier distress gone. She had a smile on her face and fierce concentration in her eyes, and Xander knew she was full speed ahead on winning this thing.

That was just one of the things he loved about her. Her determination. Her drive. She might be hurting, but she was going to be named Northwest Montana's Best Chef.

"You've got this," he said, squeezing her hand at their station. He wanted to ask if she was okay, if they were good, but this wasn't the time to talk about them. They had to concentrate on the contest.

"Let's do it!" she said, those beautiful green eyes flashing with spirit.

I love you, too, he thought. And almost said it right there.

I love you, Lily Hunt. I flipping love you!

Holy hell. He loved her!

Minutes later, he had to table that incredible revelation to focus on being Lily's assistant. He chopped and diced, he handed over the packages of meat and beans, he found the right pots and pans and utensils.

Kyle Kendrick boasted up a storm at the station in the middle, snapping at his assistant, who Xander hoped would tell him to shove it and walk out on him. But unfortunately, she kept taking his unnecessary criticism. Hopefully, she'd get sick of it soon enough.

"Ow!" shrieked the woman on the far right station. Kerry, her name was. "Burned myself a bit."

"You okay, Ker?" Lily called over.

"I'll live!" Kerry called back.

"Can I concentrate here? Jeez," Kyle complained.

"Oh, shut it, Kyle," Kerry announced with glee. Her assistant, also with short dark hair, clapped. Xander almost clapped, too. Kerry's assistant wrapped the burn in a Band-Aid, and Kerry was on the move again, dashing between stirring pots and pans.

Finally, time was up. Lily's chili smelled amazing. Looked amazing. Tasted amazing. She had to win this. She *had* to.

The three judges took their bites. Made their notations.

Hal appeared again in the front of the stations, the three judges beside him, ready to announce the results. "In third place, Kyle Kendrick!" Hal announced.

Kyle's mouth dropped open. "There has to be a mistake. *Third?* No."

"Third," Hal said, consulting his clipboard. Kyle glared at him and stared at the judges. They each nodded.

"This blows. I'm outta here," Kyle said. He stalked off, leaving his assistant just standing there.

"You deserve better," Xander said to her.

The blonde shrugged and sighed and went racing after Kyle.

"In second place…" Hal began.

Xander held his breath. He grabbed Lily's hand and squeezed, hoping he wasn't cutting off her circulation.

"Lily Hunt!" Hal continued.

What? There has to be some mistake. Second? No.

Jeez. Now he knew how Kyle felt.

He looked at Lily, who attempted a smile. "Hey, I tried, right? Second out of almost three hundred is pretty darn good, right?"

"And our winner, Northwest Montana's Best Chef, is…Kerry Atalini!" Hal said.

The judges began clapping. So did Lily. In fact, she ran over to Kerry and gave her a big hug.

"Congrats, Kerry. I can't wait to visit your café and eat an amazing chocolate croissant while I watch the little ones play trains," Lily said.

Kerry hugged her back. "Thank you, Lily. Can we keep in touch?" They exchanged email addresses and cell phone numbers, and then Lily was back over at their station.

Kerry was presented with her check for ten thousand, and Xander could feel the absolute wistfulness coming off Lily.

"I wish you'd won," he said. "You're the best chef in the world."

Lily squeezed his hand. "At least Kyle didn't win."

"True."

"Let's go home," she said. "I need home."

He nodded, and they thanked Hal and the judges, then left the kitchen and headed to the elevator.

When the door of their room shut behind them, Xander planned to grab Lily in his arms and tell her he loved her, that he'd been bursting with it ever since the start of the chili cook-off. But as she packed her things, the words wouldn't come again. They were stuck behind something.

What the hell? he wondered. *Tell her. Say it!*

If he said *Lily, I...* and couldn't get anything out beyond that, she'd have every right to punch him in the stomach.

"Ready?" she asked, overnight bag slung over her shoulder.

"You okay?"

She nodded. "I really am. I'll apply for a loan on Monday morning. There's a chance I'll get it. Of course, the bank may say I'm too young and untried and don't have enough work history under my belt. But I have a solid business plan. So we'll see."

"I'll front you the money, Lily. I believe in you and I'd be honored to invest in your business. You can pay me back in French dips, filet mignon in garlic butter and cooking lessons."

Her mouth dropped open. "You're going to just give me ten thousand dollars?"

"Yes. I am. For the reasons I just stated."

And because I love you.

But again, the words wouldn't come.

"That's incredibly generous of you," she said. "*Beyond* generous. That you believe in me means the world to me, Xander. But I can't—and won't—take your money. I might be the Rust Creek Falls Cinderella with my makeover, and I definitely believe in Prince Charming, but I'm no princess and I plan to rescue myself. Know what I mean?"

He stared at her, speechless for the moment, but not surprised.

This is why I love you.

So why couldn't he say it?

Chapter Fifteen

On Tuesday afternoon, Xander was in the barn, doing his favorite chore—cleaning out the stalls—when his mind was full of its own muck. He hadn't spoken to Lily since Saturday night, when they'd returned from Kalispell. The ride home had been on the quiet side; Lily had been clearly tired, and they hadn't talked about *them*. Or the most memorable experience he'd ever had in a chair.

He closed his eyes, remembering. Lily in that tiny white towel. Straddling him.

I'm no princess and I plan to rescue myself...

"Hey, Xander," a male voice said.

His brother Knox. "Ran into Lily in town coming out of the bank this morning. I don't think I've ever actually seen someone kick up their heels, but she truly did. I asked her if she won the lottery and just deposited it or something, but apparently she applied for a business loan yesterday and was approved today."

He grinned. Go, Lily. Yeah!

"She's starting her own personal chef and home-cooking kit business," Xander said. "Was I that focused at twenty-three?" He shook his head, full of admiration for Lily.

"Your plan at twenty-three was to date as many pretty women as possible," Knox reminded him. "So no. You were not."

Xander laughed. "Yeah, I guess so. I kept underestimating Lily because of her age. Do you know that because she didn't win the ten grand in the cooking contest, I offered her the money myself and she turned it down? Said she'd rather get a loan and take care of herself."

"She's awesome. No way around it."

Xander nodded, leaning on the rake. "I kept thinking she was too young for me. But maybe I was just using it as an excuse."

Knox rolled his eyes. "Duh. Of course you were. You got burned in Dallas and understandably wanted nothing to do with falling in love again. I get it. But then you *did* fall in love again. And you can't handle it so you're costing yourself the best thing that will ever happen to you. The woman you *love*."

Xander stared at his brother. Knox was always on the intense side, but he was talking straight from the heart right now. "I do love her. I really do."

"So go get her. *If* she'll have you."

You can't live in the past, she'd said.

I plan to rescue myself, she'd said.

What she'd done was rescue him. From *himself.*

He loved her. With all his stupid, guarded heart, which

now felt stretched open wide. He tried to think about Britney and Chase, smiling their fool faces off at the carnival. But all he pictured in his mind was a pair of flashing green eyes, those freckles and that glorious red hair. He tried to picture his mother in her yellow apron and himself waiting by the window. Again, all he saw was Lily, stirring that pot of chili, adding the green chilies and the extra cayenne pepper to infuse the food with home.

To him, Lily meant home. She *was* home.

Knox grabbed the rake out of his hand. "Almighty Lord, Xander. Go. Run."

"I have a stop to make first," he said, heading out of the barn. At the door, he turned back. "Knox?"

"No more excuses. Go!"

"No more excuses," Xander said. "I just wanted to say…thank you."

The ever-serious Knox Crawford nodded, then broke into a smile.

Cloud nine would be a lot better if Xander were up here with her, but she was so dang happy she found herself skipping from room to room of her house.

I got the loan, I got the loan, I got the loan! Lily's Home Cookin' is coming your way, Rust Creek Falls, so watch out! Or better yet, get yer bellies ready!

She turned on the radio on the kitchen counter, swaying to her favorite country station while putting together her very first Lily's Home Cookin' kit. She'd run into Viv Dalton in Daisy's Donuts when she'd taken herself for a celebratory iced mocha latte and had told her all about the loan and her new business. Viv had been so excited for her and said she'd put in an order right then. A home kit for beef bourguignon. Viv's husband loved the intensive, time-consuming dish, but they were both so busy right now, and if they could make the meal together without having to shop and prep for it, that would be ideal.

Exactly what Lily hoped many, many, many residents of Rust Creek Falls would think about her service. Lily had almost walked right into Xander's brother Knox on her way out of the bank this morning, and he said he and his family would keep her in business for years.

Which made her wonder. How was she going to see Xander every day, maybe—very likely, actually—as a customer, and not go crazy?

Stop thinking about him! she yelled at herself. Focus on the beef bourguignon. She had her little containers all ready to go—the chunks of succulent beef, the bacon, the chopped, sliced and diced vegetables, even the flour and oil. As she snapped the lid on the last container, the tomato paste, she couldn't wait to sketch designs for her own labels.

She packed up her cooler bag, included the red wine necessary to make the beef bourguignon, and added a bottle of champagne that Lily had gotten as a gift from one of her clients so that Viv and her husband could celebrate with their meal. She thought about what Viv had said earlier, that she shouldn't really be ordering something so fancy when business was so— But then she'd stopped talking and looked distracted and uncomfortable, and Lily realized that Viv's wedding planning business, which she operated with her friend Caroline Clifton, might be in financial trouble or having some setbacks.

Huh. Maybe that was why Viv had been so quick to agree to a million-dollar payout from Max Crawford if

she married off all six Crawford brothers! Not that anyone wouldn't take that deal, but Viv had sure run with
it and now the whirlwind of dates made total sense. Viv
needed that money.

If this Rust Creek Falls Cinderella had a fairy godmother, the closest to it would be Vivienne Dalton herself. After all, it was Viv who'd suggested Lily throw
herself into the dating pool for a Crawford. Viv who'd
arranged the date with Knox. Which led to her date with
Xander in the park.

Tears stung her eyes even though she was smiling at
how Viv had believed in her ability to hook a gorgeous
Crawford when she'd been a tomboy with tomato sauce
on her shirt and flour-stained baggy jeans.

I owe you, Viv, she thought, reaching into her wallet
for Viv's check and ripping it up. Lily grabbed her phone
and sent Viv a text.

I'm dropping off your beef bourguignon kit in ten minutes, as discussed. Oh, and I ripped up your check—this
special meal from Lily's Home Cookin' is on me. You're
my first official client!

Wow, really? Thanks! Viv texted back.

No, thank you, Viv, Lily thought with a smile. *I might
not have ended up with love, but thanks to you, I found it.*

With ten minutes to kill, Lily eyed the *Rust Creek
Falls Gazette* on the kitchen table and sat down to poke
through it. Ooh, she could check apartment listings! She
turned to the Apartment and Condos for Rent section,
glancing through a few possibilities. But there was a
small house for rent, zoned for business and residen-

tial use, right in the center of town off North Broomtail Road.

It was a little out of her price range, but she could cut
back in other areas. She'd hang out her shingle, and have
her customers come to her for meal kits or to place catering orders. With her loan, she could renovate the kitchen
to her specifications, but considering she wouldn't have
four hungry Hunts constantly in the kitchen and eating
up her good ingredients and leftovers, she might not even
need such a huge work space. She circled the ad for the
house, then grabbed her phone, pressing in the telephone
number for the real estate agent.

But the doorbell rang then, so she put the phone down
and got up to answer it.

Xander. In a suit and tie and a Stetson.

He took off the hat and held it against his chest. "Lily,
I have so much to say to you."

She tilted her head and waited. "I'm listening."

"I didn't come to Rust Creek Falls expecting to fall
for anyone. You know I've been burned before."

*Please don't be here to apologize for not loving me.
I couldn't take that.*

"But then out of nowhere," he continued, his dark eyes
intense on hers, "a smart, focused, talented, passionate,
honest, funny, dachshund-loving, hoodie-wearing gorgeous redhead with sparkling green eyes captured my
heart before I even knew she had it in her possession."

Lily gasped and her knees wobbled. She could barely
breathe—or speak.

"I didn't think anything scared me, Lily. But all this
time, I've been so damned afraid of how I feel about you.
And you know what?"

"What?" she managed to whisper.

"You taught me a lot about courage. And let's face it, I just love you too much to let you go."

He loved her!

"Lily, I want to start over with you. Can we?"

She couldn't speak. She couldn't move.

Finally she found her voice. "Nope, we can't start over. But we can pick up where we left off," she added with a grin. "So where were we?"

"On a chair. Naked. In a Kalispell hotel room."

"Maybe we can go back this weekend," she said. "And re-create that moment—changing what happens next."

"Done," he said. "I do want to change what happens next. But now. Not a minute later." He got down on one knee, opening up a black velvet box. A beautiful diamond ring glittered. "Lily Hunt, will you make me the happiest guy alive by becoming my wife?"

"Yes!" she screamed at the top of her lungs.

He stood up and slid the ring on her finger, then picked her up and whirled her around, smothering her with kisses.

"Yes," he repeated. "Forever."

"Forever," she said.

They delivered Viv's beef bourguignon—and the big news that Viv was two down, four to go on the Crawford bachelors. Lily held up her left hand, the emerald-cut diamond, surrounded by diamond baguettes on a gold band, twinkling.

Viv yelled so loudly her husband came running. The four of them cracked open the champagne Lily had brought, then she and Xander left them to make their romantic meal for two. With leftovers, of course.

Then Xander suggested they book a room at the Maverick Manor for a little privacy, so after surprising the heck out of their families with their big news—Knox wasn't the least bit surprised—he booked the honeymoon suite at the Manor.

More champagne. Chocolate-covered strawberries.

And the love of her life, her fiancé, her soon-to-be husband, beside her in the enormous four-poster bed.

Xander held up a chocolate-covered strawberry and dangled it in front of her mouth. "Want to know a secret? The first night I met you, I went home and thought of feeding you strawberries. Now here I am doing it."

"Ha! I knew you liked me from that first not-a-date." She accepted half the strawberry while he ate the other half, then their lips met in a kiss.

"We'll live happily—and hungrily—ever after," she said.

He kissed her again, wrapping her in his arms. "You know that little house you mentioned you saw in the paper?" he asked. "What do you think of us buying our own ranch close to town and I'll build you your own cooking studio and make you the Lily's Home Cookin' sign for it? State-of-the-art kitchen, display cases, reception counter, waiting area—the works."

"Told you I believed in Prince Charming. Here he is," she said with a smile, then burst into tears.

"I hope those are happy tears," he said.

"My cup runneth over, Xander. Thank you. Yes, yes, yes, a million times yes. Maybe while you're at it, you can build a doghouse for Dobby and Harry."

"Definitely," he said. "I love those furry little beasts."

"And I love you."

He kissed her, and they lay together for a moment. "Oh, I just remembered I brought something with me I wanted to show you." He reached into his overnight bag and pulled out an old jewel-encrusted book.

"It's that diary you and your brothers found in your bedroom!" she said, sitting up.

"Yup. I jimmied it open with a screwdriver. I figure it's the only way to find out who it belongs to so that I can try to get it back to its owner."

"Any clues?"

He opened it up to a middle page, and Lily leaned closer to glance at the yellowed pages. "I read through some of it and whoever kept this diary was seriously in love. He or she was involved in a passionate love affair with someone referred to as only 'W.'"

"Ooh, that looks like a love poem," she said, pointing to the right-hand page.

"'My fair W,'" Xander read, "'I cannot stop thinking of you, dreaming of you, wishing we were together. Soon, I hope. Forever yours.'"

"Aww," Lily said. "So romantic!"

He smiled. "I'll go through it and see if I can find some names. It's probably someone from the Abernathy family, so if I come across a first name, maybe someone with history here in town will recognize it."

"Are you going to write me a love poem?" she asked, kissing the side of his neck.

"I'm not much of a writer, but I promise to cherish you just as much as our surprise diary writer cherished the fair W."

"Me, too," she said, and they snuggled in to start the diary from the beginning.

Epilogue

A week later, Lily, in a white satin wedding gown she'd found in a Kalispell bridal boutique and had altered in record time, walked down a red carpet aisle in the Rust Creek Falls Community Center on the arm of her father, who was crying the entire way. She and Xander had chosen this venue over the swanky Maverick Manor because the center could hold the entire town—and the entire town had been invited to their wedding. Between the Hunts going back generations in Rust Creek Falls, and the Crawfords becoming famous for the million-dollar wager on their bachelorhood, everyone wanted to come. The more, the merrier.

Lily now stood with her gorgeous tuxedo-clad groom in front of the minister, so happy she thought she might burst. Xander's brothers were his groomsmen, and his father his best man. Lily's matron of honor was Sarah, and five of her dear friends who'd scattered after high school had come back for the wedding, even on short notice, all managing to find a pale pink dress and silver shoes.

She thought of herself in that pale pink dress and silver ballet flats at the Summer Sunset Dance the night she and Xander had made love for the first time. To her, that color scheme would always represent new beginnings. So she'd chosen it for her bridal party.

In a rush of words and with shimmering eyes, they were pronounced husband and wife, and Xander kissed her so passionately that there wolf whistles, and she even heard Dobby and Harry, guests of course, giving two short barks each.

The reception was held outside under a beautiful open-air tent. Lily had called for a potluck, and everyone had brought something. Food equaled love, and Lily wanted everyone's love at the wedding.

After the first dance, Max Crawford asked to give a toast, and spoke for quite a while about how love kept surprising him. First, Logan had found it with Sarah. Then Xander with Lily. "Watch out, Knox, Hunter, Finn and Wilder. It's gonna come at you hard when you least expect it, with the woman you least expect it with." He winked at Viv, who smiled back, then they all raised their glasses and drank to true love. Surprising love.

Lily smiled at Viv, too. If her wedding planning business was in trouble, at least Lily had helped by taking down one more Crawford brother—and hiring Viv to plan this shindig.

Everyone was crowding around the buffet tables, where champagne and heaps of food waited for the guests. Lily had decided to make her own chili—not the recipe that hadn't won her the cooking contest, but her mother's recipe, a chili to die for. She'd added a little of everything under the sun so that as many people as possible would be reminded of home.

"Brings me back to Texas," Xander said after taking a bite. "There go those crazy memories again. Hunter putting a frog down my shirt. Me beating Logan for the first time in a race." A look of surprise crossed his face. "Hey—strangest thing," he said. "The next memory that flashed at me was you in your T-shirt and jeans, a hoodie wrapped around your waist in the doorway of the Maverick Manor kitchen."

Lily gasped. "That was here. In Montana. The night you showed up as my date."

"Because *this* is home now. Home is always going to be where you are, Lily Crawford."

There were clinks on glasses, which meant the new husband had to kiss his new bride. Under the Big Sky Country's brilliant late-August sun, Xander dipped Lily for the kiss of all kisses, and Lily knew they had indeed found home in each other forever.

* * * * *